# Rua's Gift

# Rachel Dray

ISBN: 9798846658448

2

# DEDICATION

My thanks go to my friends and family for their love and support, and constructive criticism, during my struggles completing this novel. Particular thanks go to my mother whose belief in me has always been absolute; to my husband, Peter, who has put up with my ignoring him for days, nay weeks, at a time; to my editors, Mary Chapman and Jan Harris ; and, of course to my children, Lizzie and Chris, and their partners, Michael and Calli, for their encouragement and promises to help market my books

# Contents

Prologue - The Gift .................................................. 7

Chapter 1 .......................................................... 9

Chapter 2 ......................................................... 11

Chapter 3 ......................................................... 20

Chapter 4 ......................................................... 23

Chapter 5 ......................................................... 35

Chapter 6 ......................................................... 45

Chapter 7 ......................................................... 49

Chapter 8 ......................................................... 64

Chapter 9 ......................................................... 75

Chapter 10 ........................................................ 96

Chapter 11 ....................................................... 118

Chapter 12 ....................................................... 137

Chapter 13 ....................................................... 148

Chapter 14 ....................................................... 160

Chapter 15 ....................................................... 173

Chapter 16 ....................................................... 183

Chapter 17 ....................................................... 190

Chapter 18 ....................................................... 217

Chapter 19 ....................................................... 218

Chapter 20 ....................................................... 240

Chapter 21 ....................................................... 257

Chapter 22 ....................................................... 271

Chapter 23 ....................................................... 274

Chapter 24 ....................................................... 281

Chapter 25.................................................................288

Chapter 26.................................................................302

Chapter 27.................................................................314

Chapter 28.................................................................333

Chapter 29.................................................................344

Chapter 30.................................................................349

Chapter 31.................................................................360

Chapter 32.................................................................371

Chapter 33.................................................................376

Chapter 34.................................................................380

Chapter 35.................................................................392

About the author .....................................................413

## Prologue - The Gift

Inscription on the Statue of Rua, as translated by the priests at the Temple of Helvoa

*In the beginning was a memory. A memory of light and of life and of love.*

*The memory became known as the Goddess, the Blessed Rua.*

*The Goddess danced through the void, calling to her all which had been lost.*

*And where she danced, swirls of stars were formed, bringing light to the darkness.*

*There was light, yet there was no life for her to love.*

*And so, the Goddess birthed countless worlds to circle the stars.*

*And she waited, but no life came.*

*The Goddess despaired.*

*Our world was born in her grief, and reality splintered in her pain.*

*Within each reality lay a twin to our own world, formed by its own truth.*

*Some were barren, and the Goddess turned from them.*

*Some bore life and the Goddess was pleased.*

*She gifted part of herself to the life that she loved. This was the gift of magic.*

*And so, the Goddess watched.*

## Chapter 1

Susan's ankle twisted and she landed on the ground with a loud thump. Wincing, she sat back on her knees and brushed the dirt off her hands. Dirt! Where was the carpet of the elevator? She stared at her hands then the dusty track beneath her, with its small stones and gritty texture. What the hell?

She raised her head with a grimace, dreading what she would see, and blinked at the sunlight filtering through the gaps between the trees. Bloody trees! Her vision spun and she felt lightheaded. This could not be happening! She squeezed her eyes shut as she gulped in desperate breaths. She was having a breakdown! The stress had finally got to her! A sob escaped and she pulled at her hair. Oh God! Mr Blenchcot was going to be so angry.

In the heart of the city, Martin Blenchcot, senior partner at the law firm, Treedle, Blenchcot and Drone LLP, strode towards the elevator to take him from the fourth floor to the seventh. His personal assistant scurried behind him, taking notes on her pad while he barked out instructions.

Martin was not in a good mood, his meeting was due to start in five minutes and Susan, the junior solicitor currently working for him, was late with his breakfast. His heavy brows dipped even lower as he ended his list of tasks with an ominous, "Tell Susan to bring my coffee up to the meeting, personally." A friendly ding turned his attention to the polished steel elevator doors as they slid open.

Martin took a step back and his lip curled in disgust while

his assistant's painted eyebrows shot up. Her mouth dropped open, almost comically wide, before she glanced nervously at her boss. The elevator's usually immaculate interior was a mess. The smoked glass mirrors that covered the walls were dowsed in a brown liquid that was streaming down into a muddy puddle on the soft grey carpet. On one of the walls a white snail trail of icing led to a gooey lump that had slopped atop an abandoned attaché bag. Alongside the bag sat a plastic lid, its companion paper cup tossed across the floor. Another empty cup lay on its side amidst the growing puddle.

Martin narrowed his eyes as he looked upon the attaché bag, recognition registering immediately. His jaw taut, he spat out the words, "Shut this down and get it cleaned. Delay the meeting. I need to have a few words with Miss Susan Trabochet." He stalked back to his office but stopped before going inside. "Find her." His door slammed shut and his assistant jumped. Gripping her notes tightly, she hurried back to her desk. The momentary glance of pity she tossed towards Susan's empty office didn't prevent her from obeying his final barked command

An hour earlier and not far away, Triene sat silently atop a rock overhang, her arms wrapped around her bent knees, as she breathed in the moment of black stillness which precedes the rush of dawn. Her long woollen cloak was tucked protectively around her body. Wolf lay curled beside her, his head resting between his huge front paws.

From deep within the darkness, the melodic sound of a blackbird solo pierced the silence, only to be quickly accompanied by the repeated trill of a robin. While they sang, the blackness slowly retreated to allow the rising sun to pick out the blurred grey/green silhouette of the pine trees. A wren added its soprano to the chorus and wood pigeons cooed their percussive accompaniment. The air was filled with song and promise. Triene lifted her chin and closed her eyes as she bathed in all that the dawn offered. The smothering memories and heavy hopelessness of the night began to lift. She whispered the words of her father, her daily reminder to keep going, "You cannot change the past, but you can improve the now and the future."

She forced herself to smile and she stretched out her hand to stroke Wolf's head. He leant into her, knowing that this was part of her preparations for the day. She listened to the chorus, forcing herself to take pleasure in the sound. She felt the warmth of the soft fur beneath her fingers and the constant support of her dearest companion. Her smile softened. She breathed in the fresh air, with its crisp scent of pine and the reassuring earthy aromas. Just like the dawn, she hid her own darkness and was ready for the day. She relaxed. She would work on improving the now anyway.

Beneath the overhang, a vixen trotted past their wagon on her way back to feed her hungry cubs snuggled safely in their den. Scenting the larger predator above, she froze and glanced upwards. Wolf opened one eye, inhaled, then closed his eye once more. The fox, sensing his disinterest with relief, adjusted the rodent in her mouth and hurried away before he changed his mind.

A slight snore drifted up from beside the wagon and Triene smiled a wide and genuine smile, her slightly sharp features softening with the movement. Her green eyes sparkled with mischief and anticipation, as she nudged Wolf with her knee before getting to her feet. She stretched her muscles, which were stiff from the chill air and from sitting on the firm rock, until her long, lithe body became fluid in its motion. Wolf stood and leant back, front paws to the ground, rear in the air, as he also stretched. He gave a wide yawn that revealed his large fangs and curled his pink tongue. He looked over at Triene and she grinned at him while reaching over and tickling just behind his ear. The fresh morning dew had dampened the grass and slickened the rocks. Wolf's large, fur covered paws with their long claws found the slick rocks easier to traverse than Triene's soft and slippery leather boots. Fortunately, Triene's innate balance helped her pick her way down until they were both safely beneath the overhang and alongside the quiet horses.

The closest horse snickered in greeting before he resumed nibbling at the grass by the edge of the road. The mare lay on her side in a state of repose, undisturbed by the two walking beside her. She had long accepted Wolf as part of her herd and tended to mother him if he wasn't careful. Triene tiptoed towards the peaceful figure slumbering beneath a coarse blanket. He was on his side, his bedroll stretched out over the pebbly ground. Her brother looked younger and agreeable when at rest, but she wasn't fooled. Keeping her distance, she kicked him gently in his side with her booted foot and jumped out of reach. "Time to get up, Jael," she sang pleasantly.

Jael immediately flipped upright and crouched with legs ready to push up as he scanned the area around him. A dagger had appeared in his hand and was raised protectively. The loose blanket that had covered him pooled to the ground in comparative slow motion. Upon seeing Triene's impish grin he relaxed his grip on the dagger and slowly unfolded his large body. "Not funny," he grumbled, his now usual scowl returning to his face. Triene giggled and blew him a kiss just to add insult to injury as all good sisters should. He decided that his dignity would best be preserved by ignoring her, so turned away and started folding his bedding, ready to place in his pack.

Triene made her way across the dirt road, chuckling to herself for having discomposed her stalwart brother as she headed towards the lightly trickling stream that lay between the road and forest. Wolf lapped at the water, splashing droplets that sparkled in the newly risen sun. He spied out of the corner of his eye a dash of silver as a small fish wiggled its way up-stream. He lunged and snapped his jaws, tipped his head back and in one gulp the fish was gone. His tongue swiped his mouth with relish, and he sat back on his haunches. Triene used the icy water to wash and then ran her damp fingers through her cropped auburn curls to get them under control. She could see Jael watering the horses downstream, murmuring to them soothingly as he quickly brushed their coats and checked their hooves. He always took more care than necessary to make sure the horses were content. Triene headed back to the wagon and prepared the horses' oats, an essential supplement to the grass they had eaten, if they were to make it to the port before nightfall.

Jael checked the wagon before harnessing the horses to it. After securing their packs with their cargo in the back, Wolf jumped up and lay stretched out on them, while Triene made to sit upon the wooden bench at the front. She gathered up the reins and passed them to Jael once he joined her. With a snap of the reins and an encouraging call, the horses set off, drawing the wagon away from the rocks and toward the centre of the dirt road. They soon attained their practiced, synchronised stride and the wagon began to rock steadily in time to their swaying steps. The pace was neither fast nor slow, but that in-between tempo, which can endure for league upon league. Bred from sturdy stock, renowned for their stamina rather than swiftness of hoof, refreshed and well-fed, the large horses placidly embarked upon the journey.

The lingering dew evaporated as the warm sun promised a fine day. Soft, feathery clouds interspersed the cerulean sky over the dirt track which cut a line between the roughhewn rocks to the left and the dense forest to the right. The track trailed the course of the stream that trickled from the tops of the hills, gathering momentum as it fed from tributaries until it reached the mouth of the river where it kissed the sea at the port of Carnom. Far ahead, the boulders and forest merged as the road wound to the right and out of sight.

As the wagon trundled along the dusty track, Triene leant her head against the wooden frame and concentrated on the

14

gentle rock of the wagon and the regular beat of the hoofs and wheels as they traversed the road. She was determined to appreciate life. Her father had battled his own demons but had always taken the time to teach her the beauty surrounding them. She focused on the warmth of the sun on her face and the scents of early spring. She glanced at her brother's profile. He never used to frown so much, she thought. She sighed gently, neither could return to whom they once were.

The wagon soon rounded the bend; the horses' steady gait deceptively effective at eating up the miles. As the screen of trees unfolded, a huddled figure could be seen lying in the centre of the track. Jael pulled firmly on the reins, bringing the horses to a halt. Triene murmured her concern, while darting probing glances at the rockface, searching for warning signs of an ambush. Jael slid his sword from its scabbard, his expression troubled, eyes checking the dense trees to his right. He passed the reins to his sister and advanced warily. Wolf sniffed the still air, before springing to the ground, confident and relaxed. He padded over to the figure, reaching her before the more cautious Jael.

The woman had her eyes pressed tight and she was whimpering weakly. Her body was folded, head bowed. She seemed completely unaware of their presence. Wolf gently nudged her knee with his nose and snuffled at her face. The woman's eyes popped open, and she jerked away from him, hands scrabbling in the dirt for something she could defend herself with. Wolf cocked his head and looked at her quizzically. She stiffened and stared back. She was covered in dust from the road, it had settled in her tangled hair, and ingrained itself into her disarranged clothes. Her eyes were red and puffy, and her nose was pink and moist from where she had been crying. She had thick, black lines streaking down from her eyes and a bright red smear across her lips and cheeks. Wolf sniffed at her mouth; it smelled of oil rather than the metallic tang of blood. She didn't seem to be injured, although her leg coverings were clearly no protection as they were severely torn and exposing her flesh to the small, sharp stones on the track. One bizarre shoe with its knife-like heel dangled off the toes of one foot, while its twin lay butchered on the ground. As Wolf surveyed the carnage, the woman's eyes followed his gaze. Horror washed over her face and she gently picked up the pieces of the broken shoe and nursed it against her chest.

Having established the area was clear, Jael now approached the stricken woman, broadsword by his side, but within easy reach. "What are you doing here?" he demanded while taking in her dishevelled state.

"Is that an actual sword?" the woman exclaimed, eyes widening and clutching her shoe even tighter to her body. Jael just stared at the woman, baffled by the inane question, of course it was a sword. She took advantage of his silence and pointed to Wolf, "And is that a wolf?"

Jael took a moment to examine the strange woman and note her peculiar appearance. She looked like she had been thrown from a wagon, perhaps by a desperate relative unable to cope with her ramblings. Dishonourable and cowardly, since she would be at the mercy of brigands or wild animals out here. Pity filled him as he realised that the woman must be suffering from some kind of mental infirmity, so he answered her with a simple "Yes" in a reassuring tone.

16

"I'm in an elevator!" the woman blurted out.

Taken aback by this incomprehensible response, Jael decided to ignore it and instead introduce himself and hope the woman would be able to respond in kind. He held out his open hand and spoke calmly, "I'm Jael, this is Wolf and that's my sister, Triene," nodding in the direction of the wagon.

The woman turned her head to look at the wagon as if only just realising it was there. She slowly shook her head as if clearing her thoughts before looking up at Jael and explaining in a slightly wavering voice, "I'm Susan. I ... I ... am due in a meeting with clients at..at... 9." The woman's eyes were full of confusion. Jael felt an unexpected rush of compassion for the woman while his innate sense of responsibility tugged at him to assist her. Logically, he should leave her by the roadside as she could prove a danger to them personally or through her connections. They shouldn't take on such a liability. He glanced over to his sister and sighed. Triene would insist they help her. At least the woman didn't seem dangerous, and Wolf accepted her, which was reassuring. They could leave her at the inn, but that wouldn't be fair on Seema. They would have to take her to Carnom, but that was it. He would wash his hands of her as soon as they got there. Someone else would have to help her then. A twinge of guilt in his stomach had him scowling at her as he said, "We're going to Carnom. Would you like to accompany us?" Jael's reluctance could be heard in his voice, but the woman didn't notice.

Her forehead wrinkled in puzzlement. "Carnom? Is that a town?" she asked.

"Largest port town hereabouts."

Susan slowly looked around, taking in her somewhat isolated location before saying quietly, "I think that might be for the best," and she tentatively took Jael's proffered hand. He hauled her to her feet and quickly released her. She floundered briefly before finding her balance. She winced as she stood on something sharp and soulfully eyed the broken shoe in her hand before putting it on her foot. She then picked up the other shoe and resolutely broke off the heel. "Better than nothing.", she muttered and hobbled, awkwardly, over to the wagon. She went to the front and started to look for a way to climb up without hitching her skirt around her waist.

"Oh no you don't! You go in the back with Wolf." Jael said as he scooped her up with ease and walked with her to the back of the wagon. He hefted her into the back next to Wolf, who was already stretched out and settled for the journey. "Watch her, Wolf," Jael instructed. Wolf gave what looked like a nod and stared unblinkingly at Susan who shuffled hurriedly away from him.

Already feeling a mixture of frustration and regret at the situation, Jael leapt up to the front of the wagon and received the reins from his deceptively quiet sister. "Not a word," he warned her as he urged the horses forward. Triene glanced back at Susan; who was sitting as far away from Wolf as she could, back pressed into the wagon's side; before turning her head forward again with a roguish grin.

Susan tucked her legs tightly into her body and hugged her knees as the wagon started to move. She studied the enormous, grey wolf sprawling on the stacks of leather and rough cloth. His amber eyes examined her in return.

Susan shut her eyes and took a couple of deep, calming breaths. Janice, her Pilates teacher always said, as she took them through their initial moves, that good breathing fixes everything. Well, Susan could do with that now. When she opened her eyes again, the wolf was still watching her and for a reason she couldn't fathom, she got the impression he was amused. She spoke her thoughts out loud, as if explaining things to him would make them understandable. "One minute I was at work, the next I was crashing onto a dirt road in the middle of nowhere! It's just ridiculous!" Her voice wobbled indignantly before she continued. Wolf cocked his head as if trying to understand her. It reminded her of her mother's King Charles Spaniel, which was a comforting thought. "I'm in a coma, that must be it! The lift dropped and I got badly hurt. I'm unconscious in a coma." She nodded decisively. Unravelling her legs, she gesticulated to the wolf, "You're a hallucination......." She paused, looking thoughtful. "If it's all in my head, I'm sure I'm safe and will just wake up with the proper medical treatment?" She spoke with a confidence that was missing in her eyes. Wolf noticed her scent indicated fear with a touch of bravado. She was rather entertaining, he thought. Her anxiety spiked and she placed her head in her hands. "Oh my God! What will Mr Blenchcot say? If I'm not at work, he'll replace me with Roger!" she mumbled into her palms

## Chapter 3

Susan's thoughts drifted to earlier that morning.......

It had started as usual with the progressively loud beeping on her phone waking her and forcing her to emerge from beneath her cosy covers. She had appeared, tangled and disgruntled, then showered before making her favourite breakfast of strong black coffee and a thick layer of Nutella on toast.

The late nights working on the Frobisher case were taking their toll, giving her dark shadows under her eyes and pale cheeks . She had covered up the evidence the best she could with expensive creams and layers of makeup before tying her highlighted hair into a messy bun at her nape. She had popped the rich red lipstick that matched her manicured nails into her attaché bag, along with her keys, as she sought out her trim black skirt suit and white shirt with fine red stripes. Susan had then turned her attention to her biggest indulgence, her shoe collection. She had known exactly which pair she would be wearing. She had chosen the blood red Malone Souliers with the killer heels, and reverently slipped them onto her feet. She smiled to herself as she remembered looking in the mirror and thinking she looked perfect. The ultimate professional, clearly Associate material.

Her smile slipped as she took in her broken shoes and torn stockings. She had taken such care of her shoes as she claimed her place among the suits herded towards the underground station by the menace of failure nipping at their heels. She had danced between them as she avoided the cracks in the pavement, breaking the steady beat from the footfall of the vacant-faced commuters.

Her phone had beeped indicating another message and she had checked it before losing signal. She had quickly deleted the photos of a bachelorette party on an old school friends' group chat and read her single text message. It was from Mr Blenchcot, "Get me a large cappuccino and cinnamon bun on your way in." She had sighed and proceeded to buy them when she resurfaced into London Bridge station.

Carrying a two-cup coffee holder in her right hand and the paper bag with the bun held tightly against the leather handle of her attaché bag in her left, she had carefully weaved between the people scuttling past, and managed to get to the glass doors at the front of her office block with no mishap to coffee or shoes. She had marched past the receptionist who was partially concealed behind a mammoth floral display, and reached the elevator. Focused on keeping the coffee flat, she had reached out and pressed the button to call the lift. The doors had opened and she had carefully manoeuvred herself into the elevator. Readjusting her bag, she had leant forward to press the button for the fourth floor.

Susan rubbed the point above her nose, just between her eyebrows as she tried to focus on what had happened next. She remembered the lift rising. Did she remember it falling or shooting upwards? Her frown deepened. No. No, she couldn't.

What she did remember was her vision blurring and it seeming as if she were both surrounded by the soothing greys of glass and metal and by the strong colours of trees and dirt and sky. The greys faded and the trees came into

21

focus as she stumbled on the rough surface of the dirt track. She let go of the drinks and her bag as she wobbled. Her heel broke and she fell onto her knees. Susan rubbed her knees unconsciously soothing the fresh bruises. She was finding it hard to believe she was in a coma. She groaned and leant back on the wooden frame and closed her eyes. Just breathe slowly, she told herself. Control the breathing and you can control your life.

## Chapter 4

Susan lurched awake, eyes popping open instantly. She focused on the canvas roof of the wagon, nose twitching at the musky smell of dog. She still appeared to be in her personal version of Middle Earth. Coma induced or not, she couldn't believe that she had fallen asleep! Next to a wolf, no less! She stretched out her sore limbs, as she realised that the wagon had stopped, and the wolf had disappeared. Curious to see what was happening she crawled across the packages until she reached the door, then she cautiously folded back the cloth and peered outside.

Not much had changed, there were still rocks and trees, although the sun was higher in the sky and the air was much warmer. Susan jumped back as Triene's smiling face appeared from the side. Triene's cheerful greeting of, "Good to see you're awake for lunch." was quickly followed by a nimble leap into the back of the wagon and a firm, "But first we need to find you something suitable to wear." She searched through the packages with a swift and sure determination that sent Susan scuttling around to allow her access to the packages. Soon she had gathered up what she wanted and, just as nimbly, jumped out of the wagon.

Sending Susan an encouraging glance over her shoulder, she said, "Come and freshen up, then it is time to eat." She didn't wait for Susan to join her but rather made her way to the stream. Susan hesitated for just a moment before clambering awkwardly out of the wagon and stumbling after her.

By the time she reached the stream, Triene was already

sitting by the water, unfolding and setting out the clothes she had collected. She waved vaguely in the direction of the forest, "You can go a short distance into the trees to relieve yourself if you need to. It is perfectly safe, Wolf and I have already checked, and Jael is looking after the horses." Susan glanced back at the wagon where Jael had just stooped to check the wheel spokes for damage.

"Um…..ok ….." said Susan uneasily, as she realised that her bladder did feel a little full and the sound of the water tripping merrily over the pebbles wasn't helping. She had no option but to act upon it. She self-consciously searched the edge of the forest for a tree that would screen her from the others.

When she had finished, she carefully picked her way over the roots and plants to where Triene was sitting and knelt on a patch of soft moss so she could wash her hands in the clear water. The ingrained dirt from the road still stained her skin. "I don't suppose you have any soap?" she asked with a hopeful lilt to her voice. Triene looked at her curiously and pointed to the moss beneath Susan's knees. Surprised and somewhat sceptical, Susan pulled up some moss and rubbed it between her wet hands. The slight foam that formed began to take on the colour of the dirt and she rinsed them. She was relieved to see that her hands were much cleaner, although she couldn't help but sigh at the chipped nail polish.

Triene tipped her head to one side, rather like Wolf had done in the wagon, and asked, "You don't recognise the moss, do you?"

Susan watched the flowing water for a moment before

raising her eyes to meet Triene's and answering with a soft, querulous, "I don't recognise anything".

Triene reached out and took hold of her hand as she said firmly, "I heard you talking to Wolf earlier. This is real." She fixed her with a stare as she added, "I don't understand this, but rest assured, I will help you." Her green eyes flared as she spoke, although the determined mien quickly dropped as she continued to look at Susan. After a brief pause, she added tentatively, waving her hand in a circular motion, "Um… you might want to clean your face before we eat, you have something weird painted on it."

Susan scrunched her nose as she asked, "My face?" before exclaiming with horrified realisation, "Oh my God, my make up!" Susan grabbed some of the moss and rubbed it urgently in her hands. "Can I put this on my face?" Triene nodded while trying to hold back a smile. Fortunately, Susan was already scrubbing the foam and water on her face, so she didn't see.

"Thank goodness," Triene said contemplating Susan's sopping face. "I was scared that the markings were permanent, but they are all gone now," she teased before suggesting helpfully, "You might as well rinse the dust out of your hair too." Susan raised her hand to her hair only to feel the gritty texture and groaned. She quickly pulled out the band and pins still holding her hair up and rubbed some more moss foam into her hair. Wolf trotted over and sat down next to Triene who absently stroked his head while they observed Susan's desperate cleaning with an air of mild amusement. Taking a deep breath, Susan valiantly dipped her head into the bitterly cold stream and swished the strands in the water to rid them of the dirt. Lifting her head, she

25

squeezed out the excess water and flung her hair behind her. She gave a little shriek and shuddered as icy fingers dribbled down her back. A giggle erupted from her companion, and Wolf snorted loudly. Looking up at them, Susan couldn't help but give a wry chuckle.

Jael's deep voice called out, "We need to eat and move on." Glancing up, Susan saw him standing near the rear of the wagon and watched as he raised a waterskin to his lips and took a large swallow. He was an imposing man, she thought as she continued to watch him heft a bag from the wagon and wander over to where the sun warmed the granite rockface. Triene nudged Susan and pointed to the clothes she had laid out by the bank. "Try these on." she said, "They will be more comfortable for travelling in than, um, your current, um…". Susan looked sadly at her suit. Dust had ingrained itself into the fine weave. Her stockings were nothing more than shreds of nylon holding the holes together and her beautiful shoes didn't bear thinking about. She looked at the proffered clothing. They would certainly be more practical if she were to be traipsing through woods and clambering in and out of wagons. There were some trousers that looked like a soft suede, not dissimilar to the texture of chamois leather, but of a darker hue. A long, linen tunic top also sat beside a pair of solid leather boots which had a pair of thick knitted socks stuffed inside. "I make and sell clothes so I'm pretty good at guessing sizes…." added Triene. "Come join us when you have changed." She indicated to where Jael had settled, reclining against the rock, chin tipped back to enjoy the sun's rays. Susan nodded her thanks and gave a small, distracted smile as she worried about where she should change. Spying a large tree with a low hanging branch, she made her decision and headed back into the forest.

She hung her new clothes on the branch and slipped off her suit and shirt, tossing them to the ground. The remnants of her stockings were easily removed, and she leant against the tree for support as she wiggled on the trousers. They were quite tight around the hips, but the suede was soft and supple. The tunic was a rougher cloth than she was used to, and it felt prickly against her previously pampered skin. She liked the light terracotta colour, however. It reminded her of the pots that decorated the rear terrace when she had visited her parents for the summer holidays. They were always full of bold and joyful flowers. Geoffrey, the old gardener had taken time to teach her about the flowers, until he had had to retire, of course. The socks reminded her of his big ratty jumpers as well, she smiled to herself. His wife knitted them for him and he wore them regardless of the weather. The socks were rather warm and rough but she was glad to have something to protect her feet, as she tugged on the boots. They were a bit cumbersome, and loose around the toes, but Triene had assessed her size incredibly well. The new clothes made Susan feel brighter, and better able to face this strange reality. The discomforts and mundane needs were making her question her coma theory. She moved to join her new companions, suitably attired and with fresh resolve.

Jael was sharing out dried meat and some wild strawberries when Susan reappeared from behind the trees. He was already regretting his impulse to help the strange woman and had convinced himself that she would bring trouble to their small family. She seemed less eccentric now, but Triene's enthusiastic overtures of friendship were concerning.

He observed Susan walking awkwardly across the forest floor and stretching to traverse the stream. It was obvious she had no idea how to navigate her surroundings. Probably from a wealthy family, he thought dismissively. They tended to stay in their precious homes and towns, oblivious to the necessities of life that brought them the food for their table and clothes for their backs. He wondered where she was from If she were from anywhere around here she would have known Carmon. Still, if she were from a wealthy family she should have access to sufficient funds, he just hoped that Triene had negotiated a good price for the clothing. Watching her pass Triene her old clothes to pack in the wagon, Jael couldn't help but notice the tunic and trousers revealed a pleasing figure and her pale face looked softer now it had been cleaned of the paint that had caked it. Her hair fell down her back in gentle, damp waves. He found himself staring at her a little too long, so he took a swig of water and looked down to examine the remnants of his meal.

Triene sat on the ground beside Jael, beckoning Susan over to join them. Susan hesitated, as if unsure of her welcome. Sighing heavily Jael handed her an empty water skin. "You can fill the skin from the stream," he said in an attempt at amity.

"Um... ok, but shouldn't we boil it before we drink it?" came her worried reply.

"Nah, it's good. Just avoid the fish, they wiggle going down," came his deadpan reply.

Susan looked horrified by the prospect and squinted pensively towards the stream.

"He's joking!" snickered Triene, "Come on, I'll show you".

Triene found a spot where the pebbles created a slight decline and adjusted the stones to create a funnel for the water. She placed the opening of her own waterskin under the funnel and it soon filled. Smiling she then returned to Jael, leaving Susan to fill her waterskin and take a tentative sip of the crisp, cold water. Thirstier than she had realised, Susan chugged the bottleful enthusiastically before refilling the skin and returning to the rockface. Jael passed her some berries and dried meat and she chomped delicately on the strip of meat. It didn't break off, so she tried nibbling at a corner before giving in and tearing off a large bite. Her eyes widened as she chewed, working her jaw hard. After a while she gave up and forced a swallow using water from her skin. She managed to cough out a "Thank you" around the lump in her throat and drank some more water to wash the lump down. This definitely seemed more real than any hallucination should. She popped the small but sweet strawberry in her mouth, relieved that the flavour was familiar, and it was easy to eat.

Bracing herself, Susan decided to formally thank her new companions for their kindness to her. "I'm sorry I haven't already expressed my gratitude properly. I've been rather bewildered, but I think I'm coming to terms with all this." She waved her hands wide to emphasise the word this before she continued with an optimistic smile, "You've been very kind and generous to me, with these clothes and the ride, so I must thank...erm..." Upon seeing Jael's deepening frown, her smile faded and her words ground to a halt.

Jael glowered at Triene, who deliberately ignored him. Jael then turned his scowling countenance back to Susan and said flatly, "You'll pay us when we get to Carnom."

"Jael!" exclaimed Triene. "We can just help her".

Susan interrupted. "Oh yes, of course," she said swiftly and automatically. "I don't have my card, but my bank will have my electronic signature. I will have to order anything over £500 in." Her voice faltered as the truth began to dawn on her.

"Bank?" asked Triene,

"Pounds?" said Jael, uneasily.

"Oh God!" Susan said in a horrified whisper. "I have nothing! No money, no home, no one who knows me….." Her voice petered out. Her eyes locked on Jael's, panic rising. Susan despised feeling vulnerable and weak. She guessed it was her parent's influence. Susan had quickly learned that she needed to be strong and successful to gain their approval. She had always been academically inclined, and since her parents equalled qualifications and a well-paid job as success, she had thrown herself into her studies. This, however, was not academic. She needed street smarts and physical hardiness. She was completely dependent on Triene and Jael's charity!

Triene put a hand on her shoulder and said firmly, "We were saying we needed an apprentice just the other day, weren't we, Jael?"

"Apprentice," he stated blankly.

"Yes," said Triene firmly. "Susan, would you like to work for us?"

Jael stood up abruptly, returning to the wagon.

"Um…I don't think Jael wants that," Susan said reluctantly, as she watched him storm off.

"He'll be fine," said Triene with a dismissive wave of her hand. "He will want to help you. He just worries, that's all."

Triene looked at Susan reassuringly, "You can start by refilling the water skins and pack up the food." Susan nodded quickly and got to work. As she bent over the stream, she felt the burn of forming tears. She gave a loud sniff and tipped up her chin. She would show them her worth. She wasn't going to give up just because things were a little strange just now. Peering at the others, she could see Jael's movements were tense and abrupt as he harnessed the horses to the wagon, but he took care to reassure them with calming hands. Really, he wasn't as scary a boss as Mr Blenchcot and Triene seemed genuine in her desire to help. Susan certainly hoped so. She was going to need a lot of support if she were to understand what was going on and get back to the City. Her hands clenched and her mouth drew tight. She had worked damn hard to get where she was. Sure, the corporate work was dull, but it paid the best salaries and gave out more promotions than the private client departments. She wasn't suited for this life: she needed to get back.

Seeing the siblings climb up at the front of the wagon, Susan hurried over and scrambled into the back, using the frame to haul herself up onto her knees. Wolf vaulted in after her then lay down, resting his head beside her and somehow managing a convincing impression of puppy dog eyes. She chuckled gently as she tentatively stroked the thick, darker

31

ruff on the back of his neck. The comforting gesture, the steady sway of the wagon and the clip-clop of hooves progressively soothed her overstimulated nerves as she watched the tranquil landscape pass by through the open canvas doors.

Jael, meanwhile, was deliberately ignoring Triene, who didn't seem to notice the silence. She knew it was dangerous to befriend others, he thought. She knew she needed to keep her distance. His conscience reminded him that he was the one to offer Susan a ride to Carnom, but he had been clear on his intention to offer brief aid, then be rid of her as quickly as possible. There was no need to give her clothes or to offer her a job! Friendship led to talk, talk led to risk of discovery. His grip on the reins tensed and the mare tossed her head back in protest. He immediately loosed his grip with a guilty wince. Triene had glanced at him briefly at that, she was paying attention then. He growled in frustration.

Triene let her brother stew. She knew she was being foolish, but Susan's situation reminded her of her parents' early struggles. She couldn't justify leaving her on her own, and she suspected Jael felt the same way, deep down. He had always been a caring sort growing up. Always one to rescue injured animals so he could heal them and grieving when he couldn't. The worry and bitterness was changing him. She turned her head and placed her hand gently on his as she gave him a half smile. He saw it and rolled his eyes before giving her a rueful smile in return.

Eventually the rugged vista began to change. The rocks flattened and the forests thinned, until they were passing through rolling grasslands highlighted with splashes of golden cowslip and scarlet poppies. Trees flowed down from the adjacent hillsides, scattering as they poured into the grass. Their quiet road merged with a wider track which bore signs of other travellers in the grooves and churned up dirt. It didn't take long to have the discordant sounds of other travellers encroach upon the quiet of their journey. Susan could make out the clatter of many horse drawn vehicles and an occasional shout of greeting or a curse. The sight of other travellers came next, as their wagon passed those walking the road, most of whom bore weighty bundles on their shoulders.

In time, the sun began to dip in the sky, dragging its warmth with it. The grasslands became cultivated fields with crops sending long shadows across the track. Just as the light was fading into dusk, Triene turned around in her seat and spoke to Susan, "We will be reaching this lovely inn we know shortly. We can get some of their beer and stew, and sleep in real beds! It's just outside the town, so although it can get busy it's not as bad as the inns in Carnom. You'll love it!" Triene seemed genuinely pleased by the prospect.

Susan couldn't help but feel a bubble of anticipation in her stomach, or was that hunger? She certainly hadn't eaten much that day. Worry then clouded her features as realisation hit. "It sounds lovely, but I haven't any money, remember. Should I sleep in the wagon?" Susan tendered, the bubble turning to stone.

Without turning, Jael said gruffly, "You'll join us, it will be safer. Don't worry, you'll be working the expense later." Triene beamed at her brother and winked at Susan. "There, all sorted! You're working for us now." Jael huffed and Wolf raised his head to share a satisfied grin with Triene.

Susan felt relief surge through her veins, although the bubble of excitement remained heavy. She was totally reliant on these people. She wasn't used to being so dependant. What if they weren't what they seemed? What if they sold her into slavery!?! They didn't seem the sort, but who knew?

## Chapter 5

The promised inn proved to be a rambling building with welcoming warm light spilling from ground floor windows into the deepening shadows outside. The tempting aromas of hops and braising meats made Susan's stomach growl in anticipation. Enticing sounds of dining and general merriment drifted out of the inn's open door.

Jael steered the wagon through the cobbled courtyard towards a large barn positioned to the south of the inn. An elderly ostler, whose rotund belly was a hearty recommendation for the inn's food, welcomed them with open arms and a wide smile. "Ho, Jael! Got some more of those boots for me?" he called out. "I've just about worn through the last pair. They don't last as long as they used to. Using defective hide now?" His voice was deep and jovial.

Jumping down from the wagon, Jael handed the ostler the reins and gave him a friendly slap on the back. "You know I only use the best. You must have been abusing them, wading in horse shit all day!" he replied with a suggestion of a smile on his usually solemn lips.

Triene reached back into the wagon and pulled out a pair of boots which she tossed deftly to the ostler. Laughing she said, "Here you are, you old rogue. Sewn by my own hand with delicate stitches for your dainty feet." Joining her brother, Triene embraced the ostler enthusiastically. "It is good to see you again, Kol."

"And you," declared the ostler as he hugged her back. "Go

in, drink and eat, Seema is inside. You have chosen a good time to come to Carnom. The Coral Skies is due to dock at dawn and people are saying the crew sailed to the Isle of Rua!"

Triene looked intrigued and even Wolf seemed interested in Kol's words. Only Jael seemed unimpressed. "I suppose we could find something useful, but unlikely. What we need is dye and new cloth. The extra footfall it will generate will be welcome though." Patting the mare's neck he added, "You'll give the horses the special oat mix?"

"But of course, Jael," said Kol and he stroked the mare's nose, as she nuzzled happily into his shoulder.

"She missed you," said Triene.

"More like she missed the special oats!" he laughed. "Come on old girl, let's get you settled... Would you care for some tasty offal, my good sir?" Kol directed the latter part of his speech to Wolf who had wandered round the wagon while they were speaking. Wolf smacked his lips expectantly. Smiling, Kol led the horses towards the open barn doors, Wolf casually following behind.

"My thanks, Kol," Jael called out to Kol's retreating figure. Kol dipped his head in acknowledgement just before he disappeared from sight.

Susan had climbed out of the wagon, all but forgotten during this exchange, and wandered into the middle of the courtyard, uncertain whether to join the others or go in the general direction of the inn. While she stood there indecisively, another wagon entered the courtyard and rushed past her. She stumbled out of its path and in doing so

36

bumped roughly into a handsy couple heading home for the night. The woman giggled as the man gave Susan an impatient push towards the inn and muttered, "Not interested, love." Embarrassed and anxious, Susan backed away, her hands raising warily. The failing light cast a sinister shadow over the man's face as he grinned at her and Susan's breath caught. A touch on her arm made her flinch and cower, heart beating loudly. The man laughed loudly at her obvious discomfort until Triene stepped between them cutting him from Susan's sight. "Come," she said gently, "We are going into the inn. Join us." Susan gulped and gave an abrupt nod, while blushing furiously. She couldn't believe how foolishly she was behaving. Triene thankfully overlooked her pitiable state and gently guided her towards the inn's doorway, where Jael was already entering. At least he hadn't been watching; he didn't need confirmation of his bad opinion of her.

The inside of the inn was wrapped in a warm, orange glow from the fireplace at the far end of the room. A large cast-iron basket piled high with burning firewood was set within a segment of wall made of roughly hewn bricks. People crammed into the space, most of them seated at large wooden tables. The patrons seemed to be mainly merchants, busy networking over food and drink. Good to see some things are the same, thought Susan.

Ahead of them was a short bar behind which beer barrels and tankards were stacked. A giant of a man was filling the tankards directly from one of the casks. He then handed them to a harried looking woman, who carefully placed them on a circular wooden tray. Carrying the tray level with her shoulder, she slid skilfully between the tables, handing out beer to the patrons, collecting empties and dropping the coin payments into her apron pocket.

Jael headed for the bar and Triene and Susan pursued him, using the route he forged to navigate their way through the tight spaces. The bartender charted their approach, sombre eyes watching them from a bruiser's face. His oversized hands wiped a damp cloth across the rough timber on the bar as he watched. He paused and turned to face a doorway to his right, from which the alluring aroma of cooking curled. His strong voice rumbled one word, "Seema!". Having dealt with Jael's approach he returned to filling tankards with beer.

A plump, older woman emerged from the kitchen wiping her wet hands on her apron. She regarded the bartender with a worried frown. He tipped his shaved head towards Jael and she turned her gaze his way. Her furrowed brow transformed into a beaming smile as she pulled him in for a fierce embrace, her short stature belying the strength of her hold. The top of her steel grey bun only just reached Jael's shoulder, so she had to crook her neck up to look into his fond expression. "Jael! It is good to see you my boy." She reached up and pinched the cheek dimple that had made a rare appearance. "I have missed you. And where is my little Triene?" she exclaimed as she peered around Jael's wide chest. Spying Triene, she grabbed her and gave her a big squeeze before holding her out by her arms to examine her. "Look at you, so bonny!" She glanced curiously at Susan shifting uncomfortably nearby, before turning back to Jael. "Your room and a meal?" she enquired.

"That would be most welcome. We have been longing for your delicious fare the whole journey," declared Jael extravagantly.

"Get on with you, boy!" she said, giving Jael a playful nudge with her elbow. "Go take a seat and I will sort out some stew for you." She turned to speak quietly to the bartender before disappearing into the kitchen. The bartender moved towards the table closest to the bar. He folded his tree trunk arms in front of the men sitting there and told them to move, his words reverberating and low. The men initially looked inclined to grumble, but clearly thought better of it when they perceived the speaker. They hastily picked up their beers and shuffled over to squeeze onto a different table. The bartender then wiped the table with his well-used cloth and beckoned Jael over.

There was a timber bench placed against the log wall. Jael headed for it, using its position to survey the other people in the room. A single stool sat on the opposite side of the table, which Triene happily perched upon. Susan couldn't see a spare stool nearby and didn't want to ask the surly bartender for one, so her only option was to squeeze onto the edge of the bench, next to Jael. Their arms touched and he grunted unhappily before shifting slightly, affording her more room. He was much larger than her; and his bulk was all muscle and menace. His gaze remained fixed on the crowd, although Triene looked at her and smiled. "You will love the food. The stew is full of meat and the bread is filling. The beer isn't bad either, or at least Jael seems to like it well enough," she teased glancing at her brother. Jael's frown softened as he looked on Triene in response, before hardening as he scanned the room once more.

Triene leant forward, "Don't mind Jael, he is just wary around people. You should be too," she added, her voice took on a warning tone. "Any of them could be thieves or start a fight or worse. Stay close to Jael, he's good at protecting." Jael finally turned towards Susan, caught her eye and nodded before quickly looking away again.

Susan felt the start of a knot building in the muscles of her neck as she took time to consider anew the people enjoying the inn's hospitality. Her eyes fell on a particularly slovenly looking man with a ratty beard, acne scars and a beak of a nose. He noticed her watching him and leered at her, revealing yellow and broken teeth. Dismayed, Susan tore her eyes away and focused on the thick oak table immediately in front of her. A shadow fell over it and she started, quickly glancing up. It was the older lady, Seema, delivering a large, steaming pot of stew with three wooden bowls and trowel-like spoons.

"She's a nervy one!" Seema said to Jael, nodding in Susan's direction while placing the food on the table. "Where'd you pick her up?"

Triene interrupted with a quick reply, "Susan is our new apprentice. Just learning the trade."

"Bit old to be an apprentice," said Seema appraisingly. Susan raised her chin and held the woman's gaze, hoping to make a better impression, as she said calmly, "Pleased to make your acquaintance". The woman inclined her head, in a slight indication of approval, although she still seemed suspicious of her. The bartender moved between them, silently placing some bread in the centre of the table, his actions breaking the tension in their exchange.

Seema shrugged lightly, before handing a key to Jael. "Your

usual room, it's ready for you." She glanced affectionately at Triene, "We will catch up later this evening, yes? When I am not needed in the kitchen." She then bustled away, acknowledging one of her regular patrons with a few words as she went.

Susan eyed the stew pot suspiciously. It smelt good, but she was beginning to feel concerned about the hygiene of this place. Wooden bowls and utensils tend to hold germs. No dishwashers here, did they even have washing up liquid? To divert her train of thought, she spoke to Triene, "You seem well known here."

"Yes, we often come here. Seema's our mother's sister, and Kol is her husband."

"Oh, your aunt!" Susan said with understanding, "So does your mother live near here?"

Jael paused from filling his bowl for a moment before answering blankly, "Our parents are dead." Triene's face filled with anguish and she dropped her gaze as the darkness burst from its prison and threatened to consume her.

"I'm so sorry, I didn't realise," said Susan faintly.

Triene exhaled slowly, struggling against the overwhelming hopelessness. Jael clarified, his words stilted and tight, "It was a few years back. They were killed while we were on the road. We found them when we returned home…" He fell silent for a moment before reaching for his sister's hand and giving it a reassuring squeeze.

Uncomfortable, Susan muttered another apology, "Of course, sorry," and started filling her bowl with stew to

41

occupy the uneasy silence. In a subdued voice, Triene advised Susan to dip the bread in the stew to soften it. The uncomfortable atmosphere continued so Susan focused on her meal. She was relieved to find the meal as appetising as promised and managed to consume a second bowlful.

The waitress with the tray of beers stopped by their table a few times during the evening, and each time she did, Jael bought three mugs of beer with pieces of copper kept in a leather pouch tied to his belt. As night fell, Susan found her thoughts becoming somewhat fuddled so the next time the beer was offered, she was careful to decline. By this time, most of the tables had been cleared. The quiet room now had a contemplative air with the remaining drinkers mostly staring into their final tankard. Seema had emerged from the kitchens, casting aside her apron, and was conversing quietly with Triene and Jael. Conscious that she should not eavesdrop on their private conversation; feeling full, tired, and needing to unwind, Susan turned her focus on the play of light and shadow created by the dwindling fire.

She watched the flames lick their leisurely way around the remaining firewood. The sparkling orange embers mesmerising her exhausted mind. The fiery shapes swayed as if they were people dancing to an unheard melody. As she was drawn into the imagery the weight of the day gradually lifted and she felt her body melt into a relaxed stasis.

The longer she watched, the more distinct the people became, and what she had seen as a dance slowly morphed into a battle. A battle with bloodied weapons cleaving through the flames. Swords clashed and Susan could hear the impact in the crackle and snap of the fire. She could see the back of a man as he fended off a couple of heavy blows from a muscle bound soldier bearing a double headed axe, He was forced to his knee, one foot still braced on the ground, sword and head lowered. His attacker ruthlessly struck at him and Susan flinched, but somehow the fierce blow was deflected by a two handed, upward sweep of his sword. The man continued with an offensive as he swept his lower leg round and tripped his attacker, who flailed and fell heavily, embers flaring on impact. The man with the sword rose as his attacker fell and thrust his sword deep into his attacker's chest, the cry of pain echoed within Susan's head. She tasted bile and tried to retreat, but she was trapped, an unwilling witness to the butchery.

New attackers were cautiously approaching the man with the sword from behind. She recoiled, anticipating more bloodshed, even as she tried to warn the man. She couldn't cry out, her throat spasmed and squeezed shut. Fear trickled like ice through her veins as she froze, unable to help and unable to look away.

Sputtering sparks ripped through the last log and a young woman, who looked remarkably like Triene, rose within them. A blistering flame burst free from her outstretched hand, engulfing the attackers, who writhed and thrashed as the heat consumed them. The wood split with a jolting snap and the image disappeared. Susan was suddenly released and jerked back. She put her head in her hands for a moment, stunned, before gradually regaining an awareness of her surroundings.

She heard Triene's soft voice, suggesting they retire for the night, while giving a meaningful look in Susan's direction. Seeing Susan blinking slowly, she added gently, "You must be shattered. We have kept you up too long with our talking. You looked like you were sleeping where you sat. Shall we go to bed?" Still disorientated, Susan quickly agreed. Sleep, yes. She had had a disturbing dream. Perfectly understandable in the circumstances.

## Chapter 6

Susan jerked awake to the sound of someone moving furtively around her bedroom. Her heart hammered in her chest. A burglar! She stiffened, trying not to alert the intruder as she wondered what she could do? A sudden weight landed on her stomach, making her exhale in a rush. Her eyes flew open to see a huge dog looming over her, drooling mouth just inches from her face. No! Not a dog, A wolf. Recollection kicked in. Wolf. As if sensing her recognition, Wolf's long wet tongue flicked out and swiped her cheek, spreading saliva from chin to forehead. Grinning he stepped off her and snuggled up against Triene on the other side of the bed. As he burrowed in, his paws pushed against Susan who shuffled onto her side, allowing him sufficient space.

As she shifted uncomfortably on the lumpy mattress, she hoped it didn't have bed bugs. Oh God! Her right arm was itching. Just relax, she thought. It is just thought association. But the more she tried to ignore it, the worse the itching became. She wiggled to free her other arm so she could scratch it. The prickles dodged her nails and started inching their way down her leg and into her foot. She desperately rubbed her foot up and down her other leg, trying not to disturb Triene. The itch just jumped to her waist. Giving up and breathing heavily, she tried distraction next and took advantage of the hint of light filtering through the narrow window to survey the room.

It was a small room with a low, sloped ceiling and only the one small window tucked into the roof space. Two beds and a chest of drawers had been squeezed into the bedchamber

45

leaving only the smallest area of oiled floorboards bare. The pottery basin rested on the chest, cloth abandoned by its side, while its companion jug with its cool water awaited the morning's ablutions.

Jael was lying asleep on the other bed, his coarse weave blanket had been tossed onto the floor. They had all remained clothed, with Jael having retained his trousers and an undershirt. Without the outer clothing, Susan could verify the bulk of his physique. While less chiselled than the muscles modelled by movie stars, they were obviously powerful. Susan's gaze wandered to his face. His jaw had developed a dusting of hair during the night adding to his rugged appeal, while his chocolate brown hair tumbled raffishly over one eye. The usual furrow between his brows was smooth and his mouth soft and slack as he slept. Shame he was such a grump, she sighed to herself.

Wolf suddenly twitched and kicked as he dreamed. Susan twisted on the bed so that she could run her hand over his fur to settle him. He quickly quieted and giving a satisfied smile she sank back to resume her observations, only to see Jael's hazel eyes were now open and his intense focus was on her. How awkward! She managed to whisper a stifled, "Good morning,"

Jael seemed about to reply, but was halted by Triene's overly cheerful exclamation from behind her, "Oh, are you both awake now? Excellent!" and she leaned over to give Wolf an enthusiastic chest rub. Wolf rolled onto his back, snaking into the blanket, clearly enjoying the attention.

Jael unfolded and perched on the edge of his bed, deliberately avoiding looking in Susan's direction. He cursorily ran his fingers through his tousled hair, before stretching his neck and eliciting a loud crack. He then bent forward and started pulling on his boots. Susan gave an inward shrug and followed his lead, the rough blanket and bumpy mattress not tempting enough to make her want to stay in bed.

Breakfast was waiting for them when they made their way downstairs. A couple of other tables were already occupied, although their table from the previous night had clearly been kept available for them. As they took their seats the bartender brought them each a tankard of beer. Susan was relieved to see they also had a jug of water, even as she lamented the absence of her morning coffee. Breakfast included some fresh and warm goat's milk and some of the same kind of bread as before. Slices of some rich, dark meat and some boiled eggs also sat on the wooden platter in the centre of the table.

As they devoured breakfast, Jael and Triene discussed their plans for the day. Carnom had a market where they could sell their clothing and buy materials. Jael was acquainted with the alderman and was confident he would manage to get a spot by the auction, since it would get the best footfall. Soon, they were winding up their plans and none of them had included Susan. Concerned that they had decided they wouldn't be needing her help, she spoke up, "What do you want me to do?"

In unison, they turned to face her, Triene looking guilty and Jael looking annoyed, as usual.

"Um, I'm sure we could have help with……" Triene began and looked at her brother hopefully.

"You'll be fetching and carrying, and doing whatever needs to be done, when it needs doing," he said gruffly.

Relieved that she wasn't going to be left behind Susan replied lightly, "Oh like a gopher – go for this, go for that.....".

They both looked at her blankly before Triene said, "Yes, probably."

## Chapter 7

Plans concluded, they left the inn, promising to return that evening. Kol met them in the courtyard, Wolf by his side. He had led the wagon out of the barn, the horses already strapped into their harnesses. The younger horse tossed his head in excitement, clearly well-rested and fed, and eager to stretch his legs. The horses' dappled, rough coats had been brushed smooth and their manes and tails freshly plaited. The gelding's shod hooves clipped on the cobblestones as he shuffled on the spot. The older mare rolled her eyes at his antics, and she whinnied a soft greeting to Jael, nudging him affectionately. Jael ran a calming caress over her withers and shoulders as he quickly checked them both.

"Our thanks for your care, Kol," said Jael, as he grasped the ostler's hand, arm wrestler style, and held it a moment.

"A pleasure, my boy," returned Kol, handing over the reins. "May you have good trade today."

Out of the side of his eye, Jael saw Susan heading for the back of the wagon with Wolf. "You can join us up front today," he told her brusquely, before making his way into the driver's box. Surprised and pleased, Susan turned back and examined the side of the wagon looking for the best way to climb up. Triene pointed out a place for her foot and Susan heaved herself up and plonked down in the centre of the worn wooden seat. Triene sprang up behind her and Susan found herself flanked by the siblings. Jael gave a rapid shake of the reins, calling out to the horses, and they slowly moved off, their pace increasing to a gentle trot upon reaching the road.

Wolf prodded Susan's waist with his nose and she instinctively shifted away. He immediately took advantage of her movement and wormed his large head between the women. He rested it on the seat and peered up at Triene imploringly. Triene laughed fondly and stroked the thick grey fur between his ears. He huffed contentedly and closed his eyes. Susan shook her head at the obvious ploy and smiled. She was surprised to find herself looking forward to the day, and curious as to what she would discover. Jael and Triene seemed genuinely good people, which confused her. She kept waiting for them to do or say something that revealed some ulterior motive, but nothing had been forthcoming. She found herself beginning to think of them as friends, which was also confusing. She wasn't one to have friends, only acquaintances or colleagues, whom she wasn't sure she particularly liked and certainly didn't trust. Although she was missing things, like coffee, her bed, and a hot shower, but she was shocked to realise that she didn't have any people she missed. As she breathed in the fresh air and looked around at the landscape surrounding her, she wondered if she really missed London or her work. She gave herself a mental shake. She refused to think like that. She needed to get back.

The sun had risen an hour or so earlier, but there were still signs of dew on the grasses crowding the verge and the road was noticeably quieter this morning. As they travelled, Susan observed the hills had flattened out and the fields fed into the occasional roughly built home, with squawking chickens and sweetcorn hanging to dry on washing lines in the yard. Distant figures could be seen already working in the fields, wielding hoes to churn up the soil ready for planting or scythes slicing through early crops.

Gradually, the signs of human habitation increased, and barely quarter of an hour had passed before they reached the outskirts of Carnom. As they neared the town, she could detect rows of brick-built buildings, some painted in bright colours, and the wagon rumbled along the road as it began to have cobble stones embedded to preserve its structure.

The buildings grew sturdier and more ornate the further they traversed, while the streets bustled with purpose filled people. The clean, fresh smells of the countryside were replaced by the acrid scents of excrement - hopefully from the horses, thought Susan, remembering stories of medieval London - before they intermingled with the odours of rotting fish and seaweed as the proximity of the sea made itself known. Shrieking gulls soared overhead as the cobbled street opened up into a large market square adjacent to the harbour. The sea came into view, its placid waves lapping against the ships and stone jetty, just audible amid the sounds of market stalls being set up, and earlier buyers bartering for bargains. In the distance, the azure sea blended into a sky scattered with feathery clouds, while a grassy peninsula curled protectively around the port.

The natural harbour contained small fishing vessels bobbing merrily while an imposing galleon was docked at the wharf. The sides of the galleon rose high above the water, her hull made of gleaming timber. Three tall masts stood proudly on her deck, the square rig sails furled. Sailors were scaling the masts and yards, hollering to crewmates on the deck. A striking figurehead of a naked woman rising out of a bed of brightly coloured coral, pointed towards a platform around which crowds were gathering.

Triene indicated to the stand and explained, "That's where

the Coral Skies' cargo will be auctioned. Hardly any ships have survived the journey to the Isle of Rua. I believe the last one was two generations ago. The cargo was famous for its discovery of the statue of Rua which went to the Temple of Helvoa, of course. It's the link with the magic that encourages captains to risk the journey." This last was said with a hint of bitterness.

"Magic isn't something to discuss or look for," Jael said emphatically, frowning at his sister, as he tried to send a silent message for her to keep away from the auction. Triene chose to ignore him.

"I know, I know, sorry." But the rolled eyes directed at Susan suggested that she wasn't in the least remorseful. Triene was eager to see what the Coral Skies had discovered even as she felt anger boiling in her chest at the hypocrisy of society. There was a morbid fascination with the ancients and their magical items, yet a person with only a tiny bit of magical ability was treated as a pariah, or worse. It made no sense. She squeezed the anger back in its box and pasted an enthusiastic smile on her face. "Oh look!" Triene cried, "They are putting some goods out for the auction. Come on! We need to get over there." She pulled at Susan's hand and leapt off the wagon while Jael was still slowing the horses. Susan managed to climb down and step off without falling over, before being dragged into the crowd converging on the stage. It was soon difficult to move any further forward as it seemed everyone had crammed in place, craning their necks to see what was to be auctioned. A row of imposing men, dressed in black with an emerald green sash across their chests, stood at the front of the stage. Their posture and weaponry made it clear that they were present to guard the auction goods.

Jael and the wagon were soon out of sight and Susan felt strangely lost and vulnerable without him or Wolf nearby. She made sure to keep Triene close, needing that familiarity to steady the rising anxiety.

The babble of excited voices surrounding them quieted as a short, slight man with tufts of white hair peeking out of a bright orange hat and a long purple coat, tapped his staff on the stage in three sharp raps. He waited a few moments to make sure he had the attention of the crowd and then spoke in a surprisingly loud and rich voice.

"What wonders! What delights we have for you today!" he announced.

"Four weeks ago the Coral Skies ventured forth, from this very port, determined to locate and convey exotic merchandise from the Isle of Rua. Many ships have embarked upon this journey, but none have successfully returned since the legendary SwanSong one hundred and twenty-three years ago. So many brave souls lost in the maelstrom that surrounds the isle." He dropped his head in exaggerated sorrow and paused for dramatic effect. He then looked up and beamed at his audience.

"But this auspicious day, the Coral Skies under the infamous Captain Hrel…" At this point a man stepped forward to take a bow with a flamboyant spin of his large hat. He smiled sardonically at the cheering crowd. "… has returned triumphant. His cargo contains delights that will astound you. What will tempt you to spend your coin? I hope you have brought plenty, for I predict these rare treats will prove most popular. Make sure you speak up, don't be shy. Make your bid and take home your prize today."

A growing wave of anticipation flowed over the crowd, engulfing even Susan. Triene's feet were jiggling with delight; she was clearly eager to see the goods for sale.

"First on our list is this extraordinary fruit. Observe its bright yellow pigmentation. The colour reflects the explosion of flavour that assaults your tongue when you taste it. The strong scent is crisp and tart. To add this to a dish or drink or even a perfume would bring it a fresh and exotic aroma. I can only imagine how successful an eatery serving such an unusual fare would become......"

Susan stood there, fascinated by the ferocious bidding for the crates of lemons. The auctioneer was adept at distinguishing between the bidders, despite the confusing number of people shouting and waving their arms. The auction continued in the same vein as other goods were bought and sold.

While all eyes were focused on the next crated cargo being brought forth, Susan noticed a lad with lean and lanky limbs, his clothes just a bit too short, weaving through the crowd. As she watched she saw a flash of metal in one hand while the other swiftly caught a money pouch and tucked it in his waistband. He glanced round and saw her staring open mouthed. He gave her a mischievous wink and was gone in an instant, blending into the throng. Worried, she moved to speak to Triene, but before she did, she saw a real live dodo walking across the stage. Stunned, she whispered, "But they're extinct!"

"You know this bird?" Triene questioned.

"Only through pictures and a stuffed one in a museum," she replied, immediately amused by the confident and clumsy antics of the dodo strutting around. It was easily three foot tall with a bulbous beak and fluffy tail, which waggled comically. The auctioneer revealed a cage with about 10 such birds in it and declared it contained at least two breeding pairs.

"Who will give me 5 gold coins for the cageful?"

A voice from across the square called out, "3 gold!" and so the bidding began.

The auction continued throughout the morning. A few other animals were displayed and sold. Susan didn't recognise many of them, although she did recognise the chameleons who were extolled as magical beings able to change their appearance. Susan nodded to herself. So magic was really used for an explanation of the unknown or unusual, she thought. She mused over her sudden rush of disappointment and realised, with surprise, that she had wanted there to be real magic in this strange world.

The auctioneer then halted the sales and announced, "I have but one more collection to reveal, and I assure you that you will want to see this, but first we have a visitor that hitched a lift on the Coral Skies. We can only hope to hear how she came to be on the Isle of Rua when she speaks to us. I know you will be as excited as I am. May I introduce the renowned historian and raconteur, Selene." The auctioneer stepped back into the shadows as an elegant woman of middle age moved forward. She was dressed in a simple cloak of undyed, woven wool, that covered her completely, save for her proud and strong face. She had piercing pale eyes that scanned her audience as if seeking out someone in particular. Selene's eyes landed on Susan and seemed to hover there a fraction longer than on the others.

"Selene the Storyteller," breathed Triene, as around the stage the initial excited murmurings fell silent.

Selene then spoke. Although her voice was gentle it carried effortlessly, and had a rich timbre that drew her audience in. "As you have just heard, I have been travelling, collecting histories and accounts of places far and wide, chronicles of the past and predictions for the future," she stated calmly. "Tonight, as the moon rises, I will speak in the ruined keep. You are welcome to come and listen. But be warned, this knowledge will affect your choices and the paths you take. Only attend if you are prepared to accept the consequences." She turned then and disappeared behind the burlap drapes at the rear of the stage.

Excited voices erupted around them. "Did you hear that? The Storyteller is going to speak to us!"

"Can you believe it? It really is her."

"What do you think she means, predictions?"

"Wow, I am going to have to tell Lorn about this; he won't want to miss it."

All the voices were expressing the same wonder and eagerness. Clearly, this Selene was a bit of a celebrity, thought Susan. She certainly had a way of making her words resonate and tempt the listener. Even she had been entranced when she spoke and really hoped her companions would want to stay and hear the story.

Triene beamed at her, "Wait until Jael hears about this, we need to go find him!"

As they turned to manoeuvre their way out of the crowd, they heard the auctioneer call out... "And how am I to follow such thrilling news.... Why with the sale of ancient items linked to the rejected religion, Ruaism!  The SwanSong brought us back the statue that is said to have told the story of creation.  What secrets about the magic do these relics hide and what possibilities lie hidden in their depths to be explored by their new owners?" The reaction from the crowd was all the auctioneer could have wanted.  Shock, excitement and anger swirled within the marketplace until attention was drawn back to the front of the stage.

Triene gasped and whispered, "We have to see this!" as she turned back towards the stage. She pressed forward, dragging Susan with her. Somehow, they threaded a route through the clustered and clammy bodies until they neared the platform where they would be able to observe them better.

"The value of these items cannot be exaggerated.  The seller has placed a reserve on the artifacts.  If you don't buy now, you will lose the opportunity since the Temple will no doubt snap them up."  A man behind Susan muttered, "Bloody priests!" and a grumble of agreement accompanied his statement.

Two auction guards stood behind a small, raised display. Five gemstones, each the size of a song thrush egg, had been placed upon a black silk display cloth. Each gem had a different pattern and colouration. The auctioneer spoke again, "These exquisite gemstones were discovered embedded in the sarcophagus of one of the ancients, a leader of men and a follower of the Goddess Rua. They are intriguing are they not? Look closely. Each one is a different shade, yet all are the same size and shape." Susan found herself leaning forwards to see them more closely, succumbing to his tempting invitation. "See how the gem on the left has blue and white swirls that seem to move as you stare at them...... Look into the unfathomable depths of the navy gem..... And here, we have the mottled greens and browns of the next gem, it could almost hatch before our eyes, could it not! The vermillion gem is next, see it catch the light in its warm centre and finally, but certainly not last, we have the golden gemstone. Not made of the precious metal but easily as valuable. See the way it sparkles in the sun. Exquisite!" The auctioneer had the crowd eating out of his hands.... he should make a tidy profit out of these, he thought, eyes gleaming. "Do I detect a glimmer from within these stones, I wonder? No, it cannot be...or could it be a touch of hidden magic?" The gasp from the crowd at the word rippled to the outer edges before returning to the stage. Excellent! I've got them, he thought. "No, forgive me? I am mistaken, there is no magic, even on the Isle of Rua. We are safe." he added slyly before beginning the bidding, "Let us start with 10 gold for the first gem, with its blue and white pigmentation, what do I hear?" From the worried faces this was aiming a bit high as a starting price. He was confident that he would manage to wrangle them up to a higher sum, though. The avarice was palpable. He mentally rubbed his hands gleefully at the thought of his commission.

A richly dressed merchant, with gold chains around his many chins and ornate rings on his pudgy fingers, strode through the crowd, his personal guard in crimson livery ensuring an unimpeded passage. "I will pay you 100 gold for all the stones if you end the auction now," he said in an arrogant and indolent voice.

Everyone was now staring at the bidder, while the auctioneer merely inclined his head and said slyly, "Well now, a most generous offer, kind sir. However, it may be that I will be able to get more by seeking more bids and should surely give that a try at first."

The merchant cast a disdainful glance at the crowd. "Highly unlikely, but I will play your game and go up to 150 gold if you will cease this nonsense and conclude our business."

The people who had been bristling at his derogatory attitude, now gasped. Some of the more suspect members of the crowd started fingering their daggers in interest. In a well-rehearsed move the merchant's guards unsheathed their swords and circled around him. He remained unperturbed as he awaited the auctioneer's agreement.

The auctioneer glanced over to the figure standing in the shadows at the edge of the stage. Captain Hrel nodded. "Sold!" cried the auctioneer, who immediately beckoned the merchant over to exchange the gold for the gemstones, as if concerned he might disappear if given a moment to reflect. A servant standing close to the merchant brought forward a chest which was opened revealing many gold coins. "That's a fair bit of counting to be done," said the auctioneer with a gleam. The servant carefully removed several coins and placed them in a separate pouch before handing the chest over.

"You had better get on with it then," drawled the merchant. "I don't wish to waste any more time than is necessary on this transaction."

While the auctioneer conducted the counting of the coins under the watchful eye of the merchant's servant, the two sets of guards, one in red the other in black with green, eyed each other warily and stared warningly at the closest members of the crowd. Only the merchant seemed bored by the process as he contemplated the lace on his lavishly decorated coat.

An eager young guard jumped onto the stage, ready to pack away the gems in preparation for the exchange. The two guards already on the platform supervised this undertaking, making sure he wrapped them in the silk before placing them in their leather pouch. Having completed this task to the satisfaction of his superiors, the junior guard rose, smartly saluted and retreated behind the drapes at the back of the stage.

Susan and Triene stood to the edge of the platform observing the flurry of activity around the gemstones. "I take it that was an impressive bid?" asked Susan.

Triene gave a forced laugh, "It was indeed! Very few have that sort of wealth." She shook her head. "Ruaism discoveries generally end up stored in the Temple at Helvoa and anyone who wishes to see them are required to pay for the privilege." she said, her voice bitter.

"Do you believe magic is real?" Susan asked, struggling to keep her scepticism out of her voice.

"Elemental magic is real, even if most of the magic has been lost." Triene whispered. There was a sudden shout of anger from the direction of the platform, and they swung round to look, The merchant stalked over to the auctioneer and methodically circled one bejewelled hand around the terrified auctioneer's neck, while flourishing the leather pouch in his other. The auction guards were immediately stayed by the merchant's protectors, who brandished their swords threateningly. "Where is the fire stone?" hissed the merchant between clenched teeth. The auctioneer stretched his neck and weakly grasped the merchant's arm before beckoning to the guards that had been in charge of the stones. The first guard looked from one to the other, his face a mask of horror, "It was in the pouch, I saw it packed myself. Me and Karl here." The guard standing beside him nodded vigorously. The merchant released the auctioneer who doubled up, putting his hand protectively up to his throat and coughing.

The merchant spoke directly to the guard, spit issuing from his lips as he did so, "And where is the guard that purportedly packed it?"

The guard's eyes widened and searched the stage futilely before barking an urgent order, "Find him!" The resulting desperate hunt behind the drapes led to the reluctant and nervous approach of a guard bearing a crumpled uniform. "Er, these were found, er, tossed behind a crate," he stammered under the combined glares. "They're young Jake's. Er, he was tied and gagged and, er, shoved in the privy, sir." A tense silence followed; all eyes focused on the uniform. The guard holding it shuffled nervously.

Captain Hrel pushed off the beam he had been leaning

against and sauntered forwards. His hand rested on the hilt of his sheathed sword, but his handsome face was all amiability. He executed an elegant bow, sketching a corkscrew in the air with his feathered hat in the direction of the fuming merchant. "Well, well, my dear sir," he began, "We appear to have been robbed. You of your gem and, as a consequence, me of my gold." He placed his hat back on his head and thoughtfully stroked his fair beard. "What do you say, we agree a reduced price and conclude the transaction? I have no doubt the guards will find the gem and return it to me, no harm done," he said persuasively, addressing the merchant but looking meaningfully at the guards still standing on the stage. The first guard flinched, then dragged the other off, sending more guards running to track the thief down. Meanwhile, the merchant's calculating eyes scanned the Captain's row of throwing knives as well as the sword at his hip and the daggers tucked into his cuffed boots, before saying haughtily, "Keep the coin. The gem is mine whether the auction guards find him or mine do." He attempted to sweep out of the square although his portly frame made it more of a wobble, as his entourage followed, swords still drawn menacingly.

"A pleasure doing business with you," murmured Captain Hrel as he gathered up his new coin chest and tucked it securely under his arm. He then addressed the auctioneer, eyebrow raised and a slight smirk on his lips. "Thank you for your services this day. When you feel recovered, let my quartermaster have the rest of the profit, would you? I should be taking this to my ship before other thieves are tempted to rob me, don't you think?" Tipping his hat politely, he swaggered off and members of his crew, broad and mean, emerged from the shadows to walk with him, protecting their newly earnt wealth.

Susan and Triene exchanged a look of incredulity before Triene said, "Let's go find Jael….." Susan nodded vigorously, still overwhelmed by the sudden descent into violence. So many swords! And everyone seemed so blasé! It could have easily ended in bloodshed, yet everyone was just heading back to the market, shopping, for goodness sake! No one had called the police. She eyed the weapons everyone seemed to be wearing and thought about the guards. Private justice, she thought. Oh shit! This place was dangerous! She kept close to Triene as they navigated their way through the excited throng towards the market stalls, more grateful for her help than ever.

## Chapter 8

They discovered their stall at the corner closest to the market entrance. It displayed samples of their clothing and boots for customers to examine, with the bulk of their wares kept in the wagon behind the stall. Wolf was guarding their coin and produce by the expedient of dozing next to it; his back was warm from the midday sun, and he was enjoying an intriguing combination of scents wafting through the open canvas. Wolf was under strict instructions to remain lying in the wagon since buyers could get skittish if they noticed him in their midst.

Jael observed Triene and Susan's arrival while he was finalising a sale. He handed over the folded clothing to the young woman, who blinked rapidly as he bestowed his most charming smile upon her. As she wandered off in a daze, Jael turned to face his sister, his usual scowl quickly replacing the smile. "About time you got here," he grumbled. "You can take over the stall while I locate some new dyes and fabrics." He took off without giving them a chance to speak. Triene just shrugged at Susan and quickly explained what she needed to do. Bartering was expected and the buyers would be used to this. Susan narrowed her eyes in determination. I can do this, she thought as she watched Triene work the charm offensive on their first customer.

She struggled at bit at first, but soon got into the flow. She rather enjoyed the bartering and managed to get decent prices for the goods she sold. When Jael finally returned and Triene praised her work, she felt a satisfaction she hadn't felt in her previous job. A small frown appeared on her brow, how could that be? She was just selling clothes. Her legal work was much more challenging, and her clients were important people in big businesses, not market stalls. She shook her head. It was probably the novelty of it. She pushed the worrying thought to the back of her mind as she focused on the small box of sweet treats being offered her. Jael had succumbed to impulse and bought them from a nearby stall on his way back to them.

She inspected the lightly dusted, orange squares before picking one up between forefinger and thumb. She tentatively nibbled at a corner and the honeyed tid-bit dissolved on her tongue. She sighed and put the whole sweet in her mouth and let it melt, appreciating its silky texture and sugar hit, it being the first sweet food she had tasted since arriving in this world. She opened her eyes to see Jael frowning at her. "What?" she said defensively, "They're really good!" Then remembering they were Jael's, she quickly thanked him for sharing. A snort of laughter burst from Jael, which surprised him as much as Susan. He fidgeted awkwardly with the box before placing it securely in his pack.

Clearing his throat, he said to Triene, "I hear Selene the Storyteller is speaking tonight. I thought we might attend, if you are interested." His manner was a little too nonchalant. Triene knew it and decided to tease him.

"Oh! I don't know, I am rather tired, and Susan has had her first day trading, she must be exhausted." she said, giving Susan a meaningful stare. "Perhaps we should head back to the inn and eat." Playing along, Susan gave an exaggerated yawn.

Oblivious to the ribbing, Jael attempted to persuade them, "I guess so, but I did spy a stall serving an excellent hog roast. We could purchase that for supper. We could supplement it with some of Gileon's cider. You know you love his cider."

Triene laughed, "Oh all right! Just because of the cider then." She gave Jael's arm an affectionate squeeze. "Of course, we want to see Selene." Jael looked so relieved that Susan couldn't help but chuckle. He looked at her sidewise and his dimple twitched.

They reached the ruins just as the sun dipped below the horizon, guided by the torches lining the centre. The flickering flames cast ominous shadows against the remaining walls of the keep and contorted the faces of the expectant congregation. Voices were lowered, as they shuffled into position, some laying out blankets to sit upon, others wrapping their blankets over shivering shoulders, chilled by the bite in the night air.

Jael led Susan and Triene to where the wall had crumbled leaving a wide, uneven ledge. The fallen bricks lay on the ground, obscured in the shadows. Susan stubbed her toe and swore as she stumbled. Jael reached out to support her, but his initial concern was quickly replaced with a smirk as Susan hopped lopsidedly in an impossible attempt to rub her sore toe. Despite his amusement, he offered his hand and Susan shyly accepted his help, leaning into him as she climbed over the stones, before taking a seat. Triene had already perched on the ledge and she moved over to make space for Susan, an excited smile on her lips. Triene and Jael had, of course, heard of the famed storyteller and her reputation for brave renderings of histories. She was a scholar and an adventurer but, unlike the priests in the

66

Temple, she gave her knowledge freely, saying it was important for truths to be shared lest the people be overcome by lies.

A tall, cloaked figure glided to stand in front of the lambent flames of the fire pit at the far end of the keep, forming a striking silhouette. Her arms stretched up and her head tipped back to stare at the cloudy night sky. The hushed murmurs drew silent, as, one by one, the crowd turned to stare. The figure's hidden features scanned her audience before her command rang out clear and wide. "I am Selene. Purveyor of knowledge. Heed my words." She paused momentarily before she declared solemnly, "Tonight, I will speak of the Goddess Rua's gift – I will speak of magic." Gasps followed this announcement. Triene leant forward, her eager eyes reflecting the flames from the torches, while Jael stiffened, his frown deepening. Susan felt bewildered by the rising tension in the keep. Her burgeoning familiarity with this place suddenly proved shallow. Some fundamental understanding was clearly missing. She looked upon Selene and hoped for enlightenment.

Undisturbed by the reaction to her initial words, Selene walked serenely to the wall behind the firepit and gracefully ascended to sit upon a dais. Her strong, imperturbable features were illuminated by the fire, as she carefully picked up a small mallet, wrapped in suede and used it to strike a large, copper bowl. A rich, deep tone reverberated throughout the keep, until its echo became a memory. She rang out the note once more and while it hummed, she began to chant in a low contralto:

*"In the beginning was a memory. A memory of light and of life and of love.*

*The memory became known as the Goddess, the Blessed Rua.*

*The Goddess danced through the void, calling to her all which had been lost.*

*And where she danced, swirls of stars were formed, bringing light to the darkness.*

*There was light, yet there was no life for her to love.*

*And so, the Goddess birthed countless worlds to circle the stars.*

*And she waited, but no life came.*

*The Goddess despaired.*

*Our world was born in her grief, and reality splintered in her pain.*

*Within each reality lay a twin to our own world, formed by its own truth.*

*Some were barren, and the Goddess turned from them.*

*Some bore life and the Goddess was pleased.*

*She gifted part of herself to the life that she loved. This was the gift of magic.*

*And so, the Goddess watched."*

The final vibration of the singing bowl dispersed into the night sky, and a sober stillness blanketed the keep.

When Selene spoke again, her voice was gentle and soft, caressing the ears of old and young, of distant and near.

"The entwined magic and life surged through the seas, the earth, and the skies, filling our world with the Goddess' love. The magic gave strength to the life, and life thrived.

"In time, a new creature emerged, one that had an ability to sense the presence of the magic. This creature was named, Humanity. Over the ages humans sharpened their skills, and by the time the ancients appeared, there were some humans that had developed the ability to influence the magical elements of: Earth; Water; Fire; Air and Spirit. Yet no single human had the power to influence more than one element. The ancients named those with this power their elders, a title of respect, since the elders used their influence to care for the world and all upon it."

A rumble of discontent vibrated through the crowd, as Selene paused. Yet, Susan noted Triene had a wistful smile touching her lips.

Selene's head dropped and her shoulders slumped before she resumed her tale. "Humanity, it transpired, is a selfish creature," she stated with sorrow saturating her voice. She continued, "Some of the elders grew angry that their skills with the elements were attributed to the Goddess and sought power and adulation for themselves. They gained followers, who rejected the Goddess and began worshipping those elders, and renamed them mages. In exchange for favours, the followers began identifying and punishing those that denied the mages' new status. The greed and desire for power grew."

"We all know of the death and destruction that followed. The era of the ancients ended, and the Mage Wars began." She breathed out a heavy sigh, and added firmly, "Our

69

history lessons have a selective memory. We tell our children tales of the evil that lies in magic. We dwell on the violence, on the domination by force, and the terrors that came from its use. Yet, we ignore that the magic was a gift given in love, and that humans once used it to care and nurture. It is the nature of humanity, not the nature of the magic, that gave rise to the Mage Wars. This is the truth that has been suppressed and twisted."

The unhappy murmurs that had rippled through the gathering during the last part of Selene's speech grew louder and more heated. Selene rose to her feet saying forcefully, "I offer you knowledge, information that has been lost in the fear and bitter justifications that followed the Mage Wars. You do not have to listen, but if you remain, you will open your minds to truths forgotten and be prepared for truths to come. If you go, you will remain blinded by ignorance and fear."

While it was clear that more than a few of the people present were distressed by the direction of the tale, only a handful left the keep. The remainder stayed, whether through curiosity, fear or faith, it did not matter. They listened, and in listening they gained knowledge. Knowledge that would affect their choices, their decisions, their paths.

The disruption settled. Her audience were on edge, but willing to listen as Selene picked up her tale, "The Mage Wars ended, not with a victory, but with the sudden disappearance of the magic. You are all familiar with what happened next, and that is not a tale for today."

"My tale is of the magic, and for that we must return to the Goddess Rua ... Pained by the betrayal and corruption of her gift, the Goddess withdrew the magic, leaving just enough to sustain the life she had loved so dearly. Bitter that she had suffered the splintering of reality for our creation, only for her favoured child to turn against her, she discarded the magic on a barren twin world, where it would lie dormant without life to give it purpose. She then faded into the darkness to grieve."

"The splintering of reality had given rise to many worlds that mirrored our own, but each world has been shaped by its own reality. Some lacked warmth and have turned to ice, others melted in too much heat. Conditions for those other worlds were harsh and life could not exist upon them."

"Research has discovered that the worlds, in their own bubble of reality, exist along an endless swing of a pendulum wave. The worlds spin on their axes and swing in a perpetual motion, passing the other worlds as they do so. In passing, the worlds recall the moment they were one and are drawn closer. Sometimes they brush so close they touch, and where they touch, they share a transient reality." Selene scanned the crowd as she spoke, seeming to pause when she reached Susan. "In that moment and in that place, what exists in one world, exists in the other." Susan felt a tingle down her spine as she sensed a connection to those words, but it was quickly lost as an uneasy murmur rippled through the keep at Selene's next words, "A priest from the Temple of Helvoa has predicted there will soon be a merger with a world of barren rock, where magic slumbers awaiting the call home." Selene's voice held a warning as she persisted, despite the intensifying tension. "The priest has been commissioned to work on a precise calculation of the time and location of the merger. The procurer awaits his findings, but for what purpose?"

Selene shook her head. "I fear the purpose is not a good or kind one." The tension snapped, and fear emerged spreading tendrils of alarm in the form of quiet sobbing and anxious whispers. "We know that in the Mage Wars ancient artifacts were used to store vast amounts of magic, could it be that these will be sought for that purpose once more?"

Selene raised her hand and waited for silence. Once she was assured of her audience's full attention, she gave some much needed reassurance, her voice softening as she said, "I believe we can stop this."

"Earlier, I recited the story of creation, translated from the inscription on the Statue of Rua. Until recently, this was the only inscription."

"Last winter a prophesy engraved itself on the stone, and amazingly this prophesy was written in the modern language..." Not a sound, not a movement, interrupted Selene's next words, "It reads..." Selene opened out her arms as she intoned.

*"There will come a Time for the Stranger to Guide, and the Child to Find:*

*The Preacher for Air, the Fortress of Fire, the Weapon of Earth, the Vessel of Spirit and the Driftwood on Water.*

*Together shall they Protect and Free the Lost Gift."*

At the final word Selene bent her head and the hood of her cloak fell forward covering her face. The bewildered people stared and waited for clarification. When it did not come, they shifted self-consciously, uncertain of what this meant and what they should do.

Eventually, Selene straightened and pushed back her hood. Her cropped grey hair glowed copper in the firelight, and her mien was solemn. She carefully and deliberately, unfastened the ornate catch at her neck and removed her cloak. She placed it on the dais, smoothed it with her hand before looking at the worried faces.

"And now my telling is complete, I have given you the information you need." she said gravely. "However, the tale has not ended. The ending depends on you. On your decisions, on your actions, on your choices." Susan felt Selene's words resonate in her chest and her body tingled with anticipation, while others in the keep met Selene's words with a confused silence.

The uncomfortable quiet was scored by the shrill wail of an infant, prompting the crowd to disperse. Triene, Susan and Jael brushed down their clothes, and picked their way back to their wagon. Jael lifted a dying torch off the wall to help guide them. They didn't speak, each consumed by their own thoughts.

Without the moon's assistance it was too dark to drive safely to the inn, so they set out their blankets, under the shelter of the wagon's canvas and lay down, Wolf at their feet. One by one, they fell into dream ridden sleep.

Selene's words echoed in Susan's head as she drifted off,

*"There will come a Time for the Stranger to Guide, and the Child to Find:*

*The Preacher for Air, the Fortress of Fire, the Weapon of*

*Earth, the Vessel of Spirit and the Driftwood on Water.*

*Together shall they Protect and Free the Lost Gift."*

## Chapter 9

A row of five horses stood in the centre of the inn's courtyard. Their proud posture denoted their military purpose, while their uniform chestnut satin skin and elaborate tack shimmering in the post dawn light indicated the ostentatious wealth associated with a personal guard.

The inn was still and dark. The cheery chirps of small birds were accentuated by the occasional coarse caw of a crow and the muffled rhythmic crack of axe splitting wood from the rear of the inn. The barn door swung on its hinges with a soft creak, followed by the disquieting sounds of a scuffle, a hoarse yell and a heavy thud. Three men in crimson uniforms appeared in the doorway of the barn. Two of them were dragging a lanky youth by his upper arms, their lack of co-ordination making the movement protracted and painful for him. The boy's shaggy hair fell forward, over his slumped head, and his booted feet bumped over the cobblestones. The soldiers' struggles made them spiteful, and they thrust him to the ground when they reached their horses. The boy let out a groan of pain as he fell hard onto his knees, hands bracing his fall just before his face hit the ground. The horses looked down their long noses at the intrusion.

The third soldier to exit the barn observed his soldier's endeavours with scorn. He was an older man with lined skin and cruel lips and eyes. His face featured a sunken scar that started at his forehead, crossed his left brow and ended on the bridge of his misshapen nose. His narrowed eyes scanned the inn before he strode towards the collapsed captive. Satisfied by shadowed windows and lack of movement, he turned his contemptuous gaze to his new recruits, taking in their slovenly stance and malicious expressions, before ordering, "Search him."

The boy sat back on his knees and slowly raised his head, defiance in the set of his mouth and the flare of his eyes. A lock of dull blond hair stuck to the warm blood that trickled down his cheek from the cut next to his rapidly swelling eye. The officer's lip curled contemptuously as his hand roughly jerked up the boy's chin, "Where is it?" he demanded, his voice harsh. Aware that there was nothing he could do or say to save himself from a beating, the boy remained silent and motionless, until the swift, sharp kick to his ribs made him crumple, gasping for breath.

The door to the inn swung open and hit the log wall with a muffled thump, and Kol stepped out, followed closely by Seema, whose hands and apron were covered in flour. They had both been in the kitchen, Kol supping some goat's milk and Seema preparing the dough for the breakfast rolls, when they had noticed the disturbance out the front. Kol scanned the courtyard, his eyes taking in the soldiers and horses, before falling upon the youth at their feet. He was huddled up protectively clasping his side. Kol's face dropped, there wasn't much he could do. It was made worse by the sound of footsteps striding through the gaping doorway of the barn. Two more soldiers were heading his way, one had a smart, military bearing while the other had the swagger and appearance of a street thug with his uniform barely stretching over his wide shoulders. Kol stepped closer to him as he asked with concern, "What's going on?" The soldier merely sneered as he released a driving punch to Kol's stomach. Kol staggered backwards, doubling-up, as he let out a loud exhalation of air. He then sank to the ground, wheezing. Seema squealed in alarm and rushed over to kneel beside him, covering him in flour as she held him in a protective embrace. Her fearful eyes focused on the now smirking soldier.

The bar tender arrived from the back yard in response to the noise, just in time to see Kol fall. The wood axe that had sat in a relaxed grip by his side, rose to hip level, blade out and battle ready as he assessed the situation. He prowled towards the man closest to Seema and Kol. The soldier's smirk dropped as he took in the size and determination of the man heading his way. His more experienced companion withdrew his sword and gestured that the bar tender should stay his advance, but it was Seema who stilled him with her softly spoken, "Not yet." The bully regained his arrogant smirk and pulled his own sword, waving it in their direction in a taunting manner. The bar tender's face remained impassive, body alert and ready to fight should the need arise.

The officer cast a dismissive gaze over the cowed owners of the inn and a questioning one at the smart soldier newly emerged from the barn. "No trace of it, sir." was the brisk response, as the soldier lowered his sword, but kept it unsheathed, uncertain of the bar tender's inaction and not wanting to rely on his comrade's prowess.

Disappointed, the captain turned to face the gawping soldiers behind him. Raising his eyes to the heavens he gave an exasperated sigh before commanding them to, "Get on with the search". They jumped guiltily into action, roughly stripping the youth of his clothing and inspecting them for hidden objects. The youth cried out as his arms were wrenched up to remove his tunic, the action stretching the bruised muscles around his injured ribs. His pale torso was hairless and thin. His boots were tugged off and while one inspected them, the other tugged at the feet of the boy's trousers making his back smack into the hard cobblestones. Naked, the boy drew up his long legs and huddled them against his chest. His wiry arms wrapped around them defensively.

Kol, and Seema were forced to stay on the ground by the sword flourishing in their direction, the soldier clearly enjoying the power play. Frustrated, and silent they watched the mistreatment of the boy. The bar tender remained still but the corner of his eye twitched.

The search was completed without any trace of the object they sought. The youth scrambled around gathering his clothes and hastily pulling them back on. He was desperately tugging his boots onto his feet wanting their protection, when the officer impatient and displeased with the unsuccessful and interrupted search, snapped, "Take him with us to question later."

Upon hearing this, Kol rashly spoke up, "Wait! Please? Where are you taking him? Why are you doing this?"

The captain finally looked directly at the innkeeper and his wife. His unfriendly demeanour tinged with irritation. Deciding they might have some information that could be used, he deigned to explain, "A valuable gem has been stolen. This lad has the same look as the thief. It's my job to recover the item and get retribution for my master." He looked at the lad with distain as he spoke, the threat of violence clear.

"There must be some mistake," said Kol in an appeasing voice. "The boy is my stable hand and is a good lad." Seema blinked slowly, but otherwise showed no indication of her surprise at his words. "When and where did this theft occur?" Kol continued, shifting slightly so he could offer his palms, placatingly.

Suspicious, but beginning to think it possible that this boy might be a waste of time, the captain offered tersely, "Carnom, yesterday morning.".

Kol's reassuring response came quickly, "Then it wasn't him, he was working here all day." The boy's eyes darted between Kol and the officer, a faint hope brewing in his chest.

The other soldiers shuffled uncomfortably and looked to their captain for guidance. The older soldier, was reluctant to concede despite his doubts, so he threatened instead, "Do I detect a lie? Perhaps I should question you as well as the boy?" Seema inhaled sharply and the axe jerked in the bar tender's hand. Kol forced his expression to remain placid, although his hand moved involuntarily to grasp his wife's tightly.

The clipping sound of hooves hitting the cobblestones diverted attention to the entrance of the courtyard. A pair of black and white shire horses leading a covered wagon walked sedately across the cobblestones and pulled up parallel to the inn. Triene was holding the reins lightly in one hand, eyes focusing on her relatives with fear. An apprehensive Susan was still seated beside Triene, but Jael had immediately sprung from the wagon upon observing the strained scene. His longsword already extended from one hand, dagger in the other as he advanced confidently on the soldiers surrounding the boy.

In a simultaneous motion, Wolf had bounded towards Kol's attacker. Hackles raised, lips curling to reveal menacing fangs, he snarled and snapped at the snivelling soldier who took two shaky steps backwards, almost tripping in his haste, both hands gripping his sword desperately. The scent of urine hit Wolf's nose as the warm trickle left a damp trail down the crimson trouser leg.

The other soldier now had his sword trained on the bar tender who had stepped forwards, axe held ready to eviscerate, upon Jael and Wolf's arrival. The soldier's nervous eyes flicked over to the huge wolf and back again, as he awaited his officer's lead.

The captain had placed his hand on the hilt of his sword and let it rest there, while watching Jael through bitter and narrowed eyes. The other two soldiers just stood and stared, frozen into inaction by the unexpected arrivals.

"Greetings Kol, Seema," Jael said evenly, not taking his eyes off the soldiers. "It looks like you need some help this morning." His anger only showing in the tightness of his jaw and the flash of his eyes.

Seema spoke up, confident now her nephew had arrived. "Why thank you, but I believe, we won't be needing that help, for these gentlemen are just leaving. They had thought our stable hand was the thief they seek, but now realise their mistake." She addressed this last part to the captain who was rapidly recalculating the odds. Three of his men were embarrassingly incompetent. Newly recruited bullies with no experience of fighting against skilled opponents, let alone a wild animal. Concluding that his men would be at a disadvantage should a fight ensue he reluctantly agreed with Seema's statement,

"Aye, that we are." he said sourly. The captain swung up onto his mount, his soldiers scrambling to follow. Before they left, the captain gave a resentful, long last look around, then turning his horse's head he led them out of the courtyard and back towards Carnom.

Jael smoothly sheathed his weapons and extended a friendly hand to Kol, who lent on it heavily as he rose to his feet. Seema's watchful eyes checking his stiff but resilient movements, before she scurried over to examine the boy, He had managed to reach a lopsided standing position with one hand resting on his ribs, the other on his thigh as he caught his breath. With a concerned frown, she reached up to brush his hair back so she could see the wound over his eye. "Come inside and let me sort that out for you." she said kindly, giving him a gentle push in the direction of the inn door. The boy seemed reluctant, so she added, "I'll see about getting you some breakfast after." At that incentive the boy started forwards. To her relief Seema saw that although the rib clearly pained him, it didn't seem to be causing any significant restriction on his movements or breathing. The benefit of youth, she thought as she guided him to the table near the bar.

While Seema was busy with the boy, Kol twisted to dust off the rear of his trousers, with only a small wince, and glanced up to smile wryly at a worried Jael, who was hovering as if expecting him to collapse any moment, his concern for the older man clearly evident. "Ah, don't fuss so, I'm fine. I'll just get your horses settled and will join you inside. Get some nourishment in you and we'll see what this is all about." Jael gave Kol a final examination before nodding his acquiescence and went inside.

Kol moved a little awkwardly over to the wagon but grinned up at Triene and Susan. "Well, it's a bit early for all this, but it's been an eventful start to the day, that's for sure." Triene was gripping the reins tightly as she stared at him. Her heart was pumping and her breath was coming in short gasps as she tried to control the fear on seeing her relatives on their knees with soldiers threatening them. Kol patted her hands, gently removing the reins. "There now lass, don't fret. We are fine. It's the lad they wanted." Triene managed a soft smile as she got down from the wagon and kissed him gently on the cheek before walking to the door.


Kol held out his free hand to Susan who had remained seated. She blinked a few times before she forced a smile and accepted his assistance politely, while taking care not to put any weight on him. He nudged her towards the inn. "Go have some beer, we'll all be right as rain in no time at all." Kol then accompanied the hungry horses as they walked with purpose towards the wide-open doors of the barn.

Only the bar tender remained, having walked to the entrance of the courtyard to ensure that the soldiers had truly left. Finally satisfied, he relaxed his grip on the axe and returned to the rear of the inn. It wasn't long before the regular thud of an axe and the splitting of wood sounded once more.

Standing in the doorway while her eyes adjusted to the lower level of light, Susan observed the others for a moment. She felt like she was looking at them through a haze. This couldn't be happening. There had been swords and daggers and axes being brandished, by people she knew. Only a couple of days ago, she had been on the phone, talking about directors' duties to a CEO who had breached them. Today…. Well, today was very different!

She could see that the youth was sitting on the edge of a bench while Seema dabbed at his brow with a wet cloth, pink with his blood. Most of his face was turned from her but she could see that the flesh around his eye was puffy and red, with a hint of bruising bubbling up to the surface. The boy didn't seem fazed by his injuries but was clearly uncomfortable with the attention he was receiving. He muttered that he was alright and tried to pull away, but Seema held his head in place with grim determination.

Triene was seated next to the boy, a tankard of beer in each hand. Wolf lay at her feet, eyes closed, on the principle that if he couldn't see anyone, they couldn't see him. Seema was clearly aware of his presence, however, as her gaze kept darting towards him. She seemed to be torn between enforcing her rule that he stay out of the bar area and leniency due to his part in their rescue. Her sense of gratitude apparently won as she said nothing, taking his lead by simply pretending he wasn't there.

Susan slowly walked towards Jael, who was leaning on the bar nursing his own beer. Jael noted her approach and raised his tankard inquiringly. After such a tumultuous start to the day, Susan decided Kol was right and a beer would improve things, so she gave a rapid nod. Jael's lips twitched at her enthusiasm as he took down a tankard from the shelf and slowly filled it from the cask. Passing it to her, Jael attempted a humorous comment to lighten her mood, "Hey, no one died." It backfired. Her eyes widened, and her breath hitched as she hastily took a large gulp of the amber liquid. The combination predictably led to her coughing as she choked on the beer. Jael, looking remorseful, patted her on the back until the choking subsided. At least this cleared the fug that had clouded her thoughts.

Jael shifted to contemplate the boy, giving Susan time to recover her composure. He didn't trust him. Why was he on his own? Sure, he was young, but that didn't make him innocent. Seema and Triene were treating him as if he were a little kid, but he was easily in his early teens, 13 or 14 most likely. He had brought trouble to his family, they should treat his wounds and be rid of him. He resisted the temptation to help heal him, it wouldn't be necessary anyway. He was moving well and the swelling would go down quickly.

Red in the face and eyes watering, Susan followed his gaze. The morning's events clearly centred around the boy, in what manner needed to be discovered. She heard Triene exclaim indignantly "and said you stole from their master!" and heard the boy respond with a mumbled "I din't though", head hung with his hair dropping forward. While Susan watched, the boy lifted his head and looked straight at her. Susan narrowed her eyes. Even with the swollen eye she recognised the money pouch thief from the marketplace. Susan pursed her lips. The youth sighed as he saw recognition dawn. Deciding a partial confession would be in his favour he added, "though I don't say that I 'aven't been known to take the odd bit o' stuff, so as to eat and such."

His apologetic tone was aimed at disarming Seema and Triene, who he felt would have more sympathy for him than Jael and Susan. To augment any pity felt, he gave a wince and held his side as if his rib had pained him.

Susan moved forward, asking him with suspicion, "What did those men think you had stolen?". She thought she already knew the answer though. She'd recognised the crimson uniforms of the unpleasant merchant's guard from the previous day. The same merchant who was searching for his new and valuable gemstone.

Seema helpfully replied on the boy's behalf," They said something about a gem."

Triene looked at the boy thoughtfully. "*Are* you the one who took it?"

He replied ingeniously, "They din't find it, did they?"

Susan moved even closer and perched on a nearby table. She attempted to look approachable and friendly. She felt on familiar ground now, as she channelled her inner lawyer and began her fact finding with an affable, yet obligation inducing, introduction, "I'm Susan, this is Triene, Seema and Jael." she began, indicating to each of them as she spoke. "and you are?"

The boy paused as he decided whether he should reveal this bit of information about himself. Concluding that it was safe, he offered it with an abrupt, "Will."

Susan nodded, and gave an encouraging smile, while the others looked on fascinated by the change in her manner. "Thank you, Will." she said before she resumed her gentle interrogation. "So, we understand that you sometimes have to steal things. To eat and such, I think you said." Will nodded warily. "and, of course, having saved you from the soldiers, you know you can trust us." Will looked at Seema's concerned face, Triene's sympathetic one and then cast his uncertain gaze over Jael, who had folded his arms and was regarding him disapprovingly.

Will gulped and tendered a questioning "Yeah?"

Susan supressed an inopportune smile at his disbelieving response and instead proceeded with a statement, that didn't exactly lie, but did indicate more knowledge than she actually had, "I was at the marketplace yesterday morning, and I saw you, I know you remember me." Again, Will nodded, not knowing where this was leading. "You're the one that stole the gemstone," she stated with confidence as if she had seen him do it. She finished with, "I was very impressed by your skill!" as her voice and face took on an enthusiastic expression. "No one saw you do it, at all!"

Will's face lit up with pride at her words. Susan gave him an admiring smile, and asked, "I can't imagine how you got away. Where did you go?"

Disarmed by Susan's words Will answered, "I went to see Old Sally, as he usually pays a fair price. Only Old Sally din't want it." Will frowned. "Old Sally is a tough 'un, but 'e said the merchant's guards 'ad been to see 'im and 'ad roughed 'im up a bit. 'e said they was mean bastards and told me to get out of town, right quick." Will's earlier wariness had disappeared completely, and he now seemed keen to share his tale. "Well, if Old Sally thought I should leg it, I weren't going to stay around. I see the auction guards searching a wagon of turnips, and as soon as they was finished, I hitched a ride outta there. Only they stopped 'ere last night so I thought I would take a nap in the stable after I nabbed a bite from the kitchen…" He stopped abruptly and looked sheepishly at Seema.

"So that's what happened to the missing roast, hmmm?" was Seema's amiable response to that revelation.

Realising he wasn't in trouble, the boy gave her a cheeky grin and said "Yeah… it were really tasty! Anyways, I found a really warm spot above the 'orses and 'ad me kip, and that's where the soldiers found me. You saw what they did." He indicated to his eye and rubbed his side with a pout.

Susan prompted him to continue, "So where do you plan to go and what about your family and friends?"

"I dunno, any town'll do." he shrugged. "I dun 'ave family. Old Sally were nice tho."

Seema exclaimed "Oh my poor boy," and drew him in for a hug. He allowed it, but he looked extremely uncomfortable with the overt display of affection. Triene took his hand and looked sorrowful. Even Jael seemed distressed by Will's words, his mouth downcast while he searched Triene's face protectively.

Susan waited a moment, the only one unaffected by his words, still focused on her line of questioning. She interrupted the emotional distraction with a blunt, but important question. "Where is the gemstone now, Will?" The others straightened, mien serious once more. The soldiers were still looking for the gemstone and were not going to ask nicely. They all regarded the boy solemnly as they awaited his reply.

Assessing the change in the mood, Will shrugged and with exaggerated nonchalance explained, "I buried it outside the kitchen. A trick I learned years ago." he said loftily, "Don't let 'em find it on you."

Susan sent an urgent glance in Jael's direction, but he was already moving towards the kitchen door. On the way, he encountered the bar tender bringing in the wood for the fireplace. At Jael's unspoken direction, he released the logs into the basket behind the bar and accompanied Jael outside.

"How do you plan to avoid the merchant's men as you escape?" asked Susan worried about Will's future safety. Will squirmed, clearly uneasy at the thought, although his words were cavalier, "I'll manage, always do." He then recovered the remains of his beer from Triene and sat staring at it broodingly before swigging it down in one long swallow.

"You'll need to get further away from Carnom, and soon," said Seema glancing at Triene who mouthed a maybe in response. Will just stared at the now empty tankard.

Thinking about when Triene might be leaving made Seema suddenly jump with the realisation that the bread hadn't been cooked and breakfast wouldn't be ready for their customers. Customers who would be arriving at any moment. She bustled back to the kitchen, gathering up the bowl and cloth, stating that she would be right back with something for them to eat.

Will finished contemplating the empty tankard and moving cautiously so as not to hurt his side, he ambled over to the bar. He refilled his tankard, took a few sips, topped it up and wandered back to the table where he started to drink it, more slowly this time. Triene cleared her throat meaningfully and tapped her own empty tankard on the table. Will looked up at her confused, before realisation hit. "Oh, right!" he said and he began to take Triene's tankard to the bar, before he hesitantly asked if Susan needed some more beer. Smiling genuinely this time, she shook her head. Pleased that he had got the social niceties right, Will continued to the bar.

While he was filling the tankard the inn door opened and Kol strolled in with a puzzled expression, "Why in Rua's name, is Jael digging around in the backyard?"

Triene smiled widely and asked, "Is he getting muddy?", obviously hoping for an affirmative response.

"Not really," said Kol, taking a seat on the bench. Triene pretended to be disappointed and gave an exaggerated pout of her lip. Will returned with two beers and passed one to Triene and the other to Kol as he mumbled an embarrassed, "Thanks for saying I were your servant." Kol gave him a contemplative look. Eventually he replied with, "You are welcome young man, just remember it when you next get itchy fingers." Will looked taken aback and said "Course!" and lowered his gaze.

The conversation about Jael's antics resumed between Triene and Kol until the subject himself returned, followed by the bar tender who ignored the group to gather up the logs from behind the bar and carry them over to the fireplace. He knelt on one knee and methodically stacked the fire basket in preparation for the evening. Jael, however, came straight to their table and swung his long legs over the bench so he could sit next to Susan. He then purposefully placed a worn leather pouch, still damp from being cleaned of soil, on the table. All eyes were fixed on the find, even Will's, who was drawn in by the sense of anticipation.   Jael proceeded to remove a blue bundle from the pouch. He carefully unfolded the scrap of fabric revealing several coins and an iron ring topped by a warm pale opal, and, finally, the all-important vermillion gemstone. In the dim light of the inn, they could clearly see a sliver of light flickering, deep within the stone.

Jael held it out and twisted it back and forth as he examined it, trying to determine what it was made of.  Normally, he could sense the consistency and construction of a stone, but whatever this was, he was unfamiliar with it. He frowned, confused by the lack of information. Triene held out her hand so she could also examine it.  He placed it in her palm, but snatched it back when the inner light pulsed brighter. "It may be dangerous!" he declared as he quickly wrapped it up in the cloth once more, shoving it into the pouch and tossing it to Will.  Susan was puzzled by the abrupt change, but willing to accept Jael's assessment of the gem's potential for danger.   This place seemed to be full of danger and lawlessness. Will eyed Triene speculatively as he unwound the strap and placed it over his head like a necklace before tucking the pouch into his loose-fitting shirt.

Triene felt the palm of her hand tingle and stared at it. Magic! she thought, the stone contained magic.  She felt her gut spasm while her mind was caught up in a flurry of fear and wonder. Jael was right. If the gem truly was a magical artifact, then it was dangerous.  Very dangerous.  She could feel the heavy door slam shut on her wonder, locking it safely away. A tear formed in the corner of her eye, but she blinked until it disappeared and placed a smile on her face as she added to the conversation. "The ring was an unusual one, where did you get it from, Will?" Before he could answer, the sound of horses in the courtyard and a shouted "Ho, ostler!" led to Kol rising to greet the new arrivals.

Not long after, two cheerful travellers entered through the open doorway. They appeared eager to start their long day of riding by tucking into the inn's hearty breakfast. One, a short man with his long hair tied back in a ponytail, beard trimmed in a neat goatee, was rubbing his hands together in anticipation while the other, a taller fellow, with his hair cropped short and round glasses perched on his hawklike nose, ordered beer to accompany their feast. Brandishing their full tankards, they moved over to a window table and sat in contented companionship while they supped their drink.

They were first of many customers that either emerged from the inn's rooms or arrived in the courtyard in wagons, on horseback or on foot. All, it appeared, were well aware that the inn provided a flavoursome fare and were keen on starting their day with their stomachs full.

As the inn filled, Kol and Seema were kept busy and were unable to speak with the others, who were themselves busy consuming a substantial breakfast of black pudding, eggs and fresh bread, accompanied by some crisp, clear water in a tall pitcher. They maintained a light conversation while they ate. Susan was fascinated to discover that the water came from an underground river that flowed through a series of caves beneath the inn. The caves linked to the coast and the river flowed into the sea just north of Carnom. From

there the conversation turned to the inn's beer. The bar
tender credited the water for the quality of his brew, his
malted barley and brewer's yeast benefiting from it as well
as the beer itself. He had been the one to locate the
underground river when he arrived at the inn.

Eventually, the subject of Will's journey was raised once
more. Triene had been thinking about this while they ate.
She couldn't bear the thought of the merchant finding Will
and the gem. The merchant wasn't the sort of person she
thought should be in possession of anything magical.
Triene's voice was hushed but firm as she insisted that Will
should travel with them. "The gemstone and Will need
protection. Others might be persuaded to give them up to
the merchant for coin." Susan noticed that Triene had
prioritised the gemstone, but before she could ponder this,
Jael was hissing that to take on another passenger, one that
was being hunted, with a stolen gem no less, was too
dangerous. Jael was angry. Angry that Triene wanted to
bring another person into their circle, and angry that he
couldn't keep her protected from exposure to magic. She
was more affected by their parents' deaths than she let him
see. He knew his sister. The bubbly and cheery disposition
she portrayed was an exaggeration of the person she used to
be. He worried what lay beneath it.

Will tucked hungrily into his meal while the discussion took
place, not bothering to offer his own thoughts as he didn't
expect a conclusion in his favour. He could look after
himself, always had, he didn't need nobody. He sniffed in
defiance of the world. Wolf emerged from under the table
to rest his chin on the timber next to Will's hand. He snuffled
in the direction of the black pudding on the plate and looked

up at Will, hunger in his pleading expression. Susan surreptitiously watched Will break off a large chunk of his own portion and pass it to a grateful Wolf, who munched on it with noisy enthusiasm.

Will was an interesting young man, thought Susan, caught somewhere between cynical adult and trusting child. Her instincts were to protect him, yet she realised that she was more innocent and unprepared for this world than he was. She also found herself wanting to discover more about the enigmatic gemstone. What was it the merchant had called it? That's right, the fire stone. The merchant had obviously known something about those gemstones. He had come barrelling in with a ridiculously high bid and when he discovered one was missing he sent guards, nay soldiers, to ruthlessly search for the thief and stone. She remembered the auctioneer hinting at the gemstones containing magic, and that they had been in the grave of an ancient, probably one of the ancients that used magic in Selene's story. What was she doing? Magic and stories! What was real and what wasn't in this world? She didn't know. She needed to understand what the others believed was real. She decided to speak, but kept her voice low and quiet, mirroring the others, "I'm confused," she began. "Is Selene's story just entertainment or is it real. Were the mage wars and magic real here?" Triene lowered her head, and Jael just scowled, but Will quickly exclaimed, "Wot do ya mean, was they real? Course they was! Where you been? I dunno 'bout Selene, coz I din't go, but even I knows she tells the truth."

Jael hushed Will as he glanced around at the other patrons, making sure no one was paying attention to their conversation. When satisfied he added, "What Selene said was as accurate as you can get. If she said the magic is coming back, its because that's what is going to happen."

Will sat back in shock. "Is that wot she said? Cor!"

Triene's head remained bowed. Susan looked at her then tendered, "I hope you don't mind my putting forward my opinion, but I agree with Triene about this. We should help Will. It doesn't feel right, just leaving him." She then took a deep breath and said, "I was wondering if the gemstones might be some of those artifacts that can store magic and the merchant might be one of the people Selene was warning against. Surely if that is the case, anything we can do to prevent him getting more magic would help?" Not sure if she had jumped to unlikely conclusions or pushed her luck too far, Susan sat back nervously. Will had looked up from his meal and was staring at her curiously. Triene had raised her head and nodded her agreement, Even Wolf had cocked his head quizzically. Jael remained silent for a moment as he contemplated her words, slowly rotating the bread in his hand.

"The danger in helping him is greater than you imagine," he said solemnly, his face worn and worried, "but your point is a good one." Jael had already been wondering about the gem and Selene's story, and feared they were on a dangerous path. He wanted to ignore it and concentrate on just him and Triene, but the Goddess seemed to have other plans for them. "We'll take him with us. I'll speak to Kol and ready the wagon. Eat up, we will leave as soon as possible." He stood up abruptly and strode out of the inn towards the barn. Triene gave a slow smile, it seemed the brother she knew was coming back. Susan was taken aback by Jael's immediate acceptance of her argument, and it appeared that

94

Will was similarly affected, since he stared at the departing Jael, slack-jawed. He hadn't expected that. In his experience people didn't just help him. Wolf took advantage of their evident distraction and gulped down the rest of the food on Jael's plate, licking his lips with a satisfied grin.

## Chapter 10

The wagon trundled along the dusty road with Triene at the reins. The steady gait of the horses a soothing tempo that countered the tension seeping from Jael. Jael was seated in the centre of the driver's box, one foot resting on the board in front. All too aware of their dangerous cargo, he carefully scanned the grasslands on either side, searching the occasional hedgerows and distant woodlands for any sign of a threat while his left hand flipped and twisted his dagger dexterously.

They frequently saw other travellers taking the same route, Jael tensing at each encounter. Those riding faster horses cantered past, eager to get to their destination, while those walking were easily overtaken and were greeted by a cheery wave from Triene. They met even more people journeying towards Carnom, many of whom were travelling in a long caravan of wagons, with bored guards scouting ahead and bringing up the rear. Their horses were trudging along so slowly that children ran from wagon to wagon, laughing and playing.

It was proving to be another warm spring day, with only the hint of a cooling breeze brushing the long grasses. The sun beat down, with a few fluffy clouds occasionally passing across it, casting a temporary, relieving shade along their path.

Will was under strict orders to remain hidden within the firmly tied canvas at the back of their wagon. The warmth of the air within the enclosed space and the steady rock made his eyes grow heavy with sleep. He dozed comfortably while

Wolf remained on guard, ears and nose alert for any danger from outside while aware of the temptation of their satchel of coins to a seasoned thief.

Susan sat at the edge of the driver's box, clinging to the side of the wagon as it swayed. She found herself daydreaming, her head swimming with muddled memories and images. One moment she was reading the contract for her clients, Thompsons plc, and studying the restraint of trade clause, the next moment the clause was being read out in Selene's voice before it morphed into a deeper message, *"But how will we stop the misuse of magic, and avoid the errors of the past?.....That depends on you. On your decisions, on your actions, on your choices"*. She rubbed her temple, the combination of her confused thoughts and the rumble of the wagon over the rough track, causing a pounding headache and a queasy stomach. Her thoughts drifted again, this time to an image of Mr Blenchcot pulling a sword out of his briefcase, face turning scarlet with anger as he marched towards her. She grimaced as her unruly thoughts swirled and cavorted in her head. Regaining some focus, she looked upon the sun-bathed landscape, she thought it would have been warmer. She rubbed her hands up and down her arms and gave a little shiver.

Jael stopped the spin of the dagger and stole a worried glance at her, asking "Are you all right?"

Susan half turned to face him, hugging herself and replied, "Just a bit cold." Jael looked troubled as he examined her face, peering closely into her eyes before turning to whisper urgently to Triene. Triene pulled hard on the reins instantly bringing the wagon to a halt. Susan looked around at the empty road, surprised. "What's wrong?" she said with a slight slur to her words.

Jael climbed across the box in front of her and jumped out of the wagon. He then reached out his arms indicating for her to get down with his support. Confused, Susan started to descend, but the strength in her legs melted away and she tumbled. He had anticipated her weakness however, and he caught her securely, murmuring, "It's all right, I've got you." He then swung her up, placing one arm behind her back and under her arm, his other beneath her bent legs. Susan felt a violent shiver suddenly wrack her body. She hugged herself tighter and snuggled closer to his chest, cold and befuddled.

Jael carried her to the back of the wagon where Will had just untied and opened the canvas on Triene's barked instructions, he then shuffled backwards to make space. Jael carefully laid Susan down then climbed into the back himself so he could lift and adjust her. Hands hooked under her armpits, he managed to haul her lengthways along the packed clothing and lowered her carefully so she could lie on her side. She immediately curled up shaking and shivering. With a concerned expression, he placed the back of his hand on her clammy forehead and noted it felt baking hot despite her complaints of the cold.

"I don't feel well." said Susan weakly.

"You have a fever. You must rest." Jael said gently as he brushed away the hair sticking to her damp face. "I will keep you safe, don't worry." He smiled reassuringly, even though his mind was racing. This was bad. Jael had learnt the craft of healing from his father, who had taught him to recognise and treat all kinds of illnesses, even those that were dormant, like lefenhage. The disease had wiped out swathes of the population shortly after the Mage Wars had ended. Many cast blame on the mages for the disease, whereas others, like his father, blamed it on the loss of the magic.

Whatever the cause, those that had survived the disease had passed on the ability to survive it to their children and so on, so that now most believed it had been destroyed. His father had shrugged his shoulders at that, saying that these things usually lingered somewhere. That was why he had taught Jael the signs and treatment of lefenhage, and that was why Jael knew the violet lines streaking across Susan's eyes meant she had caught it.

When his parents had been travelling these roads alone, his father had created secret locations where healing plants could grow, and where they could safely rest. Later, Jael had taken on the task of caring for those waystations. They were about an hour's drive from the closest one. They needed to get there quickly, but first he gave Will some instructions for Susan's care. "You need to keep her cool. Wipe a wet cloth on her face, neck and arms." He handed Will a piece of material and a full waterskin. "She will need to vomit soon. Help her sit up so she doesn't choke." Jael sought out their cooking supplies, "She can be sick in this." He pulled out a cast iron cook pot. Will automatically cradled it as he stared at Susan in horror. "Can you do that?" snapped Jael.

Will jerked to attention and nodded. He grabbed the waterskin and poured some water onto the cloth before crawling over to Susan and wiping it carefully over her face. Satisfied with the determination in Will's expression, Jael tied the canvas doors shut then crawled through to the driver's box. He took the reins from Triene whose forehead was creased with worry. "I can fix this," said Jael with forced confidence and he urged the horses into a trot, frustrated that they couldn't go faster on the uneven road without the risk of a broken wheel or axle.

In the back of the wagon Will was carefully following the instructions for Susan's care. He didn't like seeing Susan sick. She had been concerned about his safety and had persuaded Jael to help him. He felt he owed her, and that wasn't something he was used to. He had only been responsible for himself since his mother had died and being responsible for another human being made his heart race and his palms sweaty. Wolf was sitting next to them both, trying to help by licking Susan's hand. Sensing Will's anxiety he gave him a reassuring bump with his head, but since it was on Will's injured side, it invoked a yelp rather than the comfort intended. Wolf sighed and lay down to continue his licking.

Susan was alternating between shuddering with cold and tossing her roasting body back and forth. When she started to cough and gag, Will linked his arm under hers and eased her up. Holding her hair back he helped her aim for the pot. The rank reek of vomit filled the warm enclosure, and Will fought against his own gag reflex so he didn't join her in emptying his stomach. Wolf sneezed and shifted his body until his head was up against the canvas wall, his nose poking out of the small gap, inhaling deeply.

Finally, the rattle of the wagon bouncing over the ruts in the road eased as the horses' trot slowed to a slow walk, a halt for a few moments while there was a creaking slithering sound, then a sharp left. Triene leaned back and swiftly rolled aside the canvas while she explained to Will that their track was clear of people. Will gratefully untied and ravelled up the rear canvas, gulping in the fresh air. A soft breeze blew gently through the open wagon, Susan sighed as it fanned over her.

The track was narrow and overgrown, but somehow the wagon's wheels didn't encounter any obstacles that could cause damage to the wheel spokes. They pulled up in a clearing surrounded by ancient woodland. The clearing was vibrant with colour and life. A small but deep freshwater pool, fed by a stream, was positioned to the far side. Above it, dragonflies swooped and darted, their bodies iridescent in the dappled sunlight. A giant crab-apple tree, resplendent in pale blossoms, reached out across the pond from the edge of the woodland, littering the grass and water with its delicate petals. Their arrival disturbed small white butterflies so that it looked like the petals swirled and danced. Beneath the crab-apple's branches, wildflowers added bright colours to the delicate hue of the fallen blossom, tempting the fluffy bumble bees with their nectar, while leafy foliage interspersed the large flat rocks that lined the edge of the pond.

Triene guided the wagon round and stroked the horses' heads soothingly while she watched Jael head for a ramshackle hut tucked a short distance into the wood. It was barely big enough to fit two people and was constructed from roughly sawn planks, nailed together. Its door was strapped to the wall with twine and leather and fastened by a hook. A bird's nest peeked out of the roof and angry chirrups emerged from it as Jael flung open the door and disappeared inside.

Triene brushed down the horses and watered them while Jael fished around the hut. As he sorted through the contents, clunks and clinks rang out, until he materialised bearing a cast iron cauldron and a long ladle, a jar of dried herbs, a pot with hidden contents and three black iron poles with a chain and hook attached to one. He set up the tripod stand and cauldron and set Will searching for kindling. Returning to the hut he re-emerged with an armful of dried wood.

It didn't take long before a fire was burning and the water in the cauldron began to boil. Jael fetched Susan from the wagon to a spot not far from the campfire. Triene had already laid out a bedroll for her on the uneven ground. She helped Jael guide Susan's limp body onto it and solicitously placed a folded jacket beneath her head. Susan's fever had worsened, her unseeing eyes wide while her lips mumbled incoherent sounds. Her body was beset by involuntary trembling just as sweat wilted her hair and ran down her temple, her sodden tunic clung to her shivering frame. Wolf lay beside her and whimpered his concern as Triene cleaned the sweat off her face.

Jael had relocated to the pool and was carefully inspecting the plants. Will was already there, busy scrubbing the cook pot clean. Out of the corner of his eye he saw Jael gently caress a fern like leaf with a bluish tint. Will narrowed his eyes as he saw the plant vibrate even after Jael had removed his hand. Jael glanced nervously at Will, but Will had years of practice in hiding his interest, he seamlessly finished rinsing the pot and carried it back to the wagon. Reassured, Jael broke off a couple of leaves and took them back to the fire.

He tore the leaves into small pieces and dropped them into

the cauldron, added a pinch of herbs from the jar and took out an orange and brown dried fungus from the clay pot before adding it to the water. He stirred the mixture and left it to boil while he checked on Susan. Triene looked up at him, eyes wide and fearful, "She's not responding, Jael."

Wandering along behind Jael, Will wrapped his arms tightly around his middle as he peered down at Susan, "Wot's wrong with 'er?"

"Lefenhage." Jael replied in a monotone before moving back to the caldron.

Will quickly backed away, "Shit! But that's been gone like forever!"

"It just doesn't kill people anymore." Jael stared at the bubbling contents of the cauldron. A foam was beginning to form, it wouldn't be long.

Will continued to question him, "Why's she ill then?"

A scum began to sit on top of the liquid as he answered, "I can only guess that it's because she's not from here." Before Will could ask his next question, Jael added, "It's ready! She needs to be sitting." He scooped off some of the scum and carried it over to Susan.

Triene was struggling to lift Susan's limp body and simultaneously raise her head. Will rushed over to help. "'Ere," he said, "I can do that." He knelt and propped his arm around Susan's back to keep her upright while Triene supported her head. Jael lifted the ladle to her lips and with his free hand pinched Susan's nose tightly. Her mouth popped open, even as her eyes rolled back, and Jael tipped the foam into it. She took an involuntary swallow and coughed, while Jael went back to the cauldron for more. After three doses, they eased her body back onto the ground and carefully lowered her head. Triene remained by her side, attempting to regulate her wildly fluctuating temperature.

Jael wouldn't know if the medicine was working for some time. He needed something to do. He glanced around the clearing and his eyes landed on the cauldron. They wouldn't be needing that anymore. With a cloth to protect his hands, he unhooked it and fished out the contents with the ladle. He placed them on a drying rack to make use of the late afternoon sun and washed out the cauldron before returning it to the hut.

While Jael had been busy with the cauldron, Will had gathered more dry wood and topped up the fire, putting the remainder to one side. Using the cleaned cooking pot, Jael put together some dried leaves and berries and made a warming tea. The camomile would help them relax. Triene joined them and they sat on their folded bedrolls, watching the fire and sipping the tea as the evening drew close. Will's stomach gurgled and he clutched at it, embarrassed. Triene didn't seem to notice, her attention flitting between Susan and the flames, but Jael stood up and retrieved the food Seema had packed for them that morning. They shared out the meat and bread, giving a portion to Wolf who hadn't left Susan's side in order to hunt. They ate slowly and with very little conversation until eventually the light began to fade. Triene added some wood to the fire before moving over to Susan to see if she could make her more comfortable.

"Jael!" she hissed, her beckoning hand urging him to join her. Jael's heart stuttered and he rushed over to her immediately, afraid of what he would see. "I think she's sleeping." came Triene's uncertain whisper. Jael was hit by a wave of relief that washed through his tense muscles as he bent down to examine his patient. She was breathing softly, its cadence finally even. Her eyes had drifted closed. Jael exhaled slowly as he met Triene's eyes and gave a gentle smile. "She is."

Triene's hand was shaking as she adjusted Susan's pillow and placed a blanket over her. She was going to be ok, she told herself over and over, as she fought to suppress the wriggle of doubt tunnelling within her darkest thoughts. She's going to die. It's your fault for liking her. Can you hear that wheeze? That's the sound of her final breath. She's dying, just like your mother, dying just like your father. The insidious thoughts burrowed into her chest and spread tendrils into her gut and up into her throat, which tightened making her breath stick.

Oblivious to Triene's distress Jael gave her shoulder a gentle squeeze. "She should be ok to travel late tomorrow," he said.

Will had followed them and was peering down at Susan with hope in his eyes, "You fixed 'er?" he asked of Jael.

"Yes!" The confidence in his voice helped Triene quieten her fears.

They returned to their bedrolls and helped themselves to another tea. This time, as they cradled their mugs, they began to talk. It soon turned to Selene's tale of the previous night, Will having missed the momentous occasion. "So, wot's this talk of the magic coming back then?" he began. Triene tried to explain as much as she could, but not having

105

Selene's talent, ended up confusing Will who attempted to clarify, "These worlds, they're all this one, but different," he paused before adding, "And they bash into each other, chucking stuff around?" This last ended up as a question to which Jael replied, "Sort of." Will scratched his head. "OK. So, the magic will get thrown back 'ere when we ends up bashing into this other one then." A grin lit up his face, "Cool! That'll get some folks really worked up!"

Triene's face fell, and Jael snapped, "and more people will die!"

Will's expression turned horrified as he realised what it could mean, "You saying, there would be another war or cull?"

Jael shook his head slightly as if to dislodge the unpleasant thoughts before he spoke. "I don't know. But there are more people without magical abilities than those with and the hatred runs deep." He adjusted his bedroll, laying it out and suggesting they should get some rest.

Will needed to speak, "The war weren't the magic's fault." He paused, concerned about the possible reaction to his controversial statement. Jael and Triene looked at him curiously rather than with fury, so he felt emboldened to explain. "It were only some of the people with power that was bastards," Will continued hesitantly, not used to sharing his deeper thoughts, "Like Jael and the soldiers back at the inn. Both had swords and strength. Right? They wasn't the same though." He kept his head ducked, and his arms wrapped protectively around his waist, uncertain of the reception his words would receive despite his suspicions.

Triene finally spoke, "I think you are very wise, Will." she said quietly before she lay down on her side, Wolf snuggling up beside her.

Jael stood up. "I'll stay awake to keep an eye on Susan." he mumbled before heading over to the horses to make sure they were settled. Will shook out his blanket and stretched out on his bedroll. The fire had almost burnt itself out and the evening chill was beginning to creep in. He put some wood on the fire, not for the extra heat since he was used to sleeping in the cold, but to disguise the lack of familiar sights and sounds of night-time in the town. Closing his eyes firmly he forced himself to breathe evenly and concentrated on the warmth radiating from the fire and the crackle and pop as the wood caught alight.

Triene continued to stare at the flames long after Will had drifted asleep and was breathing noisily through his mouth. She could hear her brother moving around the campsite, before finally sitting with his back propped up against the trunk of the crab-apple, legs outstretched. She had seen flashes of the old Jael the last couple of days. Having Susan, and now Will, travel with them was forcing him to relax some of the rules he had set himself, and while she hated that she even thought it, she couldn't help but be glad to see Jael using his healing abilities for someone else. Although, it was true that befriending others made them vulnerable in more ways than one, it seemed that it was helping them move away from the crippling effects of their memories.

The usual feelings of hopelessness that weighed her down, especially as the night took hold, were battling with other, more immediate emotions that fought for dominance. For each feeling that sent her hiding came a feeling that countered it, drawing her back. Fear that Susan would die was countered by relief at her recovery; worry that Jael would fail to heal her and what that would do to him, was countered by happiness that he had opened himself up to that risk; concern for Will's safety was countered by the desire to protect him. Wolf snuggled closer and she closed her eyes. She found herself remembering Selene's words. Hearing her speak of the ancients and their use of the magic had been cathartic. She was sick of the hatred and the fear. Her stomach clenched. What would be the result of the magic's return? She squeezed her eyes tighter as she fought the terror invoked by that thought. She searched for something else to concentrate on and recalled she was confused by the inclusion of Spirit as one of the elemental magics. She didn't remember hearing of that before and tried to imagine what it could mean. With that foremost in her thoughts, she drifted into a rare, peaceful sleep.

Jael was whittling a horse out of a thick twig. He would have to sharpen his dagger later. He lifted up the carving and examined it closely in the light of the fire before cutting into it again. He noted that Triene had finally fallen asleep. That was good, she didn't get enough rest, he suspected she had nightmares. He dug the tip of his dagger into the wood to shape the ear and sighed. He would be surprised if she didn't. His eyes wandered over to Susan next, she was still sleeping peacefully. He felt the clenching in his chest relax. The medicine had worked; he hadn't been too late. It was such a fast-acting illness, once it had moved out of the blood and into the organs there was no coming back. He inhaled deeply, as he reminded himself it was ok, he had managed to halt it in time, she was going to be alright. His breath took in the lingering scent of apple and cinnamon. He had always liked this waystation because of the crab-apple. It had been smaller, much like him, when he had first helped his father work on the plants here.

It had been in this clearing that he had declared his childish intention to be a travelling healer, thinking his father would be proud of him. His father's reply had been swift and sharp. "You cannot, son. Your healing can only be for your family." He had not understood why he had to let others suffer when he could help them. Jael gave his head an involuntary shake as he tried to rid himself of his father's tragically prophetic explanation of human nature. He had followed his father's instruction, until now. What was it about her that made him take these risks? He looked at Susan again. She wasn't insane, as he had first suspected. She was just trying to get to grips with a different way of life. Where was she from? Selene's words about the splintered worlds touching had led to Jael speculating about Susan's origins and he was now convinced that she had crossed from another world to theirs. Susan could most definitely be described as a stranger, and he was concerned that the prophesy might have more relevance to their small group than he was willing to currently acknowledge.

He returned his focus to the stick, using the limited light to concentrate on giving texture to the mane and tail while the others slept, undisturbed by his troubled thoughts.

Susan woke to a pounding in her head and pins and needles in her arm. Her body was damp and sticky. Wolf was lying alongside her keeping her back warm, which was lovely, since she felt chilled and achy. She groaned, her parched throat, cracked on the sound. Someone moved closer and put an arm behind her as she struggled to sit up. "I'll help you.

Take it easy." Triene whispered. "I've got some water if you want?" Susan managed to half open a heavy eye and looked blearily at Triene crouched beside her. It was very dark, but she could just about make out Triene's concerned expression in the firelight, before her focus zoomed in on the waterskin in her hand. Susan licked her dry lips and leaned towards the drink, Triene helped guide it to her mouth, and she swallowed thirstily. Exhausted by the effort, she sank back into a dreamless sleep.

The next time she woke it was morning, the light bright against her sensitive eyes. Although her head felt tender and her stomach hollow, the pounding headache had gone and most of the pain and aches had eased. With her eyes lightly closed she listened to the conversation. Will was demonstrating his sleight of hand and sounding rather like a stage magician talking about the hours of practice and use of misdirection. His theft of the gem had clearly been a challenge his professional pride couldn't resist. Susan's lips lifted at the corners. She peered in the direction of the voices out of half open eyes. They were sitting around a dying fire eating and drinking. Her stomach indicated its interest in Will's roughly made cheese sandwich. She shuffled and managed to prop herself up onto her elbow.

Jael noticed her movement and came over to help her sit up properly. He offered his mug and she gladly sipped from it, the fruity, herb like liquid tasted good on her furry tongue. Her stomach loudly demanded more, and Jael gave her a warm smile as he offered his bread. He has a really nice smile, she thought as she chewed, but then again she would probably think that of anyone offering her food at that moment. She alternated between food and drink until she grew weary, and her throat tightened, refusing more. She relaxed and leant into Jael who remained beside her. The morning light was already warming the open ground, providing an accent to the cool shade beneath the trees. She was soothed by the natural beauty surrounding her, muscles loosening in response. She almost forgot that her back was resting on Jael, as she relaxed.

They remained in position, with Susan dozing in and out of sleep, until Wolf sauntered back from the woods, a large rabbit dangling limply in his jaws. His long tail curved upwards, his ears pricked proudly, as he trotted towards the fire. He dropped the kill next to Triene and grinned. Triene exclaimed her delight with his gift and rubbed his ears enthusiastically. Susan opened her eyes at the disturbance in time to see Triene remove her dagger and chop off the rabbit's feet. She threw them to Wolf who chomped on them with relish, the crunching sound made Susan feel a little nauseous. Susan averted her eyes as Triene removed the head, although she was sure she could hear every slice and chop amplified. This was also tossed to Wolf whose strong jaws made light work of it, bunny ears flapping out the side of his mouth until swiped with a tongue and swallowed.

Will set to work on the fire, getting a good blaze going so they could cook the rabbit, his enthusiasm for another meal befitting for a growing lad. He then rinsed out the cook pot, added a small amount of water to it and hung it back on the tripod. Triene and Will worked together to prepare the meal, with Will adding some new potatoes from the wagon and collecting wild watercress by the pond once Jael had directed him to it. Not trusting Will's foraging skills, Jael went to gather some mushrooms to add to the pot.

111

Susan watched with horrified fascination as Triene neatly sliced the skin at the neck of the rabbit before peeling the fur from its carcass in one perfect piece, it needing just a final firm tug to pull it off the legs. She quickly turned away, however, when Triene sliced into the abdomen in order to remove the intestines and organs, not quite ready to face that reality of food preparation.

Jael had located the edible fungi immediately and returned to find Susan desperately trying to ignore the disembowelling. He handed the mushrooms to Will and hurried over. He didn't want his patient losing the small amount of fluid she had managed to consume. Eager to distract and to encourage activity he asked, "Would you like to have a wash and a change of clothes before we eat?"

Susan looked down at her sweat-stained tunic and sniffed. She grimaced as she finally noticed the acrid body odour and stench of stale vomit emitting from her. "God yes! I'm disgusting!" Susan said weakly but emphatically.

Holding back a laugh, Jael headed towards the wagon, "I will get you some fresh clothes." Susan gratefully closed her eyes and prepared herself for the effort to come. Having finished his rabbit treat, Wolf trotted over. He gave a loud sneeze and Susan cracked an eye, "Don't you start" she said, "I'm going to wash." Wolf's mouth opened in a grin, he licked her cheek before he returned to Triene in the hope of some more tidbits. "Ew! Dead bunny saliva!" mumbled Susan wiping her face with the back of her hand.

Jael returned to her, all too soon for Susan's comfort, since he immediately propped her up and carried her over to the pool where he had already laid out the clean clothes.

Although she felt embarrassed being so close to him when she was so smelly and sticky, she was glad he was willing to carry her. She didn't feel strong enough to walk just yet. Jael spoke reassuringly as he carried her, "The pond isn't deep and the water's warm." He lowered her so she could sit on a rock by the edge of the pool. Stretching over to peer into the clear water, she could make out the rocks at its base and the aquatic plants that grew between them. It looked clean and inviting. She recognised some of the soapy moss nearby and felt a burst of excitement at the thought of scrubbing her greasy skin and hair clean.

Jael was still speaking. "Leave your dirty clothes over here", he indicated to another rock, "and I'll make sure they are cleaned for you." He then shook out and draped a blanket over a long branch which overhung part of the pond. "This will screen you from the camp as you get in and out of the pool. I'll be on the other side of it in case you get into difficulty."

Susan hadn't even thought of that, thank goodness he had, or she would have stripped off in her eagerness to wash, for all to see. Not into exhibitionism she would have been humiliated as soon as she realised. The blanket seemed well positioned to preserve her modesty as long as she submerged as soon as she got in the water.

Jael continued, "You can use the blanket to dry off." He gave a worried glance at Triene who was now working on the rabbit skin, stretching and salting it. Then he blushed and shuffled awkwardly as he offered "Er, if you need help removing your…"

"No!" interjected Susan, as her own colour heightened. "I'm

good, thank you." Jael looked relieved as he disappeared onto the other side of the blanket.

Susan's feet were already bare, so she set to work wiggling out of her trousers, which left her feeling fatigued. Jael must have heard her grunts of exertion, but made no more offers of help, thank goodness. She pushed the trousers and knickers over to the rock identified for the dirty washing, then she puffed and panted as she manoeuvred the tunic over her head and added it to the pile. With a twist and unhook, her bra was flung aside and she sighed in relief. Although she felt vulnerable and exposed, she took a moment to rest before she dipped a foot into the water. Urgh! She pulled it back out with a squeal and a hiss. Warm, my arse!

Jael's voice called out from behind the blanket, "Susan, are you all right?"

"Fine." she replied in a strangled tone, before holding her breath and sinking both legs, her hips, stomach and finally her chest into the water. She gasped and swished her limbs about to try and warm up.

Now she was in the water she could see the campfire, Triene and Will looked up and waved. Conscious of the clear water, she gave a small wave back, hoping they couldn't see her breasts bobbing near the surface. Fortunately, they quickly returned to their cooking, and the process of curing the pelt.

She could also see Jael leaning back against the tree, one leg outstretched, the other bent. He was whittling away at some wood, taking care not to look in her direction. Susan wasn't sure if she was offended or pleased that he wasn't peeking.

114

Calling herself an idiot, she gathered up some of the moss and set to work.

By the time she had finished cleaning, the stew's meaty fragrance had drifted across the clearing and her stomach grumbled appreciatively. Although the effort of washing had made her tired, she believed she was feeling stronger than before. Her recovery was surprisingly rapid. Normally, she couldn't face eating and just stayed in bed after a bad bout of the flu. Yet here she was, feeling fresh and hungry already. Scooting as close to the blanket as possible, she checked everyone was looking away before she emerged from the water with a whoosh. Out of the corner of her eye she thought she saw Jael's head turn, but when she looked in his direction, he was still absorbed in his whittling.

She quickly grabbed her side of the blanket and rubbed the rough fabric against her in the hope that it would absorb some of the moisture clinging to her. When she had exhausted the cloth's potential as a towel, she examined the clothes and boots laid out for her. No bra! She looked at the dirty washing pile, but no, it would be better to go free than wear that again. Still feeling a little weak, she perched on a flat-topped rock and dressed in small increments. Once fully clothed she pondered how she would get to the campfire. She doubted she could walk without support. Feeling self-conscious, she crawled under the blanket and looked over to her friends. Triene was just dishing up the meat stew into some wooden bowls, but upon seeing her emerge, called out, "Do you need some help?" Before Susan could reply, Jael had jumped up and made his way over to her.

Before he could scoop her up, Susan tendered, "Do you think you could help me walk, please?" Jael looked at her sceptically, noting her drawn features. She held out a hand for assistance as she tried to stand. She was weaker than she had thought, but she refused to give in to it, wobbling proudly to her feet. He slid his arm under hers and pulled her close to his side to better take her weight. They inched forwards until they reached the fire, and she gratefully sank to the ground. Her shoulders sagged when Jael released her, so he edged close and allowed her to prop herself up against him. Triene looked at them, a speculative gleam in her eye before she passed a bowl of stew to each.

They all tucked into the food, enjoying the hot fare, even Susan. In fact, Susan found herself still hungry after polishing off her bowlful and gratefully accepted a second helping. While she was busy eating her extra portion, Will spoke, "You're lucky Jael knew how to fix you up, lefenhage were a real killer way back. Jael said you're not from 'ere and that's why you got ill. So, where you from then?"

Susan's head was reeling from too much exertion and now from Will's chatter, but she managed to understand enough to answer, "London".

He looked quizzically at her and said, "Not 'eard of it. I guess it's a long way away."

"Yes, it is. It's a long way…" her tired brain had a moment of clarity, "It's on a twin world!" she said eyes widening. They all stared at her.

Will was the first to recover. "Wot?" he said, "like Selene

talked about?"

"I crossed over when the worlds overlapped!" Susan exclaimed in awe.

Triene clapped her hands and said excitedly "Of course!".

Jael sat silently, resignation in his eyes. He then shook his head as if to clear it, and said, "Susan is still unwell and needs to rest while we clear up." Susan felt a wave of exhaustion wash over her as if in response to his words, and she nodded her agreement. She didn't protest when Jael picked her up and carried her to the wagon, placing her on her back and gently laying a clean blanket over her. "Rest now," he said as he left her to sleep. Her heavy eyelids drew closed and she was slumbering efore he had finished walking back to the fire.

## Chapter 11

When Susan opened her eyes, the strong afternoon's light was filtering through the cream fabric of the canvas and made a cosy setting for a nap. Wolf and Will had succumbed to the temptation and were dozing side by side in the wagon. Susan adjusted her position to relieve the knot in her back and pulled herself up to sit against a wooden pole. Whatever the medicine had contained it had been very potent. All her symptoms had disappeared, and she felt refreshed, even energised by her sleep. At the sound of her movements, Will stirred, giving a wide, open-mouthed yawn and stretched out his long limbs contentedly, barely wincing at his rapidly recovering injuries. Although Wolf's ears twitched, his eyes remained closed, while his back leg gave a double kick in Will's direction in order to get comfortable.

"You're looking better," said Will around another yawn.

"I am feeling it too. I'm surprised at how well I feel already!" replied Susan with a smile.

Will avoided her eyes as he agreed, "Yeah, the medicine was good."

His awkward response immediately set off warning bells in Susan's head. She wasn't one to leave it at that, especially since it applied to her health, so she asked, "You seem unsure, why?"

He adjusted his position a couple of times, clearly torn between telling her his idea and keeping it secret. He glanced around before giving in to temptation, he leant towards her and whispered conspiratorially, "I think Jael 'as the Earth power." Eyes flashed with excitement as he added, "You know, like the mages…"

Astonished, Susan let that statement sink in for a moment. Not totally convinced by the reality of magic, despite her acceptance of Selene's warnings, she found it hard to believe Will's assertion and asked, "What do you mean?"

Will's answer was low and confiding, "When I were little, me mum showed 'ow she used 'er Earth magic, but it were a secret I couldn't tell nobody." Will's voice got quieter but more emphatic as he continued, "Before Jael broke off the leaves for your brew, they moved, like they did for me mum. I reckon 'e gave 'em a bit of 'is magic so as the medicine would work right." His words got faster, "and I reckon 'e knew this place coz it full of Earth magic." he concluded and leant back, nodding sagely, satisfied that he had proved his point.

As Susan sat back again to ponder this information, she noticed that Wolf's amber eyes were intent upon her, ears flat against his head. Discomforted, she looked at Will yet couldn't avoid glancing back at Wolf nervously.

Will lent forward to whisper again. "I reckon they both 'ave the power." He indicated to his chest where the gemstone lay in its pouch. "The gem 'as magic, I reckon. Did you see it light up when it got near Triene, before Jael quickly 'id it away?"

Susan's head was swimming with all this speculation, but it made sense as far as anything made sense in this world. What didn't make sense was that everyone said the magic had gone so how could they be using it? She asked as much.

Will screwed up his nose and looked at the roof of the wagon as he fought to remember his mother's explanation, "There's still a bit of magic or we would 'ave died. It's the little bit left that can be used now. Me mum said it were the difference between making the apple tree out back strong and the fruit tasty by caring for it every day, and getting an orchard of apple trees to do it from a burst of magic four times a year."

"That is a wonderful gift to have!" declared Susan. "Why would Jael and Triene be so secretive about having this ability?" she asked, a confused frown creasing her brow.

Will snorted before he replied, "I thought you 'eard Selene's story?" Susan nodded slowly wondering where this was going. "Well, folks 'ate mages, don't they? They kill them," he said with a shrug. His eyes flared with anger though.

"What?!" Susan exclaimed loudly, then in response to Will's shushing her, lowered her voice. "Surely not? In the marketplace, the crowd were interested in the gemstones and their possible link to the magic!"

"Fascination with dangerous stuff, innit?" said Will wisely before adding in a falsely casual voice, "Me dad killed me mum once 'e knew. All she did was grow plants." His mouth pulled tight and he hugged himself as he said, "I ain't got no power, but if I 'adn't run, 'e'd 'ave killed me too. Tainted, aint I?"

"Oh my God! I am so sorry," exclaimed Susan, horrified.

"Ain't your fault," muttered Will. "It's 'is."

Susan wanted to grab hold of Will and hug him tightly in a

futile attempt to make things right, but of course, that would do nothing but make him squirm unhappily. The obvious vulnerability behind his nonchalant façade near broke her heart.

It was a harsh life here, with danger and violence on what appeared to be a daily basis! Even Triene and Jael had suffered the loss of their parents. Her stomach clenched. She had been so wrapped up in her own troubles when they had mentioned it that she hadn't given it a thought save for the awkwardness over dinner. When had she become as self-centred and heartless as her parents? As a child she had longed for their approval, even as she realised they only cared for status and wealth. Susan had gone into law as they had deemed it an acceptable career choice while she had been motivated by the need to promote justice, to protect the vulnerable. When had that morphed into a focus on monetary and societal success and a disregard for the underdog? For that had surely happened. Susan was mortified by this realisation. God no! How had she become just like them? Her hand shook and she felt sick. Will saw her face grow pale. "'ere, do you need the cook pot?" She forced a weak smile and shook her head, making the effort to concentrate on Will and controlling her distress. She recalled his revelations and made herself ask conversationally, while she recovered from her shock, "You said you don't have the power, is that what usually happens? It is inherited?"

Will moved away from the pot, relieved she wasn't about to be sick again. "Yeah." he agreed. "But not everyone gets it, 'course. Me mum got it from 'er dad who were a farmer."

A cold prickle formed at the back of her neck…as a dawning

121

comprehension took shape. No! Please no! Dreading the answer, she asked the question all the same, "Do you think Triene and Jael's parents could use magic too?" Will nodded curiously and waited for Susan to continue. "They were killed," she said simply. A verbal expression of the connection unnecessary.

"Ah," said Will. Further words were beyond them. Wolf whimpered and placed his head between his paws.

Will and Susan jumped guiltily as Jael's scowling face appeared at the back of the wagon, "We need to talk." were his angry words before disappearing again.

They exchanged a worried look. "Do you think he heard us?" Susan said anxiously. Will shrugged nonchalantly, but he couldn't hide the concern in his expression.

Will hastened to exit the back and seek out a secluded spot to relieve himself. Susan emerged more cautiously, apprehensive that her new friends were offended by her gossiping with Will. She squinted as she encountered the full impact of the strong afternoon sun after having sat in the filtered light of the wagon.

She could see Jael and Triene standing where the fire had been, but all traces had been cleared away. They appeared to be arguing, Triene was wringing her hands while she spoke, eyes not meeting her brother's. while Jael folded his arms stubbornly and looked down his nose. Wolf padded over to them and stood beside Triene, in obvious support. His presence seemed to give her strength as she raised her head and her voice, first stabbing her finger towards Susan and then at Jael. Susan made out the word "friends" but the remainder was too low to hear and she didn't want to intrude on the argument since it was clearly about her. She felt tears sting her eyes and through the watery haze she saw Jael glance at her before unwrapping his arms and giving a gesture of exasperated agreement.

Will emerged from the woods and started walking to them, "Come on!" he said as he passed Susan, who hastened to keep up with him. He was braver than she, although it was Susan who spoke first, "I think you heard us talking about you and the magic, and I am so sorry. It was rude and I am so sorry if I have upset you. I have no problem with magic, in my world it doesn't exist except in stories, and I think it sounds wonderful." Triene and Jael were looking at her solemnly as she spoke and didn't give any indication of their response to her outpouring so she continued, "Sorry. I hope you can forgive any offence as I think a lot of you.....I think of you as my friends.." she added hesitantly, unused to expressing real emotions and making herself vulnerable in this way.

As if Susan's apology had opened a dam, Will's words surged forwards, "I've not 'ad any 'elp since me mum. You've saved me and took me with you. As far as I'm concerned you're good people, and if you 'ave magic, then good on you. I wish I did too!"

Wolf had listened intently and nodded as if satisfied. Jael remained stony faced, but Triene had started shedding quiet tears as they spoke. She managed to respond, "I am glad to hear your words for I hope you are indeed our friends, I know that I wish for it yet we have reason to be wary." She looked at her brother before explaining, her voice small, "We have decided to trust you with our story since you have

123

already guessed much about us." Her voice broke on a sob, and she was wringing her hands. Her eyes flittered to Jael again, "I cannot speak of it so Jael has agreed to do so. I would ask you to respect our story and allow us to share it all before you respond." Once she had spoken she sat down next to Wolf and rested her face against his shoulder. She could feel her body and mind starting to shut down in preparation. Wolf pressed into her reassuringly.

Jael muttered grudgingly, "We have kept away from other people until you two, and look what happened when we didn't!" He took in a deep breath and looked down at Triene, before continuing, "It is not something that is easy for us to share but we hope you can be trusted. We have decided to tell you about our parents, since their lives and deaths have shaped our own."

Will and Susan stood motionless, afraid that the slightest sound or movement from them would stop the reluctant revelations. Jael sighed and indicated they should all sit. "It is a long story."

"Our mother told us of their early years together, as a way of recollecting happier times and teaching us caution." He glared at Will and Susan as if it were their fault he hadn't shown caution with them. He then sighed again and closed his eyes for a moment before continuing in what Susan suspected was the storytelling voice of his mother. "They were named Greta and Miln, and they came from a village called Haven, up in the mountains. The village had originally been the home of a small group of magic users hiding from the cull." At Susan's puzzled expression, Jael explained, "The cull was the murder of all magic users, regardless of innocence or guilt. It followed the end of the

124

mage wars, Magic users could no longer protect themselves with magic and most had never learnt to fight in other ways because it hadn't been necessary."

"In any case, over time, the village expanded but took care to remain isolated and hidden. The valley was surrounded by mountains with impassable ridges and the only entrance to the valley was through a narrow cave, hidden behind a waterfall, which villagers always took care to disguise. Only the most trusted villagers ventured beyond the valley so they could trade for goods they couldn't produce themselves. Seema and Kol were non-magical and volunteered to take over the inn when the previous owners grew too old, it was a place where villagers could safely stay on their journeys beyond. They had to travel wide to avoid suspicious eyes and questions from the closer villages and towns. In all, Haven remained a protected secret for over two hundred years."

"Our father's side of the family ran a farm. Family members with Earth magic were trained to use their power to protect the plants from disease and attack. The possession of Earth magic passed from generation to generation, yet an increasing number of children inherited no magical ability. Despite this, they had enough Earth magic to make the farm successful and the plants grow strong and healthy."

"Miln was the youngest in a family of six, all of whom worked the farm. Miln, it transpired, had a different kind of Earth magic. His power enabled him to sense the healing potential in plants and enhance it. This rare talent meant that he was apprenticed, at a very, young age, to the village apothecary, where he learnt about different illnesses and how to mix medicines." Susan and Will shared a knowing glance at this. "His ability to heal and his outgoing and friendly demeanour made him a popular young man with the ladies. He, however, was only interested in one. Greta, our mother."

"Greta was the blacksmith's youngest daughter. Her sister, Seema had married Kol and left the village when Greta was only seven. Greta was a quiet and gentle soul, who found making friends difficult. She had inherited her father's skill with Fire magic, but rather than work in the smithy she preferred to work with her mother cutting and sewing fabrics to make clothes for the villagers."

"Miln, was her opposite, a loud and confident fellow, having had to compete for attention with five older siblings. He was determined to bring Greta out of her shell. He encouraged her to attend the events at the village hall, where he would be found by her side to field the conversation until she felt confident enough to join it. They often went on long walks around the valley, during which he would show her the different plants and talk about their various uses. In other words, they were in love and it wasn't long before they sought permission to marry. A date was set for after the harvest, so that his family could participate fully in the celebrations. It was a time of happiness for them and their families."

"Summer came and went and soon it was time to harvest the final crops. Miln managed to avoid being drawn in to working the fields with his busy family, through the simple plan of whisking Greta away for a walk to one of their favourite woods." Up to now, Jael's telling of the tale had been steady and sure, but here he hesitated and his expression darkened. He looked at Triene who was curled in

126

on herself, her hands were in fists where they rested around her waist, He didn't want to continue, but knew he must. They had started this explanation and they needed to finish for themselves as much as for the others. They hadn't spoken of it, treating it as something best avoided. He began to suspect that it hadn't been the best thing to do as he looked at Triene. Perhaps she had needed to have it vocalised in order to come to terms with it. Perhaps he hadn't been protecting her mind, but rather allow her pain imprison it. Will fidgeted uncomfortably as Jael remained silent, watching his sister.

Jael blinked slowly and returned his attention to Will and Susan as he continued his tale. "They had travelled a considerable distance when they noticed smoke coming from the direction of the village. They rushed back to help tackle the blaze. Greta's Fire magic would be useful in controlling the flames. As they closed the distance, they heard sounds that brought fear and disbelief to their hearts. There were clashes of swords, shouts of alarm and, worst of all, screams of pain. They ran as fast as they could, breath rasping, hearts pumping, but they were too far. Our parents were still running when the sounds were replaced by an unnatural and terrifying silence."

"When they finally reached Haven, the greedy flames that had engulfed and consumed the village were dying out, leaving just the glowing shells of what had been homes and workplaces. Their steps slowed, their minds numbed as they faced the sight of men, women and even children they had known, missing limbs and heads, bloodied, hacked to death, their lifeblood draining away into the cracks between the cobblestones."

"They sought out Greta's home first and found the brick-built forge was the only thing remaining of the smithy. Greta's father lay twisted on the ground, his longsword, tarnished with blood, lay beside him. His gut had been sliced open and his entrails oozed through his clutching hand. Upon seeing his daughter his mouth moved silently, before he managed to rasp out, "Hide…hide". Greta clung to him, as he died in her desperate embrace." Susan's cheeks were wet with silent tears as she listened. "Our maternal grandmother was found splayed over the anvil, a stab wound through her chest, the sword having pierced her heart. She had been fortunate to die quickly, yet many others had not been so lucky. None of the villagers survived. The attackers had been vicious and thorough. Nothing remained. All trace of their lives, their families, their homes had been permanently erased."

"The young couple had grown up under the security and acceptance of Haven. Yes, they had known the outsiders feared the magic and had heard the stories of the Mage Wars and the Cull, but nothing could have prepared them for this. Grieving and fearful, with nothing left but what they wore, they walked away from the village for the second time that day, but this time would never return, for there was nothing to return to."

"The next few years were hard for our parents. They initially sought out Seema and Kol who grieved with them and helped them adjust to their new life. However, Miln and Greta soon moved on, not wanting to bring danger to Seema and Kol's door. They chose to live as nomads rather than expose themselves to prying neighbours' eyes. My father set up locations where his Earth magic encouraged the growth

128

of healing plants, so they had safe places to stay as they travelled."

"As is often the case, Greta was soon with child. As the pregnancy progressed, she became more and more anxious that she be close to a midwife and other women. Miln was reluctant to settle in a populated area, but Greta's rapidly expanding belly won the argument. They built a small home on the outskirts of a village called Talom. My father farmed while my mother's sewing skills became highly prized by the villagers."

"And there my sister and I were born and raised. We learnt how to farm, to make and sell clothes, and importantly, we were taught to control and hide our magic. The lesson of Haven was drummed into us, so I also learned to use my body as a weapon, so I could fight and defend my sister." He gave her a sad smile and added, "Although she learnt many such skills herself, of course."

Jael's voice faltered before he stated in a bland tone, "As we got older and started taking on the responsibility of trading, our parents seemed to enjoy the happy memories being a part of village life brought them, and they started spending more time in the village, while Triene and I still travelled and traded, happiest on the road."

Jael paused and took a deep breath. When he resumed the tale, his voice was tight and clipped with restrained emotion. "Just over four years ago, at the start of winter, we came back from a successful trading trip. Our parents had stayed home, as was usual then. They had made friends in the village and felt settled and happy, and they were even thinking of moving closer." Triene curled up into a tighter ball and gave a gasping sob.

"We could tell something was wrong as we pulled up the track to the house. The track was churned up as if heavy traffic had passed it, yet we had the wagon and our parents walked into the village. The wagon's wheels couldn't traverse the mud so Triene and I, and Wolf who had found us the year before, walked toward the house. Wolf smelled it first, of course, and he let out a pained howl. Triene cried out and tried to run to the house, but I stilled her. We carefully approached our home, fearing what we would find." Tears formed in Jael's eyes as he clenched his hands in tight fists. He stood up and paced, his anger needing a physical outlet. He spat out the next words through clenched teeth, "The rotting stench of decaying flesh hit our nostrils before we saw them. The sight of our parents tortured bodies haunts us still." Jael swallowed hard then took a sip of his water, while Triene sniffed loudly and wiped away the tears that were silently flowing down her face. Will had begun to rock as he hugged himself, his face ashen but expressionless.

"Our home had been demolished by what looked like a frenzied mob, the earth around it had been churned up and the walls and our things had been attacked with sledgehammers and axes. The attack had clearly been planned and was targeted against our family, for in front of the ruins sat a cage. A cage barely big enough to fit a wolf, and in that cage were the rotting bodies of our mother and father."

Jael stared into the sky clearly reliving the memory. "The cage had manacles attached to the bars at the top and they had put our parents' hands in those manacles so they couldn't move even within that tight cage. They had cut out their tongues so they couldn't speak. They had then proceeded to stab them. The wounds shallow but numerous. Then, those bastards left them in the cage, tied up so they couldn't hold one another, unable to speak words of love and comfort to one another, and left them to watch each other bleed and starve to death."

Susan retched and threw up before she could get out of the way and Will looked about to join her. But instead tentatively rested his hand on her shoulder.

Jael continued lost in the memory, his voice bitter, "None of their so-called friends from the village had come to free them or heal them, none had come to release their bodies and give them some dignity in their passing. They had been left there to feed the creatures that could fit through the bars. There wasn't anything we could do for them except release them from that prison and bury them together on the land we had called home."

Susan trembled and gasped for breath, desperate to escape the words, yet knowing she had to hear them. Will offered her his waterskin. "Alright now?" he asked quietly. When she took a sip the water and nodded, he said, "Come on, we need to let 'em finish this."

Susan turned back to face Jael. She saw he had sat down and was holding Triene. They rested their heads together, eyes closed, in a moment of much needed comfort. Wolf snuggled close to them both. Jael opened his eyes first and looked steadily at Susan. "I'm sorry," she said contritely, unable to more accurately express the intense emotions surging through her at that moment. Jael tipped his chin in understanding and Triene offered a small watery smile. Will waited, his water bottle gripped tightly in both hands.

"How could someone do that to our gentle and kind parents. They never said or did anything to harm anyone, but they had to live in fear and died in fear." came Triene's watery pain.

Jael's anger was still simmering, but with his sister's head resting on his shoulder and his arm comforting her, his voice was more measured, "We blamed everyone. The people who betrayed them, the people who hurt them, the people who pretended it never happened, the people who fear magic. What had their friends done? Nothing! They hadn't even buried them! I wanted to punish everyone, to make them suffer as our parents had suffered, as we suffered." His hands flexed and muscles tightened. Triene reached up to pat him on the chest even as she gulped down her sobs.

Will was also flexing his hands, jaw tight. He leant forward to speak, looking in Jael's eyes, "I wanted me dad dead. I wanted to smash 'is 'ead in like 'e did to me mum. 'E just went out and got drunk while I struggled to drag me mum's body into our small garden and left 'er to lie on the plants she 'ad cared for. I was beaten meself, and only a little'un so I couldn't bury 'er. I 'ad to leave 'er before 'e got back and remembered me. I 'ad to leave 'er." He had bowed his head during the final words, but he raised it again and stared at Jael. "It took me a while, but I got me enough coin to pay a bloke to give me dad a beating. 'E didn't kill 'im, but 'e broke 'is arm good and proper. I watched from the roof then left that town. I ain't gone back and I never will."

Susan's moral compass was spinning. His actions were simply revenge, yet without a legal system to provide

132

punishment, forget rehabilitation, his father would have killed with impunity. Her gut screamed it was justice, while her head struggled to accept this moral code.

Jael, however, nodded his understanding. A bond formed in rage and a need for revenge. "We watched over the village that first night, seeing them greet and hug and go about their lives as if there hadn't been evil lurking on their doorstep. They must have known something of the attack, even if they hadn't joined in it, our home wasn't so far from the village for something like that to go unnoticed. Our parents would go to the village most days, yet no one had gone to check on their absence. Instead, they carried on with their lives, and dared to laugh." The bitter anger from that time was still in Jael's voice. "I wanted to use our powers to kill their crops and set fire to their homes. A petty revenge compared to the horror that had been done to our family."

Susan could feel her own anger urging on this revenge, but her moral compass settled, she knew this was wrong, this wasn't justice. A rising disappointment in Jael began to fill her. She tried to quash it. She had no right to judge, but she couldn't resist the sensation. Jael's next words, however, made the disappointment disperse as easily as it had formed.

"But as we watched, we saw the children, the mothers and fathers. How could we wreck their lives? How could we perpetuate the injustice and pain? … And so, we just left." The difficulty of that decision was written on his face, in the tightness of his jaw, the furrowed brow and the eyes closed tight.

He forced himself to continue and looked sternly upon Susan and Will as he spoke, "We have deliberately kept our lives separate from others. You are the only people we have shared our travels with, and we are trusting you with our most painful secrets and with our lives."

Will burst out, "I may be a thief, but I ain't no magic 'ater! I'm with you all the way!"

Susan's words were quiet and emerged through tears of pride and relief in his decision, "I have nothing but gratitude and respect for you, for your kindness to myself and to Will, for the familial love and support you have shown and for the fortitude and generosity of spirit in such terrible circumstances." She took a gulp before adding, "You can most assuredly trust me, as I have and do trust you with my life. Thank you for everything and thank you for sharing this with me." Fat tears were rolling down Susan's cheeks now and she was glad she had managed to get the words out before the lump in her throat had appeared.

Triene had lifted her head as Susan spoke and a fresh flow of tears was streaming down her face, although this time the tightness in her chest was from her hope of friendship. Even Will roughly brushed his eye and looked away. Jael stood up under the pretence of needing to check on the horses, while Triene and Susan hugged and sobbed together for a while. When they were finished and had blown their noses and splashed their faces with water they were gently smiling.

"We aren't far from the next village, probably two to three hours ride." said Jael relieved to be talking business again now the tears had dried. "We usually stop and sell some of our clothing to the villagers when we take this route. It is only a few items, usually, but it is a convenient place to stay the night before we head for the next big town. They have an inn that serves food, but we will have to sleep with the wagon."

"Sounds good." said Susan with a soft smile at him.

He acknowledged her agreement with a nod before looking at Will, "You will have to stay hidden as we aren't that far from Carnom and this is a popular route for travellers." Will's face fell but he indicated his acceptance of the plan.

As they started to climb up into the wagon, they heard a distant rumble coming from the direction of Canorm. Triene and Jael exchanged a look and Triene quickly disappeared down the track.

Will moved fitfully as they awaited Triene's return and Susan could see he was nervous. "What is it?" she whispered urgently, not recognising the sound. Will stopped moving and stared just above her head as he listened intently. "Lots of 'orses, moving fast, Lots of 'em." Uneasy, they waited and listened as the rumble became the more distinct sound of hooves kicking up the dirt track as they galloped towards them. To Susan's ear, it sounded like the regular rhythm of an old train, traversing the iron rails, getting closer and closer to the station. The snap of reins and the rattle of wheels followed the horses as the sound raced past their location without any sign of slowing.

Triene re-appeared when the hoof-beats had become a distant echo, distractedly brushing bits of shrubbery from her hair and clothing. Will and Susan observed her vexed expression with concern. "The merchant's carriage and about fifty of his soldiers just rode in the direction of the village." she said irritably.

"Damn it!" exclaimed Jael in frustration, as Will struggled to hide his apprehension. "They are bound to stop there. There's nowhere else they, or we, can travel to before sunset."

## Chapter 12

"We will have to stay here." stated Triene. They all agreed, none of them wanting to risk encountering the soldiers again.

Wolf thought he might as well use this time to find the next meal, so he padded towards the woods. He fancied some squirrel and there had been plenty scampering around the trees earlier, so he was confident of success. Will looked inclined to join him. Wolf rolled his eyes, thinking of the noise the boy would generate. Actually, he could use that to get his prey to run towards him…hmmm…as long as they were kept near the ground it could work. He stopped and beckoned with his head for Will to follow him. Will grinned and jogged to catch him up and they headed into the woods together.

Jael unhitched the confused horses while Susan and Triene prepared a small fire. Susan was surprised to see Triene use a flint and steel but said nothing, thinking she probably had got into the habit of it since they had to hide their powers. Susan felt there were still lots of gaps in her understanding of the magic and said as much to Triene.

Triene thought for a moment then tried to explain how it worked, "Magic is part of the fabric of life, it infuses all living things. The power to control and manipulate the magic only exists in a few humans. Those of us who can, inherit different levels of control, and it is dependent on the magic around us, in the rocks and earth or the heart of a flame, the breeze or the flow of water in a stream. Each of us are connected to just one of the elements, Jael's is Earth and mine is Fire." Triene's eyes dropped to the ground and her mouth turned down for a moment. Susan was puzzled, why was Triene sad when speaking of her magic? Had something happened?

Triene continued, making her voice brighter and lifting her chin. "Our mother was able to tell us about the ancients, but most of the histories were destroyed with the Mage Wars and the cull. However, we learned that the elders, and therefore ourselves, were the caretakers of the Goddess Rua's gift. That we were chosen to look after the world and the life upon it."

"What about the artifacts? What were they and how were they used?" asked Susan thinking of Selene's words.

Triene concentrated, trying to remember, "I don't think our parents knew much about them, to be honest. I recall mother telling us that they were rare but gave access to much greater magic than an elder could normally use. I don't know much more than that."

Susan was nodding, her mind connecting Selene's story with Triene's. "Then some of the elders got greedy and used those artifacts in warfare," she mused out loud.

Triene nodded, "Yes, that's what we were told. By the end there were only four mages involved in the war and they were believed to have artifacts because of the power they wielded, but their empires fell as soon as the magic disappeared."

"At first elders and non-magic users fought the mages' armies together, but soon the people turned on anyone who had any magical ability. The resulting cull was bloody and

138

brutal." Triene shook her head as if to dislodge her disbelief.

Jael had wandered closer and now he took over the explanation, exasperation coating his words, "The cull was caused by the mages' use of the magic. The people had suffered for decades at their hands. A whole generation had only known the evil perpetuated by the mages and their soldiers." Jael continued to pace. "The mages were known to rip apart the ground, swallowing up homes and farmland, or flames soared through crowds trying to resist the mage's control. Tornados whipped through villages and giant waves drowned sailors or coastal towns. The mages destroyed many, many lives." His anger was palpable. "Who could blame people for fearing magic? Was what they did wrong! Of course it was! But their fear and loathing had an easy and immediate target, and they took out their rage on anyone with a trace of magical ability, even children." He spat out the next words, "for what they could become..."

Triene's expression was grim. "There is no reason to hold on to that hatred now," she said fiercely, "As Selene pointed out, the mages were the abomination, not the magic. People need to learn the truth about the magic, learn about the ancients and the good magic can do."

Jael was nodding, but pointed out bitterly, "That isn't going to happen while the knowledge is kept in the Temple of Helvoa and is only available at a hefty price."

Susan had been largely ignored during this interaction; her initial question forgotten. The horrors of war seemed universal, she noted sadly. Here they were perpetrated by magic, on Earth by science and engineering. People's greed, fear and hatred were the common denominator. She feared that her own focus on success and influence at work, and disregard of others' difficulties or loss bore an uncomfortable similarity to the desire for power of a dictator. She shook her head, no more. She had recognised it and wouldn't repeat it.

She focused her attention on Triene's description of the magic, and the elements of Earth, Fire, Air and Water. She was perplexed by a significant omission in Triene's description of the magic, for Selene had mentioned an element of Spirit when speaking of the ancients and it was a vital part of the prophesy. She asked them how the elemental magic of Spirit worked.

Triene exclaimed, "I don't know anything about it!"

Jael nodded, a frown of confusion on his brow as he added, "Spirit elders weren't part of the Mage Wars and never featured in any of our mother's tales of Haven or the ancients."

"I wonder what they could do and what happened to them?" said Susan quietly. Jael and Triene shrugged, clearly nonplussed.

Will returned from the woods, proudly displaying the three squirrels dangling from his hand by their tails. Wolf sauntered along behind him, allowing the boy the glory from the kill. He had already eaten two of their catch and was feeling magnanimous. While Triene and Will skinned and gutted the animals, Jael showed Susan how to use a machete to clear the bark off a long stick and to create a sharp point at one end. Susan's first attempts ended up slicing the stick in two or taking too much off, but Jael was patient and merely retrieved more sticks for her to work on. Finally, all was ready and the squirrels skewered, resting in a sort of wigwam over the fire to roast.

They were silent as they waited for the meat to cook. So much had been said, they needed time to just reflect. Even Will was still and staring into the flames. Susan's mind was busy compartmentalising the wealth of information she had received since arriving here. She was good at that, at sorting through the data until she had determined what was important and what needed to be actioned. Normally, she would record her conclusions on the computer, but she didn't have lots of cases to juggle now, just one world and one important component to deal with. Everything kept circling back to it. The magic was returning to this world and danger would come from it. Especially, if the wrong person had an artifact.

She wondered how much magic could be used through the artifact, would someone be able to trap all the magic if they were at the point where the worlds met? She felt a prickle of fear travel down her spine and across the tops of her arms. That had to be prevented at all costs. Trite words, but she felt a burning need to stop it consume her. Perhaps she had been brought here to stop it! She scoffed out loud at her grandiose thoughts. Who was she to do anything? She was a stranger to this world, she was weak and ignorant. The desire still burned though.

Her thoughts stumbled, stranger, wasn't there something about that in the prophesy? Was she part of the prophesy? She concentrated and tried to recall Selene's words, muttering them out loud as she thought. "The Stranger to Guide, the Finder Child." Her eyes went wide and focused on Will. "You "found" the red gemstone!" she exclaimed making the others stare at her in confusion. "We could be the prophesy!" she said, blinking rapidly. She pointed to herself, "The Stranger," then to a confused Will, "The Finder Child". She moved her eyes to rest on Triene, "The Fortress of Fire, and the Weapon of Earth!" she concluded as she rested her gaze on Jael, who was the only one without shock on his face, but rather had a weary expression as if he had already come to that conclusion and was unhappy about it.

"We don't know that for sure," he muttered, reluctant to accept what it would mean. "It is vague and could apply to lots of people. We don't match the rest of the prophesy either."

Susan's face dropped to a frown before determination drove her to look directly into his eyes, "That's true, but like Selene said we all have choices to make and perhaps our choices will help prevent another war, whether we are linked to the prophesy or not."

She felt herself trying to bulldoze her way through Jael's caution and checked herself. Her friends had experienced the real dangers and losses of such choices, she needed to respect that. "Sorry, I was getting carried away by the idea, you are right, we must take care. You have a much better idea of what that would mean." A sense of rightness came with those words. Anyway, she thought with a mental shrug. If she were the stranger in the prophesy, she was meant to be a guide, not a bulldozer!

Jael turned away, his thoughts in disarray. He feared that Susan's presence meant that they were indeed part of the prophesy. He had certainly trained and fought enough to justify the label warrior. He felt it was forcing a fit to say Will found the gemstone, when he clearly stole it, and how was Triene a fortress for goodness sake! There was no sign of any Air or Water elders, and they didn't even know what a Spirit elder was, so how would they find one? Perhaps that was what Will was supposed to find. Gah! He couldn't believe that he was even considering this. He glanced across at Triene who was sitting quietly with Wolf's head resting in her lap. Her fingers were stroking the fur behind his ears.

Triene was thinking about her magic. She hadn't used it since finding her parents. She wasn't even sure she could find it again if she wanted to, she had locked it away so securely. They were in trouble if she were part of the prophesy. She didn't believe it, of course. Her wish to help was just that, a wish. She was broken. She knew it and accepted it. She looked at Will talking to Susan. He was eager to be a hero. She gave them a small smile, amazed that Will had retained such optimism. Susan hadn't mentioned much about her life, but she seemed a determined sort of person, if a bit out of her depth. Jael was right, they weren't the ones in the prophesy, they couldn't be. She wasn't a fortress. She was a crumbled wall.

"Do you really think me nicking the gemstone makes me the Finder Child?" Will asked wistfully.

Susan's answer was apologetic, worried she had misled him, "I really don't know. It just seemed to make sense in the moment. I just thought our coming together was almost like fate deciding it.." she said sheepishly as she realised how foolish she sounded.

"You mean like the Goddess planned it. Planned me to save the world?" Will scoffed, while his eyes blazed with hope.

Susan laughed, "It's far more likely than me saving it!" before adding, "What can I do? I can't fight, I can't do magic, I don't even know the name of this world let alone the country I'm in."

"Yeah" said Will his smile diminishing. "We're no 'eroes". Then he added with a smirk, "You 'appen to be in this mighty country of Ellada, on the planet Ruanh. So now you know that at least."

Susan gave him an amused smile. "Now I know. Thank you."

They fell silent as they ate their meal.

Susan's thoughts had progressed onto the gemstones. The red one had seemed to react to Triene, and if Will was right, there was magic contained within it. What if all the gemstones contained magic? They had been hidden away in a burial chamber of an ancient elder, they were clearly regarded as important. Perhaps they had been hidden to prevent the corrupt mages from finding them. Susan slowed her thoughts, this was speculation, she told herself, but this did nothing to quell her growing conviction that they were ancient artifacts that could be used in some manner to enhance a mage's power. Susan's heart was pounding now. She was certain that the merchant's desire to purchase them was for a nefarious purpose. She curled her lip. He didn't seem the sort to be interested in being a caretaker for the world. Damn it! He still had four of the gems.

"We must rescue the rest of the gemstones!" she declared

out loud. surprising herself and the others.

Triene's eyes widened at Susan's sudden and unexpected announcement and Jael started to chuckle, before his jaw dropped, "You're serious?"

"I am," said Susan firmly. "It is like Selene said. Now we know the magic is coming back, we have a responsibility to do something to prevent its misuse, whether we are part of the prophesy or not. The gemstones have got to be ancient artifacts. I know you sensed the magic in them." she declared as she recalled Jael's panicked reaction to it glowing. "The merchant is not a good man, that much is clear, and whether he is planning on using them himself or has a buyer that wants them, he cannot be allowed to keep them!" she exclaimed, her breath fast and shallow in her consternation.

Triene and Will exchanged uneasy glances, while Wolf raised his head and fixed her with a curious stare. Finally able to speak, Jael spluttered, "I have no idea what makes you think we have any hope of getting close enough to find the gemstones, let alone escape with them."

Susan regarded him earnestly, "We need to try. Imagine the harm he would inflict when the magic comes."

Jael was getting angry now, "Look at us! Do you honestly think we could take on fifty soldiers and a possible mage?"

"Of course not! I'm not suggesting we engage in a fight, but rather a different kind of attack."

"A sneak attack!" declared Will, excitedly.

"Exactly," replied Susan.

Jael was frustrated. Susan had no idea what she was suggesting. She obviously had some half-baked notion of noble quests and had no concept of the danger it would entail. Will was no better. He looked to his sister, at least she would show some sense.

Triene was clutching a fist in front of her chest. She could feel something like excitement churning within it. It was overpowering her fear. They should at least have a look and see if they could come up with a realistic plan to recover the gems. The idea of rescuing an ancient artifact was building an unexpected sense of empowerment that was being pumped through her bloodstream, chasing away the negativity. She lay her hand on her brother's arm. "The merchant is close. I think we should consider the possibility, Jael." she added gently. "If we don't, then who will?"

Jael looked down at her, exasperated, "It'll be too dangerous." Then he added in a lower voice, "and I have vowed to keep you safe."

"I know." said Triene softly as she hugged him tight. "I know." Jael sighed as he returned her embrace, laying his cheek upon the top of her head as he breathed, "I can't lose you as well."

Triene spoke into his chest, so quiet only he could make out the words. "I need to do something Jael. I need to do something to make things right." Jael's heart clenched at her words, he understood what she meant. Revenge hadn't been the way, but perhaps this would be.

Wolf clearly decided to add his own opinion to the discussion by padding over to Susan and turning to fix Jael with an intense stare, Jael glared at him in return as he muttered, "I can't believe I'm considering this madness."

Susan moved closer to him and lightly took his hand, saying sincerely, "Thank you." Jael shook his head but kept his hand in hers, worried eyes locking with her solemn ones.

## Chapter 13

The large shire horse moved cautiously through the gaps in the trees, his riders hunched over his back to avoid wayward branches. Susan's head rested against his neck, white knuckled hands in a death grip on his braided mane, too worried about falling off to feel embarrassed by Jael's body wrapped snugly around her. Jael leant slightly, directing the gelding to come to a stop where the line of trees met the rolling meadow beyond.

They had decided to approach the village indirectly, not wanting to draw attention to their arrival. Their assumption being that the soldiers would be screening all newcomers. Their plan was basic so far; sneak in and sneak out with the gemstones. They were hoping more details would come to them when they found the merchant. Will was happy with this plan, since most thefts were based on opportunity and adaptation, but the others felt discomforted by the lack of clarity. Susan in particular was a planner. She liked to plan every detail of every encounter in advance, although she was learning to react more out of necessity.

Jael dismounted easily and assisted Susan in her ungainly slide down the gelding's back and onto wobbly legs. She retained her grip on the mane until her nerves settled and her legs steadied. She remembered why she had refused to continue with her riding lessons now. She gave a tentative pat on the horse's neck, recalling others doing so after the lessons. The gelding gave a dismissive snort and tossed his head. Unable to resist grinning at Susan's indignant expression, Jael handed the horse a piece of apple. He eagerly snuffled at it, using his flexible lips and chomped

148

happily before wandering off to nibble at a patch of tasty grass at the edge of the field.

Triene and Will soon joined them, riding in on the slightly shorter mare. Jael greeted them with a raised hand while offering another piece of apple to the mare and murmuring soothing words in her ear. Triene joined Susan, as they watched Jael. She said in a small voice, "He's saying goodbye to them in case we don't make it back."

The reality of the danger they faced hit Susan then. Her blood ran cold and her limbs felt weak. What had she got them into? She watched Jael give the mare a last tender pat and turn to join them. Triene was standing beside her, solemn and still. Susan forced herself to speak, "We don't have to do this, I should never have suggested it. I'm just a stupid idiot, overly influenced by a rally cry!"

Triene grabbed her arm and turned her to face her. Her green eyes flared as she fixed her with a stare. "You merely put words to it. Each of us has chosen this path, knowing the danger. If you do not wish to go on, you may stay, but I will continue."

Jael's hazel eyes were more soothing and comforting as he spoke, "Your fear is understandable, and you can wait with the horses. We will not think less of you."

"That's not what I meant." mumbled Susan, "I shouldn't have dragged you into this. You have already been through so much." Her own eyes dropped to the ground.

Will piped up, "Don't be daft! We ain't being dragged into nothing! Let's get on with it before it gets dark." He was jiggling impatiently. The intensity of the moment was

149

broken, and even Susan managed a smile as she apologised, before declaring, "All for one and one for all!" while holding out her hand for a high five. They all gave her a strange look, before turning away and heading towards the far edge of the trees. Ah, yes. They wouldn't know the Three Musketeers here, thought Susan, slightly embarrassed.

It was now late afternoon, and a few heavier clouds were starting to cross in front of the lowering sun making the air chill. The breeze was also picking up, causing the topmost branches on the trees to creak and the long grasses in the field to bow their heads. The sun sat behind them, that meant they were heading eastward, at least Susan thought that was how it worked. She took careful steps, trying to avoid the dips and trips between the trees. Luckily, her boots didn't rub, but they also didn't cushion the impact, and she soon felt the jolt of each step in her heels and knees.

Before they had left the wagon, they had changed into darker clothes to help them blend in with the woodland and to keep hidden in shadows. It would be most useful when it was night, but it still helped them blend in. That had been Will's suggestion, of course, being the most experienced at sneaking. They had also filled a backpack with essentials and placed weapons about their bodies. Susan had only one machete since it had been the only weapon she had ever held, and that only for whittling!

Wolf was nowhere to be seen, his fur being much better camouflage than their clothing. He knew where they were going and would keep close.

Reaching the edge of the wood they were faced with a pasture sprinkled with steaming cow pats. Huge, thickset cows with bold red and white hides grazed the lush grass placidly. Jael waited for the others to catch up then spoke quietly, "We will need to pass through this pasture to get to the cover of some more trees. If you look there is a farm at the far end of the field. We don't want to be seen so we are going to need to move quickly and try and use the cows as a screen. Now, when we reach that thicket..." Susan's eyes followed his gesture and saw that the trees were much smaller and further apart. "We will be close to the village and there isn't much cover so we will need to keep low to the ground. Are you ready for this?"

They all nodded, but Susan eyed the cattle suspiciously, noting the sharp horns curling back from their white, rectangular heads. She remembered hearing that more people were killed by cows than sharks and looking at these creatures she could believe it. She watched Jael move quickly towards the nearest heifer. He halted when he stood alongside the cow, in a contorted crouch, soothing her with a touch when she turned to examine him, mouth rolling as she chewed. Satisfied that he wasn't going to disturb her peace, she ducked her head and continued grazing and Jael darted over to the next cow. Triene quickly followed his lead, then Will, until the three of them were ducking behind a cow each, who were all but ignoring them. A snort of laughter escaped as Susan watched her companions bobbing across the expanse with the occasional look of surprise from the cattle as they passed. The ridiculous sight had the effect of diminishing the anxiety that had beset her. She took a deep breath and rushed forward, trying to project a non-threatening aura to the nearest animal.

Up close the heifer was enormous, easily five foot tall. For some reason she had imagined cows would be a lot smaller than a horse. The points of the horns seemed to glint in the sun threateningly. The heifer raised and stamped a front hoof, then started to walk. Alarmed, Susan tried to keep pace with her while remaining tucked up against her warm, flatulent body. Relieved to note she was walking in the right direction, Susan decided to stay close and allow the cow's movement assist her in the safe traversing of the pasture. To her left she could see the others still darting from cow to cow but soon she and her cow caught them up and even overtook them. She patted the cow's shoulder and smiled as they headed straight for the trees. The cow mooed softly in response and kept up her steady pace, head bobbing as she walked. They reached the point at which the pasture ended and the trees began. Susan was so pleased with her helpful giant, she reached out and tickled her behind her fluffy ear. With a soft exhale the cow's large tongue extended and slowly swiped over her arm, taking the fabric along with it. Susan chuckled softly before she ducked into the trees and waited for the others.

Most of the trees in this thicket had spindly white trunks with peeling paper like bark Their fine long branches reached upwards and were topped with light green leaves and cottony yellow catkins. The ground beneath them was carpeted with the deep green leaves and merry flowers of hundreds of bluebells. While a charming sight the protective cover was limited, and Susan could clearly see the others heading her way, even though they kept low to the ground. Jael stopped before they reached her. He had found traces of a dried-up brook which over the years had cut a path through the copse as it had trickled down the gentle slope. The banks were far enough apart to allow a person to lie flat, and the occasional rocks embedded in them would make good hand and foot holds for someone crawling along it. Jael decided to test the additional cover it could provide. Crawling over to it he lay himself along the dip, face down, and using his elbows, hands and feet, shuffled along the path of the rivulet.

Susan crawled over to them when she saw Jael lay flat and disappear from sight. The plants on either side effectively hid him unless you were looking along the line of the crevice. Triene waved her on to go next. With a small sigh, Susan scrambled to follow his lead and with some difficulty managed to wiggle downstream. She had to fight down her rising bottom as she shuffled, and more than once her foot or hand slipped, and she twisted awkwardly before righting herself. She forced herself not to squeak or cry out, even when her hand caught on a sharp rock edge and cut open slightly. She gritted her teeth and continued wiggling. She could hear the breath of her companions as they followed behind, although Jael had managed to scramble his way much faster and was some way ahead.

Not long into this uncomfortable process, they started to hear sounds of habitation. Uncertain as to the source or whereabouts of these sounds, they took great care to move as noiselessly as possible, stopping frequently to listen and assess their relative location. Soon the sounds grew louder and indicated a significant amount of activity ahead. They had reached the edge of the copse and Susan thought they must be right on the edge of the village. Jael had managed to squat behind a low but dense shrub and beckoned for her to join him. His dagger was palmed and he had a deep frown furrowing his brow. Worried, Susan shimmied herself up the slight bank, squashing the grasses by its side as she tried to avoid scraping herself on the protruding rocks. Once beside him she sat and looked up expectantly. He needlessly put his finger to his lips to ensure she didn't speak, then he mouthed "Soldiers". Her eyes widened and she paid closer attention to the sounds now she didn't need to focus on moving. She thought she could make out the sound of metal clashing against metal and grunts of exertion. Then came a frustrated raspy shout, "No, no, no. Not like that! Give me that!". The clash of swords recommenced and was immediately followed by a cry of pain and a thump. "Now, try again!" the voice commanded.

As they tried to distinguish what was going on beyond the fight training, they were joined by Will and Triene whose alarmed expressions revealed they had recognised the significance of the sounds. It was hard to make out, but eventually they could discern the clamour of soldiers setting up camp. Was the merchant with his soldiers or in the village? Susan couldn't imagine the merchant slumming it with his soldiers, and the decision to set up camp by a village suggested his demand for a bed.

Jael indicated that they should stay put while he scouted and then disappeared into the shrubbery. The three remaining companions hunkered down and waited, anxiously listening for sounds of alarm which would indicate that Jael had been spotted. Triene rested her head back against the dark, waxy leaves. Although her eyes closed, she remained alert and she held her dagger firmly. Her mind was focused on the sounds in the camp. She was ready to fight to the death, knowing that not doing so would lead to worse. Will was obviously having more difficulty waiting, he was like a coiled spring, wound tight as he fought the urge to move around. Instead, he focused his energy on methodically stripping parts off a leaf so that only its skeleton remained. Susan watched him for a while, before closing her eyes.

This necessary silent stillness proved difficult. Susan fought with her imagination which was determined to think of as many unpleasant outcomes as possible, and cleaned out her cut. It wasn't as deep and long as it had felt, thank goodness. It throbbed but the bleeding had stopped. She was covered in tender bruises from the crawling and her muscles were burning. Gym classes didn't prepare one for this sort of physicality. She sighed again.

With the sinking of the sun and darkening of the skies, the fight training concluded. Without the noise of combat, they could make out the sounds of the camp settling into its evening calm. The tearing scrape of a sword being sharpened, the rumble of male voices followed by a bark of laughter at an unheard joke. The saliva inducing scent of roasting hog being slowly rotated over a wood fire wafted in their direction teasing them with its tempting aroma.

The sun finally dipped over the horizon and there was still no sign of Jael. The silver light of the moon took the place of the sun, while the orange light of campfires glowed from the other side of the shrubs. Only the occasional sound drifted over to them from the soldiers. Susan was having to move more now, since her knees and back were beginning to cramp and stiffen in the cool air.

A gentle rustle behind them had them alert and fearful, until Jael came into sight. An involuntary sigh of relief expelled from Susan, while Triene frowned and shook her brother's arm for having left them for so long. He ruffled her hair then pulled her close for a short hug and gave Will a manly nod in greeting over Triene's shoulder. As soon as he had released his sister, Susan flung her arms around him and held him tightly, as if to prove to herself he was back and safe. Although initially surprised, Jael returned her hug before pulling back self-consciously. Concerned they had made too much noise, they froze for a moment and listened for sounds of soldiers nearing to investigate.

When it was apparent that they hadn't been heard, Jael brushed an area of ground clear of debris and, using a stick, drew a basic map, the moonlight enabling them to make out the shapes. He drew a cross and whispered, "Us." Then drew a line to indicate the direction of the village and the fact that the soldiers were camped in between. So faintly they could barely hear it, he said, "Patrols here and here" as he used the stick to point to where he had spotted the soldiers circling the camp. Unfortunately, it appeared that they would be unable to avoid passing close by.

Jael had thickened the shrubs reducing any gaps. That would help hide them. He brushed clear a bit more ground and drew some rough rectangles before drawing an arrow pointing to one. "He's here."

"His guards," and he proceeded to mark the corners of the rectangle with crosses, and then put crosses inside the shape.

"I can get in," said Will. Jael looked at him then nodded.

"Let's go!" Susan whispered confidently. Jael tipped his chin in response and turned to lead the way.

Crawling low to the ground, the lush grass cushioned their

156

hands and knees while softening any sound. They reached the point where the patrols had just met, before moving out again. They remained immobile, waiting for the opportunity to continue.

"Anything?" asked one soldier.

"Nah. Course not! What we doin' patrolling 'ere?" replied the other bitterly.

"Yeah, I know. We should be downing a few in the tavern, not stuck out in this 'ere field," added a third.

There was the sound of metal on flint then a sickly, sweet smell that faintly resembled burnt rope filled the air. There was a loud inhale, followed by a slow exhale.

"You better not let the Commander catch you with that." said the first voice again,

"Eat my dick!" replied the other, while the third man gave a crude chuckle.

An exaggerated sigh was followed by fading footsteps." 'Ere, give us a puff?", a pause was followed by an increase in odour as the two men lingered until the joint was finished.

When the soldiers finally moved off, they resumed crawling. There was a short gap between the shrubbery and the hedgerow bordering the village. They stilled and listened. When they were confident that it was clear they crossed it as quickly as they could and sat behind the hedgerow breathing heavily. The pale light of the moon picked out the line of brick and stone buildings with their small holdings laid out to the rear. The main street lay to their right, just beyond sight.

Jael silently indicated the route he had taken just beyond the gardens, hugging the hedges that bordered another field. They would need to crouch low as they walked. Susan held in a groan. Her thigh muscles were already trembling with overuse and her back felt like it wouldn't be able to straighten again. Bracing herself mentally, she took a deep breath and made to follow Jael once again. He didn't seem to be discomforted by the awkward movements and angles, even though his bulk and height meant he had to hunch even more than the others.

Without warning a huge creature with gleaming teeth loomed before them. He trotted towards Triene who greeted him with a big embrace and a whispered, "Wolf." A quiet whine of pleasure emitted from his throat, and he snuggled deeper into the hug. Relieved to have Wolf back with them, they continued their half crouching walk.

Some of the buildings were unlit, but most had the soft glow of candlelight warming them and although the occasional silhouetted figure passed the windows noone stopped to look out. One garden contained chicken huts where the birds were already roosting. A dog lay half in a kennel, guarding the huts from foxes and other predators. He scuttled inside and whimpered as Wolf walked by.

Jael called a halt to their progression as a large and well-lit house came into sight. It had two stories and its brick work had been rendered and painted a charcoal grey. The ornate casing around the windows and doors were painted white as a stark contrast. A four foot wall ran the perimeter of the property, interspersed by tall pillars topped with gleaming white spheres, It was clearly the home of a person of wealth and importance in the village, and just the sort of building that would attract the merchant. That alone would have drawn her to the building, but the crimson clad guards at the back of the house confirmed the merchant's presence within.

Adjusting their approach, Jael led them through the vegetable plot behind a more modest house two doors down. The fence between the gardens helped conceal their presence, and they quickly moved to stand in the narrow passageway between the two buildings. They stood pressed into the deep shadows of the alley. There weren't any windows to overlook them here. It was time to work through the most dangerous part of their plan.

Adrenaline flooded Susan's body, panic rising as her heartbeat raced and she gasped for breath. Triene pressed a calming hand on her shoulder. Responding to the external pressure, Susan began to control her breathing and gradually the sense of panic subsided. Embarrassed, she whispered, "Sorry." Triene squeezed her shoulder reassuringly then released it, letting her hand fall to her side.

Triene's own emotions were under control, all the combat practice, and the need to constantly hide who she was, proved good training for this moment. She was focused and alert. Jael, however, had been distracted by Susan's distress and Will had taken advantage of it. With a fleeting glimpse of his blonde head as he exited the alley, Will slipped out into the silent street.

## Chapter 14

Jael fumed when he realised that Will had snuck out of the passageway. Will had better know what he was doing or they would all be caught. They strained to listen for the slightest sound that would indicate what was happening, but the only sounds came from someone moving around in the house to their right. Susan held her breath as she listened, until she realised what she was doing and took a large gasp of air. Jael turned and gave her a confused look. Feeling awkward, she tried to mimic his soft breath, mere whispers of sound, but she struggled to focus on both breathing noiselessly and on attending any indication of trouble. "Way to go, Susan." she thought negatively, "Can't even listen and breathe at the same time!" At least there wasn't any shout of alarm.

Keeping to the shadows and staying flat against the wall of the house, Will exited the passageway and scanned the quiet street. The dirt road that sliced through the centre of the village was lit by a silvery sheen of moonlight, while deep, black shadows engulfed the buildings on either side. Perfect, Will thought. Strangely, the street was completely clear of people, it appeared that the villagers were huddled in their homes to avoid the attention of the soldiers. The tavern at the end of the village had been busy earlier that evening, their kitchens having been commandeered to prepare an elaborate meal for the exacting merchant, but its windows and doors were now shuttered tight.

Will shuffled along the wall. A single candle cut a delicate sliver of warm light, through a gap in the curtains draping the furthest window. He twisted and took a surreptitious peek through the gap. There was a mature couple sitting on a pair of high-backed chairs placed in front of an unlit fire. They appeared to be having an earnest conversation, punctuated by nervous glances.

Using his long fingers to grip between the stones and his soft leather boots to wedge in the larger gaps, Will scuttled up the wall, past the window, and clung to the corner just under the guttering. He found a sturdy piece of pipe to help take his weight and stared at the grandiose building housing his quarry. From this advantageous position he could see the two austere soldiers standing guard at either side of the large, ornate stone doorway. Unlike those he had encountered at the inn, these soldiers were alert and business-like. The merchant clearly kept his best guards closest to him. While Will watched, the guard furthest from him shifted his feet and shoulders, gearing up for action. He then moved purposefully around his half of the garden, his sharp eyes searching the hidden areas between the plants at the base of the perimeter wall and then over the wall at the street. Having completed his scrutiny of the grounds, he returned to his station at the doorway and stood silently observing while the other guard completed his own circuit. Will continued to watch them. They were irritatingly thorough in their observations. Will couldn't see a route to slip past them unseen. Undaunted, Will counted down the three stages of their routine and was pleased to note they took a similar count for each part. A weakness he should be able to use. He continued to inspect the property.

Unlike the house he currently climbed, the walls were sheer having been smoothed and painted. The stone decoration around the windows and door would, however, be ideal handholds, but the guards would inevitably notice should he attempt to use them. Annoying, since there was a tempting window at the top left, that was slightly ajar. How could he get to that window? The tiled roof was an encouraging prospect. It sloped down towards the front of the house and had a sturdy looking stone ridge gutter decorating its edge. The ridge ended about three feet above the top of the window, which in turn looked to be a further four feet to its sill. That was a possible route, but how to get onto the roof?

The perimeter wall with its ornamental pillars kept the roof a good distance apart from the neighbouring properties so it wouldn't be possible to jump from one roof to another. Will considered the wall further. It wasn't particularly high, being about four feet tall but the supporting pillars were higher and topped by smooth spheres that rose above them. Standing on the one closest to the corner of the house would get him almost level with the lowest part of the roof at full stretch. Shame the passageway between the wall and the side of the house would prevent a simple climb from one to the other. He contemplated the distance for a few more moments. Satisfied he had seen all he could, Will shifted his weight, the pain in his ribs wasn't bad now, and extended his right leg sideways until it found a gap in the stone where he could wedge his toe. His hand soon followed suit and he carefully edged along the top of the wall, back to where the others still waited.

Dropping down at the entrance to the alley, he absorbed the impact in his legs so his landing was virtually silent. Even so, he managed to startle Susan with his sudden appearance, and she began to expel a scream. Jael was ready and he quickly placed his large hand over her mouth muffling the sound. Susan managed to swallow the scream and Jael gently removed his hand, watching her face for signs of anger at his rough treatment. Instead, she mouthed her thanks and turned to look at Will. Jael's surprised eyes remained on her for a fraction longer before he too, examined the irritating young man. Somehow, Jael managed to refrain from shaking the lad and listened instead as Will spoke under his breath, "There's an open window on the top floor. I can get inside but you'll need to get the soldiers outta the 'ouse.", he explained. Then, looking at Triene, he asked, "Could you light something on fire?" Jael started to bristle, but Triene brushed his arm reassuringly. She looked across the street. Even if she couldn't use her magic, she could use the flint and steel. It would be harder to control the flame, but a distraction would be possible. "I could set fire to that stable." It wasn't attached to any houses so she should be able to stop the fire spreading.

Jael looked up and down the street for a moment then added, "Presumably his carriage is in there. That would definitely distract him".

Susan was worried, "Can we free the horses first? Then we will need to agree a place to meet Will afterwards."

Going back past the soldiers wasn't an option. Not with the chaos the fire would cause. Jael tried to recall what lay beyond the village. "There's a thick forest at the end of the village, on the right. That would be easiest to get to. We could meet there."

Will looked worried, he didn't like the idea of getting lost in a forest. "'Ow am I gonna find you?"

Jael gave this some consideration and suggested, "Third tree along, tenth tree deep. We'll meet you there." Will was happy to agree, but Susan's experiences of hiking on holiday made her wonder if that would be as easy as it sounded, yet before she could question this Will had disappeared again.

Wolf bumped Triene's arm then he too disappeared. He would find them again, he always did, but his absence left her feeling less assured. Flint and steel, she thought. She could do this one way or another.

Will slid along the wall of the house, ducked under the window and waited in the shadows where he could make out the heads of the guards. The closest guard was completing his circuit of the garden. Will bounced on the balls of his feet and shook out his arms as he waited for him to return to the doorway. He did a final check of the street then focused his attention on the pillar and sphere near the edge of the house before looking up to the corner of the roof.

The guard reached the doorway and as he turned to face the front, Will expelled the breath he had been holding and burst into action, while mentally counting down the moments before the other guard would turn to face his direction, 1...2....3.... In five long strides he sprinted towards the pillar, keeping his landings light and silent. His open hands were already reaching out as his back leg powered him into a leap, so that they braced on the side of the sphere as the toes on his front foot pressed against the pillar. Using the momentum of the run, Will kept moving, his other foot rising to rest on the top edge of the pillar as his hands gripped the top of the sphere. In a continuous motion his lower leg pushed up to join his hands on top of the smooth surface. 9...10...11...

His eyes were trained on the corner of the stone guttering. As his trailing leg lifted and his hands left the surface his body uncoiled like a spring and propelled him across the passageway. His arms lifting, legs swinging forward, his feet gently bounced against the corner of the house before gripping either side of the corner. Hanging from the stone guttering by his left fingertips, he stretched up his right hand to grab hold as he scuffled his feet up the wall. 15... 16...17... He pulled himself up onto the roof and crouched like a gargoyle while he caught his breath. The guard on the right shuffled as he prepared to move. 18... 19... then the guard stepped forward.

Will took his time as he carefully made his way across the roof top to the point just above the open window. Experience had proved loose tiles were liable to tumble to the ground in a loud explosion. By the time he had reached his destination, the guard had approached the point where he would be turning to face the house once more. Although Will was high up, he didn't want to risk being seen so he lay himself flat against the slate, face down, hands tucked in, so as to form a dark silhouette. He had started counting again when the guard had commenced his walk and waited until he had counted to 42 before he checked the other guard had started his circuit again. Then he counted out the next circuit before he began to move into position.

The guards were both standing in the doorway and Will had a count of 30 before the first guard would be facing the house again. He swung his legs over the edge of the roof and dangled them while he took the weight of his body on his straight arms. This bit would be harder as he had to move slowly, no momentum to help, using the strength in his wiry muscles to control his descent. Leaning slightly forward, he gradually bent his arms and felt for the top of the window frame with his toes. 7...8...9... got it! In a well-timed jump and release, he bounced downwards so that his hands gripped the top of the window frame and his feet rested on the larger windowsill. He couldn't avoid the sigh of relief when he made it. 12...13...14...

The sash window was only open a fraction, he needed to raise it quite a bit higher if he were to squeeze inside. Will widened his stance so that he could squat and grip onto the side of the window frame with his left hand while he pulled open the window with his right. 15...16... The window wouldn't budge so he pushed harder. He wobbled, but he quickly regained his balance. 21...22... He would need both hands to lift the window. He made sure his body was central to the window as he deepened the squat, leaning as close to the window as possible. He released the side of the frame and quickly,with both hands wrapped underneath the window, he slid it upwards. 24... 25... Will was still gripping the base of the window as he pushed his feet through the gap, his body and arms quickly following, 28...29... He whisked round and slid the window back to its original position before crouching in the dark room while his racing heart steadied.

While Will was finding his way onto the roof of the house, the others had been making their long way round to the stables. Distancing themselves from the watchful eyes of the guards, they followed the shadows along the line of houses. Careful to avoid catching the attention of a worried villager who could alert the soldiers to their presence, they swiftly crossed the road and passed the houses and backyards. From there, they doubled back, heading rapidly towards the rear of the stables, concerned that any delay by them would put Will in danger.

Sitting alongside the timber wall of the stables was a box shaped carriage. It had obviously been a prized possession and well cared for until it had been unceremoniously discarded to make room inside the stable for the merchant's carriage. Now it tilted on its rear axle and the lovingly painted crest had been badly scratched. The driver's box had become detached and it listed at such a severe angle it was surprising that it hadn't already fallen to the ground. Thick grooves had been dug into the high grasses as the soldiers had manhandled it into its current position.

The stables themselves were a sturdy timber building with wide doors opening onto the street that could swing aside and allow the passage of a large vehicle and the horses pulling it. There were no windows, the building being designed to house sleeping carriage horses and their charge. Behind the building lay a track that led to a wide pasture for all the village horses. They could see six horses in the field, rough blankets flung over their backs, while make-shift shelters were positioned at the far end, for the storage of straw as well as chilled bodies. A large door at the back of the stable, big enough to guide a single horse through, faced the securely fastened gate to the paddock.

Triene found the bolt on the back door and pulled it aside. Jael remained beside the stable and crouched behind the ravaged carriage to stare at the large house. Over the top of the wall, he could see one of the soldiers heading back towards the house, clearly inspecting the surrounding area for signs of intruders. As the soldier stationed himself beside the front door, a previously hidden, shadowy figure unfolded on the roof immediately above the slightly open window. Relieved that Will had his part of the plan under control, Jael ducked back behind the stable and through the back door to help with the distraction.

Triene and Susan had entered the stable somewhat tentatively since it wasn't as dark as they had expected. The light source proved to be the innocuous remains of a candle burning in a lantern at the rear of the building. Triene exhaled in relief. It would be much easier to make use of the candle whether with magic or on its own.

The faint light highlighted the gold decorating the merchant's dormeuse carriage, which took up most of the floor space. Susan thought it resembled a traditional Silver Cross pram, it even had a mattress laid out within. One of the merchant's trunks remained affixed to the roof, while another had clearly been removed, as the leather straps for it hung loose. Triene scrambled up to quickly examine the contents of the trunk, although it was highly unlikely that the merchant would have left the gems unguarded.

Susan sought the animals she needed to release. She noticed that the ornate gold and crimson leather tack for the four horses had been carefully hung up next to the stalls. It had replaced the plain breast plate and harnesses of the overseer's horses, which had been thrown onto the dirt floor. The sleek, ebony coats of the merchant's thoroughbreds merged into the dark depths of their stalls, although as she looked, one sauntered to his stall door, to see who had arrived and disturbed his rest. Susan unbolted his door first. He didn't move, clearly waiting for instructions. She tried to encourage him to come out with a beckoning motion and kissy noises, but he merely looked bemused. Panicking slightly, she grabbed hold of his long nose and tugged on it while whispering a firm, "Come on!". He easily pulled his nose free from her grip and stepped back to observe her warily. She now had an audience, as the other horses had woken and rested their heads on their stall doors, curious to see what she would do next.

Entering the stable, Jael observed her failed attempt to move the horse and quickly suppressed a grin. Joining her he whispered reassuringly in her ear, "Go open the gate to the paddock, I'll bring them out to you," The smirk broke free at her obvious relief as she hurried out of the stable building. Still grinning he patted the horse's shoulder and said, "Get out there, mister, if you don't want to be cooked." The horse began to walk obediently to the door only to stop as a pair of long johns were flung from above and came to a rest hanging over one ear and eye. Triene, peered over the open trunk, down at the horse, "Oops!" she said as she rapidly descended the carriage and plucked it off him. He gave her a long, cold look before resuming his dignified exit.

Jael busied himself releasing the other horses and he gave Triene a worried glance as he walked them to the door. She nodded confidently at him, saying, "Get them out, I'm ready!" Reluctant to leave her, knowing she had struggled to use her magic, but determined to respect her decision, he guided the horses outside and across the track to where Susan was waiting by the gate. They trundled obediently into the paddock and Susan shut them in. They turned towards the stable. Susan slipped her cold hand into his, both seeking and giving reassurance. He gently wrapped his fingers around hers and clung on to her as they nervously waited.

Triene needed to overcome her fear and use her magic if she were to have any control over the blaze. The locals had decided to store foods here as well, and the flour could explode endangering the villagers. She needed to create a line the flame would not cross.

She trembled slightly as she recalled trying to find the magic shortly after her parents' death. Her darkness had engulfed her in painful memories, telling her magic was dangerous and wrong. She had failed and ended up wailing in despair in her brother's frightened arms.

That was then, now was different. The darkness had retreated slightly over time, and with Selene's tale and Susan and Will's acceptance she was feeling more confident to try again. Will was depending on her.

Trying to remember a time when she enjoyed having the power of fire, she recalled how her mother had encouraged her to originally coax out her magic. They had been travelling as usual. Greta had taken a flame from their campfire and had balanced it in the palm of her hand. She had made it roll into a ball, grow fat and wide, tall and thin, to the delight of a very young Triene. She had told her to go looking for the magic in her mind. It was there she said, just waiting to be introduced to her. Triene remembered sitting cross-legged on the ground, face screwed up in concentration for what felt like a very long time, until she discovered it cowering like a little tabby kitten hissing and showing its claws. She did as her mother had advised and introduced herself. She showed it the flowers she had seen on the walk to the campsite and told it how her mother had picked an orange one and tucked it behind Triene's ear, saying it glowed like the fire of her hair. She showed it her enjoyment of fruit, freshly picked, and pictured her fingers covered in blackberry juices, and she showed it her silly big brother as he pretended to be a horse so she could ride on his back. With each image the magic had crept forward until she could reach out and pet it. She then showed it how her mother had shaped a flame on her hand. Excited and eager to help, the magic had helped her create her own warmly flickering flame. Triene had wanted the flame to look like the kitten and the flame had shaped itself, to Greta's immense surprise, and Triene had made it pounce and strut on her palm.

Triene smiled at the memory. How could she have gone so long without her dear companion? The day she had buried her parents the fear and blame had begun, and soon the magic had slunk away to hide behind a door in her mind, a door she had avoided ever since. She owed it a massive apology, if she could only open the door. Triene closed her eyes and gingerly approached it. A crack of welcoming light immediately shone light through her darkness and the door opened a fraction. A sense of shared pain and of acceptance washed over her and the door suddenly burst open so the magic, full of love, could soar through her willing mind and tingle its way around her eager body. The suffocating blanket of fear Triene had been sheltering beneath disintegrated and was replaced by a feeling of strength and stability, and of peace. This was right. This was who she was. She was a mighty tower, a wall of strength. She had buried a part of herself with her parents. No more! She raised her hand and the little flame from the candle danced excitedly over to sit in her palm, growing bigger and stronger the closer it got. She watched it twist and turn in her hand and willed it to grow hotter. The flame grew still and fierce as a core of blue-white spread up to its tip. The flame roared as it sought more fuel to burn. She sent it arrowing towards the bottom of the carriage where it easily ignited the straw and began to eat its way into the wooden structure.

Triene pictured the carriage on fire, flames licking up its sides, then imagined the straw and hay in the stalls and stored against the wall catching alight, the rapidly growing fire spreading to the structure of the building next.

Then came the important part, the hardest part to control. She pictured the storage area where the food was kept, and the area outside the building, the grassy track, the tree and the houses nearby. She visualised sparks landing but extinguishing instantly. She focused intently on the image of the building aflame, but carefully contained. Not a single flame travelled beyond the line she drew in her mind. She felt her magic pulse in understanding and knew that it would do all it could to control the extent of the fire. As she left through the doorway, she took further comfort from the knowledge that the flames would soon be seen, and the villagers would take urgent steps to put it out. She just hoped it would provide the necessary distraction for Will to grab the gemstones and escape safely.

## Chapter 15

Will was inside the house. The room was dark, but his eyes quickly adjusted to the limited light coming from the window and seeping in from the gap along the bottom of the door. It was enough for him to determine the rough layout of what appeared to be a child's room. Will quickly decided that it was an unlikely place for the merchant to store any magical items. He therefore crept over to the door and pressed his ear to the split between frame and door and listened. He could hear distant murmurings, but nothing indicated anyone was close. He didn't have time to listen for longer, so he cracked the door open and peered with one eye. A candelabra with three lit candles sat on a side table, its light spilling onto the matching porcelain dish beside it. Additional light flickered up from the hall downstairs, caught in the draught from the partially open front door. The voices were more distinct now, enough that Will caught some of the words stated in a commanding baritone, "the morning" and "ready the troops". Then came a sharp flutter of light and the distinct sound of the front door shutting behind a set of retreating footsteps. A second set of footsteps walked decisively to an internal door, and knocked twice, the sound more a demand than a request to enter. The merchant's arrogant voice drawled out, "Permission granted." The footsteps hesitated as if annoyed by the condescension, before walking into the room, followed by a sharp click of the door catching.

The coast seemed clear so Will opened the door enough to squeeze through and carefully pulled it closed behind him. Testing the floorboards for a tell-tale creak, he crept along to the next door. Listening once again before he slowly opened it, he noted that this appeared to be the master chamber. The four-poster bed had plush drapes dripping braiding and beads onto a sumptuous royal blue bedcover. An extravagantly decorated rug lay on the polished floorboards in front of a muted fire, which had been lit to reduce the chill for the merchant's comfort that night. A large travelling trunk lay open by the bed, and a nightgown and cap had been placed on the stool beside the bed.

There didn't appear to be any other items added to the room, but Will had a cursory look anyway. His focus returned to the trunk, and after checking his hands were clean, he delicately lifted the remaining items to feel for any pouch or other container that might hold the gemstones. His questing fingers latched onto a small chest and he gently set aside the linens so he could extract it. Despite its size, the chest was of a sturdy design, with a strong iron hinge and catch. There was a lock, but no trace of a key. Undeterred, Will reached up to the back of his neck and from beneath his sandy locks he removed a thin clip. Opening up the clip revealed a sliver of sturdy metal with a slight bend at the tip. It didn't take Will long to find the trick of the lock and with a final wiggle the chest was open. He carefully replaced his clip and rummaged through the jewellery the chest contained. Not one to pass up on an opportunity, he slid a decent selection into the pouch around his neck. The magical gemstones weren't there, however, so he replaced the chest in the trunk, careful to make it look undisturbed. Time was moving on and he hadn't found any trace of the gemstones. If they weren't in the bedchamber, they were probably in the merchant's possession. Will looked out of the window and thought he could detect a faint glow coming from the stable, and he knew it wouldn't be long before the fire would draw attention. He could only be ready to take his chances when it did.

He exited the room and stood at the top of the stairs taking in the view of the hall below. The wide, glossy oak banister curved to the right until it reached the front door where it ended with a scroll effect newel post. The owner of the house clearly liked his home to display his obvious wealth. The front door had a large, egg-shaped urn placed on either side of it. Next to the urns were high-backed, formal chairs. There were paintings on every wall, and side tables loaded with more ornaments and candelabras. Normally, Will would be smuggling out as many objets d'art as he could, but not today. Today his only concern was to avoid knocking into them and warning the soldiers of his presence in the house.

The closed door, behind which the merchant and at least one soldier resided, was on the wall to the right of the front door. The door opened into the room, rather than the hall, and was surrounded by a solid looking frame. Will peered down at it, contemplating the best method of access.

"FIRE!" came the anticipated call from outside, and the alarm tore through the village in the predicted chain reaction. Will ducked back just in time as one of the guards from outside opened the front door and the Commander marched through the internal one. Will only caught a glimpse of the crimson uniform and a full head of dark brown hair. The Commander was swiftly followed out of the room by another crimson clad guard who left the door open. A quick, urgent conversation ensued just by the front door, during which the Commander expressed concern that it was

175

a ploy to leave the merchant exposed. "Clever one, that," thought Will, making a note to keep far away from him. Will felt twitchy, despite the flames the soldiers hadn't left and the merchant was still in the room. There was no way he could get in there. Fortunately, the merchant wasn't as astute as his soldiers and wasn't one to listen to anyone's recommendations. He pursued his guard out the door, face puce with rage. His shrill and vibrato voice screamed at the soldiers to go and save his damn carriage. The ordinary soldiers backed up in the face of his fury, while the Commander moved tactically to one side. The merchant strode down the garden path gesturing that they should get over there without delay.

This was his chance, Will jumped lightly onto the banister and, half-squatting, arms out to the side for balance, he surfed down it, his boots sliding on its smooth, polished surface. He trained his eyes on the open door and as he drew level, he bunched his leg muscles before propelling himself forwards. His lean fingers grabbed the top of the doorframe and he swung into the room. He landed in a starting line crouch, which absorbed the shock to his knees as well as the sound of his landing. The position also meant he was able to move as soon as his feet touched the ground. His eyes had been scanning the room as he swung and now he had the contents of the desk in his sights. He whisked off his neck pouch as he moved. The four gemstones had been placed on the desk in a neat line. A thick, ancient tome lay open beside them. It was obvious that the book had something to do with the gems, but it was too big and heavy for him to escape with. Running lightly, he scooped up the gems, two in each hand, and stuffed them into the pouch, securing it as he continued towards the window. He raised the window just

176

as the merchant returned, having sent all, but one guard, to tackle the inferno. The garden was clear.

Standing in the doorway, the merchant's eyes locked on Will and he halted in horrified disbelief. The following guard withdrew his sword and struggled to squeeze past the merchant's rotund frame. That gave Will enough time to escape through the window, run across the garden, and leap onto the wall. Easily maintaining his balance, he sped along the wall as the guard followed him out of the window. Less nimble, the guard stomped through the flowerbeds trying to catch him and calling out for the Commander. Will had a good head start and could see a route across a low roof on the next building. He jumped and sprinted across the next garden. Raising and bending his right leg, he placed it on the side of the house and pushed off, using his momentum, to run up the wall. He grabbed the roof ledge and pulled himself up and onto the roof. He ran across it, not caring about dislodged tiles this time, until he reached the next house and dived across the gap between them. He ended on a shoulder roll which allowed him to push up and keep running. He heard the pursuing guard yelp in pain as he leapt over the wall and landed face first in a blackberry bush.

Out of sight, Will used his heels to control his slide down the back of the roof and dropped onto the thin, wobbly wooden fence, then into the garden. From there he jogged towards the back fence and side jumped over it, continuing to run until he had passed two more buildings.

Moving slowly and cautiously now, Will used this time to catch his breath, nothing more suspicious than breathing heavily when there is a chase going on. He walked between the houses, stopping when he faced the street so he could ascertain the situation. The villagers had turned out of their houses and many were forming a line to carry water from the well to the stables. A couple of the crimson clad soldiers were at the front of the line while another was trying to break down the stable doors. Will winced as he anticipated the flames rushing out at the man when he succeeded. Clearly, the more intelligent Commander wasn't supervising their actions. Concerned, he looked around the street, but couldn't see any more soldiers. He didn't like not knowing where the Commander was, but he needed to move.

Spying an open door to the house on the opposite side of the street Will walked over to it. He gawped, like the other villagers, before he stepped into the empty house. He trotted up the stairs and into the bedroom. There he rummaged through the clothes hanging up until he found a blue linen dress that would be a fine fit. Pulling it over his head he expertly did up the fastenings and shook out the long skirt to make sure it covered his other clothes. He then pulled out a shawl and wrapped it over his head and shoulders, as if to stave off the evening chill, and exited the house. He wandered over to join the villagers. There were a group of women off to one side, similarly attired, watching the efforts to put out the fire. He stood slightly behind them, but as if part of their group, and took a moment to ensure his pursuers were otherwise occupied.

The flames in the stable were beginning to burn out, and had not spread, a sign of Triene's control over her power, Will thought. Soon the observers would be heading back to their homes and he would stand out. The soldiers would be searching hard for him so he had better make a move. He could see the guard that had pursued him meeting up with the others in the street. He was gesticulating insistently at the roofs while the others listened. The guard that had been trying to break down the stable doors was now gaping at the roof so someone had clearly had the foresight to stop him.

The youngest of the soldiers was a handsome man with a pleasant face which for some reason set off the hairs on the back of Will's neck. He was listening intently, but while he listened his intense eyes were flicking over the people around him as if he could sense Will was nearby. His gaze returned to the speaker who finished with an apologetic shrug, and without a change in his expression, the man's right hand raised and struck like a snake, across the guard's face. For a moment the guard just looked stunned then a thin line of red appeared. He clasped his face and gibbered as bright blood started to ooze through his fingers. The other soldiers instinctively recoiled, but at a questioning look from his attacker quickly recovered their stoicism. The handsome soldier began giving orders to the others who split up and started pushing their way through the villagers, seeking out anyone who looked vaguely similar to Will. So, that was the Commander. Yes, he definitely wanted to stay clear of him.

The group of women were still focused on the stable fire which was now well under control. They started to shuffle as if about to head home. He followed their lead and moved purposefully, as if heading towards a building, so as to avoid raising suspicion amongst them. He made sure he remained in their peripheral vision and as soon as the soldiers' attention was engaged he ducked behind the nearest house and proceeded through the shadows to the rear yards. He then ran, the best he could in the dress, to the end of the village and the start of the evergreen forest. Checking no one had seen him, he then counted one, two, three trees, and walked determinedly into the darkness.

Only a couple of trees deep into the forest, the tall pines effectively prevented the moon from lighting his way. Invisible to his straining eyes, the pine needle cushioned ground was scattered with ferns that tangled his feet and with raised twisted roots ready to trip and stub. Will shuffled along, despite his desire to get far away from the soldiers, the long skirt proving hazardous. He dare not shed the dress and leave a trace of his passing, however. The leaf bearing branches started well above his head so he didn't have that to contend with, but the trunks bore sharp twigs to catch him unawares. His arms were outstretched, hands feeling the way through the darkness while his anxious ears were alert for sounds of pursuit. He twitched at every rustle of nocturnal creatures scuttling in their search for food. The tenth tree was deeper in the forest than he had expected, there being spaces to traverse between each sturdy and furrowed trunk. Was he even following the right line of trees? What if he couldn't find the others. A wash of fear trickled over him. That familiar numbing of his limbs had him unable to continue. His thudding heart echoing loudly in the dark had him reliving the terror of hiding from his drunk father, the angry sounds and quiet whimpers that came before the gentle times with his mother as they nursed their injuries. The memories left him shaken and uncertain. "Guys?" he hissed desperately. "You here?"

A tiny spot of light appeared some distance to his right and he gratefully stumbled towards it. As he neared the source he could see it was a tiny flame swaying in the palm of Triene's upraised hand. The trees should prevent the light from being seen in the village, but the smaller the flame the better. Will was so thankful to see Triene he flung his arms around her and gave her a hug, to both their surprise. Smiling with a combination of relief and embarrassment, they moved apart and Triene ruffled his hair like a fond older sister, before leading the way to the others. Her eyes sought out the small piece of cloth tied to one of the bare branches, which she had affixed earlier to mark out the start of the route. As they passed it, Will untied the rag and placed it securely in his trouser waistband. Even with the light, the journey was laborious as they picked their way over the roots and between the trees, searching for the next marker.

Eventually, the sound of whispering reverberated from within the darkness and Triene smiled at Will reassuringly as he flinched. A large, stern form emerged from the shadows before Jael's relieved face flickered into view. He gave his sister a quick, firm embrace and took Will's hand and pulled him in for a friendly shoulder slap. Susan appeared from behind him and while giving her own hugs, whispered, "Thank goodness you are both safe. Are you ok Will? What happened?"

"I got em!" he replied proudly, "but I were seen so we got to get out of 'ere." he added.

"That's amazing Will! No one else could have done it." said Susan giving Will a tighter squeeze.

Jael added his own praise, "You did a good job." Then he noticed Will's attire and his eyebrows raised. He refrained from commenting and merely suggested, "You might want to put your dress in one of the packs and ride for a while. You're probably tired." Will started to protest but Susan urged him to take up the offer. Will reluctantly agreed, although deep down he was pleased for his muscles were tight and aching and his ribs were sore. He assumed they had stolen the horses from the stables, but as Triene's light illuminated them he realised they were the shire horses from the wagon. Jael saw his surprise and laughed quietly, "I know!" he said with satisfaction in his voice. "Wolf retrieved them and circled the village to get them to us. I guess they're part of his pack and he didn't want them left behind." As Will climbed up onto the gelding, Jael pointed out, "It's a bit tricky getting them through the forest and we can't ride them properly, but I for one am glad we have them with us."

"Me too," whispered Will under his breath. He wiggled into position, lying flat along the back and neck, holding onto the braided mane. "'ow will we know we 'ain't going in circles or 'eading back to the village?" he suddenly worried.

Jael replied, "I'm using my Earth magic to sense our position in the forest. We will be fine."

"That's really cool." Will said with awe. "Can you get the soldiers lost?" he asked hopefully.

Jael shook his head even though they couldn't see him clearly. "I can disguise our trail a bit though."

"Nice!"

Triene took the lead and they slowly made their way through the trees, heading towards the coast and away from the main route across the country.

## Chapter 16

Raul was fuming. He had spent a fortune on that artifact and his pitiful excuse for soldiers had let a scrawny looking lad get in and run off with them. He paced the room, his corpulent body, unused to the exercise, rippling as he moved. His face turned red with anger and exertion, while a bead of sweat gathered at his temple and made its way down his flaccid cheek. His chubby fingers, decked with opulent jewels, flexed and clenched as he paced.

He needed those gemstones. His beady eyes narrowed as he glanced at the desk. His enemies missed a trick, leaving the book with all its secrets behind and he couldn't believe the thief hadn't grabbed the other artifact. He stopped pacing and contemplated the oval stone resting on the open page. The idiot probably thought it was a decorative paperweight. The stone was some kind of amber, with pale buttery shades at the outer edges leading to a deep ring of auburn as it gravitated towards the centre of the stone. At its heart, the stone appeared hollow, so dark was its hue. He scoffed over its fanciful name, the Eye of Rúa. The ancients and their stupid beliefs held no interest for him. The only thing that mattered was that the artifact could draw in the magic for him to use. That thought reminded him of his loss and he resumed his pacing. What were his men doing? Surely, they could catch the thief quicker than this?

He paused by the window and glared at the burnt-out remnants of the stable. The blackened beams rose out of the ruin like ribs from a half-eaten carcass. His carriage completely destroyed as the fire had consumed it first. It had cost Raul many golds to get to his current state of comfort and now he would have to put up with one of the local's inferior vehicles. The thought that his horses had also burned made him shudder, he really didn't want to be lumbered with some bumpkin's old nags.

He stomped over to the desk and squeezed into the worn leather chair which creaked its protest. Damn chair is too small, he thought, as he wiggled to fit his ample rear between the arms. He dragged the book towards him, its weight coming from robust iron bindings and thick layers of parchment. He removed the artifact and examined the open page. It had a row of symbols etched upon it, and beside them writing in the ancient language. A loose piece of parchment inscribed by a scratchy hand was liberally splattered with dried blood. Raul had paid for a translation, but the damned Commander hadn't taken care when he had retrieved it and now he had no means of understanding this page. All he could decipher were the words: *And so the Goddess generously gifted to a chosen few the power to guide the life-giving rain and to deflect the destructive storm, the power to breathe life into those struggling with the same, and the power to reach the highest peaks and furthest lands in the search for* ...and from there the ink had been mixed with the blood and smudged beyond recognition. This part of the translation was pointless anyway without the gemstones. He slammed the book shut and wisps of dust puffed and settled back onto the desk.

Raul tapped his bejewelled fingers on the wood impatiently before glancing at the Eye of Rua. Damn incompetent soldiers meant he had to waste his energies. He placed a hand on the amber and drew in a wheezing breath. Raul pulled at the small amount of magic hiding in the artifact. It struggled and resisted but was dragged into Raul's lungs before being expelled into the air with a silent command: "Seek." The magic twisted and wrapped around the desk, getting the taste of the thief, then shot out into the gardens, flowing onto the wall then up and across the roofs. Raul slumped in the chair, the effort having exhausted him. With the return of the magic I will be stronger, he consoled himself. His plan to eliminate his competition would help. It had proven to be a successful endeavour, which the Commander had embraced enthusiastically. The ignorant masses had of course helped, with their fear and suspicions, unaware they were helping him, an Air mage. He smirked briefly, in satisfaction.

The Commander's neat form appeared in the doorway and he cast his gaze over Raul, slouched over the desk. The Commander's soft brown eyes and relaxed features remained impassive as he entered the room. "The man is impudent," thought Raul, "When I have my full power I shall school him in the correct subservient behaviour owed to me," he decided, unaware that his face revealed his inner scheming to the intelligent soldier. The Commander raised an eyebrow and smiled at the merchant before speaking, his voice rich and deep,

"I've had my men gather everyone resembling the description of the thief. Would you like to see if you can identify him, sir?" The tone was respectful, yet the words held an edge of sarcasm. Raul bristled and with some difficulty forced himself out of the chair. He raised himself up to his full height and puffed out his chest, although this merely pushed out his already extended paunch. "Bring them in." he said in a voice that cracked.

The Commander repeated the instruction, his voice ringing loud and firm, while he kept his eyes on Raul. Five youths, four boys and one girl entered the room at sword point. Their eyes were downcast, shoulders sloped, and more than one looked on the verge of tears. The youngest, who could only be about ten, was snivelling quietly, snot running over his quivering lips. Each was thin and had sandy coloured locks. Raul's desperate eyes searched their faces for some similarity to the thief only to be disappointed. "Fools, he is not here." he spat out. "How could you be so incompetent?"

The Commander's face turned stony as he interrupted the harangue with a quietly spoken, "This is but the start of the hunt. You know I never allow a slight to go unpunished." Raul flinched, for even he was aware of the threat that accompanied the Commander's words. Maintaining some illusion of control he squeaked, "Do it then," and gave a dismissive wave of his hand. The Commander nodded, "You can be sure of it" he said coldly, before he turned and strode out of the room. His men quickly followed, nudging their prisoners forward with their blades. Raul's heart fluttered as he hurried back to the desk and put his shaking hand on the Eye of Rua, but it was, of course, empty and silent.

The street was now lined with soldiers summoned from their camp and in front of them the villagers who had been perfunctorily driven out of their homes. Some of the soldiers bore flaming torches that highlighted the frightened faces. The younger villagers looked around confused and concerned, while the older villagers eyed the soldiers with the fearful suspicion experience brings. An oblivious toddler escaped the safety of his mother's arms and ran.

186

About to give chase, the mother was stayed by a dagger jabbed towards her ribs. She froze, while her distressed eyes stared past the sneering soldier and watched as her baby was grabbed by the arm and carried back by a second man in uniform.

The Commander emerged from the house and strode to the gates before smiling in greeting at the crowd. "Thank you for all coming here to sort out a little problem we have encountered during our stay," he began amiably. A soldier sniggered but was silenced by a pointed look in his direction. The Commander continued as the prisoners were brought out and positioned beside him. "A youth, with a passing resemblance to these helpful volunteers," the Commander swept his hand to indicate the prisoners, "has taken something from my esteemed employer and he would like it returned." Some of the more impressionable villagers listened eagerly, while those who had borne witness to the more violent activities of the Commander and his men remained reticent and wary.

"The youth is probably hiding, regretting his impulse," the Commander grinned, "A feeling many of us will have encountered at some point." This raised a few chuckles, mainly from his soldiers. "I am merely concerned with the recovery of the item. I am sure we can work together to resolve this easily." The Commander waited and watched the villagers expectantly as they looked around at their fellows, whispering urgently and shaking their heads.

The Commander spoke again, allowing some disappointment and incredulity to creep into his voice. "No one can assist? Surely, someone must have seen something."

A man in a mud-coloured jacket spoke up, "I saw someone running out back, through my vegetable patch. He jumped over the fence afore I could see his face though."

"And where might I find this… vegetable patch?" replied the Commander.

"Over there" and he pointed to a house a couple of doors down.

An older lady piped up, "I was in my bedroom just there," she used her cane to point to the next house, "and I heard a terrible clattering on the roof!" she declared.

The Commander's smile was beginning to look a little false now as he gritted out, "How about now, does anyone know where he is now?" only to face a sea of shaking heads. A gleam appeared in his eye as he said in a querying tone, "Perhaps we need something to help you focus." He looked sideways at the boy who had been snivelling while in the house and beckoned him over before bending down slightly to talk to him. "Do you want to help people focus better?" he asked him gently as he brushed a stray hair back from the boy's face. The boy briefly met his eyes before seeking his parents in the crowd. Finding them he looked pleadingly towards his father who nodded encouragingly. This was noticed by the Commander who gave him an approving nod in response. The boy gulped and nervously turned to face the Commander, murmuring a muted "Yes?". The Commander beamed at him, "Good lad," he said before he straightened and drew his sword.

The boy's father cried out "No!" and lurched forward but was instantly restrained, while his mother screamed and reached out helplessly. The villagers found a sudden wall of soldiers blocking their way as they shouted and pushed. The boy's eyes widened as the sword swept across his neck, slicing through his artery and windpipe. Hot blood spurted. The Commander, having anticipated this, had jumped clear, only catching the slightest splatter on his lip and cheek. He dragged his tongue across his lip, savouring its taste, as the boy's knees folded and he fell face first into the dirt, his remaining blood rapidly pooling beneath him.

The boy's mother was still screaming, while his father sagged helplessly within the restraining grip. He was suddenly released and he tumbled to the ground where he sat numbly staring at his son's prone body. The remaining villagers fell silent. The Commander raised a sardonic eyebrow and looked at the soldier closest to the wailing mother, "Some quiet would be appreciated." he said. The soldier started, then raised his sword arm and hit the woman soundly on her temple with the hilt and she crumpled to the ground. The Commander sighed in satisfaction at the cease of sound, then addressed the stunned crowd.

"I do hope you now have something more useful to tell me. But never fear," he added as if promising a treat. "I have created a most beneficial means of tapping into those reluctant recollections. Allow me to show you." He walked over to a waist high rectangular object over which a checked horse blanket rested. Grabbing hold of a corner he tugged at the rough material and revealed a slightly rusted iron cage. He pointed to the two sets of manacles attached to the top. "Note that it is designed to hold two people because I have found this adds to the mental anguish." He explained to the terrified villagers. He then tapped the bars, "Of course, the gaps are wide enough that small predators or scavengers, such as rats, may enter and feed." The Commander gazed upon his transfixed audience. "Now, let's see if you can recall where the scoundrel is, or perhaps it's time to make use of this?" he said patting the cage fondly.

Chapter 17

A subdued version of daylight sifted through the high branches, coating the forest floor in a speckled grey. Jael and Will were guiding the weary horses now the night had receded and with it, the need for Triene's flame. After her exertions, Triene was enjoying a much-needed rest on the solid back of the gelding. Her head reclined against his gently nodding neck and her eyes were shut in repose. Plodding behind them came Susan on the mare. Susan's eyes were open, but unfocused as she drifted in and out of slumber, desperately tired but feeling too vulnerable to completely relax. She had felt joy when she had seen the horses waiting for them, relieved she could leave the guilt she had been carrying behind her. Thank you, Wolf! She was even beginning to trust them to carry her safely, well trust the gentler mare anyway.

After having benefited from a few hours riding at the start of their foray into the forest, Will felt well-rested, but he slumped his shoulders and kicked his feet amongst the pine needles and soft ground, bored by the repetitive backdrop to their walk.

Jael hadn't rested, his Earth magic was still a necessary part of their journey. His previous stamina training meant the long hours hadn't adversely affected him, especially since he was able to rely on his magic to sense and choose the best route through the forest. There was no hesitation, no pause in his steps even as he let his mind relax and the magic take over. Wolf, who had spent the night padding around the trees, snuffling the scent of nocturnal prey, had finally decided to walk beside him. He had recently snared a decent snack, unaffected by the fierce competition between the local foxes, badgers and owls, although one particular sow had been rather vocal about his arrival near her carefully guarded sett. His stomach wanted him to find a place to settle down and digest his meal. Perhaps he could do so when they exited the forest. The others would need to break their fast. He was pleased to smell the sharp tang of the sea, an indication that the forest would end soon. He expected the others would notice it shortly.

The series of warm spring days had been replaced by a damp chill. The tops of the trees creaked, and the spiky leaves gave a dry rustle as the wind, with its salty hint, stirred them, high above the calm at the forest floor. The gentle pitter patter of rain could be heard, but not felt. A sudden strong gust whipped around Will's hair, ruffling it, and he quickly reached up and patted it down. "Where did that come from?" he exclaimed and looked around as if he would be able to see an answer in the trees. Jael stood still while his Earth magic tasted the lingering essence of the Air mage's spell as it disturbed the forest in its flight back to the village. Jael said urgently. "It was sent to find you by an Air mage. We have to get out of the forest."

The sharp snap of his words woke Triene and Susan whose

sleepy demeanour was instantly replaced by alarm, while Will's face dropped in absolute horror. "They can do that?" he muttered. "Shit!". Triene and Susan slid off the horses so they could pick up their pace within the canopy of the trees.

It wasn't long before the trees thinned, and the wind and rain began to make itself known, soaking into their linen clothing. Fat raindrops rolled down branches before combining and dropping down on them in large wet plops. The sounds of the sea mingled with the rustling of the trees and as they reached the edge of the forest, they heard a strange growling chorus. Wolf cocked his ears to listen but was unable to recognise the sound. It didn't seem threatening, in fact it was a sort of comforting sound, almost like the purr from hundreds of contented cats. They stepped out of the line of trees and onto the crest of a jagged, grassy cliff that overlooked a lightly choppy sea. Above it, the sky was thick with black and white birds, swooping into the waves before soaring back to their pufflings, nestled deep in the burrows dug into the soft earth on the cliff face. The growling sounds were reverberating from within those burrows.

A dumpy puffin waddled past them, head down as if saying "Don't mind me, just passing through", as it headed for another section of cliff. Susan thought its colouring and movement resembled a penguin save for his bright orange beak which was nearly as large as his head. Wolf bent his head, and almost touching its soft down, gave the puffin a good sniff as it passed, intrigued by the combination of bird, fish and brine. The puffin gave a quick sideways hop before continuing, otherwise unphased by the encounter.

Triene suddenly exclaimed, "Oh look! A ship!" and pointed

to an anchored galleon tucked beyond the rocky outcrops. Susan moved closer and stared out over the sea,

"They might 'elp us get away!". Will stated enthusiastically, from his spot further along the cliff, conscious that the soldiers would be heading their way now he had been traced.

Jael hated to disappoint but he was concerned by this sighting, "This isn't a port. So why is the ship here?" The others looked at him blankly, so he continued. "It could be pirates." Will beamed at him until Jael added, "Pirates who won't be happy we have found them... We need to get out of the open before we are spotted."

"Um. I think we might be too late." said Susan eying three burly sailors emerging from a hidden path just beyond where Will was exploring. Jael spun, placing his hand on the hilt of his sword, but the first sailor already had his cutlass raised. He grabbed hold of Will, putting his thick arm around his neck to hold him in place.

"Put the toothpick away," he said addressing Jael. "Our Captain wants to speak with ye." Clearly at a disadvantage, Jael let his hand drop in apparent submission, while he rapidly assessed different attacks where he could avoid Will getting hurt. But when Susan stepped within range of the sailor, all such plans ceased. Damn woman! He couldn't fight them now. He had to hope that in wanting to talk rather than kill them immediately, they might be willing to negotiate passage. The fact that they didn't strip him of his weapons was a positive sign, he supposed.

The sailor indicated that Jael should lead the way down the path while he followed, keeping his cutlass ready, wisely mistrusting Jael's easy compliance. Then came Susan with another sailor behind her. The rain made the rocks and sandy soil slippery for the horses, so Jael set a cautious pace, while Triene and Will also protected them from the vicious thorns that hid beneath the delicate silver leaves of the sea buckthorn growing beside the path. The third sailor brought up the rear, oblivious to Wolf who hunched low behind the shrub as he stalked them.

The path opened into a crescent shaped cove, with a deep stretch of dark gold sand. Rocks had tumbled down to form ridges that bridged the splashing waves and puffin filled cliffs. Dragged up onto the shore lay a long rowing boat with several oars safely stashed within. A thick rope attached it to a square raft still bobbing in the shallows. A couple of sailors were unloading crates and barrels from the raft and carrying them to the back of the cove before disappearing behind the rocks. Another man stood upon the rocks, overseeing their efforts.

Upon observing their descent, the man hopped off the rock and greeted them as they reached the bottom of the path. "Well, this is a pleasant surprise!" declared the man brightly. "I wasn't expecting guests, especially such lovely ladies and handsome young men." He then waved them over to join him on the rocks as if he were entertaining them in his home, instead of sitting on seaweed and mollusc encrusted boulders, clothes clinging wetly to their chilled bodies and limp hair dripping water into their eyes.

"I must say you provide me with quite the predicament. I mean, what am I to do with you?" he said and rested his elbow on his bent knee while he pulled lightly on his beard, wary eyes examining them. They remained silent, unsure

194

what the best answer would be, until Susan, who had been staring at him intently, suddenly exclaimed, "Captain Hrel of the Coral Skies!"

The Captain remained seated but gave a brief smile and a flourish with his hand as he replied, "At your service."

"Thank goodness." Susan sighed, "We were worried that you were pirates and would kill us."

Hrel gave a depreciating smile. "Oh, but we are pirates. We just pretend to be merchants sometimes," Hrel confided amicably.

"Oh dear," said Susan before going quiet, while Jael rolled his eyes skyward.

Will piped up, "That's so cool!"

"Indeed?" responded Hrel, turning his attention to the lad.

"Yeah," Will continued happily. "I'm in the same line of business, you might say." he declared boldly. "We was 'oping you might give us passage to your next stop. We 'ave jewels to pay you."

"That is possible,." said Hrel tapping a finger on his goateed chin thoughtfully while the wind tousled his damp blonde curls. The companions waited as he paused for a moment. "But why won't I just kill you and take the jewels anyway?" he said finally, looking at them as if genuinely interested in any contrary argument.

Jael and Triene appeared to be expecting this comment from Hrel, but Susan flinched visibly, while Will seemed unperturbed. "Why would you kill us?" he scoffed.

Hrel looked amused, but his astute eyes were gauging their reactions to the conversation. He wasn't the only one conducting such an assessment, for Susan was already contemplating the pirate Captain. He appeared to be relaxed and jovial, but his bright blue eyes told a different story. She tried to consider the situation from his perspective for a moment, despite her growing fear. A necessary process if she were to succeed in this negotiation.

Being captain of a pirate ship must be a bit like being the owner of a small business enterprise in that he was responsible for the safety and well-being of his crew as well as making a profit. But in this world, his decisions would determine life or death on a regular basis. Susan couldn't imagine pirates tolerating someone inept as their Captain. Hrel must be astute, ruthless and decisive. The fact that he had chosen to converse and allow them to state their case, rather than kill them and steal their weapons and gems, suggested that he was willing to listen and negotiate. She just needed to work out what they had to offer that he and his crew would be interested in.

She studied the galleon. There must be at least 100 people on board, probably more. They had sailed to the Isle of Rua, which was famed for its danger and difficulty. They were self-declared pirates, and pirates fought other ships. This Captain and his crew were adventurers, drawn to danger and excitement. From what Selene had announced, a return of the Mage Wars was likely and Susan couldn't imagine the pirates welcoming the tip in the balance of power and disruption on the seas that would ensue. Imagine what they could achieve in protecting the magic with the pirates on their side!

Convinced that they should try to get Hrel to help them for more than safe passage, Susan decided to reveal their recent actions in relation to the magic and discuss the concerns they had over the dangers linked to its return. If they could get the pirates to help them, they could do so much more than protect the gemstones. Not entirely confident in her own idea, she began carefully with, "While she was in Carnom, Selene told of the magic's imminent return." She felt and ignored the tensing of Jael's muscles and his sharp look in her direction.

"Selene, you say. She didn't tell me this while on board my ship," Hrel said thoughtfully. Then he asked casually, although his eyes sparkled with interest, "While that must have been an interesting story, what does it have to do with you and, more importantly, me?"

Susan tipped up her chin and said firmly, "She explained that we are all responsible for protecting each other and the magic from those who would misuse it, and to take steps to avoid the mage wars of the past. We are taking that responsibility seriously." She paused before acting on what she believed she saw hidden within the ocean depths of his eyes, "and I believe that you would take it seriously too."

Hrel's eyes flickered up to the sailor standing behind Jael, arms folded, expression stern, then his gaze travelled past Will's eager face, Jael and Triene's similarly concerned frowns before landing back on Susan's nervous but earnest expression. "Forgive me, my dear but I don't see how this affects our relationship."

Here it was, the crux of the matter, did he have the inclination to protect the magic and fight to prevent a mage war? She saw Jael's grimace. Any decision she made would affect him, Triene and Will too. But what were their options? She was sure Jael and Wolf would be able to fight well, but there were several pirates and each of them gave off an air of strength and menace. In a fight there was a real risk one or more of their small group would get hurt or killed. Even if they were to prevail, the pirates on the ship would probably hunt them down and kill them later.

So, if they didn't fight, they needed to convince Hrel to either help them or to let them go, although if he let them go, they would soon have the merchant's soldiers bearing down on them since the Air mage had traced Will. They really needed to get on the ship and out of here. She had to be very convincing. She suspected Hrel was interested in the magic, even though he tried to hide it. She needed to use that to get his help.

"We stole the magical gemstones you sold to the merchant." she began. "We believe he is seeking artifacts so that he can channel the magic and become a powerful mage. Selene warned us about this. We want to prevent him and others using that power for selfish and cruel means. It is obvious that he is both of those." she ended in an impassioned rush...

A crooked smile crossed Hrel's mouth as she spoke, his expressive eyes lit up with humour as he responded with, "Thieves and adventurers indeed!" He then added, "I hope you forgive me, but I would like to verify the rather dramatic statement that magic will return, thereby making the gemstones dangerous in the wrong hands." Susan nodded, relieved that he appeared intrigued by her argument, enough to find out more at least.

Hrel spoke to the golden skinned pirate with the shaved head standing behind Jael, "Uisca, didn't some of the men go to listen to the storytelling in Carnom?" Uisca grunted an affirmative and nodded over to one of the sailors carrying a load towards the cliff. Following the movement, Hrel called out to the man, "Ahoy, Larven. May I have a word?"

The man carefully put down his crate and walked over, his expression surly, "We haven't finished yet."

"My sincere apologies Larven, this lovely lady," he gestured towards Susan, "has made a reference to Selene's storytelling in Carnom. I understand that you attended and might be able to confirm some information for me."

Larven's face softened as he said, "Aye, that I did."

"Excellent." Hrel gave him an encouraging smile, "I have been informed that Selene announced the magic is returning. Is that correct?"

"Aye," was the simple reply.

"Goodness! How unexpected! What else did she say?"

"She said it were up to all of us to stop the mages getting the magic."

"How interesting."

"Aye, but the best bit were the prophesy."

"A prophesy?"

"Aye. I remember it coz it mentioned finding Driftwood to help save the magic". He shifted, clearly having had enough chat, his face turning surly again, "I need to get finished

199

here."

"But of course,,. and thank you, Larven." Hrel waved him away with a smile, although his eyes were sober. Regarding Susan seriously he asked, "Do you recall this prophesy and the mention of Driftwood?"

Susan frowned in concentration, as she tried to remember the words of the prophesy. It had gone round in her head many times, but she wanted to be sure she recollected it correctly. Closing her eyes as she concentrated, she said, "I believe it went something like this:

*"There is a Time for the Stranger to Guide, and the Child to Find: The Fortress of Fire, the Weapon of Earth, the Vessel of Spirit, the Preacher for Air and the Driftwood on Water.*

*Together they will Free the Lost Gift."* As she drew to a close, she opened her eyes to discover everyone staring at her. Jael looked reluctantly impressed, while Triene was nodding her agreement. Hrel rubbed his beard thoughtfully as he mulled over the words.

After a moment, Hrel cleared his throat and speculated out loud. "The prophesy refers to the five magical elements plus a child and a stranger." Hrel's gaze quickly brushed over Will, as he said the word child. "Each of the elements probably relates to a person with the relevant elemental magic, and each person has an additional description. Water is linked with Driftwood..." He fell silent for a moment. "If I am not mistaken, it would appear that the prophesy needs these people to keep the magic from being used for evil." He looked up at Jael who was eying him suspiciously, and

200

he added with a wink in his direction, "Another Mage War would ruin our livelihood and we can't be having that now, can we?"

Hrel faced Susan once more, "Tell me more." He steepled his fingers and peered over them as he waited to hear what she had to say.

Susan took a deep breath and declared, "I think that I am the Stranger mentioned in the prophesy." Her own involvement was one she was ready to reveal, but she would keep Triene and Jael's secret. "Selene explained that the sister worlds cross and when they do they sometimes transfer something from the other world, I think I was transferred from my world to here."

"That really is something." Hrel said with genuine astonishment. "One day I would like to hear about your world, but I suppose now is not the best time." He sat back and contemplated each of their group with solemn eyes. He considered Susan first, staring into her eyes for some time before nodding. Jael's hand clenched and Uisca placed a warning hand on his shoulder. Hrel noted the movement and a wry smile crossed his face as he observed Jael's protective attitude. Triene held her head high as Hrel examined her, meeting his speculative blue eyes with her own defiant green ones. Hrel smiled fully at her before casting his gaze onto Will, who grinned back and enthused, "Susan has some cool ideas, like nabbing the gemstones. I bet she has more ideas too!"

"I'm sure she has...." Hrel chuckled now before he declared, "I do believe you have another member of the prophesy present." Jael and Triene froze and Susan looked stricken, but Hrel continued as if he hadn't noticed their unexpected reaction, "I am known by the name of Hrel Driftwood to my crew and you could say I'm usually on water," he indicated in the direction of his galleon. "I also have a connection to Water magic." Hrel noted, that Triene and Jael visibly relaxed when he identified himself as the Water mage in the prophesy, while Will exclaimed, "Nice one!"

"I knew it!" declared Susan, her face lighting up. "So, you will help us?" she added.

"I will," he agreed modestly.

Jael lifted a sceptical brow, "I don't get it. It's too easy, why should we trust what you say?"

The large pirate was still standing behind them and at these words he moved ominously towards Jael, but Hrel waved him to stay calm before saying with a shrug, "Why not?"

Hrel turned his attention to the other pirates standing on guard and suggested that they help unload the raft. He then patted the rock beside him and said to the last, "Come sit with me, Uisca, these are friends now." The large pirate gave them a dubious look as he sat down on the flat rock next to Hrel, who was saying, "There. That's better, isn't it?" From the deep scowl Uisca was exchanging with Jael, Susan wasn't so sure it was.

"Like I said, I have a bit of skill with Water magic," Hrel continued. "It helps us navigate the seas safely.  It is the main reason why my crew decided I should be the Captain. On pirate ships the nomination Captain is a matter of a vote, you know. My crew have trusted me with this role for fifteen years now. In truth, though, I think that the crew merely regard me as a sort of good luck charm." He gave a merry chuckle and Uisca's expression softened as he glanced towards him.

Hrel's face lost its jovial expression, however, as he leant forward and stated firmly, "I'll not have my men endangered as part of a power play using the seas. I will protect them. Whether it be from a maelstrom, a sea monster or a mage." His serious tone didn't last long however, as he soon sat back again and said with a smile, "but I can do that a lot easier if we stop the mages before they get too strong, eh?" He then added, "So how are we going to do that?"

Susan's stomach was broiling, full of excitement and apprehension at this exchange. It was happening, the prophesy was coming together. "I'm not sure yet, but I'm sure we will be able to figure it out if we put our heads together." She looked hopefully at the others. Will was grinning happily, his dream of becoming a pirate seemingly close to fruition.

Triene and Jael were still wary, their habit of distrust hard to shake, especially when outnumbered. The Captain could have killed them and taken the gems, if he wanted to gain the magic for himself, however. He had let them keep their weapons too. It was looking like a safer proposition than waiting for the soldiers' arrival.

Jael glanced at Susan. He had been afraid that she had been about to spill their secret, but she hadn't. Instead, she had forged a connection with the pirate Captain which had garnered his assistance. He hoped the prophesy knew what it was doing!

Hrel turned to Uisca, "We will need to call a meeting when we get back on board," Uisca nodded and with a final glower at Jael, stood and went to see how the unloading was progressing.

"The caves go a long way and branch out several times before you get to our hoard, Hrel commented as he watched Uisca walk towards the cliffs. "It shouldn't be too long, though, before we can return to the Coral Skies."

Jael looked over at the ship apprehensively. "I'll not leave the horses."

Hrel, looked at them assessingly, "They should be fine on the raft, if you can keep them calm"

"Wolf can do that." piped up Triene.

"Wolf?"

At the sound of his name, Wolf appeared from the direction of the path and trotted towards them, leaving a trail of disappearing paw prints in the wet sand. He sat next to Triene and fixed Hrel with an unflinching amber stare. To his credit, Hrel's initial dismay at the predator's arrival was rapidly replaced with his usual composed demeanour and when his crew emerged from the caves, he blithely jumped up to lead them all over to the boat and raft. Jael glanced up at the tops of the cliffs. The magic sent to locate Will meant that the soldiers would soon be hunting them amongst the trees. He sighed. The only sure way to get beyond their reach would be to accept Hrel's invitation.

They guided the horses to where the raft rested on the lapping waves. Wolf paddled confidently and calmly stepped onto the swaying squared timbers. Two of the pirates were already standing at the front corners of the raft, each holding a paddle which they dug into the sand to minimise the raft's movement. Their eyes bulged and their arms tensed as Wolf came to stand between them. Wolf paid them no mind and simply sneezed encouragingly at the horses. The mare immediately stepped onto the raft which dipped. She kept moving forward until she came to a halt just in front of Wolf. They gently touched noses. Hrel declared the process "Impressive!" as he admired the manoeuvre from the shore.

The gelding was more suspicious of the raft, and his tentative step onto it was quickly taken back when the raft shifted. Triene stroked his nose and whispered reassuringly as she walked backwards onto the raft herself, encouraging him on. He whinnied, then put both front feet onto the raft and kept going despite the movement beneath him. Continuing to encourage him, Triene backed up until the gelding stood nervously next to the mare. The whites of his eyes were showing as he tossed his head in distress. Wolf stretched up and bumped noses with him too, huffing gently. The gelding dropped his head and huffed back, his body visibly relaxing at the comforting gesture. Triene glanced over at Jael who was standing hesitantly on the shore. "We will be all right, Jael," she assured him, as two more pirates stepped onto the raft and stood at each rear corner, releasing their paddles.

Triene had been feeling happier since using her magic. The darkness had, for the most part, been chased and locked away behind that big door in her mind. She was focused on her role in this adventure and, despite the natural concerns over putting herself in the hands of pirates, she was feeling genuinely optimistic. Hrel's openness about his magical ability and his accepted, nay valued, status as a result gave her hope. Not that she was going to reveal her own abilities just yet!

The rowing boat had been pushed into the water, just beyond the raft. The rope between them had been repositioned and now had very little slack. Susan and Will were already sitting on the bench in the centre, with two pirates in front of them and one behind. His pairing was standing in the water ready to push them deeper out before they started to row. Jael waded through the icy water until it was just above his calf then climbed in to sit on the small seat at the stern of the boat. Hrel sat at the bow, unlike his men he was facing the sea, his head tipped back slightly, as he smiled contentedly.

The pirates readied their oars while they were pushed out until the sea reached the wading pirate's waist. He then hauled himself easily on board, as the others counterbalanced the boat, and placed his own oar above the water. Uisca shouted "Heave... ho....," and they all dipped their oars into the water on the ho and pulled backwards on the next "Heave". Their shoulders and biceps flexed as the boat began to move forward. Those on the raft dipped their long paddles partly to guide its path and partly to encourage its forward movement as the rope between them tightened. The oars and paddles soon built up a steady but powerful rhythm as they used the ebbing tide to ease them out to sea and towards the galleon.

Salty spray splattered its passengers as the boat dipped and rose over the waves. The previously enthusiastic Will was now silent and had his left fist pressed to his mouth while his right hand gripped the edge of the boat tightly. His skin had a green sheen. Uisca noticed and laughed good naturedly. He called out to him. "Don't worry lad, ye'll soon get your sea legs." Hearing this the other sailors glanced in Will's direction and chortled merrily.

Behind the boat, the raft cut a harsher path through the waves, washing water over its wooden floor. A puffin plopped into the sea beside Triene and she stared into the shadowed depths, waiting for it to re-emerge. When it finally broke the surface of the water, it was bearing several small fish in its large, triangular beak. It flapped and splashed along the sea's surface until it scooped up into the sky, flying back towards the cliff face.

The pirates continued to row, their strokes smooth and powerful, heading towards the galleon which loomed up like a timber cliff, waves crashing dramatically against its sides. When they drew portside, thick ropes dropped down from the waist of the ship's deck and the pirates got to work fastening them to the boat and raft. Those on the raft also wrapped some of the rope around the horses in a form of harness and indicated for Triene to wrap her leg around a rope and hold onto Wolf. Uisca hollered: Ready to haul" and a loud voice called back, "Haul" while another laughed, and called out "Hold tight or ye'll be tasty morsels of shark bait." With a creaking jolt, they lifted out of the water and lurched their way up, with the occasional stomach churning bump and spin. The petrified horses dangled from their harnesses, legs stiff. Not even Wolf's serene presence could overcome their terror as their ears twitched, eyes open wide, and their braided tails tucked low.

When the vessels finally reached the deck, they were helped on board by members of the crew. Hrel leapt on board with ease, slapping the shoulder of the grey-haired pirate who was coordinating their retrieval, and greeting him with a hearty "Ahoy, steward. We have some portly birds for the cook," here he handed over a large sack, "and some guests to entertain. We also have horses that will need stabling. I trust I may leave it with you to sort out?"

"Aye," the older man replied, as he beckoned over a ship's boy to take the sack of puffins to the kitchens. The boat and raft were quickly stored under the main sail while the unsettled horses were encouraged to travel down to the hold where the livestock were kept, Wolf following protectively. The pirates he passed gave a double take but were surprisingly quick to continue their activities, their previous adventures having included some interesting sights.

The human guests followed Hrel to the quarterdeck and stood by the rail as he checked in with his quartermaster and boatswain. Uisca joined him and they were soon in a detailed conversation which included glances out to sea and gesturing at the sails.

Will bent over the portside rail, hands covering his bowed head. Moaning sounds emanated from beneath his fingers as he rocked back and forth. Triene's stomach was also rolling slightly, and she had a lightness in her head that made her feel off balance. She imagined Will was suffering from a worse form of the same. She wanted to distract him and herself and so glanced around for something to grab her attention. The dark, rain filled clouds had finally drifted inland leaving cottony clouds to intersperse the sky. Gold touches gave them a luminous warmth, in a lightened sky, sprinkled with swirling puffins. "Look Will!," she said pointing to the shore. "Doesn't that look beautiful?" Indeed, it did. The crest of the waves twinkled brightly as they crashed onto the gilded shore, even the rocks gleamed wetly. Will managed to peek over at the cove, but less impressed than Triene, he cast his gaze out towards the horizon. Perhaps that wasn't such a good idea, there was only the rolling sea in that direction. Will gagged.

Jael was also standing against the rail staring at the shore, a worried crease lining his brow. Susan moved closer and tentatively placed her hand so it was touching his. He gazed down at her with a question hovering on his lips, but she wasn't looking at him. Her gaze was fixed ahead, so he resumed his contemplation of the cove, but his frown had eased.

"Which is worse, having to trust a stranger or missing your connection to the land?" asked Susan quietly.

Jael chuckled wryly at her insight. "That obvious, huh?"

She squeezed his hand. "I really think we are on the right path." she said earnestly, looking up at him. "I think Selene was talking to us that night. Earth, Fire, the Stranger and the Child and now Water. It seems like our group is coming together in line with the prophecy."

It does seem rather more than mere coincidence," Jael acknowledged reluctantly.

Susan nodded slowly and whispered, "I think we have an obligation to follow the prophesy." They both stared ahead for a moment, unsure how that would actually work. Susan's heart, which had been racing all the time she had

209

been speaking with Hrel, finally settled into a state of calm acceptance as she obtained comfort from Jael's proximity and the play of light on the constantly shifting sea. She had always loved the sea. Some of her happiest childhood memories were of holidays on her parents' yacht. The small crew had taught her how to sail, while her parents sunbathed and drank cocktails. She had really missed the crew when her parents had sold the yacht to buy a second home in Greece. She should have kept in touch with them, but she had let the friendship drift as she focused on her degree and career. She wasn't that different from her parents after all. She raised her chin. That was before. Now she had the opportunity to do things right, and this time she was determined to put people first. Especially her new friends.

She raised her eyes to Jael's firm profile, noting the slight bump in the ridge of his nose, and the hint of the playful dimple in his cheek. It wasn't playful now though, rather Jael seemed lost, almost lonely. Susan asked him cautiously, "So, does water block the Earth magic?"

"What? No." said Jael confused as he turned to look at her.

"Oh. I guess you have to be really close to the earth you are connecting with then." she continued.

"Yes, but not completely. I could sense the end of the forest long before we got there although I couldn't affect it. Where is this going?"

"Well, I was just wondering why you seem so lost," she said, before gently pointing out, "The earth is beneath the water too."

"It is, but... I ...." he paused, startled by the thought, before

210

he concentrated sending his magic searching. Down, through the surface of the sea where the sun's rays brightened the jellyfish floating in its warmth. Down, through the darker and colder waters where fish darted between the brown-green kelp undulating above the sand and rock, where crabs scuttled, and an octopus hunted. His magic snuggled into the earth and revelled in the connection. Jael smiled sheepishly at Susan, "I can't believe I didn't think of that."

"You're welcome." she said with a smirk, before slipping her free arm around his waist and giving him a friendly hug.

Jael gazed down at her amused expression. His free hand brushed back a damp lock of hair before gently caressing her cheek. His hand then dropped to her waist as he pulled her closer, eyes resting on her slightly open lips. Her breath caught as she anticipated the kiss, but they were interrupted by Hrel's approach as he said in a teasing manner, "So much sexual tension! If I weren't already taken, I would ask to join you for a threesome," He laughed loudly as both blushed and stepped apart. "Come along, we are going to eat and discuss our plans before we hold the crew meeting." As he walked past a scowling Uisca he playfully tweaked his nose and said softly, "I'm running a rig. You know I only want you."

They followed Hrel down the steps to the Captain's quarters where they were joined by Wolf. Will clung to the ropes as he descended, feeling dizzy and unbalanced. Unused to being unsure on his feet, he swore soundly making Uisca chuckle before he turned away and dropped down another level.

Hrel opened the door to his quarters and invited them in. His

211

quarters were a combination of board room and bedroom. The room was well lit, with leaded windows all along the rear of the ship, revealing an uninterrupted view of the sea. A large bunk was placed port side with an ornately carved chest at its base. Starboard, there was a highly polished desk and leather chair. Upon the desk lay an ink well sunk into a base that allowed it to move with the ship, a white quill and a worn, leather-bound journal. Behind the chair was a bookshelf containing more such journals and parchment scrolls, containing a selection of ancient and recently drawn maps.

In the centre of the room was a large, oak table, with matching chairs placed at intervals around it. The table was empty but obviously more frequently used than the desk. Ring stains and grooves marked its top, and the polish was so worn it was difficult to ascertain its original colour.

Wooden panels lined the walls and gilt-framed oil paintings provided colour to the room. The strong lines and vivid hues managing to catch the flavour and vibrancy of life in a port town. Hrel saw Susan admiring the one of Carnom. "Uisca likes to capture the likeness of each place we visit."

"He is very talented."

"Yes, he is," said Hrel, his face lighting up with pride.

Blissfully unaware his artistic endeavours were the centre of attention, Uisca arrived in the doorway bearing a tray piled high with steaming food. Its appetising aroma instantly grabbed the notice of the hungry travellers who turned to look at the plates with anticipation. Young kitchen hands accompanied Uisca and hurried about, setting the table.

Jugs of fresh water were added before they scurried away.

Hrel took the seat at the head of the table, with Uisca on his right, and he gestured the others to join them. As they hastened to take their seats, stomachs rumbling, mouths salivating, Hrel started carving the cooked bird and placed the slices on the plates. He added some of the kelp and mashed potatoes to each and indicated that the full plates should be passed round, saying, "Enjoy your meal, my friends!" Hrel then passed the remaining bird to Triene with a smile, "For Wolf" he explained. Surprised by Hrel's thoughtfulness, Triene nodded and placed it on the floor next to her, where Wolf lay waiting. Not one to pass on a tasty meal, he promptly devoured the bird despite his earlier feast. Licking his chops happily, he settled back down to rest while his gut set to work.

Will eyed the food suspiciously although he did take sips of the water, until Uisca advised him roughly, but with gentleness in his eyes, "The sickness will pass in a couple of days, ye'll need to eat before then." Will groaned at the thought of it lasting for so long, but nibbled on a small portion of meat, earning a nod of approval from the pirate.

Susan, on the other hand, was ravenous and convinced she had done more exercise in the last day than she had in the rest of her sedentary life. She took an enthusiastic bite of the meat, expecting the puffin to be rich and greasy like duck. Instead, the bird had a distinctly fishy flavour that worked well with the salty seaweed and fluffy potatoes.

While everyone tucked eagerly into their breakfast, Hrel wiped his mouth on a napkin and leant back in his chair, eying each of the companions until his gaze finally landed

213

on Susan, as he asked, "So what's the plan?"

She had just put a particularly large bite in her mouth, and now everyone had turned to stare at her. She chewed and chewed, the mouthful seeming to increase in size and become harder to swallow the longer she chewed. At the same time her mind was whirring as she tried to think of something. They had already got the gemstones, what next? She picked up her glass of water and took a sip to gain more time as she felt the pressure of the expectant gazes. There must be a reason the prophesy identifies magic users. Throat finally clear, Susan shared her thoughts, "I think the prophesy indicates that magic users with altruistic motives are needed to protect the magic." She saw Triene and Hrel nodding which encouraged her to continue. "Those identified in the prophesy will need to be strong and will need to access the magic in the gemstones."

Hrel agreed, but regretfully pointed out, "I tried to use the gemstones, of course, but although one glowed brighter when I held it, I couldn't access any magic. I assumed with the magic gone from the world, their use as artifacts had been lost."

Susan was convinced now she was on the right track and responded, "I think we need to understand how the artifacts work."

Will added, "The merchant 'ad an old book that looked important. I bet that's what 'e was trying to do." He looked crestfallen, "I should 'ave grabbed it."

Susan gave him a stern look, "Do not think for one moment that you should or could have done more. It is amazing that you got the gemstones and you escaped. You couldn't have done that if you were trying to carry a book as well." Jael and Triene added their agreement. Will's face flushed scarlet at her praise and he picked at the food on his plate self-consciously.

Triene had been sitting quietly, but Hrel's actions had been reassuring and she was beginning to feel more confident. She proffered her own idea, "Selene mentioned a priest at the Temple in Helvoa. Perhaps we can find the answers we need there?"

Susan scrunched up her nose and asked, "What is this Temple? It has been mentioned before."

Jael replied with obvious distaste, "The Temple was set up to research Ruaism, magic, history and science. It's a place where the wealthy can seek and buy that knowledge."

Hrel exchanged a look with Uisca and stood, placing his hands on the back of his chair. "I shall seek the agreement of my crew to this plan. Helvoa is two to three days sailing from here. We have no other plans for the moment, and I expect they will enjoy spending their recently earnt coin in the city. Please remain and enjoy your meal. We shall return shortly." With a courtly bow, he left for the meeting on the deck. Uisca followed, sending a warning look towards Jael as he left.

Jael kept his eyes on the pirate until the door was shut, then turned to face his sister who smiled at him reassuringly. "I think we have found more new friends, Jael."

He snorted, not yet convinced. "Let us hope so. They have certainly been courteous for pirates."

Will sighed, "I always wanted to be a pirate, but seems like the sea and me don't get on so well."

Susan leant over and patted his hand. "It will get better, I promise," she said sympathetically. "I got seasick at first too. You will soon be living the pirate life, I'm sure." She twisted to face Triene, "I think you are right, we do have new friends to help us." Then fixing her eyes on Jael she added, "We need them if we are to protect the magic."

Jael held her gaze as he replied, "but who will protect us from them, if you are wrong?"

## Chapter 18

The magic reluctantly weaved its way back through the forest. It had found the thief's location and was being drawn back to the Air mage who commanded the artifact. The mage's elemental power had shaped the magic and tainted it with the acrid taste of his greed. The Air mage was better than the other one, though. The magic shuddered, disturbing the pine needles coating the ground, as it recalled the moment the Fire mage had briefly held the artifact. No, the taint of the Air mage was a much better option.

Leaving the forest, the magic sensed the grief and fear that now shrouded the village. It slipped through the sobbing families huddled in the street, past the metallic stench of blood and snuck past the hard-edged soldier positioned to the right of the door. It found the Air mage staring out of the window, twisting the rings on his fingers as he watched. Eager to end its venture, the magic dived into his lungs on an inhale, quickly releasing images of the boy. As the last of the images faded, the command concluded and the magic was drawn back into the safety of the artifact, where it curled tightly and hid.

Raul turned from the window his thin lip curled, as he demanded of the guard in the corner of the room, "Summon the Commander. I have found the thief....."

## Chapter 19

The waking sun stretched out his rays from behind the horizon, his light glinting on the softly, undulating waves. Susan felt the gentle heat on her back as she watched the morning glow reveal the opulent magnificence of the harbour and walled city of Helvoa. The city had spared no expense in creating its carefully calculated impression of wealth and power. The wharf that jutted out into the deep waters was as impractical as it was beautiful, with its gleaming bleached timbers and polished mooring posts. Elegant vessels lined its length, while smaller trading boats hugged the busy quayside where the merchants readied their loads for the day's trade inside the city.

Where the wharf ended, the sandstone path to the city began. The path was already populated with travellers and traders, who were dwarfed by the towering gates set in the centre of the warm sandstone wall, their burnished bronze furnishings sparkling in the sun. A pair of giant guardians flanked the gate, reminding Susan of the lamassu in the Assyrian section of the British Museum. Hewed on the same theme, the guardians had the standing body of a winged lion and a stoic expression on the face of a bearded man.

As soon as the ship reached the wharf, the pirates swarmed, ensuring she was secured. Men swung down knotted ropes to the docking bay before using the same ropes to moor them, while more hefty fellows, including Jael, carefully eased the weighty chains that lowered the anchor to rest on the seabed. Will scampered along the rigging, helping secure the furled sails, he had quickly recovered from his malaise, and Triene was assisting Uisca pack his navigation

218

tools while chattering to him happily. Wolf lay spread flat at her feet, basking in the morning light.

Uisca was silent as he worked, rolling the parchment maps, cleaning and folding the compass callipers and sextant, before passing them to Triene to store them away in the leather trunk. Triene had seen something of her brother in the gruff navigator, and had been drawn to his side. To Uisca's alarm, she had decided to assist him during the journey, and he often found himself the recipient of a one-sided conversation. She had been enamoured of his maps that depicted the changing landscape as the ship skirted the coast on its journey, believing it a skill that could be used when travelling the roads. Uisca hadn't protested too much when she pressed him to help her create some of her own, secretly appreciating her enthusiasm for his craft. He did find Triene and Susan's fascination with his paintings in the Captain's quarters uncomfortable, however, squirming when they started discussing it in front of him. Triene was talking about his artwork again now, "You said that you have been to Helvoa before, so why haven't you painted it?" she asked him, pointing to the striking scene before them. Uisca glanced dismissively at the stagey exclamation of wealth and shrugged before replying, "I did a painting, just not that."

"Ooo, which one?" Triene said excitedly, demanding his reply with her stare.

Uisca sighed, he couldn't understand her fascination with his paintings. Like his maps, they simply recorded the places he had been. His hesitant brown eyes met Triene's expectant ones. Knowing from experience, she wouldn't give in, he stated flatly, "The flower stall." in an attempt to end the discussion quickly. He should have known better by now.

"I love that one! The girl selling the flowers is clearly exhausted, but is putting a smile on for the customers. It's such an empathic painting!" she declared.

Uisca merely grunted noncommittedly and hefted his trunk down the steps, pursued by a loquacious Triene.

The Coral Skies had set sail three days ago, the crew clearly excited to be off on another adventure. Hrel had immediately introduced the companions to the boatswain, a petite woman with iron-grey hair tied up in a tight knot. Her voice was a powerful contralto which issued rapid orders from her position beside the main mast. Upon their presentation, she circled them, her shrewd eyes assessing. She allocated Will the job of rigger, Jael was sent to the carpenter to help with the ship's maintenance, and she had accepted Triene's prompt request to be navigator's mate. A crease appeared on her brow as she eyed Susan for longer than the others. Susan managed to remain still, although she did jump slightly when the woman pinched her upper arm and shook her head. Susan was put with the pre-teens, working as swabbie, which involved keeping the deck wet and the timbers swollen to prevent leaks. Her hands were now rough and dry, the years of expensive manicures finally surrendering their influence. She didn't begrudge the work, but she did wish she had had Triene's foresight to volunteer for a less physical role.

The companions were on the daylight shift, so they were able to meet up for food as the sun set, and to sit beneath the stars listening to the pirates tell tales as they drank their hot grog. The sweet spices and treacly scent of rum mingled in the shadows, while the flickering lamplight combined with the creak of the masts. Influenced by their new adventure, the older pirates shared tales of the dark days that came with the Mage Wars. There were stories of unnatural storms that broke masts and washed sailors overboard by sea swells shaped like hands, of hungry fires that engulfed ships and seamen in their blazing maws and of colossal waves that snatched and carted ships far inland, depositing their broken hulls in forests and on hilltops. When the stories had finished, the impressionable youngsters huddled as they plotted how they would fight the mages on their quest, with declarations of bravery that made the older pirates share a smirking smile over the tops of their mugs.

When the evening's entertainment was finished the pirates found their way to their beds. Other than Hrel and Uisca who shared the Captain's quarters, the only separate quarters belonged to the boatswain, the carpenter/surgeon, the cook and the quartermaster. Everyone else slept in communal quarters, where Susan had been relieved to see cots rather than her imagined hammocks. They had been supplied with fresh linen and clean clothes which had been laid out for them on their first night. To Susan's amusement, she noted that the sleeping quarters for those with babies and toddlers was situated at the opposite end of the ship to the others.

Hrel's role on board was not as Susan had imagined it would be. It transpired that the day-to-day decision-making was largely undertaken by the quartermaster, a stern giant of a man, with a gnarled face and fists the size of boulders. Although it should be noted that his fearsome features hid a lively sense of humour, which could be seen sparkling in his eyes, if one dared to get close enough to see. Although Hrel consulted with the quartermaster frequently, most of his day was spent sauntering around the ship, speaking to members of the crew who welcomed him with enthusiasm, eagerly demonstrating the results of their labours for his approval. His encouragement left a trail of good humour in his wake.

All in all, the pirate's life seemed to be a good one.

The pleasant but labour-intensive interlude in their quest was over now that they had arrived at Helvoa. During their planning meeting it was evident that the appearance of wealth would be necessary in order to gain entry to the Temple. It was imperative that they succeed in entering the inner sanctum if they were to access the information they required. The Temple guards were the initial screening process, and they would have to be persuaded that they bore sufficient riches to afford the Bishops' levies to get inside the Temple door. Hrel had approached this challenge with enthusiasm, engaging with his steward in the selection of appropriate disguises. The results of their efforts were now awaiting them in the Captain's quarters.

Susan turned from her quiet contemplation of the city, and curious about the guises that had been obtained, she descended in order to join the others in the quarters. Pulling open the door she encountered a swirl of fabric and anticipation. Hrel and Triene had taken control and were thoroughly enjoying themselves as they rummaged through the clothing and accessories heaped on the large table. They were picking up items, rapidly agreeing their use before placing them into discrete piles. Uisca was leaning against a wall, arms and legs crossed, observing their antics with an amused expression. An expression that was reflected in

Wolf's eyes and open jaw as he sat companionably beside Uisca. Will shared the excitement demonstrated by Triene and Hrel. Eyes sparkling, he unabashedly stripped and slipped on the guise of a servant which merely consisted of a tunic and trousers in shades of brown, although the fine weave of the fabric was designed to denote the wealthy status of his employer.

Jael, on the other hand, was not amused. He was positioned to one side of the table, next to one of the growing piles, his arms folded tightly across his chest. A frown furrowed his brow and his mouth turned down as he eyed the items that made up his disguise as a personal guard. Susan slipped unobtrusively through the doorway and sidled towards Jael just as Hrel spun round bearing a leather strap containing a row of throwing knives. Surprised, Susan took a step back, while Jael unfolded his arms and moved protectively between them. Hrel smirked knowingly before exclaiming, "There you are!" to Susan. "Triene has your dress ready." He nodded in the direction of the table. Then fixing his stare at Jael, "and you, my good fellow need to remove that tunic and pop this on." He waggled the strap at him.

Jael's frown deepened. He scanned his disguise which consisted of black leather hose, embossed arm guards and scabbard, and a pair of black boots. "I'll need a top underneath it". he said firmly.

"Where's the fun in that?" declared Hrel teasingly, eliciting a grumble from Jael, before Hrel reached for the black linen shirt he had kept separate anticipating Jael's refusal to bare his chest.

Meanwhile, Triene had spied Susan and hurried over to her

bearing a woven silk dress. She held it up for Susan to admire and its folds flowed to the ground. The silk had been dyed to mimic a setting sun starting with a rich indigo around the neckline and shoulders blending into salmon pinks, lilacs and a buttery yellow at the hem. Triene's eyes lit up as she held it against Susan and sighed, "This will look perfect on you." Eagerly pressing the dress into Susan's arms she lifted the seam of the dress and pointed out the tiny, even stitches. "This is so beautifully made." she said breathlessly before swirling back to the table. "Here!" she said retrieving a soft leather corset of burnt sienna and some matching boots. "You tie the corset over the dress." Triene explained, while demonstrating its purpose by placing her hands on her own body. Sharing a quick grin, Triene then grabbed her own outfit and ushered Susan to the screen placed by the bed.

Ducking behind the screen, Susan gently placed the dress upon the neatly made bed and quickly removed her tunic and trousers. It didn't take long to shuck on the loose-fitting dress. Its full-length sleeves were narrow at the shoulders but hung wide and low over her hands. The dress had little shaping around the body and was overly long. She could see why the corset was needed. She loosened the laces and slipped it over her head, wiggling it down to just below her breasts. Then working down the laces, she tightened them so she cinched in her waist and plumped up her breasts. She then adjusted the scooped neckline so that it was even and made sure the top of the dress billowed softly out over the corset before glancing over at Triene. Her duplicate dress was of an olive green, with a corset of black and she was just adjusting the shoulders and running her hands lovingly along the smooth material. Looking up at Susan she grinned guiltily, caught in her momentary indulgence. Susan grinned back and they both sat on the edge of the bed to put on their boots. After finger combing each other's hair and twisting Susan's to rest on one shoulder, they emerged from behind the screen, heads high, backs straight. Ready to be admired.

Susan sought out Jael and found him standing by the door, scowling, arms folded in front of the rows of throwing knives crisscrossed across his chest. The shirtsleeves pulled taught, the fabric revealing the strong musculature hidden beneath it. He looked every bit the intimidating guard he was meant to be, that is until his eyes met Susan's. They widened momentarily before they narrowed into a smoulder and a satisfied smile turned up his lips. Her body responded with a wave of warmth before Hrel's visage cut the connection. "Delicious, my dear lady" said Hrel, raising her hand to his lips. Still holding her hand, he frowned and stared at it in horror. Susan tried to remove her hand and flushed uncomfortably, but he held on determinedly. "My apologies for the labour that has caused your delicate hand such damage." he said contritely. "Allow me to rectify the matter." As he spoke, the water from the jug sitting on his desk rose and arched its way towards him. Taking hold of her other hand he raised it alongside its companion, and his lips twitched mischievously as, to Susan's open-mouthed amazement, the water formed a transparent shell over her hands before it was slowly absorbed into the skin, rehydrating it instantly.

Jael had moved closer and was watching suspiciously, but on observing Susan's glowing delight, his expression softened. Hrel released his hold and Susan twisted her hands

225

to examine them. "Amazing!" she whispered to herself. Hrel then reached up, fussing over her hair before pulling back to admire the result. Raising a hand to touch her hair, Susan felt the bejewelled clip he had placed there. He then draped a pendant adorned with precious stones around her neck. Raising her eyes to Jael's she couldn't help but grin as she said playfully, "You will have to guard me well now I am a wealthy lady."

His eyes serious and fixed upon her own, Jael replied, "Always." Taken aback by the intensity of his response, Susan dropped her gaze and smoothed her skirt, saying awkwardly, with an attempt at lightness, "I might just hold you to that."

While Susan had been holding Jael and Hrel's attention, Triene had been swishing her skirts and twirling gleefully towards Wolf whose body shook as he made a chuffing sound that resembled laughter. She rubbed his head as she said, "I bet you wish you could come with us and don a disguise. You would look dashing as a pony!" she laughed. He snorted and rolled his eyes.

Triene then swirled her skirts over to the table and peered into the mahogany chest. The chest contained both coins and jewels and the plan was for Will to carry it into the city. It was large enough to indicate affluence, but small enough for Will to convey in his arms. The leather straps were undone and the lid open wide for her to fish out an onyx pendant. Will scooted over and examined the contents.

"There's some nice stuff in there." he said knowledgably. His brows pinched together and he added, "We shouldn't take all of it though. What if we get robbed?"

Uisca had moved forward as Will approached the chest, and rumbled ominously, "We'll have members of the crew nearby should anyone be tempted by them."

Will stood back, holding up his palms in a gesture of innocence, "We're on the same side, you and me. No worries, 'ere."

Uisca gave Will a sceptical look and seemed about to comment further when his attention was caught by Hrel's reappearance. He was now attired in his rich man finery. A white knee length coat shimmered with blue semi-precious stones that picked out the sky blue of his silk shirt. His knee breeches were the dark blue of the sea at night and tucked into the cuff of his boots. He still wore a sword at his side, but the hilt and scabbard had been wrapped in a soft blue leather to co-ordinate with his outfit. He swaggered towards the others, and on passing the table he scooped up a wide brimmed hat of blue decorated with a large white feather. Sporting a mischievous grin, he spun it in his hand as he brought it up and placed it rakishly upon his head. The ladies playfully oohed and ahhed, while a fond smile hovered on Uisca's lips. Will and Jael simultaneously rolled their eyes, but neither could suppress their smile at the flamboyance of his approach.

Hrel's grin dropped and his mien turned serious as he addressed them. "We need to maintain our roles once we leave this ship. The bishops take their protection very seriously. Don't be fooled by their foppish uniforms, the Temple guards are well armed and well trained and known for their sharp justice. If they suspect us of any misdeeds or deception, we will be in danger." The frivolity disappeared before the importance of their task. Uisca held open the door as they passed through, steady and determined. As Hrel passed Uisca, the large pirate frowned and lowering his voice said, "Be careful," while looking meaningfully at the others. Hrel nodded and winked at him before following them to the gangway set up for their descent to the dock.

The gangway was a rough construction of wooden planks and hemp rope. Will took the lead and trotted down it confidently with Triene following more cautiously, picking up her long skirts and watching her steps. Susan looked uneasy as she watched the gangway sway each time the waves crashed into the ship, so Jael slipped his arm around her waist in support. Smiling gratefully, she straightened her shoulders as she leant into him, more than willing to accept his help. After exchanging a few words with Uisca, Hrel brought up the rear, his step light.

Uisca and Wolf stood watch on the deck as the others made their way along the wharf to the city gates, Hrel on point, with Susan and Triene hooked on each arm. Will and Jael walked behind, as befitting their subordinate roles. Hrel led them up the path, past the queue of visitors and traders, who eyed them with jealous hostility. At the gate, they were brought to a halt by a mean faced guard, his threatening manner necessary in order to counter his otherwise ridiculous appearance. Someone had inexplicably decided that the gaudy combination of orange and lime green would be appropriate colours for a uniform, and that a puffed-out cap would provide a suitable accent. The pike he bore, however, looked sharp and used. Hrel inched closer, some coins balanced on his open hand. Sniffing, as he looked down his nose at the offering, the guard deigned to accept the payment and placed it in an already heavy purse, before indicating to his fellows that Hrel and company were to be permitted entry. Passing through the towering gates they found themselves within the hubbub of the city.

The sandstone path arrowed for the Temple, cutting through the largest marketplace Susan had ever seen, the lack of the permanent shops explained the vast swathe of traders clamouring to enter. The rapid influx made the large number of guards necessary as they directed the traders to their allocated sections and kept any scuffles in check. Fruit stalls were placed next to fruit stalls, those with livestock were kept together and so on. No doubt, the plan was to maximise competition and minimise the prices for the Temple residents. A sound economic strategy that the servants making their way to the stalls, empty baskets in hand, would take advantage of, in the hope of making a little profit for themselves.

The Temple itself spanned the width of the city, dividing the enclosure in two. All the residents of the city lived and worked behind its polished marble wall. More guards were marching in formation in the space between the market and Temple, the calls of the drill instructor ringing out above the sounds of stalls being set up and the calls of traders promoting their produce.

The central path to the Temple was lined with stalls aimed at the wealthy visitors and residents. Rich cloth and seductive scents were displayed to draw in the passers-by, though many of these traders were still unpacking, their leisurely pace surprised into hasty preparations on spying Hrel and company. One intrepid trader snatched up a delicate amethyst bottle decorated with gold filigree and scurried towards Susan, brandishing it eagerly. Jael took a step towards him, dagger in hand, scowl on his face. The man's eyes widened as he leant back from the weapon.

Quickly intervening, Hrel waved his hand in Jael's direction and stated firmly, "Stand down, 'tis only a perfume." Still suspicious, Jael placed the dagger back in its sheath and backed up slightly, allowing the man to address Susan. The trader's voice had a faint quaver as he began extolling the exquisiteness of the scent, sending a worried glance towards Jael's grim features when he removed the stopper and wafted the bottle towards her. When Jael didn't react, he relaxed slightly and continued, "The floral notes are obtained from the summer jasmine and" he lowered his voice conspiratorially, "the rare tiger orchid."

The perfume was fresh and delicious, Susan couldn't help but exclaim, "That's lovely!".

The trader smiled encouragingly "It is very expensive to make and is only available to the most discerning customer. For you, I could sell it for two gold." he said hopefully. Susan's smile fell from her lips as she stuttered, "Oh, oh, I…."

Hrel interrupted with a haughty, "Since you seem to like it, my dear, we will take it. Will, pay the man."

Will carefully removed two gold coins from the chest and handed them over to the excited trader, who quickly passed Will the bottle and hurried away with his profit. Hrel leant into Susan and said under his breath, "Please don't admire anything else, or we'll be coinless before we reach the Temple." Gulping, Susan gave a brief nod in guilty agreement. The other traders had indeed been encouraged by their compatriot's success and soon crowded around them as they tried to continue their journey. Polite and not so polite rejections failed to deter those determined to achieve a sale. In the end, they had to rely on Jael using more physical tactics in order to proceed.

The white marble Temple wall loomed ahead, the lack of windows made a stark and inhospitable impression, especially as the sun reflected brightly off it. Beyond the wall, the roofs rose and fell, interspersed by tall narrow towers with swirled pinnacles. A lone iron door sat in the centre of the wall, flanked by two guards. As they approached, the guards crossed their pikes in warning and demanded, "State your business."

Hrel arched his brow and stated sardonically, "I would have thought that obvious, I wish to obtain some information."

The guard who had spoken, curled his lip into a sneer and stated, "Information costs, as does access." Hrel sighed dramatically and indicated that Will should open the chest. He made a show of fishing around for a gold coin, which he then proffered in payment. The guard pocketed the coin, but the pikes remained crossed. Hrel sighed again and handed the guard a further coin which proved sufficient to get the guard to sound the bell hanging by the door. Its deep toll echoed against the surrounding walls, drawing stares from the marketplace as well as the clip of footsteps from within the Temple. Feeling exposed, Susan felt sure her agitation was obvious to the guards, but she resolutely placed her hand on Hrel's sleeve, cocked her hip and tried to plaster a look of boredom on her face as they waited. Jael, smothered his burst of laughter at her efforts behind a cough, earning a glare from Triene and a curious side eyed look from Will.

231

The scrape of an internal bolt being slid open was followed by the door slowly opening with an ominous creak. It revealed a small, elderly man with a balding pate and a web of broken veins on his pale cheeks. His nose was bulbous and purpling on its tip. He was dressed in a robe of mustard yellow that covered him fully although its hood rested on his slightly rounded shoulders. The interior was made of the same white marble as the exterior, covering both walls and floor.

"State your area of interest." The man enquired pompously.

"Ruaism." Triene blurted out before Hrel could speak. Hrel glanced at her and gave a small smirk as he agreed, "Yes, indeed, the history of the ancients and their religious beliefs is of great interest to us."

"That Bishop is unavailable at present," the little man said with a false smile, "in the meantime, a tour of our collection is possible, for a fee….." he added.

Having expected something of the sort, Hrel opened his hand and revealed a large sapphire in a gold ring. The man licked his dry lips and snatched it, hiding it somewhere under his robe. "There is, of course a fee on entry as well," he said, a crafty look crossing his features. Hrel merely raised an eyebrow and stared at the man. Realising that he wasn't going to receive further remuneration, their new guide turned and called out, "Follow me." and hurried away.

Stepping into the Temple corridor they kept pace with their guide who whisked them past the flaming torches which lit the windowless corridor until they reached a junction where natural light filtered in from the right. Turning the corner, they found themselves walking alongside an open courtyard, where the wall to their right was replaced by intricate columns and arches. Their guide slowed the pace checking the wooden doors on the left until he found the one he sought and stopped, placing his hand on the doorknob. Will had been surreptitiously sliding on the marble floor and bumped into Triene as she came to a halt. Jael pulled him back and with a strategic prod and inclination of his head suggested Will examine the layout of the courtyard.

Will's eyes flickered as he surveyed the open square, noting the low roofs that tipped down towards it and the rocks placed within sections of pale sand. In one of the sections, a robed priest was painstakingly raking patterned grooves in the sand. Their guide gave a genteel cough and announced, "Here we are, our Ruaism collection." Then holding the door open for them he encouraged them to step through with a flap of his other hand. Jael took the lead to check for threats as warranted by his role as guard, before nodding for the others to file in behind him.

The circular room was packed with exhibits surrounded by stacked bookshelves that stretched up to the domed ceiling overhead. Golden pillars accentuated the shelving and evolved into thin golden beams that crossed the dome. A couple of carved lecterns were strategically placed for visitors to stand and study the valuable manuscripts.

Their guide manoeuvred himself to a position in front of the first exhibit, "Behold the statue of Rua, which was discovered on the Isle of Rua by the famous explorer..." Susan found herself staring up into the alien eyes of the goddess as the guide informed them of the statue's history and the challenges in translating the inscription upon it. "The

233

carving was made in soapstone, hence its green hue and smooth texture, using tools......." Susan wondered how the sculptor had determined Rua's form. Unlike the Christian god, she didn't resemble a human, but rather was an ethereal creature that was made up of the elements. Her face was featureless save for the disproportionately large eyes that expressed her compassion as a single teardrop hung suspended in perpetuity. Framing her face were flames, flickering in if caught in a strong wind. From her neck, her body split into four creatures, a mammal, a lizard, a fish and a bird whose feet or pelvic fin became roots which dug deep into the earth beneath her. The inscription containing the story of creation was engraved on the column upon which she perched. Beneath it was the prophesy.

She heard Jael ask in his deep voice, "Who is Father Danin?" and took her eyes off the statue to focus on the answer. She should have been paying more attention.

"Father Danin is our current expert on Ruaism. He was novice to poor Father Culdric, may he rest in peace. He is currently working on the multiple worlds theory."

"Father Culdric was the only other expert but he has died?" asked Hrel,.

"Why yes! Father Culdric was working on the translation of one of the books in our collection. He had nearly completed his work and had discovered how the artifacts were used by the ancients, I understand. So tragic!" the little man shivered.

"What was so tragic?"

"Why the theft of the book and his translation, of course!"

234

he declared, as if it were obvious, before adding, "Poor Father Culdric was killed during the theft."

"He was murdered!" exclaimed Susan, while Triene looked sickened. Jael and Hrel were listening intently.

Will blurted out, "Did the book have iron clasps and was this big?" he moved his hands to indicate its size.

"Why yes, young man, have you seen it?" their guide fixed an intent stare on the supposed servant.

Realising his mistake, Will glanced nervously at Hrel, and said in an apologetic tone, "I…. I heard of it, from my previous employer who visited the temple when he was young." Will bluffed before Hrel distracted the guide,

"Yes, well, that is all well and good, but it's no longer here for us to see, you said?"

Their guide was eager to expand upon the theft. "It is indeed gone, along with the Eye of Rua, an artifact Father Culdric was examining at the time of his death." The man leant forward and whispered conspiratorially, clearly more interested in this topic than the museum pieces, "Poor Father Culdric's throat was slit, from ear to ear." He made a motion with his hand against his neck as he spoke.

"That must have been very unpleasant for you and whoever found the body…." said Susan sympathetically.

"Oh? Oh, yes, Father Danin was very distressed, he has since locked himself up in his workroom," he gestured to another closed door to the side of the room, "and insists on having food left in here so he doesn't have contact with anyone."

"Gracious, was he harmed or a witness to the murder as well?"

"Oh no! But he is convinced he is next because of his studies, the Bishop says it's nonsense but it's been several months now and he hasn't come out."

Susan looked at the door curiously, "He's in there now?"

Pleased to have such a receptive audience, the man expanded, "Oh yes. Like I said, the Bishop is very angry because Father Culdric's translation was lost as well as the book, which meant he didn't get the final payment from the merchant Raul. He even had to refund some of the down payment. He is insisting on Father Danin working extra hard so he can make up the loss."

Hrel looked around the windowless walls. "How did someone get inside to kill Father Culdric or was it someone from inside the Temple?"

"Oh dear, it wasn't a priest, oh no, no." said the guide, quite flustered by the suggestion. "I understand a man came seeking information on Ruaism, very much like yourselves. Fedao let him in and let him examine the collection. He said he was a very polite and charming young man. He had no worries leaving him to his contemplation of a text," he indicated to a lectern, "Which is where he was, when Fedao returned. The gentleman even thanked Fedao with a small gift as he exited as if nothing untoward had happened. It wasn't until poor Father Danin went into the workroom to talk to Father Culdric that we realised something was amiss." The man shook his head angrily, "The guards should have stopped him …"

"Indeed!" said Hrel in a dismissive tone, thinking that the guide was about to enter a tirade against the guards. Seeking to change the subject so as not to raise suspicions on their particular interest in this event, he pointed to another exhibit and asked, "What is this item?"

The guide hurried over to the object and said with a proud smile. "Why that is the dried hand of the infamous Ypis, the Fire mage that controlled much of this part of the world during the days of the Mage Wars." Indeed, it was obviously a hand, now they looked at it closely. Most of the digits were folded over, but the thumb was extended in a gruesome parody of the Like button on social media, thought Susan. Triene's nose curled as she asked, "Why did someone keep his hand?"

The man shrugged, "A trophy, I believe, from one of those responsible for his demise. I understand other body parts were also dried, but we have not yet discovered their locations."

Hrel looked around the collection, "Do you have any other ancient artifact, now that the Eye of Rua has been stolen?"

Their guide's expression turned sour, "No! It was one of the most lucrative items as well."

Triene was still circling the hand as she casually asked, "How did the ancient's use the artifacts?"

The old man's face turned sly, as he said, "Is that your question for the Bishop?"

Triene laughed and said, "You've got me. But I thought the expert was Father Danin not the Bishop."

"That's right, but you have to ask the Bishop, who then instructs Father Danin to provide the answer. The Bishop will take your payment, half on asking and half on receipt of the answer."

Hrel spoke then, "What is the fee for such a question?"

"The Bishop will explain when you see him." A peel of bells rang out and the guide added with a satisfied smirk, "That won't be today though, as all the Bishops are now convening for a meal and unavailable for the rest of the day. You will have to come again tomorrow."

Hrel laughed loudly, "And you are, no doubt, the doorman again tomorrow and a further payment for entry is expected?"

"That would be correct, sir."

Hrel shook his head and gave the others a meaningful look as he stated, "I think it is time we return to the ship."

They were accompanied through the corridors to the external door, and then walked silently past the guards and through the trading section, and successfully negotiated their way past the insistent traders and out through the city gates. Still silent they strolled down the dock and boarded the Coral Skies. Once they had met up with Uisca and Wolf and entered the Captain's quarters, Hrel finally gave acknowledgement to the idea that was already forming in each of their thoughts, "I do believe we need to pay Father Danin a visit."

Susan sighed, relieved she wasn't the one suggesting the dangerous escapade this time. It made sense to go straight to the source.

Jael nodded his agreement and said, "I will go, and I would appreciate the benefit of your skills, if you are interested, Will?" he added.

Flushing slightly, Will preened and declared boldly "Too right, I'm interested! You're going to need an expert to get you in and out of that place."

Hrel added matter of factly, "I will also go. I think three will be more than enough, though, don't you? More and we are going to find it hard to remain hidden."

"Agreed," said Jael, crossing his arms and tipping up his chin decisively

"Agreed," said Will emulating Jael's reply and posture.

## Chapter 20

It was a moonless night, beset by a dampening drizzle, as Jael, Hrel and Will skirted the city wall. The land around the wall had been cleared of shrubs and rocks, and the grasses cut short to expose anyone seeking surreptitious entry to the city. Fortunately, the cloud filled skies and their all-black clothing made them virtually invisible to searching eyes, although when combined with the rain, the darkness increased the difficulty of their venture. The city had been emptied and the entrances were well guarded. The only way in was straight up. The gaps between the sandstone blocks, their narrow treads.

Wary of the light from the quayside they edged along the wall until it was out of sight, coming to a halt beyond the scope of prying eyes. Jael made sure that his rope was looped and tightly secured over his shoulder and across his chest, and that he had his wax pouch of powdered chalk firmly attached to his belt. He stretched out his muscles, rising onto his toes and flexing his fingers, hearing the subtle susurration of Hrel and Will's own preparations.

Jael had never tried scaling anything like this before. The height and steepness of the wall was daunting enough, without the need to climb it blind. Taking a deep, calming breath he pressed closer to the wall and ran his fingers along its slick surface, using a combination of touch and Earth magic to sense the size of the large sandstone blocks. The dry-stone construction meant there were plenty of holds, albeit narrow and shallow for the most part. He placed some chalk on his hands and reaching up, felt along until he found a suitable grip for his right hand. He then located a secure foothold for his left leg, about knee high, from which he would be able to power up. On an exhale he bunched his arm muscles, pulled on his fingers and pushed down on his toes. As he lifted off the ground, he sought further grips for the other hand and foot, stretching up and out. Remembering Will's advice, he twisted so his hip was close to the wall and his feet facing the same direction. He took smaller steps, keeping his arms straight and legs bent. It was slower going but Will had assured him that he would appreciate it at the later stages of the climb and it would help prevent his feet slipping. The sound of a faster scrambling came from nearby, Will, of course, and the occasional subdued scuffle and sigh from Hrel. They were really doing this. Jael thought as a blast of exhilaration filled him. This is what he really wanted, not to run from shadows, but to run at danger, sword in hand. He had his responsibilities and had to protect his sister, but this…this is what drove him.

Will swung his left foot up to rest his heel on the nook he had found and twisted his hip inwards to rest the foot more firmly before changing his handhold. He was worried about the others. Hrel had a good sense of balance and had been climbing ropes most of his life so should have the flexibility needed for the climb, but the techniques were different. He had done his best to explain the differences and ways to deal with them and hoped that Hrel would be able to remember them during the climb. The pads of Will's fingers lodged onto the ledge, thumb clenched over the knuckles firmly as he hung there feeling for the next hold. Jael wasn't used to climbing though. He didn't have the experience or physique for it. All that bulk meant there was more to lift and less flexibility. He had tried to give him techniques to help keep his body close to the wall anyway, but he could hear him mutter an oath under his breath as he struggled to find another hold for his larger fingers. Will's toes wedged into a crevice and raising his heel to put more friction on his toe, he focused on the climb.

Jael could feel the burn in his bent left arm as he fished around for a crevice with his right hand. He knew it was there. He gritted his teeth and forced himself to keep searching, pushing higher on his right leg so he could seek further along the wall. He felt his boot slip and he shifted his weight back onto his left, muttering a curse. He couldn't see the drop but he could imagine it! Stretching his right hand vertically, he tucked his hips back against the wall. There! His fingers finally found the ledge and he wedged them in as far as they would go, scraping some more skin. He took a deep breath and let his weight rest there for a moment, his heart pumping pure adrenaline.

Hrel was slightly ahead of Jael and he could hear Will moving confidently up the wall. Oh, to be young! Hrel, on the other hand, could feel his muscles tiring, it had been too long since he had been a rigger and his unpractised muscles were protesting their use. Fortunately, he could see the outline of the wall now, the faint light cast from the torches in the Temple cutting through the black of the night. Not far to go. The thought spurred him on.

Will reached the top of the wall and sat upon it, letting his muscles and breathing settle for a moment. The wall was four blocks wide and provided plenty of room for him to stretch out. That was some climb! he thought with satisfaction. He could hear the others still climbing, their breath a bit ragged. They were doing well. He grinned with pride. Using the limited light, he looked down upon the

Temple roofs. Most were flat, which would make their route to the courtyard easier. He thought the source of the light below was coming from there. The building layout was patchy though, with varying heights and angles to traverse. He needed to work out a route down into the courtyard and to find a place to secure their ropes, ready for an urgent escape should the need arise. A bit further along the wall there was a taller building in jumping distance. Will walked along the wall, until he drew alongside the building and reached into his chalk pouch before squatting and marking the inside of the wall with a large white X. He then removed a small metal hammer and a U-angled piton and ring, from his pack. Adjusting his body so that he was lying face down on the wall, he placed the piton against a      solid block of sandstone and carefully hammered it in so that it wedged itself deeply into the rock. He wiggled a bit further along the wall and repeated the exercise with a second piton, then a third and finally, a fourth, making sure they were secure. By the time he had finished, Jael and Hrel had joined him and were carefully threading rope through each piton's ring. Will proceeded to thread his own rope through the final ring, making sure the ends were of an even length. He let his rope drop down the inside of the wall while holding tightly to both ends.  Looking sideways he could see the other three pitons were similarly prepared although their ropes had been carefully coiled to rest on the wall, ready to fling outwards on their return. Nodding to the others, Will stood up, feet together, arms moving to the side and then up as if he were about to dive into a pool. He then sprung forwards, tucking in his elbows and head, as he curled into a ball, dropping the rope onto the roof and rolling as he landed.   Quickly scooting over to the rope, he wrapped it around a small chimney that sat squatly smoking in the centre.

Jael shook his head at Will's theatrical dive, bunching his own leg muscles before taking a powerful leap, soaring towards the roof, legs moving as if running through the air before he landed on both feet, knees softly folding into a squat, hands out to brace his forward motion. Beside him, a smiling, Hrel dived and rolled onto his shoulder before springing up and beaming at Jael, who rolled his eyes and sought out Will.

Will was looking speculatively at the corner of a roof quite a few feet away. The roof was lower than theirs and its edge had a slight lip, it was this lip that Will was eyeing. As they approached, Will whispered, "This way." and running off their own roof he leapt forward, catching the lip with his fingers and pressing his toes against the wall. He bounced backward, simultaneously twisting to the left as he dropped, reaching out to catch the edge of another roof, positioned at a right-angle to the first and even further down. Heaving himself up, he stood looking over at them and gave a thumbs up before tripping lightly along the roof and out of sight.

With eyebrows raised, Hrel looked at Jael, who was frowning at Will's disappearing form. "After you," Hrel murmured with a wry smile. Jael turned his frown to the buildings, working out the layout. The first building ran parallel with theirs, ending with the corner that abutted the second, much lower building. If he could turn the corner on the first, he should be able to drop down onto the other without any fancy tricks. He took a couple of steps back, then with a running leap, reached out and firmly grabbed hold of the lip with his right hand, but his left hand missed, and his body swung perilously above the massive drop. His fingers strained to maintain their hold. Refusing to fall, Jael planted his toes on the wall to gain friction. He exhaled hard as he stretched up with his left arm, fingers just brushing the underside of the lip. "Come on," he muttered to himself as he pressed his hips forwards and pushed up on his heels. This time he managed to grab hold. With a sigh of relief, he started to swing his body side to side to help him inch his way to the corner. Reaching it he placed one hand on either side and glanced down. He needed to move further along. Arms burning with the strain, he somehow managed to shuffle even further... That would have to do. Looking at the roof below, he relaxed his body, released his grip and fell. He landed softly and quickly stood up, unfolding from the crouch, glad to be back on his feet.

He squinted down the roof top for a sight of Will, but he had vanished, presumably he had headed to the lit space up ahead. It looked like that was the courtyard they were aiming for. Hrel came to stand alongside him and acknowledged their destination with a tip of his chin. Together, they jogged lightly along the roof until they could see into the courtyard below. It was empty of people although the torches still burned, casting their flickering light across the rocks and sand making the patterned swirls and loops dance like waves on the ocean. Jael tried to make out whether Will was lurking in the deeply shadowed corridor, just as Will's head popped round a pillar, and he beckoned for them to follow before merging back into the darkness. Lowering themselves down, they entered the corridor and found themselves opposite the large open door to the Ruaism collection. A light was emanating from within. Jael approached the door cautiously and peered inside. Will was standing beside one of the exhibits bearing a lit torch. Hrel pulled the door closed with a click. They remained motionless until Hrel gestured towards the second door. This was why they had come, to speak to Father Danin. They moved towards it. Jael already had misgivings about this plan, why on earth would the priest speak to them, surely, he would just raise the alarm and they would have to subdue him. What had they been thinking? He shook his head. They were thinking they need this information!

The door had a faint light outlining it, suggesting Father Danin was still awake. They hesitated, unsure how to approach the priest now that they were here. Will brushed his gaze over Jael's large and forceful presence, and Hrel's pleasant countenance but not so pleasant knives. He decided to enter first and tried the handle, expecting it to be locked, but it opened easily and silently. He took a tentative step forward as he rapidly assessed the small room and its contents. A bronze oil lamp balanced atop a tower of books and manuscripts on a laden desk. Unable to support them all, documents were strewn across the floor and even the small cot had papers and parchment piled high upon it. The room smelt of leather and dust.

The priest was partially hidden as he sat hunched over the desk, scratching away on a piece of parchment, the quill quivering as he wrote. The white of his robe was peppered with ink spots, the cuffs more black than white. He had a pair of square glasses perched on the tip of his nose and his large dark eyes peered through them as he worked. His rich dark skin glowed warmly in the lamp light, while his hair was a mass of tight, black curls spiralling wildly from atop his head.

Will gave a gentle cough. The man's head shot up surprised, and his hand recoiled defensively, catching the pot of ink.

246

As the ink pooled and crept towards his work, the priest frantically mopped it up with a much-stained rag, inadvertently soaking his already abused sleeve. He paid no attention to Hrel and Jael as they came up to stand behind Will, who shrugged at them nonplussed. Jael spoke softly, "Father Danin, my name is Jael, this is Hrel and Will." The priest continued to clean, but the edge of his mouth twitched in response as Jael continued. "We have come to speak to you about your prediction. We want to protect the magic when it arrives."

The priest put the rag to one side and still looking at the parchment said in a clipped baritone, "Have you come to kill me? Father Culdric was killed because the magic is coming back."

"Not at all," Jael reassured him. "We didn't kill Father Culdric and we want to stop the people that did. We will need your help though." Will and Hrel nodded their agreement, even though the priest wasn't looking at them.

Father Danin, stood up and started to pace. He was tall, slim and younger than they had expected. "They will come for me next," he said, almost as if talking to himself. "They want my research. They mustn't get it. The Bishops have my notes on the location, but I have got more information on the merging, the magic and the artifacts that they mustn't find." He stopped pacing and fixed an earnest stare in their direction. "Will you keep my research safe?" he asked.

Jael was startled that this priest would just trust them at face value, especially since his colleague's death, but he wanted to get the information he offered so he said, "We will try to keep both you and your work safe, if you wish to come with us." Hrel raised his eyebrows but didn't object.

The priest cast his eyes back at the parchment. "Alright," he said matter-of-factly as he sprinkled sand on it before gathering it up, along with one of the manuscripts, and pushed it into an already full bag.

Alarmed, Hrel explained, "We can only take what we can easily carry on our backs."

"Yes, yes, of course, I have packed the bags already." Danin gestured to three more heaving bags lying beside his cot.

Somewhat bewildered, Jael examined the top bag. It was sturdily built and was designed to be worn on the back, with straps over the shoulders and a tie across the chest. Each bag was exceedingly heavy. He sighed. This was going to be hard going. Hopefully all this stuff would be useful. He passed a bag each to Hrel and to Will and they watched with fascination as Danin slung the heaviest bag onto his delicate frame and looked in their direction expectantly.

"Right!" said Jael, drawing his attention back to the need to escape, "let's go…." and turned to exit. Hrel and Will watched as Danin extinguished the lamp and then, slowly and deliberately tipped it up, spilling the flammable liquid over the documents on the desk. He then trailed the oil along the papers on the floor and out the door. Hrel and Will exchanged a look of concern before following him out, taking care not to step in the oil.

Danin had walked up to the Statue of Rua and was caressing the soapstone sadly. Will stood poised with the torch above the oil in the doorway, not completely sure the priest wanted him to light it and glanced at Hrel, worried. Hrel coughed,

"Ahem!" Danin turned to face them and nodded slowly, his mouth turning down. Will lowered the torch to touch the oil and the orange flame chased back into the room. Hrel closed the door and they moved back scooping Danin away from the statue and towards the exit.

Jael went through the door first to ensure it was still clear, Will and Danin followed close behind. Gently pulling the door shut behind them, Hrel whispered to Danin, "Can you climb?"

Danin examined the closest pillar and then looked up at the roof, "No. Can't we use the front door?"

Will snickered, "I think them guards might object."

"True. I must try then." Danin walked pensively around the nearest pillar while Jael glanced around, conscious they shouldn't remain so exposed.

Hrel whispered to Jael, "We can lift him." Jael nodded and moved towards Danin while Hrel pulled himself up the adjacent pillar and lay flat on the roof, Will quickly scooted up behind and sat on Hrel's legs while Jael crouched and encouraged a willing but surprised Danin to sit on his shoulders. The robe proved cumbersome and Danin shrugged it off to reveal a pair of dark trousers and a bare torso. Danin put his bag back on while Jael kicked the robe behind a rock. They tried again and this time Danin quickly managed to get seated. Jael rose up, arms wrapped around a swaying Danin's shins while Danin reached up to meet Hrel's outstretched hands. Grasping hold of Danin's wrists, Hrel hauled him up as the sound of approaching footsteps echoed on the marble floor. Jael hastened to reach the roof, flattening out just as two guards turned the corner. Shit! He could see that part of the robe was still exposed. He held his breath as the guards' grumbling neared, "and so I told him that I wasn't up for that, I was going to stick with my one and that was that."

"He needed to know that. He's full of bullshit."

"Yeah. Full of it." the voices and steps passed by, the robe unnoticed, as they focussed on their petty grievance. Jael crept away from the edge, heading towards the others.

"Here, can you smell that?" one guard said, his footsteps halting. Jael paused to listen, heart pounding.

"What?" said the other confused.

"Smoke!"

"Nah. What you going on about?"

Jael and the others jogged along the roof careful not to make a noise, until they came to the base of the next wall.

The guard retraced his steps and sniffed loudly. "Here! There's smoke, I tell you." The other guard joined him, snuffling.

"It's in there…. !" he exclaimed reaching for the door…

Will and Hrel swiftly scaled the wall. Ready for the lift this time, Danin promptly climbed onto Jael's shoulders and in short shrift they were all on the roof.

Calls of "Fire!" were answered by feet pounding down the marble corridors and barked orders to "Get the damn water!".

Getting ready to traverse the gap between the next two buildings, Will untied his final rope, and handed Hrel one end. Shaking loose the rest of the rope he wrapped the other end around his wrist before taking a running leap toward the opposite wall and pushing upwards on his extended leg in a running motion as soon as it touched the wall. Stretching up he managed to grab hold of the ledge and pull himself up. Resting his hands on his hips he gave a big exhale before raising his thumb. Not doing that again, he thought, adjusting the weight of the bag on his back. He then tied the rope to the chimney with a secure bowline knot. Hrel secured his end similarly.

Danin eyed the rope warily as Jael attempted a reassuring smile, despite the urgency of the situation. He explained how to cross the rope as he demonstrated the actions, "Hold on with your hands and hook your ankles over the rope. Then just crawl along." He hung, sloth like, before he started to move along the rope. As he climbed, he could feel the heavy backpack pulling him down. It wasn't enough to be a problem for him, but he faltered as he regarded the bag on Danin's back. Hrel was on it. "I'll get it across" he said as he slipped the bag off the priest's shoulders. Anxious eyes fixed on the bag before flickering up to meet Hrel's then down again. Danin gave a brief nod then wiggled to get into position. He gripped tightly as he felt his weight rest on his heels. Then carefully he released his left hand and right foot and moved them a fraction further along the rope. The rope bobbed and he gulped. "That's it! Keep going!" said Hrel in a strained voice, as the sounds of alarm mounted behind them. They needed to get out of here.

Danin continued along the rope, moving faster as he gained

confidence. Impatient, Hrel stared at Jael and motioned to speed it up. Jael leant down over the rope, ready to grab Danin and drag him over as soon as he could. Hrel could hear voices yelling about a kidnapping, calling out more guards. They must have found the robe. It wouldn't be long before they started searching the rooftops. He slipped Danin's bag onto the rope before Danin had finished crossing. As soon as Jael had pulled him up, Hrel was crawling along the rope, pushing the bag ahead of him. He traversed the gap at speed and slashed through the rope before dashing across the roof to join the others. The rope they had left to help them scale the wall and escape was being attached to Danin while Jael climbed it, tucking the rope around his legs and feet as he hoisted himself to the top of the wall. Will took the bag off Hrel and indicated that he should join Jael. Hrel rapidly scaled the rope, like the rigger he once was, leaving Will to fasten the bag and then swing a startled Danin and himself towards the wall. He held his feet up high, and they bounced gently off the wall, absorbing the impact for Danin. He felt the rope tug upwards as Hrel and Jael began hauling them up and used his feet to walk them up in a controlled ascent. Danin clung onto the rope, wide eyes staring at the guards appearing on the rooftops, spreading out and searching for him.

Close to the top, Will latched onto the wall and scooted across to wipe away the remaining traces of the chalk cross while Hrel helped Danin untangle himself and place the bag on his back. He then threw the rope over the other side of the wall and showed Danin how to create a harness out of the rope that would support and slow his descent. The lesson was sharp and urgent, and Hrel remained close to Danin as he descended.

The last to begin the abseil, Will grabbed the final rope, stepping between the two strands and wrapping them around his waist. From up here he could see and hear the shouts of the guards. They were getting closer. He brought the two new strands forward and stepped over them, so his feet were on the outside before bringing the strands up to form a harness around his crotch. His leather trousers should reduce friction burns, but it was a long way down. Poor Danin would need some ointment. Holding the two strands of rope in his right hand he leant out, almost horizontal to the wall, gently edging the rope through his hands. He controlled his descent, by walking against the wall and using the friction of the rope.

He could hear the shouts of the guards as they found the ends of their first rope. He began bouncing off the wall, dropping faster. Sod the friction burns! When his feet finally touched the ground, he could have bent down and kissed it. Instead, he unwrapped the rope from his legs and pulled one end free from the piton to tumble down beside him. He then checked the others had done the same. Danin was hobbling slightly, but he didn't complain as they ran blind, following the line of the wall towards the noise and light of the quayside.

It didn't appear that the guards had left the city walls yet, but it wouldn't be long. Hrel whistled a lively sea shanty, and one by one, members of his crew started to move away from the crowd to mill around closer to the wall. They greeted each other with loud laughter and congregated as if ready to head back to the ship together. Hrel and the others were soon engulfed and herded towards the wharf as part of a jovial group, at the end of a night's revelry. The gates were opening as they approached, and their group mimicked the other merrymakers who stopped and stared at the unprecedented event. Guards poured out of the city and surged towards the quayside while those bearing torches searched around the wall. A unit of five guards headed in their direction. Closing in tighter, Danin was shielded from their sight.

A couple of female pirates sashayed towards the guards with a drunken giggle, calling out, "Have you finally been let out to have some fun?" While the other brazenly said, "I've always wanted to see what's under those uniforms."

Ribald laughter accompanied this, as another pirate shouted, "Probably some frills and lace!"

The guards ignored the drunken jesting. "Have you seen anyone suspicious carrying or dragging a young man."

An inebriated man from an adjacent group piped up, "Plenty of people have needed carrying back to their ships. The beer is cheap tonight!" Another burst of laughter followed this.

"Where have they been taken?" the guards' focus now settled on the other group. Taking advantage of the distraction, the pirates continued their light-hearted journey along the wharf, keeping Danin safely hidden within. When nothing useful was forthcoming from the other group, the exasperated guard waved his unit to move on towards the quayside and the next group of partygoers.

Uisca was pacing the quarterdeck, throwing anxious glances towards the guards searching the city wall, while Susan and Triene sat with Wolf lying across their feet, silently watching and waiting. They heard the pirates climbing aboard and eagerly ran to the waist of the ship to greet them.

Hrel was the first of the adventurers to reach the top and he dropped his bag onto the deck sinking into Uisca's open arms. Then came Will, tired but excited, and he was scooped up in a celebratory hug by Triene, who had deliberately let Susan greet Jael first. Danin and Jael came up the gangway together and while Danin looked around with interest, Susan wrapped her arms around Jael's waist and pressed her cheek into his chest. He held her in a tight embrace. "I'm glad you are safe." She whispered tipping her face up to stare at his weary expression. He leant down to kiss her forehead tenderly. The Steward nudged them aside as he and two other sailors worked on returning the gangway to the ship.

Hrel led the way back to his quarters and the bags containing Danin's papers were placed on the large table. Danin hurried over to the first bag and started lining up the contents. As he worked, his mouth moved in a silent vocalisation of the system he followed. Susan reached for a bag to help, but Danin squealed at her and snatched the bag away. She slowly backed up and stood with the others giving Jael a questioning look. Jael shrugged non-committedly, but Will nodded sagely and advised, "I seen this before. There was this old bloke, down in Carnom, who had to sit in the same seat and 'ave the same food every time 'e went to the The Flying 'Orse. 'E'd lay everything out on the table, and clean 'is fork before putting it down. 'E'd then separate all the food on the plate and eat each bit, one at a time. 'E ate it in the same order every time. I reckon this is a bit like that." They watched Danin frown and rearrange two of the books.

Uisca cautiously leant in to move the discarded bags out of his way. Danin didn't appear to notice, but when he had emptied the final bag he passed it directly to Uisca. Eventually all the contents were laid out in a manner to Danin's satisfaction, and he plonked his rear into the nearest chair and regarded them over the top of his glasses.

"Why aren't you sitting down?" he asked curiously. They hastily found and sat in the chairs near the table and faced Father Danin, who spoke as if they were already in the middle of a conversation. "It will continue to guide us, I'm sure." He nodded vigorously at them.

Confused, they glanced at one another before Hrel asked, "What will guide us?"

"The prophesy, of course." Danin exclaimed as if surprised by the question.

"You know all about the prophesy?" asked Susan, eager to hear more.

"Why yes, Selene and I had a very interesting discussion about it when we met last year, and here we all are." He nodded rapidly before continuing. "I'm the Preacher for Air," he pointed to Triene, "the Fortress of Fire, and the Captain here must be Driftwood on Water". He then indicated to Will and Susan, "The Child, the Stranger." He waved his hand at Jael who was standing next to Susan, his arm around her shoulder. "The Weapon of Earth, of course." They were all looking at Danin in surprise, but at his next words their mouths dropped open in shock, "the Vessel of Spirit" he pointed to Wolf, who was stretched out on the rug but raised his head to acknowledge his inclusion.

## Chapter 21

Triene spluttered, "But how can Wolf be a Spirit elder? He's not human!"

Father Danin frowned at her, "Of course he is human." he stated as if her comment were absurd. He then continued, "We need to consult the lost Spirit elders. We have until the autumn. That should be time enough, although we should start soon." He looked expectantly at the others.

Hrel was the quickest to recover from Danin's revelations, "The lost Spirit elders? But if they are lost how will we find them? I haven't even heard of them before!"

"Indeed, they have been a most interesting omission from our histories. The Spirit elders kept themselves apart from the rest of humanity once the other magic users started straying from the path of Rua." Danin pushed his slipping glasses higher up on his nose. "As a consequence, only the oldest scrolls mention them."

"What do those scrolls say about them?" asked Susan.

Danin bobbed his head as he expounded on the subject, "A most interesting area of study, which Father Culdric was working on in his spare time. He was kind enough to share some of his findings with me and, if I do say so myself, I was able to provide assistance in clarifying some of the text." Hrel coughed meaningfully, but Danin didn't take the hint, merely saying, "I recommend some water to refresh the throat, that does the trick for me when I get an irritating cough. Now where was I?"

Susan quickly offered, "You were explaining what the scrolls said about the Spirit elders."

To their relief, Danin got straight to the point this time, "The Spirit elders were described as humans that shared a spirit with an animal. Their physical form could shift between the two, at will. Both aspects of their being were said to be present in each form, with the animal's unique senses and abilities being heightened in the human form and the human ability to think tactically and imaginatively present in the animal form." All eyes, save Danin's drifted to Wolf who was still lying on the floor although his ears were pricked as he listened to the priest's words.

Jael directed the conversation to their current problem, "So where are they now and why do you think they can help us?"

Danin adjusted his glasses again, and addressed his answer to the books on the table, "Father Culdric's research suggested that they had the closest bond with the magic. He was working on a theory that they were best placed to use the artifacts, despite the writings never mentioning their interaction with them... of course, the Spirit elders didn't keep written records, so we don't know for sure. The other elders were focussed on their own communities and rarely mention them; however, the earliest chronicles do suggest a greater empathy with the magic. It is highly probable that their lack of contact with others will have preserved their understanding. Yes, yes, they are the ones best placed to help us." He nodded his agreement with his own advice, before adding, "We need to head to the Wuhynga islands." He finally looked at Jael, confident that he had explained matters satisfactorily.

Hrel glanced at the other confused faces before voicing his concerns, "Please forgive me if I have misunderstood, but the chance of getting help from them appears slim. Furthermore, the Wuhynga islands are volcanic and considered uninhabitable. They are also a good month's sailing hence."

Danin frowned at Hrel saying firmly, "Father Culdric was a respected expert in his field, I have no doubt his suppositions are sound. You are already following a prophesy, and my own theories with regards to the merging of the worlds, I consider this expedition a mere extension of this activity."

Hrel gave a half smile and held his hands up in mock surrender. "I guess we are sailing to the Wuhynga islands," he said, turning to look at Uisca who nodded and went to seek out the appropriate map from behind the desk.

Triene finally spoke up, her voice a little shaky as she tore her eyes from Wolf's furry face. "Wolf hasn't ever shifted, are you sure he is a Spirit elder?"

"Oh yes, the prophesy is clear. I expect it takes more magic than is in the world at present, to shift from one form into another."

Susan gasped, "You mean he is stuck in a wolf's body!"

Danin snapped his brows together, "Have you not been listening? He is both the spirit of a human and a wolf, regardless of the form his physical appearance takes! It matters not which form he is in."

Susan murmured an apology and stepped back towards Jael. Uncomfortable, following his outburst, Danin faced the table and began straightening and touching his writing materials and parchments, his movements jerky. It was obvious that he would not be speaking to them for a while.

Hrel turned to face Jael and said teasingly, "Earth elder, eh? Well, we are a talented lot. When did you plan on telling me?"

Jael managed to look sheepish, but Susan jumped to his defence, "Not many people are as accepting of magic as your crew are of yours." To her annoyance, both Hrel and Jael looked at her with amusement, Jael's mouth twitching to reveal his dimples. Fortunately, they were interrupted by a knock at the door before Susan could express her indignation.

The quartermaster walked in, his face serious as he announced without any preamble, "The guards be boarding vessels now. They still be bothering the traders, but it won't be long afore they reach us." This immediately got everyone's full attention. "We can try an 'ide 'im" he nodded at Danin and the laden table, "or set sail. There's only a couple of ships 'tween us and the open sea, and if there be any smaller vessels, well, they shouldn't be out there at night." he added darkly.

Hrel glanced over at Uisca, "Are you in a position to navigate?" he asked him, his voice all business now. Uisca gave a brisk nod. Hrel turned back to the quartermaster, "Well then, let us set sail!"

"Aye, Cap'n," he said, before casting a fatherly look over Hrel's worn features. "Ye need sleep." Then looking around at the others he added brusquely, "Ye should all sleep."

With that advice given, he spun on his heels and headed for the deck, Uisca following, his bag and maps in hand.

"You heard the man, off to bed and our gentle slumbers," said Hrel drolly, then looking at Danin, "We need to find you a cot."

Later that morning the companions gathered once again in the Captain's quarters. Danin had been the first to wake, and he had wandered into the cabin unannounced, settling into his work while Hrel slept. Hrel woke to the sound of quill scratching parchment, as Danin toiled over his latest translation. Somewhat bemused, Hrel wrapped his sheet around his waist as he rose from his bed and wandered over to his chest of clothes. Fortunately, the screen hadn't been removed so he ducked behind that and quickly dressed. Danin seemed oblivious to Hrel's preparations and jumped when Hrel finally greeted him with a jovial, "Good morning, Father Danin".

"Oh, um. Yes. Good morning to you too. Hrel, isn't it?" Danin replied, pushing his glasses up as he looked in Hrel's general direction.

"It is indeed. Hrel, Captain of the finest ship, the infamous Coral Skies, pirate king and...." Hrel began, but Danin's attention was already back on his work, so with an amused shrug, Hrel moved over to his own desk and started completing his journal entries, recent events having delayed them somewhat.

They were in this state of quiet study when Uisca entered bearing breakfast and went to sit with Hrel at the desk. He was soon followed by Jael and Susan, Will, Wolf and Triene who all took their places around the main table. They had also brought food and drink with them and offered some to Danin, who absently nibbled on a corner of hard, yellow cheese as he worked.

While they broke their fast, Will tipped the five gemstones onto the table and they peered at them curiously, wondering how they worked. Triene was again drawn to the red gem, and she reached out and laid her hand above it. The pulse of magic brightened, and she could feel a tingle in her palm. "May I hold it?" she asked Will. She could sense the magic hiding in the stone; perhaps if she held the artifact, she would be able to connect with it.

"Course!" he declared, and immediately put it into her hand.

"It's beautiful," Triene breathed. She could feel the magic pulsing within the stone, as if it were alive. Her own magic danced in her mind, sending the remaining darkness scurrying, the whispered messages of danger, of loss, drowned out by the cries of excitement. She tilted her head slightly and a delicate frown creased her brow. Her eyes narrowed in concentration, but it was no good, "I can't communicate with it."

Hrel bounced over and snatched it from her hands. "No, no, no!" he exclaimed. Jael stood up ready to snatch it back, Wolf's lips curled and his hackles rose. Even Triene looked annoyed until Hrel quickly explained, "Fire on a ship is the stuff of nightmares, I beg you refrain from experimenting with the magics until we reach land, my dear Fortress of Fire." Jael sat back down with a nod of acknowledgement and a shaken Triene apologised, "I'm sorry, I didn't think."

"All's well, just don't do it again while on board my ship, dear heart," he said, placing it back on the table.

Danin had noticed the exchange with interest and added, "Yes, indeed. The first time using the magic within an artifact can be most unpredictable."

Since Danin had put his quill down and seemed willing to communicate, Susan decided to ask him, "Would you be able to explain the artifacts to us? We really don't understand much about them except that the ancients and mages were able to use them to access or channel more magic."

Danin made a beeline for a large book at the bottom of a pile. He carefully removed each in turn until he reached the one he wanted. He pulled the large leather-bound tome towards himself and replaced the other books in the same spot, ensuring they stayed in the same order. The others waited, unsure whether Danin planned to use the book to answer the question or to resume his studies. Uisca pulled up a chair and joined them round the table with a questioning look at Hrel who merely shrugged. Danin flicked through the pages and finding the one he sought, held it open to show them all a diagram of a red rock, surrounded by writing in the ancient language. Danin pointed to the text as he stated, "This entry is of particular interest as it describes the finding of the first artifact, the Heart of Rua." Danin then added with a tinge of annoyance, "The book with most information on the artifacts was stolen, of course, but fortunately I recall some of it and will include it in this discourse."

He put the book down on the table and pressed the tips of his fingers together to make a steeple of his hands and closed his eyes. Realising that this was going to be a long explanation the others made themselves comfortable. Wolf lay down on the floor between Will and Triene, head resting on his front paws. Jael slipped his arm around Susan's shoulders, and she leant into him, while Hrel leant back in his chair and put his booted feet on the table, crossing them at the ankle.

Danin opened his eyes and began, "In the time of Intuiqui the Third, the ancients were guided by the elders, those with the power of the magic. The elders were responsible for the worship of the Goddess Rua and maintaining balance. One of the responsibilities of the Earth elders was mining. They used their magic to sense the item sought and could control any necessary crack in the earth. They would repair the fissures and encourage plant growth to minimise the disruption caused by their mining.

"On one such mining expedition, the Earth elders detected a magical pulse buried deep within the rock. They excavated and in doing so discovered the source of that magic, the artifact they later named the Heart of Rua. It was the first such find and was treated with a great deal of reverence. It was regarded as a gift from the Goddess; some even declared it to be the Goddess' actual heart." Danin paused before clarifying, "Father Culdric determined that the stone is in most likely carnelian." Satisfied that the actual structure of the Heart had been made clear, he continued. "The elders built the first shrine of the ancients and placed the Heart deep within it. As news of the artifact spread to other settlements, pilgrims regularly visited the shrine to pay homage."

"The ancients now actively looked for similar artifacts but it

264

took more than a century for the Mouth of Rua to be found. The Mouth was described as an extremely large black rock, probably an onyx. The next artifact to be discovered was the Eye of Rua, which we had in our collection until it was stolen. The unique colouration within the amber was obviously the reason for its name. The Ear of Rua was discovered shortly thereafter and was the most delicate of the artifacts, namely a mother of pearl shell. I fear that it will not have survived the subsequent centuries, although I remain hopeful that the magic was sufficient to protect it." Danin sighed. "Of course, the last documented find was regarded as the most powerful of the artifacts. It was called the Hand of Rua because it was made up of five stones, each representing one of the elements."

Hrel dropped his feet to the floor and leant forward as they all stared at the gems on the table. Danin didn't give them time to ponder this disclosure, however, as he continued. "It wasn't until the time of Babayeye the First, some two hundred or so years later, that the elders found a way to access the magic in the artifacts. It was an Air elder that first discovered it when handling the Ear of Rua. He accidently created a storm that nearly wiped out the village before he gained control of it. He reported on this in the Chronicles of the day and soon after, other elders conducted experiments to access the magic in the artifacts.

The additional power the artifacts provided proved useful when nature unleashed its full force: the Chronicles record Fire elders controlling the flow of lava so that it avoided a settlement; Air elders dispersing a hurricane and so on." Danin shook his head slowly as he added. "Of course, you will be aware of the more recent Mage Wars, when the artifacts were used to create much devastation."

"True," agreed Jael solemnly.

Susan's curiosity bubbled up until she had to interrupt, "How did the elders access the magic in the artifacts? It must have been difficult if it took so long to discover." The others all leaned forward, eager to hear the answer.

"Father Culdric had been researching that for the Bishop, and his work was largely based on the contents of the stolen book. He did discuss his research with me, of course, but I don't have all the information I am afraid." Danin looked crestfallen at this lack of knowledge, "This is why we need the Spirit elders, you see?" he stated earnestly.

Susan reassured him, "We are seeking them, but perhaps, in the meantime, you would share what you do know…"

"Of course, of course!". Danin's eyes squeezed shut and his mouth trembled slightly as if repeating a remembered conversation. With a start, he opened his eyes wide and provided the information, "The elders discovered that the magic within the artifacts is similar to the magic that resides within an elder. Magic is drawn to the artifact and stored there. It needs to be persuaded to leave it. This can be a difficult task."

"I can imagine," mumbled Hrel.

"The process requires a delicacy of touch."

"Of course it does," grumbled Jael.

"How is it done? I haven't seen a way of communicating with the artifact magic. Is it because most of the magic has

266

gone from our world?" asked Triene.

Danin pondered this before advising, "That could be the case, but is unlikely, since only the magic within a mage is required for the connection." Danin continued, "The writings indicated that the initial connection is the hardest one, and once the connection is made it becomes easier to control."

Susan commented, "That makes sense."

"I haven't attempted it myself, despite the temptation. The Bishops were most adamant that magic users were a danger to their authority. Furthermore, I understand that the process of gaining that first connection requires complete relaxation of the mind, which I was unable to achieve while in the Temple."

"Meditation!" exclaimed Susan. The others looked at her with puzzled expressions. "Meditation is a practice in my old world where people focus on balancing their minds and bodies to attain a complete state of relaxation. It is said to give a state of heightened awareness and focused attention."

"Yes, indeed. That does sound appropriate. How does one meditate?" inquired an intrigued Danin. The others' attention was on Susan now, and her eyes flicked from one hopeful expression to another. Oh dear, what had she got herself into now?

"I used to do Pilates classes. Our teacher used to stress the link to meditation as we moved and held different positions."

Triene asked eagerly, "Can you teach us this Pilates?"

Susan replied, "Er, I can try. I'm not an expert but I can show you some of the techniques".

"That is excellent news!" said Danin rubbing his hands together. "We should start immediately".

Hrel interrupted the resulting excitement, "As Captain of this ship, I must dedicate some of my day to my duties. Perhaps we should undertake our work on board, before we meet again this evening?" he suggested with an amenable smile. "Poor Uisca will also need some sleep before navigating tonight." Uisca gave a big yawn on cue and Triene apologised to him for their thoughtlessness as they exited the quarters. Danin remained at the table and was soon absorbed in his work once more. Uisca ignored him and simply headed for bed.

Jael tugged Susan to one side just outside the door. He had been trying to kiss her for days and this seemed to be a good opportunity. She had been snuggling into him a lot and her greeting when he returned last night made him think she shared his ambition. They let the others pass by and make their way to the deck. As soon as they were alone, he pulled her in close, slipping one large hand gently around her waist, the other up to caress the base of her neck. He examined her face to make sure she was happy with this, then bent down to kiss her softly. She wrapped her arms around him, smoothing her hands along the strong muscles of his back as she returned the kiss, sighing into his mouth.

Jael pulled his head back slightly to look at her again. She gave him a sappy smile and he was sure his own smile looked just as sappy. It wasn't just sex, he thought, although his eyes dropped to her chest as his hand slid up to caress her breast through the material. He loved her breasts, they were soft and full and jiggled beautifully as she moved. She blushed slightly but pressed into him, sliding her own hands lower to rest on his arse.

Susan's pulse was pounding furiously as she moved closer to kiss Jael again. He was the sexiest man she had ever kissed, but hell, he was also the kindest. What a combination! She was a goner for sure!

Their lips met and this time the kiss was more urgent than before, however, the sound of approaching crew members had them pulling apart and standing awkwardly, feeling oddly guilty. The pirates nudged each other and chuckled at their flushed faces as they passed. Susan giggled; they were being ridiculous. Acting like teenagers caught making out by parents. Jael responded to her laugh with his own sexy grin before giving her a gentle kiss. His husky, "Later?" was faintly uncertain as if still unsure of her. Susan flushed brightly, as she nodded enthusiastically. His grin widened, his voice confident now as he whispered in her ear, "I can't wait."

"Me too." Susan replied shyly, reaching up to pat down her mussed hair. She really wanted to continue this later, her blood was on fire from just a couple of kisses! She watched him walk away, eyes dropping to his tight butt cheeks. She was still breathing heavily when she reached the deck and reported for duty. She was going to enjoy every minute of her time with Jael. She really liked him, he was kind, caring, tough and strong. Wow! Scarily perfect! Well, he was a bit of a grump but hell, that was sexy too!

She set to work sluicing the deck, a mindless chore that

allowed her to daydream and worry. The daydreams were sexy, and not appropriate for the company she kept on this job, and the worries were her age-old insecurities of being unlovable. Bloody parents started it and her lousy choices in bedfellows perpetuated it. To be honest though, the latter was at least partly her fault. She hadn't really been willing to invest in a relationship then. She sat up. Was that what she was doing now? Looking for more from Jael? Oh God! She was!

The girl working beside her gave her a vicious prod with her elbow and Susan gave her an apologetic smile and got back to work. Her mind still reeled from her realisation though and her insecurities flooded her thoughts. New start! She told herself over and over again. She would not be tied to her old life and her old failures. She would embrace this opportunity, and if it didn't work, then, well, she would do her best, whatever happened. This wasn't just sex. Jael knew her and still liked her. He seemed to find her amusing and wanted to be with her in other ways too. God, he was so hot! she sighed. Her mind continued in this vein and the day progressed until she started worrying about the Pilates. The need to prepare for the lesson replaced her other concerns as she focused on remembering Janice's classes.

## Chapter 22

Raul tottered through the corridors of the inner sanctum, his bejewelled, heeled shoes clicking on the marble, his breath coming in gasps. He was flanked by two of the Temple guard who loomed over him and walked faster than was comfortable. His body was getting damp from having to take two steps for each of theirs. His personal guard knew to walk at a proper speed, but they had had to remain in the outer rooms. Ridiculous! Not far along the corridor they came to a halt outside a familiar door, Bishop Istane's rooms of business. One of the guards knocked briskly on the door and waited for permission before opening it and allowing Raul entry. The guards filed in behind him before pulling the door to and standing either side of it, while Raul walked towards the two seats in the centre of the room. An older man, with a trim salt and pepper beard sat in the plush, plum velvet armchair. His plain black robe fell open at the neck to reveal a silk shirt of shimmering silver and a large opal pendant. His elbow rested on the arm of the chair, and he casually held a pewter goblet in his hand. A matching opal ring encircled his finger.

The Bishop nodded his acknowledgement of Raul's presence, before saying with an ironic quirk of his lips, "Ah, Raul, a pleasure as always." Remaining seated he took a deliberate sip of his drink, as he watched Raul shuffle his ample rear into the opposite seat. A low table crouched between the chairs, upon which sat a decanter of wine and a bowl of sweet treats. There was no second goblet and no invitation to partake. Raul reached over and took one of the treats anyway. The Bishop reacted much as he had hoped.

Eyebrows snapping together, he set the goblet down with a sharp clunk.

"I have come to collect," Raul stated arrogantly.

"It is not ready," retorted the Bishop sharply. "You will have to wait."

Raul frowned, "Our deal was that it would be ready today. The information is time critical."

"With the loss of Father Culdric we only had one priest able to conduct the research. It is not ready," the Bishop restated, chin raising until he looked down his nose at the impertinent merchant.

Raul shifted forward in his seat. "This is the second time you have failed to comply with our contract," he sneered. "Take care or your Temple will gain a reputation for reneging."

The Bishop gripped the arms of his chair tightly, knuckles whitening as he hissed, "I believe it is you that need take care, Raul. You do not want to make an enemy of the Temple." He took a breath and consciously relaxed his grip, leaning into the comforts of his chair before declaring, "In any event, we have a new priest in charge of the work and he is sifting through the remains of the fire before he can complete the research."

Raul exploded out of his seat, spitting as he yelled, "Fire! Have you lost my information?" The guards were beside Raul in an instant, pushing him back into his chair. Shaking with fury, his face turning an unpleasant shade of puce, Raul spluttered, "I will take my initial payment then. Once again you have wasted my time!"

The smug Bishop gave a faux smile, which revealed yellow, uneven teeth. "I do have the first report, of course. It contains the general location, I believe."

Raul eyed the Bishop bitterly, "And for this limited information you will keep my payment, I suppose?"

The Bishop's smile widened, "That would be an appropriate fee for the satisfaction of this aspect of the agreement."

Raul pushed himself out of his seat once more, his anger barely contained, and held out his shaking hand. "Very well, hand it over," he growled. The guards had remained close and their presence ensured his restraint as the Bishop smirked and withdrew a single sheet of parchment from inside his robe. He handed it to a guard who then passed it to a Raul. "This is it?" Raul asked his lip curling, as he crushed it in his hand.

"The research was most challenging," replied the Bishop haughtily.

Raul turned his back on the Bishop and stormed towards the door, where he stopped and, in a futile attempt to exert control, declared, "I will expect the rest of the information by the end of the second week." He then exited the room, head held high.

## Chapter 23

Back at the camp, a mile or so away, the new recruits were busy. The lucrative pay and the opportunity for violence had proved appealing to so many that the army had grown tenfold. The crops in the commandeered fields had been flattened and ground into the mud by repeated attempts at disciplined drills and combat training, the swathe of crimson attire and the clash of swords a promise of the bloodshed to come.

The Commander was sitting alone on a stool near the edge of the camp, honing and sharpening his sword. His uniform jacket had been tossed onto the dirt and his white linen shirt was untied at the neck. His shirtsleeves were rolled up to over his elbows, revealing strong forearms with a light dusting of hair. He fished the coarse whetstone from the bucket of water between his feet and began sliding it diagonally across the blade's edge. His movements were firm and steady, as he worked on smoothing away any kinks or nicks. The grinding against the steel made an even and satisfying sound. The merchant's carriage and entourage returned from the Temple, invoking a flurry of activity, but the Commander paid them no heed. Wiping the blade with the dry rag draped over his thigh he checked the new edge by sliding his thumb along the fuller and then by holding the sword up and watching how the light reflected on the steel. Pleased with the results of his inspection he replaced the coarse with the fine grain whetstone and proceeded to use it to make the edges razor sharp.

Raul squeezed himself out of the carriage's narrow door and tottered down the step, abusing the servant attempting to assist him. "I can get out of a damn carriage! Move away!" he shouted impatiently, although it should be noted that he placed his sweaty palm on a nearby shoulder as he descended. He demanded of his servant, "Get me refreshments." As the servant ran to get the supplies, a soldier accompanied Raul to his tent and stood guard outside while Raul stormed within.

The Commander dropped the whetstone to the ground beside the bucket and wiped the clean cloth over the blade, taking care to remove the remnants of the water and stone from its surface. Once polished he held it up for a final inspection, the cleaned steel glinted in the sun. With a satisfied smile, he slipped the sword into its scabbard before checking the leather bindings on the grip. No repairs required, he stood up and secured the scabbard around his waist and thigh. Rolling down his sleeves, the Commander walked unhurriedly towards the merchant's tent.

As he drew alongside some of his soldiers training the new recruits in the use of a broadsword, he halted to assess their calibre. The instructing sergeant's eyes flickered nervously towards the newcomer and he immediately shouted some directions to the recruits, "Pagd, keep on the balls of your feet... Yinle, keep your eyes on his shoulder not his hand." The recruits barely acknowledged the instructions, their efforts continued to lack focus and lustre as the experienced soldiers took them through various manoeuvres.

The sergeant trembled slightly at the Commander's prolonged silence, unable to tell what he was thinking from his placid expression. When he chose to speak it was in a pleasant tone, "Get your men to cut them," he suggested. "That will inspire them to heed their lessons."

The sergeant immediately cried out the order, "Aim to wound!" relieved that he was not the recipient of the Commander's displeasure on this occasion. The first cry of pain from a recruit brought a slight smile to the Commander's face, and he resumed his journey towards the tent. He was still smiling when he stood in front of the flap that served as a door. Without looking at the guard he gave the quiet order, "Dismissed." and the guard scurried away. The Commander brushed aside the flap and entered the tent.

Raul was reclining in a long chair, his bare feet barely reaching the end. He had a goblet of wine in one hand, resting on his raised belly, while a half-eaten sugary confection was in the other. White sugar powdered his lips which he licked nervously as the Commander came in, smiled and took the seat beside the small table. Impertinent! thought Raul, although something in the Commander's manner made him hasten to put the goblet and leftover cake down and wipe his sticky fingers on a cloth napkin before dabbing his chin and tunic, not quite removing the residue. The Commander waited patiently, noting as he did so, that a new parchment was sitting on the table next to the Eye of Rua and ancient tome. When Raul had finished cleaning up, the Commander asked encouragingly, "How fared your trip to the Temple?"

Raul licked his lips again, then explained with an indignant wobble of his chin, "The fools had a fire and lost the research. All they gave me was a vague location!".

The Commander's smile slipped and with a concerned furrow of his brows he stated, "Just a location, no date"

Assuming the Commander shared his own disbelief at the

Bishop's incompetence, Raul replied, "No, indeed! It is appalling and I shall complain to the Archbishop. This is the second time they have failed me!"

The Commander gently pointed out, "Yes, but the first time, wasn't really their fault, now was it?" and he inclined his head towards the table's contents.

Raul spluttered, "That's not the point! I paid for information, and they didn't provide it!"

Uninterested in Raul's pique, the Commander picked up the parchment, "Does this have the location details?".

Raul's expression turned sullen. "Yes, for what it's worth. We still need the rest of the information."

"But this is all we have...It will have to do." The Commander skimmed the writing before he slipped the parchment inside his shirt. Raul's eyes widened at this blatant challenge to his authority. The Commander watched Raul pleasantly as understanding of the danger facing him began to dawn on the merchant and waited to see if Raul would make the first move. Raul shifted on the sofa, uncertain eyes darting between the Eye of Rua and the Commander's sword. The Commander continued speaking. "It is a shame the rest of the information is unavailable, but at least this will get me to the right area." The Commander then deliberately moved to rest his elbows on his thighs dropping his clasped hands between his knees. Raul's eye twitched as he stared at the hands, indecisive as ever.

The Commander sighed inwardly, what would it take to get the idiot to act? "I guess, this is the end of our agreement, then," he said agreeably.

Raul winced, his breath coming faster. He tried to bargain, the merchant in him stronger than the mage, "but you need my wealth to pay the soldiers and feed them." His voice came out whiney and desperate.

"My dear, dear friend," said the Commander reassuringly, "I already have your wealth."

Raul tried to give a whimsical laugh, as if the Commander were joking, but it turned into a cough. Pure panic was coursing through Raul now, and he tried to draw in as much air magic as possible. Unable to reach the Eye, he was limited in the power he could control. Shooting a mini tornado towards the Commander, Raul pushed himself up from the chair as he shouted, "Help! Help me!" to the guard he believed was still outside the tent. The slow bob of his paunch hindered his movements as he tried to run.

Finally! thought the Commander as he easily dodged the spinning air. The tornado ripped into the now empty chair, smashing it into kindling before it dwindled to a mere breeze that fluttered the tent walls. The Commander moved in a graceful arc as he slid his sword from its casing and spun, slicing into the back of Raul's knees before coming to rest with the sword held out at a right angle to his waist, arm fully extended. A red streak followed the sword's path and Raul's legs folded, his face hitting the edge of the table as he collapsed. The impact broke his nose with a loud crunch, before he landed face down on his prized rug, his belly bouncing the rest of his body as he landed. He emitted a bubbling sound as blood poured from his nose, flooding his mouth and pooling onto the rug.

The Commander stood over him, watching with amusement as Raul stretched out his hand, grabbing at the rug in a helpless attempt to escape death. Using the point of his sword, the Commander, caressed Raul's inner elbow, deepening it as he reached the inside edge in order to detach the tendon. He then crouched down, taking care to avoid the blood, and spoke quietly in Raul's ear, "I thank you for your contribution to my success in this venture." He then rose and used the sole of his boot to roll the merchant onto his side to face him. He made sure Raul was watching him as he formed a flame in the palm of his hand. Raul's pain filled eyes widened in final understanding. The Commander sent the flame to light the rug at the furthest corner. Raul stared as the flame slowly ate its way towards him, spreading in an ever-expanding triangle as it consumed the fabric. He desperately tried to wiggle away, but the table blocked him. He could only watch the flame expand as it grew closer, the heat sizzling his silk robes even before it reached him. He screamed.

The Commander gathered up the Eye of Rua and the book and exited the tent without a glance back at the merchant. He had got what he wanted. As he walked out, the tent fabric caught alight. The red and purple flames licked up the side walls, the acrid scent of burning canvas filled the air. Soldiers were advancing on the tent with water to deal with the fire, but the Commander halted them with a raised hand and a gentle command, "Carry on with your training. We will be marching on the morrow." The worried soldiers quickly obeyed, dropping the buckets, spilling the water on the thirsty ground, mere feet from the tent.

A drawn-out gargled scream mingled with the crackle of the

flames and the occasional pop of spitting fat. The tent collapsed and its remaining cloth dipped into the fire and burst alight. The appetising aroma of charcoaled steak combined with seasoned woody notes as the contents of the tent cooked. The soldiers carefully ignored the bonfire, finishing off their work and preparing their evening meals, until, at last, the final embers of the fire burnt out, just as the sun dipped below the horizon. The Commander stood on the edge of the camp, watching the flames. A dark, silent figure with fire dancing in his eyes.

## Chapter 24

That evening, when their shift had ended, it was time for them to make their way back to the Captain's quarters. Danin had remained there, of course, working on his research papers. Susan was the first to arrive and, to Danin's dismay, she insisted that the large table be moved. Uisca had dragged the heavy table to the side of the room with very little need for Susan's attempts at assistance. Danin had hovered while the table was in transit and pounced as soon as possible, to fuss over a toppled pile of books and shifted inkwell. No longer needed, Uisca lay down on the cot, keen to continue resting before nightfall. His eyes closed and he turned his back on the rest of the room.

Susan directed Danin to sit on the floor, closest to the table, and made sure he could stretch out easily. Her own back was pressed up against the wall so she could face the others. She removed her boots and encouraged Danin to do the same. While Danin was absorbed in untying his laces, Will sidled into the room looking uncertain. With an encouraging smile, Susan shuffled along the wall so he could sit beside her. Will quickly sat down and started removing his own boots and tucked them under the table next to the others, their unpleasant odour following them. Susan screwed up her nose and held her breath, hoping the smell would dissipate before the deep breathing exercises began.

Hrel was the next to arrive. He raised an eyebrow as he observed the others sitting on the wooden floorboards, feet bare, toes wiggling. He unbuttoned his jacket and hung it over the back of a chair. He was pulling off his boots when Wolf and Triene arrived. They all settled on the floor in front of Susan. Triene directed a wide smile in Susan's direction and wiggled excitedly as she waited. Wolf's posture was more restrained, although his ears were tipped forward and his amber eyes alert. Susan's eyes widened. She hadn't realised Wolf would be participating. Of course, he would be, she thought, annoyed with herself. He was a Spirit elder. She had no idea how to adapt the Pilates positions for him and could only hope he would manage.

Jael was the last to arrive. He had taken time to quickly wash down and grab a fresh tunic since his shift had been particularly strenuous. He was still drying off as he entered the room, not wanting to keep the others waiting. He rubbed a rough cloth over his hair leaving the damp strands in disarray. Throwing the damp cloth to the side, he began to pull his clean top over his head, hazel eyes searching the room for Susan. He caught her staring wistfully at his bare chest. He gave a smug smile that made his dimples pop. She quickly looked away but not before she had returned his smile with a cheeky grin of her own. He finished straightening his tunic and positioned himself in the space next to Triene. He was now eager for the lesson to be finished as soon as possible.

Susan swallowed around the sudden lump in her throat. What if she wasn't able to teach meditation? Goodness knows she wasn't the best at it herself! An impatient Will nudged her with his foot. "Come on then!" he said prompting her into action. Yes, just get on with it. She could only do her best and it would be better than nothing.

Channelling Janice, she moderated her voice to a lower and slower pace than normal. "Lie on your back, with your knees bent and your feet flat on the ground. Rest your arms alongside your body, hands facing down." She adjusted her position as she spoke until she was lying on the floor as described. The others stared at her before shuffling into position. Wolf lay on his back, exposing a white fluffy belly, his back legs dropping loosely, his front legs flopping by his chest. Somehow, Susan managed to suppress the giggle that bubbled up at the sight, before she continued, "Breathe slowly in through your nose… 2….3…..4….and out through your mouth…2…3…4… As you breathe in, feel the cool air fill your lungs with goodness….. As you breathe out feel the warm air expel impurities from your lungs… ". She glanced around to check everyone was concentrating before she continued, "Keep your focus on your breathing, as you move and as you stretch."

Will snickered as Wolf gave a big yawn, already very relaxed. Susan smiled, but added, making her voice even slower and drawing out some of the words, "If something catches your attention…. just acknowledge it………. then let it go…. let it float far away on your breath as you exhale."

For a couple of minutes Susan let the soft huff of breath combine with the distant sounds of life on board, and the gentle rocking motion of the sea. She then spoke quietly and evenly as she instructed them to "Gently bring your chin down to your chest… then slowly raise your chin and press the back of your head into the floor. Keep doing this as you breathe and feel the stretch in your neck. Feel it elongate and loosen." Susan watched as they started the stretch, her eyes first resting on Jael's controlled movement, lingering on the stubble clinging to his jaw, before she forced herself to look at the others. Wolf's head was tipping back and forth in an easy motion, his jaws were open and his tongue lolling to the side. She noted, however, that Hrel's brow was creased, so she added smoothly, "Feel the muscles around your eyes and your forehead soften and ease." Hrel's brow immediately relaxed. Pleased, she moved her gaze onto Danin whose head movements were jerky and tense. She crawled over and placed her hand on his neck to show him how to slow the pace and make the movement fluid. He flinched but managed to follow her lead, the tension only really easing when she released him and moved away.

Susan got back into position before continuing, "Now, find that middle point and rest your head there, feeling the weight of your skull, and the looseness in your neck muscles." She paused for a moment. "Now concentrate on the feel of your shoulder blades where they come into contact with the floor. Feel the light pressure on the bones, and muscles there." Another short pause. "Continue breathing softly and slowly…. in through your nose….. and out through your mouth…" she repeated, remembering Janice doing this reminder in her classes.

For the next hour, they worked their way through simple movements, focusing their attention on their bodies and their breathing. They all took it very seriously. Even Wolf, who participated as much as his different shape would allow, although he couldn't help but wag his tail when they all ended up posing in a play bow. They finished the session by sitting back on their heels, or haunches, backs straight and taking three final deep breaths. Feeling somewhat lightheaded, they reorientated themselves and put their boots back on in silence.

Jael was the first to speak, his tone serious and thoughtful, "That was very useful, I use a similar mental technique during combat practice, but this was more focused."

Hrel nodded, "Yes, thank you, Susan. I can see that this will be a very useful part of our daily training." He then started to chuckle softly as he beheld Will's prone figure. He was still lying on his side, eyes closed, mouth open as he breathed softly. Susan rolled her eyes, but couldn't help a fond smile. Triene grinned widely at his sleeping form as she and Wolf got up and padded out the door.

"Come on, lad. It's time for dinner," said Hrel gently shaking Will's shoulder,

Will mumbled, "Just breathing, not 'sleep."

"That's right, lad. The lesson's all finished now though," said Hrel as he stood and looked out the window to where the sun had lowered in the sky. Uisca would be needed soon. He glanced over to the cot and saw Uisca was already moving. He would be searching the skies soon enough. Uisca gave Hrel a nod as he hefted his bag of equipment and made his way towards the quarterdeck.

Hrel then turned his attention on Danin, who had pulled a chair over to the table and had already opened one of his books. "Danin!" Hrel called out, "Shall I have your evening meal sent to you or would you care to join us this evening?"

Startled from his contemplation of the text, Danin looked up at Hrel with a somewhat bewildered expression, "Oh, yes! That would be most convenient." Immediately resuming his examination of the book. Hrel gave an amused smile and retrieved his jacket.

Will was hurriedly pulling on his boots. "I don't s'pose you know what's for dinner, do you? I really 'ope its stew and bread, though a roast would be cool.... What do you think it is?" Will enthused, jumping up eager to get to the galley.

Hrel clapped a hand on Will's shoulder and said, "Cook doesn't let me in on that secret, I'm afraid. But we can go find out. Shall we?" They headed out of the room and down the steps, Will leading the way.

Jael and Susan had already left, following Uisca's footsteps up to the quarterdeck. They continued past the navigator and quartermaster who were already deep in conversation, until they reached the polished rail. They stood there unwilling to let go of their peaceful mood, as they watched the changing skies reflect on the soft wake. Jael rested one hand on the rail and wrapped his other arm around Susan's shoulders. She snuggled against his warm body, placing a hand on top of his much larger one as they soaked in the striped colours of the setting sun. The darkening sea reflected the pale orange of the horizon and shone with the burst of yellow that separated the orange from the cobalt sky. The wispy clouds cast shadows that hinted at the darkness to come.

"I love my life here," declared Susan suddenly, addressing the expanse of water in front of them. Jael watched her profile for a few moments before carefully saying, "I'm glad you are happy here. Since meeting you I.... I feel like I have been able to be myself again. I haven't felt that since my parents....." Susan glanced at him briefly and squeezed his hand. He was facing the sunset again.

The sky darkened until there was just a warm amber glow left, and Jael turned back to look at Susan once more. She was still looking at him, her eyes soft. He gently brought his hand up to cup her cheek. "I care for you, Susan," he said quietly.

She pressed her face into his hand, as she whispered back, "I care for you too." He folded her into his body, and together they watched the amber glow lower and disappear into the sea.

After a few moments, Susan stepped back from the embrace and looked up at Jael appraisingly. He dropped his arms, confused by the sudden change in her mood. With a mischievous smile she cocked her hip and said boldly, "I wonder where couples go to be alone on this ship?"

Jael's expression cleared immediately and with a wicked grin he said, "Funny you should ask that, I have discovered just the place".

"What are you waiting for, let's go take a look?" said Susan pulling on his hand. Still grinning, Jael guided her below deck.

## Chapter 25

The first night of their journey had been favoured by starlit skies, steady winds and soft sea swells. This optimistic beginning was set to continue as the warm morning sun peeped over the horizon. The crisp voice of a single tenor rang clear above the baritone creaks and groans of the ship, "Oh, blow the man down, bullies, blow the man down". The rousing response of the shanty, "Way aye, blow the man down." swirled up into the open skies, and skipped across the bobbing waves. Some of the bright notes drifted through the timbers stirring the day shift from their slumbers.

Triene tugged on Susan's blanket. "Time to wake up!" she said firmly. Susan grabbed the top of the blanket tightly and squeezed her eyes shut in a stout refusal to be woken. It didn't work, of course, especially, when Wolf gave her exposed toes a nibble. Pulling her foot away and grumbling incoherently she sat up and peered at Triene under a heavy frown. Undeterred, Triene continued speaking, "Something's up. It's not time for work yet.". Then giving Susan a poke on the arm, "Come on, get up." Susan opened her bleary eyes, not regretting her late night, but definitely feeling the effects of her lack of sleep. Peering around the quarters she noted that the rest of the crew were getting ready to leave. They seemed relaxed though, and she could hear the strains of the morning shanty filtering down, so she didn't know what had got Triene fussing. She dragged herself out of her cot and washed in the cool water set out for that purpose, her treacherous mind, still half asleep, lingered on memories of steaming hot showers and coconut scented shampoo.

Sighing loudly but clean and dressed she returned to her cot and discovered that Jael, Will and Danin had joined Triene. Jael's face lightened and a secretive smile touched his lips as he glanced her way. Noting her sloped shoulders and the downturn of her mouth, his smile turned sympathetic as he opened his arms so she could snuggle against his warm chest.

"Good morning," he murmured softly against the top of her head. She burrowed into him a bit more, her frown lifting as she mumbled against his shoulder before kissing it. Will made a fake gagging sound.

"Are you unwell?" asked Danin, backing away slightly.

"Eh?" said Will confused, "Oh, nah. It was just a joke, Danin."

"A joke?" he replied, looking at Will askew. He then addressed Triene since she seemed to be the only sensible one this morning, "First shift isn't due to start for another three hours. Why are we not sleeping?" Triene gave a shrug to indicate her own puzzlement at the situation. "We should find Hrel," Danin decided.

"Agreed!" came Jael's deep, husky voice from behind him. They started for the door, but Susan spied a dawdling Shivro and waylaid him before he left the quarters. Catching up with the others as they reached the bottom of the steps to the main deck, she explained what she had discovered. "Apparently, on longer journeys the crew do fight practice before their shift begins."

"Combat training!" said Jael, his eyes lighting up. "That makes sense." Susan raised an eyebrow at his evident

289

enthusiasm, her own feelings more trepidation than excitement.

Noting the tension around her friend's jaw, Triene edged closer saying in a whisper loud enough for Jael to hear, "Oh dear, he's about to show off!"

Susan couldn't help but smile at his indignant expression and immediate reply, "I'll have you know that I do not show off. Being prepared for combat is a very serious and important matter." He glared at Triene who merely smiled innocently, pleased to have had the twofold effect of annoying her brother and amusing her friend.

A loud battle cry resounded above, and the training began. The metallic ring of blades clashing and the thud of fists hitting flesh made Susan flinch, just as it made Jael, Will and Wolf bound eagerly up the steps. Triene linked her arm with Susan's and calmly followed. It was time Susan saw this since their quest would most likely involve a battle of some sort. She needed to face that unpleasant reality. Triene suspected that Susan's previous existence had not involved violence of any kind. Her unfamiliarity with weapons certainly suggested that. Triene could fight, but had relied on Jael these past few years, unwilling to see blood after... She reached out to her magic for support and it purred comfortingly inside her mind. This was just training, not real. She needed to overcome her fears, she was the Fortress of Fire, she could do this.

They met Hrel near the top of the steps. He was standing on a large wooden crate, watching over the proceedings. He greeted them with a friendly wave and a cheery, "Ah, there you are! Just in time to enjoy the entertainment."

Will was standing beside the crate bouncing on his toes as he observed the sparring with excitement. He glanced up at Hrel and asked hopefully, "Can I 'ave a cutlass?"

Hrel gave a chuckle and nodded, "Of course! Once you prove to me you can handle one."

"Sweet!"

Triene moved to stand beside Wolf who was following the fighting with a glow of anticipation in his amber eyes. Susan let go of her arm when she felt Triene widen her stance and clench her hands into fists. Stepping to the side, and sweeping her gaze over the deck, Susan took time to absorb the sight of old men and women, and even children as young as four, engaging in the training. They were on the quarterdeck, holding short sticks, as they moved in a harmonious rhythm to the barked orders of their instructor. The newly risen sun cast a warm glow on their intent features. The young knew this wasn't a game, that it was a serious lesson they had to learn.

The jarring sound of blades clashing drew her attention to the area around the main mast where the best were doing battle. Here, the pirates swung their weapons freely, relying on their skill to avoid serious injury. Susan winced as a well-aimed blow with a cutlass swept through the air where an opponent's head had been a second before. A cheer rang out. The night crew had congregated by and on the rigging, out of the reach of those sharp blades, to enjoy the sport. They were laughing and taking bets on who would win individual bouts. When one of the sparring pirates had his cutlass twisted out of his hand, a rough voice called out from among the sails, "Oi! Calid, I've seen a jellyfish with a better grip than ye!" A rumble of laughter erupted from the appreciative audience. Calid turned and gave the heckler the finger before picking up his cutlass and resuming his practice.

Susan had never been involved in a fight, nor had she witnessed one before. The closest she had got to it was when the other girls at the boarding school had manhandled her before locking her in the toilets. She hadn't fought back, merely sobbing and pleading until a member of staff had rescued her with a contemptuous sniff. She thought that Danin had probably been the victim of bullying too. She looked for him hoping for some shared sympathy. He wasn't with them. Where was he?

Peering down into the dimly lit area below deck, she saw him still standing at the bottom of the steps. He had cupped his hands and placed them over his ears to block out the sound. His body was anxiously rocking back and forth. She made to go to him, but Jael reached out and rested his hand on her shoulder mistaking her move as an attempt to escape. "It is as well that you learn to defend yourself" he explained gently. Susan turned back surprised and saw deep concern in his hazel eyes.

"It's Danin," she blurted in explanation and pointed down the stairs. Jael's gaze followed her direction and landed on the priest.

"That's not good." he said, a crease furrowing his brow.

Will saw them facing the stairs and came over to see what was more intriguing than the fighting. "What's going on, then?" he asked as he looked down the steps. "Danin, you alright?" he called out. When there was no response, Will contemplated Danin's rocking form then looked behind him at the training. "I reckon it's the noise that's got 'im," he said knowledgably. "Leave 'im with me. I'll sort 'im out." He then skipped down the steps, turned Danin around and guided him to Hrel's quarters. Danin kept his hands over his ears as he allowed Will to manoeuvre him through the door. Shutting the door behind them to reduce the noise, Will pointed Danin in the direction of his research. Danin pulled out the chair and sat down, running his hands over the leather bindings of the books as he systematically straightened the piles.

Will went over to Hrel's desk and plopped down into his chair while he contemplated Danin. The loud noises had disturbed him badly, but he seemed ok with this lower level of sound and the comforting familiarity of his things. Will's sharp eyes scanned the contents of Hrel's desk. Spying a half-drunk bottle of rum he pulled it towards himself and removed the cork. He examined it, turning it around in his hand thoughtfully. He glanced over at Danin who had already calmed and was reading over his latest work. Will nodded to himself and started carving the cork, initially cutting it in half, then shaping it.

Back on deck, Hrel had summoned over a few pirates to train with the others. Allocated to spar with Jael were two brothers, Labanan, who had tattoos covering his muscular arms and bared torso, and a heavy scowl on his face, and Matigas. Matigas wore a malicious grin, revealing a golden front tooth that glinted in the morning rays. He tapped the hilt of his sheathed cutlass menacingly. Jael returned the grin with a wide smile that displayed his dimples and made his eyes twinkle with mischief. He had his longsword and dagger strapped to his legs and he was keen to release them. Before he did so he ran an eye over the pirates paired up with Triene and Susan. Triene's partner, Wawhai, was a tall young man with ebony skin, a smooth, shaved head and a flirtatious manner. He had taken Triene's hand in his own and had bowed his head to bestow a kiss upon it. Triene was smiling politely, but Jael recognised the ruthless determination in her posture and in the tension around her eyes. She would be fine. Susan had been paired with a slightly older woman, with leathery, tanned skin and brown hair that was flecked with grey and cropped short. Her muscular physique spoke of her strength and her movements of her control. Her eyes were kindly though, and when Jael explained, "She needs to build strength and stamina and learn to defend against an attack. She's had no experience, so start slow." she waved him away impatiently, but smiled reassuringly at Susan as she said, "Ye got a protective one there, luv. Ye don't need it though. Ye'll be fine wi me. No blades at first, luv, just fists, eh?"

First, she showed Susan how to position her body to keep her balance and to be able to move quickly, placing her feet one in front of the other but at a diagonal, with her knees slightly bent. "Keep yer feet like tha' as you move aboot. Ye can dance aboot, but keep yer feet like tha'," she explained as she demonstrated what she meant. Susan attempted to mirror her movements but when she moved her feet so they weren't on a diagonal, the woman, whose name was Kiki, pushed her roughly with one hand. Susan stumbled and fell onto her rear with a loud oof! "Keep position!" said Kiki calmly, helping her stand up. "Or ye'll fall over easy like?

Susan, brushed the seat of her trousers and mumbled, "You could have just told me".

Kiki laughed, "But ye'll take more care now" she replied. Susan acknowledged this with a reluctant nod and took up her stance again, raising her hands into what she thought was a good defensive position, fists held directly in front of her face. Kiki's hand struck out and impacted with her fists and Susan's own hands bopped her in the face making her nose tingle painfully. "Keep yer hands out fron' more, watch me shoulders to see what's comin'." Susan sighed heavily but tried to do what she said.

While Susan was learning the basics, Triene was busy sparring with Wawhai, his flirtatious behaviour having quickly disappeared as he attempted to land the first blow. His long reach and greater strength meant that Triene was at an apparent disadvantage. But Triene danced out back, reading his intentions before he began an attack and watched for an opportunity. He lunged forward and flung a powerful punch towards her head. Dropping low, she slid in close, jabbing up into his exposed armpit while delivering a vicious kick to the side of his knee cap. His leg buckled and he cried out. Triene regained her balance and used the power in her legs to follow through with an uppercut to his descending jaw, before twisting and pushing away. His head snapped back even as his hands were reaching for his injured knee. He bent his head and put one hand up in submission. Triene stepped back suspiciously and waited, used to Jael's tactics for getting her to drop her guard. Poor Wawhai, however, hobbled towards Xilm, the carpenter/surgeon and sank to the ground, waiting his turn for treatment.

Triene didn't have long to wait before a new sparring partner approached. Dava's cool and calculating eyes arrowed in on Triene. Dava's platinum locks had been pulled tight against her head and up in a high ponytail making her angular features stand out on her pale skin. She was of a similar height and frame as Triene, but bore more muscle. She held her cutlass in her left hand and took a couple of practice slashes in the air before moving closer and waiting to see if Triene accepted her challenge. Triene removed her own short sword from its scabbard and positioned it so the hilt was at her hip and the blade tilted up towards Dava. They began to circle one another cautiously, assessing before engaging.

Jael and the brothers had entered the area beside the main mast, a silent acknowledgment that there would be no holding back. The pirates already present made room for them, aware of the brothers' reputation. Those on the rigging fixed their gaze on the newcomers and fell silent, not sure whether Jael would be able to hold his own against one of the brothers in a fight. Labanan stepped forward taunting Jael with the edge of his cutlass. Jael responded with a cocky grin, "Let's even up the odds a bit, why don't I fight the two of you?" Bristling, Labanan growled, and Matigas unsheathed his own cutlass and advanced.

Jael held his longsword in a two-handed guard in front of his chest and face as the brothers separated and circled him. Rather than wait for them to commence their attack, Jael ran towards Labanan while raising his sword up and over his shoulder. He then swung it downwards in an arc using the dual momentum of his swing and his run to slice at Labanan's neck. Labanan only just managed to slide the blade off his own as he staggered back and into another pirate, who roughly pushed him off and swore. A combined gasp of disbelief broke free from the spectators.

Aware of Matigas' approach from behind, Jael immediately spun, bringing his sword back in a one handed backswing to deflect the blow aimed at his ribs, as Matigas advanced and slashed with his cutlass. Still spinning, Jael brought his empty hand up and connected a ferocious blow to Matigas' cheek, knocking him sideways. Jael danced back, raising his pommel to his chest, the blade pointing forwards as he watched Labanan cautiously advance, his own blade held upright. Labanan's eyes flickered to the side, giving away his brother's attack from the right. Jael quickly retreated as both charged.

Jael swung his long sword in the direction of Labanan's chest in order to redirect the man's advance before blocking Matigas' low arc with the sole of his booted foot against the flat of the cutlass. His eyes were back on Labanan as he regained his footing and skipped to the side. He slid his sword along the blunt edge of Labanan's cutlass, towards its hilt, and twisted. The cutlass was ripped from Labanan's grip and cluttered to the floor. Jael unsheathed his dagger as he swivelled away from Matigas' rising blade. The cutlass missed him and sliced the air as Matigas' arm continued rising. Jael used Matigas' momentum to cut through the man's shirt in a move that would eviscerate had it been deeper. Matigas' eyes widened in shock, then he straightened, lowering his blade in acknowledgement of his defeat.

Rather than retrieve his cutlass, Labanan had also palmed a dagger and was circling Jael who followed his movements suspiciously. Labanan tipped his chin in a silent question.

Jael responded by sheathing his sword and adjusting his grip on his dagger. Labanan closed the gap, arm held rigidly in front. In contrast, Jael's arms were relaxed as he watched and waited for Labanan to make the first move.

It didn't take long. The impatient pirate lunged forward thrusting his dagger towards Jael's gut. Jael trapped Labanan's wrist between his crossed arms, blocking the move successfully, and releasing the hold as Labanan pulled back. Labanan immediately lunged again. This time his dagger stabbed towards Jael's neck while his other hand grabbed Jael's right bicep to restrain him. Jael stepped back with his left leg and at the same time blocked the thrust with an upward and outward sweep of his left arm. He bent his right arm and wrapped it over the top of Labanan's forcing the man's elbow to lock and his shoulder to twist forward. He added pressure on the elbow by grabbing Labanan's forearm and used his body to force Labanan's head and body to drop and face away. Labanan grunted as both arms were rendered useless by this position. Jael maintained his grip on the forearm using the weight of his body as he removed his right arm so he could press his blade against Labanan's exposed neck. The spectators roared their approval as Labanan mumbled, "Bilge rat!"

Smiling, Jael released Labanan from his hold and helped him up. Grinning cheerfully, Matigas came over and slapped Jael on the back, "Aye, Yer did that roight handsomely!" Even Labanan gave a reluctant nod of agreement as he shook out his sore shoulder.

While they were engaged in their sparring Wolf had been lamenting his lack of willing opponents. Hrel hadn't found anyone for him after his first bout. It wasn't Wolf's fault.

298

The man needed to work on his skills and attitude. Admittedly he was at a disadvantage, despite his cutlass but he could have at least shown some fortitude. When Wolf had crouched down, baring his teeth with a snarl as a polite prelude to his attack the man had started shaking. When Wolf had pounced and knocked him to the ground, gently placing his mouth around his neck, he had simply dropped his weapon and started gibbering. The puncture wounds were superficial, but he had cried when he saw Wolf clean the blood from his lips. Hrel had taken the man away and had yet to return with a replacement.

Wolf decided to overcome his difficulty by stalking and attacking random crew members while they trained. This proved much more satisfactory as he was faced with multiple opponents who quickly teamed up to face him. He released his hold on the latest pirate's throat and stepped back, licking his lips at the salty flavour. The man scooted backwards, hand on his neck, eyes wild. He had been the last one defeated in this alliance, the other pirates were still taking time to recover and regroup. Wolf scratched his ear, one of them had managed to nick it slightly, then padded over to nudge the nearest pirate who was nursing a disjointed shoulder. The man looked at him with eyes wide. Wolf cocked his head and scratched at him with his paw to encourage him to get up, but he didn't seem keen, glancing desperately at his fellows. Oh well. Wolf curled up and closed his eyes for a moment while they worked on their tactics. He could wait a few minutes.

Will returned with Danin partway through the training session. At the bottom of the steps leading to the deck, he handed the agitated priest the two pieces of cork and nodded encouragingly. Danin took them and placed a piece in each ear, giving them a twist as they went in. He was holding his notebook in a tight grip, another suggestion of Will's. Closing his eyes, he listened while Will waited hopefully. After a few moments, Danin opened his eyes and nodded. His deep brown eyes were still unsettled but his movements were more composed. Will grinned widely and gave the priest a friendly pat on the back, eliciting an automatic flinch from the man, before beckoning him up the steps. As they emerged onto the deck, Danin's chary eyes scanned the scene, and gradually curiosity began to war with wariness.

Hrel spied them and called out a cheery, "Greetings!" as he hopped down from his crate to join them, perceiving the improvement in Danin with surprise. He lowered his voice as he praised Will, "Well done, my lad! Very well done!" and raised it again as he suggested to Danin, "Why don't you stand with me a while, and watch Will fight?"

"'E can't 'ear you," explained Will, "I bunged up 'is ears"

Hrel focused his attention on Danin's ears and saw the tops of the corks sticking out and laughed. "A truly ingenious solution, my good fellow! Go train with Vei, I've got Danin" he said, as he waved at Danin to come stand beside him.

Satisfied that Danin would remain, Will turned to find his partner and saw a cinnamon skinned man leaning carelessly against the crates. He bore the sort of muscles that come with years of use, the sort that have strength and stamina rather than showy bulk. The years had also touched his temples with grey and his eyes with fine lines. He tipped his chin at Will in greeting and said gently, "Can ye fight, lad?"

Will answered with a cautious, "A bit." Without warning, Vei lunged for Will, cutlass in one hand, the other reaching for Will's arm. Having learnt to escape his father's fists then how to fight on the streets, Will was ready for the surprise attack. He sprung out of his attacker's path and leapt onto a crate grabbing and swinging the barrel resting on top of it at the pirate. He didn't slow to see whether it hit its target as he was focused on getting behind and above him. Vei had quickly recovered from his miss, and swivelling he managed to track Will's ascent. He saw the barrel heading in his direction and jumped back as it landed on the deck and bounced heavily. He had lost sight of the lad. Where had he got to? He was too late, for Will suddenly pounced and landed on Vei's back, clinging on with one arm around his neck and his legs wrapped around his waist. Will's dagger pricked Vei's throat. The pirate chuckled deeply as he said, "Aye, ye can parry a bit, can't ye?" and dropped his own weapon to indicate surrender. Will slid down and stood slightly apart just in case the pirate wanted to seek revenge, but the man simply straightened his tunic and looked down at him with approval. "I'll be ready for yer tricky ways now, son!" he said waggling his finger and grinning.

Will smirked back, "You've not seen my tricks yet, old man!" he retorted, as he moved to put further space between the pirate and himself before they continued to spar.

## Chapter 26

After nearly four weeks on the open seas, the days had turned sultry and the skies had begun to release a light, warm rain that sizzled on the cooked decks. Sweat drenched bodies laboured under the burning sun as the muggy air sucked on their energy and wrung out their thirst. The supplies of fresh drinking water were running low. Hrel kept what remained clean, but this humid weather meant they would need to replenish their supplies soon. The eagerly awaited call of "Land Ahoy!" from the lad perched high up in the Crow's Nest was therefore greeted by the pirates below with loud cheers.

Danin emerged blinking into the bright sun and joined Uisca at the bow. Without speaking, Uisca offered Danin his leather and brass telescope, pulling it open before placing it in his hand. Danin leant his elbow against the foredeck railing as he put the telescope to his eye and peered at the islands. Uisca had spread out the map and pinned the edges down with his heavy brass equipment. He had a quill and ink set up and was making some quick alterations to it based on his own observations. The map depicted the outer islands of the archipelago and the tip of the larger, central island. However, the detail of the interior had not been captured. The reason for this became apparent as they neared.

The archipelago was encircled by a wall of islands that jutted from the sea. They were little more than giant rocks with sleek steep slopes that provided a safe haven for the sea birds congregating around their tuffs of greenery. They allowed no more than teasing peeks of the islands within. Near the centre, the concave tip of a volcanic island rose above the island wall, steam clouds releasing into the cornflower blue sky. The Coral Skies spent several hours sailing the perimeter, seeking signs of human habitation or at least a reasonable route inside, but the outer islands formed an effective barrier and the glimpses between them only revealed more of the inhospitable and barren rocks.

The excitement among the crew had palpably diminished as they circled the islands. Their early enthusiasm silenced. Hrel had joined the others on the foredeck and was using his own telescope to try to survey the interior and even his brow was creased.

Susan attempted to voice their concerns, "Do you think there may have been a mistake? Maybe the islands were hospitable once, but ..." her voice petered out.

Danin considered her question for a moment, his eyes narrowing in thought, before stating, "It is possible, of course, that the volcano wiped out the colony or they had insufficient resources for a prolonged existence on the islands." His tone was contemplative rather than concerned. "It is also the case, however, that any habitation would be hidden from the external aspects of the archipelago, or their presence would have been more widely documented over the years." He concluded with, "The only way to know is to enter the inner isles".

Susan tucked herself up against Jael and whispered, "I can't see any big enough gaps for the ship and it doesn't look safe to use a rowing boat." Jael rested his chin on the top of her head and drew her closer. Together they watched the waves burst into clouds of spray as they crashed onto the rocky cliffs before smashing into the backlash of surf from the neighbouring islands. The sea surrounding the islands was a bubbling mass of foam with churning currents that would easily rip and render a small boat against the rocks.

Hrel lowered his telescope and stroked his beard thoughtfully before turning resolutely to find Uisca, "I can sense a route, but it will be tight." he said while staring into the distance. "We must take a vote." Uisca noted the determination in the tilt of Hrel's chin and gave a brisk, "Aye Cap'n", before leaving the deck to organise the furling of the sails and lowering of the anchor ready for the meeting. Hrel then addressed the others, his focus narrowing in on Wolf, "My crew have placed their lives in my care, and I will honour their trust. The decision will be theirs." Triene had her hand resting on Wolf's shoulders but at this her fingers tightened, pressing deep into his soft undercoat. She felt bile rise in her throat. To be this close without exploring further wasn't fair on Wolf. Ignoring Triene's obvious tension, Wolf tipped his head so his arcane eyes deliberately met Hrel's resolved ones, and he slowly bowed his head in understanding. Hrel acknowledged this with a sympathetic nod of his own.

Triene started to pace the deck as they waited. She still cared desperately for Wolf, but the simplicity of their relationship had been affected, on her part at least, by the knowledge that he was also human. What did that even mean? How would they both react if he managed to shift into a man? She had no idea and had been fretting about it since discovering his secret. No, not a secret as such, he had always known he was a Spirit elder, she guessed, he just couldn't tell her. Whatever happened, his happiness was important to her. He was staring at the islands. He obviously wanted to meet others like him. He must feel so lonely. Triene's heart twisted, she just hoped that he wouldn't leave her.

The main deck steadily filled with young and old, while the more agile lounged on the rigging, Will among them. Eventually Uisca returned and confirmed, "All present, Cap'n". Hrel moved to the edge of the foredeck and surveyed their expectant faces. Throwing out his arms as if about to embrace them, he called out, voice loud and clear, "'Tis time for a vote." There were some murmurings from the deck. "Ye can see the danger," Hrel began, slipping into the vernacular as he waved in the direction of the islands. "I can sense a way in, but there be little room for error." Then he added bluntly, "Davy Jones be rubbing his barnacled hands, hoping to get the Coral Skies at last."

"Why give him that hope?" he asked rhetorically, and immediately provided the answer, "'Tis not for riches, nay the treasure be noble!" he paused as there was a rumble of laughter at the word noble, before he added grandly, "Yer quest is for freedom. Freedom for magic, and freedom from another Mage War." The pirates shuffled uncomfortably at the mention of the Mage Wars. Hrel looked at Danin and asked him under his breath, "Will you explain to them why you think the Spirit elders are here and how they may help us?"

Danin gulped and nodded nervously as he scanned the crew. He tried to raise his voice, but his throat tightened so that all that came out was a small, cracked sound. Some of the crew shifted impatiently. A childhood memory rose to the surface. He had been careful not to use his magic once he entered the Temple, the intolerance having been drummed into him during his training. That hadn't been the case when

305

he was younger. Then, his Air magic had been his solace, indeed he had never really fit in with his family or the village, so it had been his only comfort. The memory was of a time when he had been hiding behind the goat shed, crouched low and trembling. One of the older boys had been looking for him again, ready with his mean words and hard fists. The magic had helped him throw his voice so that it sounded like he was calling for his mother at the other side of the village. It had worked. The boy had hurried in that direction, and Danin had made his escape. That would help him now. Danin breathed out his magic and it carried his softly spoken words so each member of the crew could hear him clearly.

He started on a stutter, but the familiarity of the subject relaxed him. "M...m...my fellow priest f..found evidence of sailors that had traversed islands such as these, m...many years ago. The islands were described as having a barrier, much like a wall of island rocks, which made entry treacherous. They breached the barrier and within they discovered a hidden world. A world which contained a society where people and animals lived as equals. Disappointed by the lack of more material wealth, they left the islands, suffering significant loss of life and damage to their ship. A small number of their crew made it to safety, the Captain's most recent journal with them in their boat. Their recounting of their adventure caused some attempts to rediscover these peoples, but none returned. Soon the encounter became a mere tale, designed to entertain, until it eventually faded from memory. All that remained was the journal entry which came into the possession of the Temple, as such items tend to do." Danin paused and fixed his gaze on the furled mainsail.

"The Spirit elders did not participate in the ancient's habit of chronicling their activities, so information about them is limited. It is clear, however, that they were once an important part of the ancient's society and regarded as having the closest ties to the magic and therefore the Goddess Rua. As humanity became more secular the Spirit elders drew apart from the rest of the ancients, and by the time the Mage Wars were waged, they were nowhere to be found."

"Their existence remains the least known or understood from the ancient period, although it is believed that they were shapeshifters, sharing the spirit of both animal and human. When my fellow priest read the journal, he was convinced that he had discovered where the Spirit elders had gone and so worked tirelessly to identify these islands as their final location."

"We cannot verify this further without entering the archipelago. If there are Spirit elders here, it is probable that they will have retained their connection to the ancients' beliefs and knowledge, unaffected by the Mage Wars and the effects of the Cull. Our quest to protect the returning magic is hampered by our limited knowledge and experience of the magic due to these events. This is an opportunity to reduce those limitations." Deciding that he had explained matters sufficiently, Danin breathed the Air magic back in and blinked rapidly.

Hrel was watching Danin with approval, "Thank you for your honesty and respect for my crew" he said quietly and sincerely. Somewhat startled by the praise, Danin gave a jerky nod before wandering over to the rail to look out over the islands once again.

Susan now stepped forward, her worried brow warring with the determined set of her mouth. Hrel glanced at her curiously as she looked to him for permission to address his crew. He inclined his head, and she took a deep breath before raising her voice. She attempted to speak to the adventurous nature of her audience as she shouted, "Are we lily-livered land lubbers who piss in the wind … or are we brave buccaneers who give no quarter?" Susan really hoped she had understood the meaning of these phrases correctly. "I say we pursue our quest and find these Spirit elders. Who's with me?" She took heart from the calls of "No quarter!" and "Aye!" that followed her cry. Shaking slightly, she retreated.

Hrel was hiding a smile under a raised hand as he stepped up, although it quickly disappeared as he announced solemnly, "Ye have heard what we have to say, it is time for ye to vote. Bow in favour, stern against."

The main deck became a hive of activity as loved ones and friends were sought out and their views ascertained. Some members of the crew shared their opinions loudly, while others deliberated the problem as they gazed out to sea. Susan watched them uncertainly and asked Hrel, "Does it have to be unanimous or a majority for the vote to carry?"

"It largely depends on the reason for the vote. For this, I'll want them all in favour, if possible."

Gradually, the crew members started shifting towards the bow, some standing in the middle uncertainly until they settled to the fore. Only a handful of the crew stood at the rear. "Does that mean we are going ahead?" whispered Susan. Hrel's brow was furrowed, however, as he contemplated those standing to the stern. Rather than declare the result, he descended onto the main deck and made his way over to speak with them.

Susan watched as he rested his hand gently on the back of one woman who had her young son cradled in her arms, while she shook her head in frustration. She was paying attention to whatever he was saying, as were the others huddled around him. There was no sign of animosity in the group, indeed they seemed embarrassed by their decision, with their heads bowed, feet shuffling and apologetic hand movements. Hrel responded to their comments with open arms, reassuring hugs and a ruffle of the toddler's hair before he returned to the foredeck. As he returned, the handful of pirates made their way forwards to join the others and were enfolded into the crowd.

Hrel cried out, "To the islands!" and the crew echoed, "To the islands!" with a roar. Some of them punched fists or cutlasses into the air in defiance of the danger they faced, before they hastened back to their workstations. Hrel turned and quietly issued his orders to Uisca who responded with a gruff "Aye, aye" and made his way to the waiting quartermaster, exchanging a few words with the boatswain on the way.

As his crew readied themselves, Hrel positioned himself in the centre of the foredeck, where Uisca and the boatswain could see him without obstruction. He closed his eyes for a moment and sent tendrils of his magic into the sea, to dart among the currents and eddies surrounding the islands. He felt the eager rush of the water as it charged towards the rocks and the chaos as it crashed back down. He kept searching... Ah... There it was! The tug that flowed

309

between the islands, the dash of the waves was superficial there. The gap was narrower than he would have liked, but the water ran smoothly, with no hidden rocks to snare the hull. They needed to catch the current and it would help them through. He breathed deeply and raised both arms, holding them out to the side, the agreed signal for straight ahead and waited for his ship to move into line with the current.

Uisca shouted a brief command and one runner set off for the helmsman, another for Jael and the other deckhands raising the anchor. The boatswain set the riggers in motion, ensuring the mainsails remained tightly furled and the lateen sails on the mizzenmasts were adjusted to use the light winds. Below deck, the helmsman adjusted the whipstaff to lever the tiller, which in turn adjusted the rudder. Only a small adjustment was needed, and the Coral Skies moved slowly forward.

Uisca kept his eyes locked on Hrel, watching for the movement which would herald a change of direction, while Susan joined Triene and Danin to press against the rail, ensuring that she kept out of the way. Her eyes followed the line of the bowsprit which was pointing directly towards a particuarly intimidating isle. She gripped the rail as she watched the jagged rocks come into focus. Susan knew Hrel had his magic, and his crew clearly trusted him, but ships were ponderous creatures and slow to change direction. What had she been thinking, encouraging the crew to do this?

Hrel lowered his right arm and a buzz of activity followed. The ship edged starboard and caught the current. He raised his arm again so that the ship straightened and indicated with

310

a circling of his arm that the lateen sails should be reefed, reducing the amount of sail catching the wind. The ship drifted forwards, rocking as she was buffered by the surf. Spray filled the passageway, veiling what lay beyond. Susan told herself that Hrel would be able to sense any hidden obstacles, but her treacherous heart pounded its disbelief. Wolf had no such fears. He was still standing beside Triene, nose twitching in anticipation. His attention was suddenly caught by a large sea eagle that circled their ship before flying back to the islands. Wolf grinned before lowering his head and nuzzling happily against Triene's waist. She ruffled his fur affectionately and smiled softly but cautioned, "We might not find any Spirit elders, don't forget." He snorted and rolled his eyes. Just a little longer to wait.

The ship was buffeted by the turbulent waters as they neared the cliffs, which loomed menacingly, their rockfaces glistening and slick. She tipped precariously, sending stinging spray over her deck. The crew clung tightly to ropes and rails as they were drawn towards the passageway. The tip of the main mast scratched along the sheer walls of rock until the ship suddenly bobbed upright. The gap between the islands narrowed and they bumped against the sides as the ship was dragged along on the current.

There was a loud crack as the main mast snapped; pirates fled to escape the falling tip. It crashed into the deck, splitting the wood, jutting out of it like a giant spear. Hrel remained calm, arms raised. He could feel the current smoothing ahead of them. Before they reached the end of the passageway, he indicated that they needed to adjust the rudder, for a sharp starboard turn. His crew responded immediately, their faith in him complete. The ship nudged out from between the islands and navigated past the skeleton of an older and smaller ship.

It lay partially grounded on the rocks; a tragic reminder of the danger faced. The sunken timbers had been devoured by shipworms and the exposed timbers rotted by decades of rain. Pungent red algae clustered around the wreck combining unpleasantly with the acrid odour emitted by the steaming volcano.

Hrel continued to give instructions as they sailed around the central island, navigating the gusts and new currents that accompanied each of the surrounding isles. Eventually, they rounded the island and were faced with a large rock archway that spanned the waters between two islands, effectively blocking the route of their large ship. The anchor was lowered as they stared at the hidden land beyond. A bay of black sand gave way to trees, although they couldn't see much further. Hrel murmured, "We appear to have found them!"

Danin pushed his glasses higher up on his nose as he peered through the archway. "Indeed, this is most promising!" He rubbed his hands excitedly. "I must collect my things," he said as he hurried back to the Captain's quarters to collect his backpack.

The two large rowing boats were dragged onto the shore until they were high above the tide line. Wolf had bounded out of the boat before it had reached the sand, splashing in the lapping waves and heading for the coconut palms. The others struggled to keep up with him, their feet sinking into the coarse sand. Wolf stopped suddenly and tipped his head back to look up at the skies. Triene was the nearest to him and she followed his gaze to see an enormous black and white eagle swooping towards them. Susan grabbed Jael's hand as the eagle's wings cast a shadow over them, before they folded into her body as she landed several feet in front of them. Will peered at her nervously from behind the now stationary and awed Hrel, while Danin continued walking forwards, oblivious to her arrival. He was halted by Jael's outstretched hand. Danin blinked in surprise and pulled away before he noticed the eagle, watching him warily through piercing eyes. Will remained at the back, not trusting the oversized hooked beak, and large bumpy feet with long sharp talons, so hard to ignore with their bright yellow colouring.

While they had been fixed on the eagle's arrival a tall man had emerged from behind the trees and he came to stand beside the eagle  The man was naked, his sepia skin accompanied by greying black hair. His eyes were set deep above a high aquiline nose,  his mouth pulled in a taut line as he observed the newcomers.  He stared at Wolf for a moment, then indicated that they should follow him as he walked back towards the trees. The eagle took a couple of hops to the side before stretching out her wings and soaring into the sky. Wolf trotted behind the man confidently, while the others glanced nervously at one another before following them, Will taking a final glance at the eagle's disappearing silhouette before moving forward.

## Chapter 27

The man guided them deeper into the island, the narrow trail passing through a semi-cultivated area where ripe red fruits hung from tall lycée trees, and spiky pineapple plants with their golden fruit rising from their midst were crowded by the ivy-like leaves of sweet potato plants. Danin's fascinated gaze took in the squat trees with their succulent leaves all the way along their branches until their tip, where a flower exploded in a puff of vibrant red.

They emerged into a wide clearing. On the furthest edge was a cluster of shelters made from a reddish-brown hardwood, although looking around, the inhabitants seemed to prefer life in the open. There were indications of communal outdoor living in the shaped logs and palm frond blankets laid over soft moss cushions. There was no sign of the usual occupants, however. In the centre of the clearing sat a stone firepit loaded with logs and the fibrous golden trunk of the palms. Immediately around the firepit, the area had been laid flat and topped with some of the black sand from the beach.

The man took a crouched position in front of the firepit and faced them. His head tilted slightly as he observed, with interest, the visitors' shuffling search for a suitable place to sit. Wolf, of course, had no such difficulty and immediately sat on his haunches, taking in the scents of those lurking in the shadows as he waited. Triene knelt next to Wolf and slowly ran her hand down his back, needing the reassurance of that contact as she tried to supress the gnawing anxiety that Wolf would choose the Spirit elders over her. Sensing her worry, Wolf pressed his large head against her and gave the tip of her nose a quick lick. She sighed and rested her head on his.

The eagle from the beach landed lightly on the sand. She folded her wings as she skipped over to stand next to her human and joined him in contemplation of their visitors. She stared at the warrior with the dark hair and scowling expression. He had found a log to perch on and was leaning forwards, hands resting between his knees as if at ease, but his muscles were tense and his eyes and ears were scanning for signs of danger. His mate assumed a position on the blanket beside him, her feet curled to one side. She was smiling in anticipation as she leant against the log and wrapped her hand around her mate's calf. The touch seemed to soothe him.

The eagle transferred her focus to the Commander of the ship and evident Water elder. She had observed his interaction with his crew and was impressed. He had demonstrated a parental leadership not unlike that of the Spirit elders. He was currently lounging against another log, one of his long legs outstretched, the other bent. His relaxed pose was deliberately deceptive since his eyes were assessing and his hand hovered close to the hilt of a dagger. This caution did not worry her, it was only sensible for him to be wary in the circumstances. The eagle was more intrigued by the choice to include the other two visitors, she tipped her head and eyed the youngling and the man with the bag. They were sitting together on one of the blankets. The youngling looked poised to run as he watcher her with wide eyes. He seemed disturbed by her predator status. Strange since he was evidently comfortable with the Spirit wolf elder, a much greater threat to a human. She also wondered why a youngling had been brought to this initial encounter. She expected all would become clear in time. The man beside him had sat back on his knees and was rummaging inside his bag. She tensed until he brought out a notebook, travelling quill and ink and carefully laid them out in front of him, adjusting the inkwell slightly. Ah! She remembered her lessons. He sought to record their meeting in the way of the ancients. She would have to decide whether or not to allow such a record to be kept, much would depend on their reason for seeking them out.

She turned her attention back to Wolf who was providing information about his companions and their quest. He had been without another Spirit elder for a long time, and his communication was rushed, like an excited hatchling. She soothed his thoughts, and he took a calming breath before continuing. He seemed a loyal and determined male, his mate was lucky. She glanced at her own human, even more lucky if the magic returns their shifting ability. The news of its return was bittersweet. It would be fulfilling to have a complete life, yet the risk of war sounded as likely now as it was when their people first retreated to the islands. Her male gave her a mental prod. She had been inattentive for a moment and had missed something of importance. What was that?

Wolf explained it again. We seek your help to understand the magic and how to use the Hand of Rua in our quest.

They confirmed they would be willing to assist, but they wished to greet the rest of their visitors first. Wolf agreed to translate for them.

The others had been watching the silent exchange with

confusion when Susan suddenly exclaimed, "They're telepaths!"

Triene turned her attention away from Wolf's back, looking at Susan with a puzzled frown. "What do you mean?"

"They communicate in their minds!" she explained excitedly, lowering her voice so as not to interrupt them. Danin picked up his quill, dipping it urgently into the ink before scratching eagerly in his notebook.

The man cleared his throat before speaking out loud in a rough, unpractised voice,. "I am Bilqi, Spirit elder." He nodded to the eagle beside him, "She am Bilqu. She am Spirit elder." The eagle bobbed her head in acknowledgement of his words. He checked with Wolf before speaking again. "Wolf say you are yujin... friends." He stared at them, his expression stern, clearly awaiting a response.

Danin replied enthusiastically, recognising the word from the ancient language, "Yes, that's right! Yujin. I am Danin." He then resumed writing. Bilqi was obviously expecting him to continue with the introductions, his eyebrows rising the longer Danin remained silent. Susan hastily intervened, pointing to each person as she introduced them, careful to keep the language simple since it appeared Wolf was translating, "I'm Susan, this is Jael an Earth elder, Triene is his sister and a Fire elder. Wolf is a Spirit elder." She included him even though it was clear Bilqi knew who he was. "Danin is an Air elder." Turning to see the others she continued, "This is Hrel, a Water elder and over here we have Will." She took a breath then added, "We would indeed like to be your friends." Bilqi had briefly turned to

Wolf for a translation as she was speaking, now he looked back at Susan and nodded. Susan took courage from that and added, "We need help protecting the returning magic." Bilqi nodded again. Relieved that Wolf had apparently explained why they were here, Susan leant back, relaxing again against Jael's leg, on a big exhale.

As if they had been waiting just out of sight until the status of the visitors had been confirmed, others started joining them from both the air and the surrounding foliage. Hrel and Jael tensed at the movement but took their lead from Wolf who remained calm. Will scooted back as more eagles swooped down into the clearing, only to come across sleek black panthers slinking out of the cover of the rich vegetation. Racoons scampered over the logs into the clearing and amongst them all, came humans. The young of all species gaped curiously at the visitors as they arrived, staying close to family for protection. Susan shifted, made uncomfortable by the naked human bodies. She needed to sort out her priorities, since the women's nudity around Jael bothered her more than being surrounded by so many dangerous animals! Clothes were the unnatural thing here! Noting her distress, but mistaking its cause, Jael cupped her chin and tipped her head up to look at him. "It is safe," he said softly. Susan blushed and managed to say, "I know, thank you."

All around the clearing the newcomers settled into various groups containing sea eagles, humans, racoons and panthers. There was no segregation of species, although Susan supposed that was because they were all Spirit elders with the commonality of that overriding their physical appearance. The differences she perceived were based on

318

her own assumptions. There were no wolves or other creatures, Susan realised. What had happened to the other Spirit elders?

Not far from her, Will was trying to remain calm. He was a town lad, born and raised. He didn't like being at a disadvantage, and the lack of man-made structures was unnerving. The locals could blend into the surroundings or swoop down from the sky with no warning. He felt exposed and vulnerable, and he did not like that feeling at all. He knew they were like Wolf, Spirit elders, but he had shared the streets with dogs before, they were alright. Cats now, they were spiteful and unpredictable, and these cats were bloody enormous. And he had never seen a bird as big as these ones neither, just look at their vicious beaks and feet. They could swoop down and grab hold of a person before he knew it. The gulls in Canorm had done that to some food he had been holding once, before he got wise to their tricky ways.

A curious young panther decided to join Will on the moss blanket. She was smaller and slimmer than some of the others and her black fur had darker spots, an indication of her jaguar heritage. She sat next to him and stared. Will froze and looked away, as if by doing so he would render himself invisible or uninteresting to the panther. Wolf had padded over while the Spirit elders were arriving, and he huffed in amusement. Wolf bowed his head to the panther in greeting, and she bowed her own deeper still, quivering with excitement at the contact with the new Spirit elder. Wolf turned to Will and gently nudged his chest with his nose, coming into contact with the neck pouch. Will's eyes widened as he realised the Spirit elders were about to demonstrate the gemstones' use, and eagerly lifted it over his head. Wolf carefully took the strap in his mouth, letting the pouch dangle from between his teeth as he trotted back to Bilqi.

Will's attention was so focused on Wolf that he momentarily forgot the panther beside him. This peace didn't last long as she tried to snuggle against him while vibrating with a deep and loud purr. Will flinched and gave a smothered yelp, bumping into Danin, who didn't look up but shuffled sideways, carefully moving his ink along in front of him. The panther was undeterred, and she rubbed her face against Will's shoulder possessively. Trapped between her and Danin, he tentatively reached out to stroke her warm, silky fur saying hopefully, "Nice kitty!" and she purred again. Strangely reassured by the rumbly sound, he cleared his throat and resolutely focused on Wolf and the gemstones.

Bilqi reverently held up the Spirit gemstone from the Hand of Rua. He hadn't expected to have the opportunity to see and hold one of the sacred artifacts of the blessed Rua. The gemstone glowed boldly, its magic reacting to the presence of so many Spirit elders. Its golden light easily visible, despite the brightness of the sun. He could feel the magic within the artifact and wondered whether he would have enough magic to effect the shift? His heart beat faster in anticipation. His eagle had always been a part of him, yet he had never been able to change forms, no one had since the magic had gone. He glanced at Bilqu who was watching him intently. He would like to be able to shift, if only for her. Bilqi carefully placed the gemstone on the ground and rested his foot on it since his wings would be unable to hold it if the shift were successful. He closed his eyes and concentrated on the gemstone, feeling the magic within it eager to help. He felt it meld with his essence, adding to the magic that was at his core. He felt stronger but would it be enough? His internal struggle was open for all the Spirit elders to feel as he focused on his eagle. The light within the gemstone expanded, enveloping him. His body wavered on the edge of the change. To Susan and the others, he remained a shadow at the light's epicentre, which blurred as it alternated between human and eagle as if unable to decide a form. The light flared and when the glow subsided the human remained. Bilqi was smiling, although clearly tired from the effort. Despite not having kept the change, he had momentarily managed the shift of forms and his eagle had been released. Bilqu sent him a wave of love, with a compliment for his eagle. Bilqi returned the love, with the promise......Soon.....

The Spirit elders shared his elation, even as they watched Bilqi push the gemstone towards Wolf. He had provided Wolf with the necessary understanding, now he sent encouragement. That encouragement was echoed by each of the Spirit elders present, although the youngsters' boisterous enthusiasm had to be quieted so Wolf could concentrate.

Wolf sat in front of the gemstone and placed his massive front paw above it. The gemstone snuggled between the pads. He had sensed Bilqi's struggle and thought he had unwittingly held back from the shift. He would get it with practice, but for now it was Wolf's turn. Triene moved back and clasped her hands together as if in prayer.

As with Bilqi, Wolf was soon wrapped in the bright light from the gemstone, and his shadowy outline began to blur.

321

Sooner than expected and without any warning, the light disappeared leaving Triene with a temporary blindness. She rubbed her eyes, desperate to see, and as her vision slowly returned she could make out the shape of a man sitting where Wolf had been. Triene gasped and pressed her hands to her mouth. Her eyes wandered over the smooth cinnamon skin that stretched across compact and powerful muscles. Straight blue/black hair flowed down to rest on his shoulders. He was squatting on the ground with one large square hand in the sand, the other resting lightly on the gemstone, and his head was bowed. He slowly unfolded his long limbs and stood upright, reaching his arms to the sky and tipping his head back as he howled, the sound from his human throat, deep and melodic.

Cries of elation echoed his howl as the Spirit elders celebrated the first full shift in living memory. Tears were shed and people were hugging. Susan clapped her hands excitedly, while Jael and Will looked stunned by the transformation. Triene was torn. This man, he was her Wolf. She knew it, but how could it be? She stared, unable to move.

Bilqi clasped Wolf's shoulder proudly, and Wolf returned the gesture awkwardly, still unused to this new body. As soon as he could, he turned to seek out Triene, concerned that she would be finding this difficult. Observing her awed expression, he gave her a wide grin, cocking his head to the side, pride radiating from him. With that, oh so familiar, action, recognition flooded Triene and she ran towards him, stopping just short. She raised her hands to cup his face and scrutinised his new features. She saw the long strong nose, and familiar wry smile, she saw his amber eyes, full of

322

affection and humour and she flung her arms around him, pressing her cheek against his shoulder. On a sigh of relief, Wolf wrapped his human arms around her and held her close.

When Triene pulled back she stared at his face again and said with satisfaction, "My Wolf." His eyes sparkled as he gave a lopsided smile before replying in a rumbling baritone, "Yes, your Wolf." Triene's eyes widened at hearing him speak, then she hugged him again.

The next time she pulled back Triene noticed his naked state. "Um, perhaps you could put some clothes on?" she said blushing and turning her face away. Wolf shook as he huffed with laughter. The human locals didn't seem to be bothering her with their nakedness, but to please her he looked around for something to put around his nether regions. One of the racoons pointed to a blanket of palm fronds and he wrapped it around his waist like a sarong. Relieved although still a little embarrassed, Triene moved back in close, automatically stroking his arm before leading him to the others.

Jael greeted Wolf with a slightly bewildered air, clasping his arm in greeting as he searched his face. He seemed unwilling to let go until Susan brushed between them to enthuse about Wolf's transformation, her recent experiences having prepared her well for the more unusual events. Wolf listened politely to her familiar chatter, pleased to note her easy acceptance of his new form. Jael was a good man and would soon recognise his old friend. Wolf's gaze returned to Triene. She was clinging to his arm as if afraid he would disappear if she let go. It was difficult for her. She had only known him in wolf form and although they understood one another, communication had been limited. He would help her, of course.

It was time to return the gemstones to Will's keeping. Triene remained attached as he made his way over to an open mouthed and unusually silent Will. Wolf was glad to have this moment of peace before Will's inevitable inquisition. He lifted his hand, offering up the neck pouch, Triene's own arms rising with his rather than letting go of his forearm. Will stared at the leather pouch and gulped. He didn't move to take it, as if he was only now realising the power that lay within. Wolf took Will's hand and placed the pouch in his palm, folding Will's fingers around it, before wrapping his own larger hand over the top of both for a moment. Will looked up at him uncertainly and Wolf squeezed his hand reassuringly. With eyes still slightly wide, Will took the pouch and pulled the strap over his head before carefully tucking the pouch in his shirt. He looked up, returning Wolf's serious regard with an upwards tilt of his chin. Satisfied with Will's resolve, Wolf nodded his approval. Will pressed back his shoulders and stood a little taller.

Wolf noted Danin was still busy recording the transformation in his notebook and hadn't acknowledged their presence. That was good, he thought. Danin's acceptance of him was clearly not an issue although he may want more information from him for his notes later. Best avoid that for as long as possible. Wolf then fixed his amber stare on Hrel, who was still lounging by his log nonchalantly, but his sparkling eyes gave away his enjoyment of recent events. He gave a half smile as he declared dryly, "Well, Wolf, you are as handsome a man as you are a wolf." Wolf inclined his head politely to acknowledge the truth of this statement. Hrel chuckled, his face breaking into a genuine smile as he suggested pleasantly, "Why don't we all sit together for a moment?" Wolf thought this a most sensible idea, Triene needed to have time to rest and reflect. He carefully removed Triene's hands from his arm and placed them in one of his own as he guided her onto a soft seating area. She sank down, still clinging to his hand. He joined her, awkwardly trying one seated position after another. He could see why humans used chairs. The legs didn't know how to fold properly in this form. He settled on emulating Hrel, stretching out one leg and leaning against the log, much to Hrel's further amusement.

While Wolf was getting comfortable, Hrel had waved Susan and Jael to join them, and Will had encouraged Danin over by simply picking up his ink and moving it. Danin quickly followed. The young panther had gone to celebrate with her family when the shift had been completed. Will was glad to be rid of her, of course. It was only because she had been such a pest that he kept looking round expecting her to be sitting next to him.

They all gathered in quiet companionship, absorbing the impact of the intense morning, and taking the opportunity to relax. This was wise, thought Wolf. Hrel was a good leader. He always ensured his pack was cared for. Wolf stretched out his back, which was considerably less flexible in this form, and lay down next to Triene, adjusting until he found the most comfortable position which entailed resting his head on her lap. Triene seemed surprised at first, but the familiarity of it soon meant she was caressing Wolf's hair while she spoke.

"I can hardly believe this is happening!" she declared, softly shaking her head. "Do you think they will help us use the artifacts?"

She started as Wolf rumbled from her lap, "They have agreed."

Hrel looked at the position of the sun in the sky and at the island's inhabitants who were either settling for a siesta or off hunting. He asked Wolf, "Should we return to the ship?"

Wolf yawned and said drowsily, "We eat and sleep here."

They all looked at Wolf expectantly, but he had shut his eyes, having finished with the conversation.

Susan asked, "Are you sure they are ok with that?" as she glanced worriedly at the others.

Wolf re-opened his eyes and looked at her, his brow furrowing with confusion before realising she simply needed reassurance, so he explained soothingly, "It is known." He closed his eyes again, before adding, "We begin lessons at sunrise". He then fell asleep, his breath coming even and light within moments.

Taking care not to wake him, Triene whispered, "I guess we will just see what they have in store for us. They have been most welcoming and helpful." The others murmured their agreement. The conversation quieted once more. Susan and Jael relaxed against one another while Triene settled back against the log, Wolf sleeping soundly beside her. She closed her eyes. It had been a rather exhausting morning, she thought, a rest was a lovely idea. The relief of Wolf still being her Wolf, made her fall asleep much faster than she would have expected.

Will's eyes darted around the clearing. He observed the mix of Spirit elders settling down for a nap, before glancing thoughtfully at Wolf, sleeping next to Triene as usual despite his human form. He looked again at the panthers and humans lying side by side. While he sat in quiet contemplation, his nimble fingers ran a pebble up and down his knuckles, until he too, began to relax.

Hrel watched as one by one they began to fall asleep, frowning slightly as he noted the strong sunlight upon their exposed skin. He glanced up and saw that some of the locals had created artificial shade by attaching the sewn palm fronds to tall branches and propping them up against the logs. He carefully stood, trying not to disturb the others, and started to gather up the spare fronds. A couple of kindly racoons showed him the trick for tying them to the branch and helped him place it beside their little group. He settled back, noting with amusement that Danin was still industriously writing in his notebook. Perhaps he could persuade him to complete his journal when they were back on the ship! It was still hot under the shade, but at least it prevented most of the sun's rays from reaching them.

Eventually, Danin closed his notebook. There had been much to record, it had been a most enlightening day, he looked forward to learning more. He raised his head and looked about the clearing. How strange, his companions were all fast asleep, as were the Spirit elders remaining in the enclosure. The moist heat was rather draining, however, there was too much to discover for sleep. He pulled out his large water bottle from his bag and gulped it down. That

327

would keep him sufficiently hydrated as he explored. He noticed some movement in the undergrowth and set off to investigate. Wolf opened one eye and watched him leave. After checking that the Spirit elders busy harvesting for the evening meal would ensure his safety, he adjusted his body before resuming his much-needed siesta.

The late afternoon passed peacefully.

Susan awoke from a deep sleep to an alarm of hammering and industry. After blinking and gently rubbing her eyes she sought the source of the noise. There was a buzz of activity all-round the clearing as the celebratory evening meal was being prepared. Even Danin was involved. He had a stone hammer and was in the process of hitting something small, that he had rested on a large flat stone. He seemed engrossed in his task. Jael was no longer beside her. She found him sitting with some panthers. He had a knife while the panthers were using teeth and claws, and they were in the process of gutting and beheading sea birds, fish and lizards. Beside them were a couple of humans and racoons in charge of plucking or skinning. Jael spied her watching and waved a bloodied hand in her direction, inviting her to join him. Yuk! No way! She waved casually and hurried over to join Danin in his task instead.

As she approached, she could see that he was now using large leaves to handle a yellow pear-shaped fruit. He pulled something off the bottom of the fruit and placed it on the large stone. He placed the fruit in one wooden bowl, then took up his hammer and struck the object on the stone. The hard shell broke and he carefully picked up the shell with the leaf and put it in a second bowl and the contents in a third. Peering at the third bowl Susan was surprised and

328

pleased to see that the contents were cashew nuts, one of her favourites. "May I help you?" she asked politely. Danin ignored her and began the same process with a new fruit. Surprised, Susan moved closer and asked again. This time Danin spotted her and jumped. He reached up to his ear and took out his ear plug. That explained it. She asked again, "May I help you?" This time Danin responded by offering her a leaf and pointing to the hammer, as he explained, "The shell contains a potent irritant."

Wolf had been lazing in that pleasant sleepy but awake state scenting and listening to the activities surrounding them. Now he stretched before sitting up. His limbs and back were surprisingly stiff from lying on the ground. This form was not convenient in many ways, but at least the reduced coverage of fur was preferable. Unlike the panthers, his fur was better designed for colder climes. He cast his eyes over Triene, who was still asleep under the shade. Her mouth was slightly open, and she was snoring delicately. He was reluctant to wake her, but she had been requested. He leant over and gently nudged her awake. She yawned widely before opening her eyes. The slight start on spying Wolf quickly transformed into a sleepy smile. Wolf felt his heart stutter. Enough, he needed to inform her of her duty. "It's time for the fire," Wolf said looking at the firepit then back at her.

"Oh! Oh yes, of course," she said, fully awake now. She rose smoothly, glancing around at the Spirit elders who were all watching with eager expressions. It seemed that they wanted a demonstration of her fire magic! Triene's stomach clenched at the thought of using her magic so publicly. She told herself to relax, these people were unlike the others.

Here, magic was revered as Rua's gift, not an evil to be wiped out. She was safe. She took a steadying breath and held out her hand. The small flame formed in her palm. She heard a gasp and excited movement. Her audience were already entertained, but she smiled to herself, let's see what they think of this! The flame expanded and morphed into the kitten which pranced proudly atop her hand and ran up and down her arm. Pleased with the chuckles and huffs, she sent the cat pouncing onto the logs. As it landed, the flame divided, seeking the driest kindling and soon the fire had taken hold. She walked back to Wolf who was smiling proudly, her answering grin was one of relief as well as amusement.

To her surprise, many of the youngsters rushed over to sit with them. Some were fascinated with Wolf's altered appearance, but most wanted to examine Triene's hand, and were disappointed when it was empty, turning them both over and sniffing them. Laughing, she waved the children to sit down, getting Wolf to translate for her, "Make sure they keep their distance. It doesn't hurt me, but it will burn them." He did as she asked. When they were sitting quietly, Triene began to tell them about the kitten, which Wolf translated the best he could. The kitten of flame emerged out of Triene's hand and walked over to a rock, where it sat and began grooming its ears. The children giggled, and Triene found herself smiling widely. The raccoon kits covered their faces with their paws as they snorted their laughter. "Meet Roary. You can say hello, but be warned, he doesn't like being touched." The kitten flame went from sitting placidly to an enormous roar of fire, then back again. The children had leant back as the heat had blasted them, and were now staring at Roary with wide, starstruck eyes. Wolf chuckled and regarded Triene's mock horror with affection. "Oh, I am so sorry! That was very rude, Roary!" she chided. Roary turned so he was sitting with his back to her and continued cleaning. The children were giggling again. "Well, as you can see, Roary can be rather naughty at times. Why! I remember when I was just a child myself and I had decided to go into the woods at the back of our home..." Triene's voice stumbled to a halt. The kitten flame walked over to her hand and butted it with its head, as if asking for a pet. Triene smiled and pretended to stroke the flame to the delight of her audience. She forced herself to remember her home when it was a happy place, full of love, and used that memory to squash the one of destruction and pain. "Roary, here, wanted to come out to play. I told him, "You can only come out if you promise not to run away!". Well, Roary promised so I let him out and he climbed up to sit on my shoulder as I walked through the woods." The kitten flame promptly ran up her arm and sat proudly on her shoulder, to the excited squeals of the children. Wolf was also huffing gently at her antics. Triene will make a good mother, he thought.

The young panther had wandered over and sat next to Will to watch Triene's display. Although he still glanced warily at her sharp teeth and hidden claws, he had managed to come to terms with her dual nature. He introduced himself, "Me name's Will, I don't 'ave magic, but me mum were able to do Earth magic. I'm a thief by trade, well a pirate now, I 'spose." The panther stared at him without blinking. Will wiggled uncomfortably before asking, "Wot's it like being a Spirit elder? It must be weird being two people inside but only one on the outside." He chuckled nervously before adding, "I 'spect you can't understand me coz you speak in the ancient language or panther or some such." He tentatively reached out a hand and stroked her head. When he stopped she rolled into him, pushing his arm up, indicating that he should stroke her again. He did so and she rubbed her face against him, rumbling and vibrating with every breath. "You like that, I guess," he said with a shy smile.

Soon it was time to eat. Dinner was a joyful occasion. The Spirit elders being keen to welcome their guests, they plied them with many delicious dishes and fruit based drinks. Hrel added some rum to the pineapple juice, and the locals had enthusiastically partaken, the poor raccoons becoming drunk rather quickly. When the sun dipped below the surrounding islands the locals divided. Those interested in nocturnal adventures merged into the foliage, eagles flew off to roost while many of the raccoons were already slumbering. The visitors were allocated the shelters and they quickly settled down for the night. Their bellies were full and despite their afternoon's slumbers, they quickly drifted off to sleep. Wolf was the last to succumb to sleep. He listened in on the nocturnal activities until the early hours, the conversation evoking nostalgic memories. Perhaps he would join them another night. It would be good to be in a pack again.

## Chapter 28

Dawn arrived with a flurry of activity. The youngsters ran around their busy parents' legs while they emptied the clearing and laid more sand. Leftover food was stuffed into hungry young mouths as they chased each other squealing and laughing. Wolf, still in his human form, was watching the preparations for the morning's magical practice from a carved log positioned in front of the shelters. It appeared they were going to have an audience. He hoped his friends would understand and accept the Spirit elders' enthusiasm for the magic. Wolf gave a lopsided smile as he remembered Triene playfully entertaining the little ones with her fire magic the previous evening. Triene already understood.

Hrel and Jael emerged from the huts and joined Wolf in watching the preparations, their offers to assist having been firmly rejected. Triene was next, coming out of the shelter tentatively, eyes searching for Wolf and her smile uncertain. She felt strangely awkward and shy. Wolf scented her anxiety so stood up to greet her. Pushing his unbrushed hair away from his face, she stared at him intently. He rolled his eyes and hugged her. It was Wolf, he was Wolf, she snuggled into his chest and hugged him in relief.

Will had snuck out of the hut much earlier and had been getting the lie of the land. Although, it wasn't his usual set up he was feeling much more confident, and indeed was ready and eager to see what the day would bring. He sat next to Hrel, "This is gonna be fun!" he declared, wiggling in his seat. He saw Danin on the opposite side of the clearing and waved, although Danin was engrossed in his notebook, as usual.

Jael was feeling strangely nervous about using the artifact. He didn't want to accidently damage the island or set off the volcano by moving the earth.    Perhaps he could do something more like his usual use of the magic, something less weapon like. He saw a half-eaten fruit, maybe......? He collected it and tucked it against his seat. That might be a better start, he thought. He looked back at the shelter where Susan still slept. He might need to go wake her, she really didn't like mornings, but wouldn't want to miss this. As he dithered, the object of his dithering emerged, blinking blearily. His heart beat faster, at the sight of her wild hair and seductive pout. She glanced about and he waited for her to notice him. But he wasn't her target, the washroom was, and she headed towards it with purpose. Jael snorted a laugh and turned back to face the clearing.

Will had sorted through his reaction to the Spirit elders during the night and was able to greet Bilqu with a smile when she landed beside him. Pleased he had adapted well, she dipped her head and shuffled her wings in greeting. Not sure what the eagle wanted, he looked to Wolf for help, but he was occupied with Triene. "Sorry, Bilqu, I dunno wot you want!" he said with an exaggerated shrug. Bilqu tipped her head and stared at the pouch around his neck and waited. He was a clever youngster, he would work it out. Understanding dawned quickly and  Will tipped the gems onto the ground.

Bilqu examined the gems carefully. On the other side of the clearing, Bilqi had stopped to watch, his expression intense. Bilqu delicately placed a claw on the golden Spirit gemstone, careful not to damage it with her sharp talons, and focused. Will held his breath as he saw the light from the gem encase her and her form shimmered. The light dimmed and the eagle hung her head sadly. Bilqi turned away on a sigh and continued setting out the palm fronds. Bilqu wasn't about to give in though. She had felt the change was close, her human form eager to be revealed. This time when the light flared the transformation began, and when it dimmed the eagle had been replaced by a woman with deeply bronzed skin and a shock of white hair. Her golden eyes were piercing above her long aquiline nose and thin lips, which broadened into a wide smile for Will. She gently returned the gem to him then turned to face Bilqi who was staring at her in disbelief. He ran across the clearing, and she fell into his open arms. They held each other tightly, tears dampening their cheeks.

Wolf blinked slowly and Triene's hand squeezed his before eventually giving him a shy smile, "It is beautiful!" she said softly. Susan had returned in time to witness the change and sighed loudly as she clasped her hands together. Wolf suddenly cocked his head and stated, "We follow and listen now." Without further explanation he guided Triene to the centre of the clearing. Bilqi and Bilqu walked just ahead of them, holding hands and smiling. Curious, Will followed next, while Susan gave Jael an encouraging nudge forward. She planned to stay behind since she didn't have any magic, but he took her hand and helped her up, walking her into the clearing with him. Hrel stood, adjusted his sword and sauntered along behind, glancing around at the occupied seats surrounding them. It appeared their audience were in a jovial mood. Some had even brought snacks. He smiled wryly. He hoped it wouldn't turn out to be a comedy they watched.

Wolf stepped over to join the two Spirit eagle elders. It appeared that he was going to act as translator. He glanced at Danin who was still reading his notebook and making alterations to his entries. Will noticed and rushed over to get him. Danin looked up surprised as Will pointed out the group in the centre of the clearing. He set about carefully packing away his things, ensuring the ink had dried, stoutly refusing Will's urgent offers of help. He then walked over to join them, his face full of expectant interest.

Once he had arrived, the lesson began. Wolf spoke, his deep voice, soft and slow. "Magic is life. Just as the sap flows through the tree, the blood in the deer, magic flows through life. It is the heat in the flame, the wind in the sky, the eddies in the sea. Spirit elders know this, feel this. Just as we are human and animal, we are magic. Using the magic is the same as using legs to run or walk, or lungs to breathe. The magic is a part of us just as our muscles, our eyes and our minds are a part of us."

Wolf paused and listened for a moment before continuing, "When elders used the magic to harm and destroy, they had to force the magic, for it was unnatural and wrong. Like prising an unwilling tooth from the mouth, this unnatural treatment pained the magic. Rua's gift was misused, so it was taken away." Wolf looked at Bilqu who nodded. "The Goddess still loves life. She left part of the magic so life would not die."

Wolf listened again, then explained, "Before the magic was taken, life had excess magic. Elders sought out the extra magic and stored it in the artifacts. The magic slept in the artifact until an elder drew on it for the most difficult of tasks."

336

Triene burst out, "That's what they did during the Mage wars!" eyes flaring with anger.

Wolf's answering look was grave, "It is why we must protect it. All the magic will be in one place. The mage would have too much power."

Susan felt her stomach clench and bile rose to her mouth. She was not the only one affected by Wolf's words. Jael's hand on her waist tightened and Will cupped his fist, mouth forming a grim line. Even Hrel's usual amiable expression had turned sombre, while Danin, who was standing to one side of the others, slowly nodded his agreement.

Wolf continued, "Most artifacts can only be used by one elder and that elder's element. The Hand of Rua is different. Each stone represents one element and all five stones can be used together."

"The prophesy has brought us together, Spirit, Fire, Earth, Water and Air. We need to learn why."

Bilqi stepped forward and offered his palm to Triene. She placed her own hand on top of his and glanced at Wolf for reassurance. This was it, she was going to use the magic in the artifact. Wolf gave her a lopsided smile, his amber eyes shining with pride. Triene pushed her shoulders back and inhaled deeply. Meanwhile, Bilqu was smiling at Will and miming the removal of his neck pouch. Will quickly obeyed and he offered the open pouch to Triene. She already knew which was the fire gemstone. She pulled out the vermillion gem and cradled it in her free hand. The others made their way back to the shelters, and soon, Triene was standing alone in the very centre of the clearing, the artifact resting in the palm of her raised hand.

Triene concentrated on Wolf's earlier words and on her breathing as she allowed herself to relax. She heard the magic purring contentedly at the back of her mind. That wasn't right, Wolf said that her magic wasn't separate. As she focussed, the neat form of the cat dissolved into sparkling motes that spread out, infusing her body and mind. Her eyes popped open; realisation reflected in their depths. The magic thrummed throughout her. The gemstone flickered in response to the change, and she inspected it. Unlike previous times when she had examined the gem, she could now feel the substance of the magic within it. She touched that magic with her own and gently guided it into herself. She immediately felt stronger and her thoughts were clearer. The final darkness that had lingered in the back of her mind sizzled away under the onslaught of the magic.

She was the Fortress of Fire in the prophesy, she could feel it in her soul. She smiled, and with a mere thought she created a wall of flame that shot up from the ground, up and up until it towered higher than the trees. There were gasps of fear and excitement, but Triene ignored them as she concentrated on the flames that rippled up the wall in a constant flow of heat. She wanted to aim that heat out, away from herself and anyone she would be shielding. She narrowed her eyes, and the magic responded, the volcanic sand on the other side of the wall began to melt and merge.

A wave of exhaustion hit her, and she quickly extinguished the fire, not wanting to lose control of the flame. She sagged, and her knees buckled. She sank to the ground, she just wanted to sleep. Wolf rushed over and supported her as a loud cheer rose up from the watching crowd. She managed to give Wolf a beaming smile. "I did it!" she said breathlessly.

"You did," he confirmed, as he picked her up and walked her over to the seats. "Next time make a smaller wall," he added drily as he lowered her to the ground. Jael and Susan knelt beside her, concern on their faces.

Triene looked at them, "I'm the Fortress!" she mumbled, still beaming widely.

Jael smoothed back her hair, "Yes, yes, you are. Rest now though, little one," he said softly, and leant her against him while Wolf walked into the clearing with the gold gemstone. He practiced switching between forms, the transformation becoming swifter and easier. Finally, in his wolf form, he padded over to Triene and stretched out beside her on a sigh. She relaxed into him, a sleepy smile on her lips, arm resting on his back so she could sink her fingers into his familiar ruff, and together they watched Hrel enter the clearing.

Hrel had selected the deep blue gem which had called to him when he first found the gemstones on the Isle of Rua. He had been unable to connect with it then and had assumed it powerless. Not his brightest moment, he thought. He hoped it didn't bear a grudge. He struggled to let go of his responsibilities and focus on the here and now. He had been using his magic since he was little and had never reached that state of complete union described by Wolf. He doubted his ability to do so now. He could feel that doubt holding him back. He fought against it, but fighting wasn't what he needed. That was the way of the mages. He tried to concentrate on his breathing, uncomfortably aware of his audience and the time he was taking.

Bilqu approached him and placed a soothing hand upon his forehead. He stared into her golden eyes, her eagle close to the surface. She whispered a word, "Heiwa." and his mind lowered the final barrier allowing his magic to squash his doubt as it flooded his senses. He felt the magic in the artifact swirl with his own until it filled him up. He tipped his head back and laughed, the joy of it bursting out of him. He felt free and light. He saw a group of giggling children, kits and cubs and knew what he was going to do.

He called to the sea and gathered it up into a bubble which bounced over the trees until it rose above the youngsters who squealed in delighted alarm. The water burst over them as they jumped away. Laughing and wet they ran over to Hrel and shook their bodies sending water droplets flying. He joined their laughter and ruffled their hair or fur fondly. All the while the exhilaration and magic flowed like a gushing river through his veins. He felt the artifact's magic return to the gemstone and made to give it back to Will.

Will shoved a small neck pouch at him. "'ere, this is for you," he said awkwardly.

"Why, thank you!" said Hrel, touched by the gift.

"'s nothing. I made one for each gem since you're all gonna be using them now," he muttered, uncomfortably.

"It was most thoughtful, Will." He looked at the carefully stitched leather, "Well made too. I thank you again." Will nodded his head, blushing brightly at the praise and hurried away. Hrel smiled at his retreating form.

Luncheon came and went, then it was Jael's turn. He had already chosen his gemstone and, after quizzing Triene on

340

her experience, he had stood aside from the clearing to surreptitiously connect with the artifact while the others finished off their meal. His stone was speckled with the rich browns and vibrant greens of nature, and it glowed warmly in his hand. He knew what he was going to do. He walked to the edge of the clearing and bent down onto one knee. He used his magic to dig a hole through the sand, down into the earth below. He then buried a shiny, chestnut brown seed and sat back. He focused on the new life within the seed, encouraging it to grow. He felt it vibrate and split, sending roots into the soil and a shoot up into the air. The seedling that burst forth grew taller and wider under Jael's care, eventually gaining a thick grey trunk, with brown branches that sprung from it, high above Jael's head. As they watched, leaf buds formed and unfolded into oblong leaves. Jael took a deep breath. A bead of sweat had formed on his forehead, and he wiped it dry before concentrating again on the tree. Clusters of thin branches sprouted amongst the leaves and hundreds of tiny white flowers bloomed, releasing their heady scent, before dying back and forming the lychee fruits. Jael exhaled loudly. It had been hard work, but he had managed it. He stood back proudly.

Many of the Spirit elders moved closer to examine the tree, awe on their faces. They had expected a show of strength from the Earth elder and were moved by his choice. Susan came to join Jael, slipping her arm through his and declaring, "That was amazing!"

Jael tipped up his chin, "Not a warrior move, I know, but this felt the right thing to do," he said simply.

Susan rubbed his chest, "and that's why I love you," she murmured back.

Jael's arm gripped her tighter, and his eyes locked with hers. He saw her look of shock as she realised what she had just admitted. His smile widened, and he bent in for a brief kiss before whispering against her cheek. "I love you too!" Still slightly embarrassed but heart racing with pleasure, Susan slapped his chest gently as she said, "Of course you do! I'm very loveable." Taken aback by the thought, she realised she did believe she was lovable! Amazing! She sashayed back to their friends with Jael laughing as he followed.

It was Danin's turn, but the priest didn't seem to realise it as he was still scribbling in his notebook. Susan leant over and gently tapped his arm. He jumped and stared at her, eyes wide and confused. She indicated to where Bilqi awaited him in the clearing, and Will handed him the final gemstone of swirling white and blue. Danin took it automatically but didn't seem to notice it in his hand. Instead, he peered at Bilqi over the top of his glasses, his eyes worried. Bilqi smiled reassuringly but Danin didn't seem to be comforted and remained where he was.

Will eyed him, then he suggested lightly, "You better go get done with the gemstone. You'll have even more to add to your book, after," he said.

Danin stood up at that, "Yes, of course! I must use it so my research is complete." He hastened over to Bilqi, holding his gemstone in front of him. Bilqi stepped back and allowed Danin space. Danin concentrated, The Spirit elders had said that the magic was not different to a muscle in his leg, he thought. I just need to use it. It made sense, he had always known this, he had just been taught to quiet it, to hide it, just like his questions or thoughts. Even the Temple hadn't wanted his real thoughts, just the ones they told him to have.

He looked at the gemstone in his hand and he bonded with the magic in it easily. He created a breeze to create shapes in the sand, rippled lines and spirals, like the ones raked in the courtyard back at the Temple. They were meant to represent the ocean, he thought, but the ocean moves. He directed the breeze to make the grooves fluctuate giving the impression of flowing water in the sand, rippling outwards from him to the edge of the clearing. The sudden explosion of appreciation had him stopping abruptly and putting his hands over his ears. Will scooted over to him, and prised one hand away to pop the cork plug in Danin's right ear before doing the same on the other side. Danin blinked and pushed his glasses up his nose. Will waved at him to go back to the others and Danin followed, flattening some of the ripples he had made beneath his boots.

## Chapter 29

That night and through the following morning, dark rain clouds besieged the sky, bringing rumbling rolls of thunder from across the sea, and blinding flashes of lightning to the island. Everyone crammed into the shelters, which did well to keep them dry since the rain was sharp and strong.

While they took refuge, Danin used the opportunity to explain his calculations for the merging of the worlds. It was a long and detailed explanation that had Susan's mind spinning. Will's eyes had glazed over, and if Jael wasn't mistaken, he was on the verge of falling asleep, luckily he was being propped up against the wall. Jael had managed to follow some of the information, and just ignored the bits he didn't understand on the basis that Danin understood it and that was all that mattered.

When Danin finished his discourse, Hrel sought confirmation of the date. Then he said, "It will take us three weeks to reach the coast, and we will then need time to travel to the plateau. That means we only have one week to train before we leave."

"Indeed, that is the case, since we must reach the plateau before the magic's arrival," confirmed Danin.

Susan was concerned about the second stage of the journey, "There is no other option than to make a path through the rainforest?"

Danin gave her a nod, pleased that she had understood. "That is correct."

Hrel attempted to reassure her, "Several members of my crew have experience of the terrain and will be able to help. They believe the trek will take about two days before we reach the plateau."

Ah yes! thought Susan, the climb. The plateau jutted high above the rainforest, its sides sheer and smooth. She had visited Yosemite National Park on a geography school trip to California and recalled the glacier cut rockfaces. Beautiful to see, impossible for an amateur to climb. They were expecting to complete a similar climb without modern equipment and after 48 hours hiking through a tropical rainforest! Jael's promise to help with the climb didn't reassure. What was worse, the mage or mages they were planning to stop could already be there and they would have a battle as soon as they reached the top! All with just one week's practice with the Hand of Rua, since they wouldn't be able to practice on board, and as yet without a clear strategy for using the artifacts together. Susan sighed and rubbed her neck. She was feeling nauseous with this headache. Jael added his hand and firmly massaged her shoulders.

They sat quietly now, listening to the rhythmic patter as the rain bounced off the roof. Jael continued to rub Susan's neck. She was so tense. She was worried about their quest, of course. She was a planner, she liked to organise everything down to the last detail and if she couldn't, she got anxious. Jael believed in being prepared, but he knew that life couldn't be controlled. All you could do was prepare yourself physically and mentally for the worst you could imagine happening, then deal with life the best you could. When back on the ship he would get Susan and

Triene climbing the rigging and they were already working on their strength and stamina. He could also use his Earth magic and the artifact to make the trek through the rainforest and the climb easier once he got a feel for the composition and layout. They would be as ready as they could be.

Will had started snoring and Hrel looked across at the lad. He was a good lad and made for a solid member of his crew, he had real potential for a leadership role on board and he and Uisca had discussed training him up should he decide to remain on the Coral Skies. They needed to succeed in this venture first though. It wasn't going to be easy, but his crew always did like a challenge. They would be taking turns in fight training against the magic over the next few days. That would be useful for them and useful for those trying to throw magic at them. It wouldn't be much, but it would be better than nothing.

Susan was worrying… Damnit! She was supposed to be the Guide in the prophesy, although clearly not in the map sense. She could only think that she must be the one to guide them to success. The only problem was she didn't know how! She had been worrying over a particular problem for some time now, and Wolf's explanation about the magic yesterday had only made the problem worse. She needed to put it out there in the hope that together they could find a solution. "I spent most of last night trying to come up with a strategy for using the magic in the fight." She placed a hand over her stomach and took a deep breath before continuing. "I realised that I was trying to kill people with it. That isn't what the magic is for! The mages forced the magic to destroy and if we use it for that purpose, we would be doing the very thing we are trying to prevent!" She looked helplessly at the others.

Will had woken upon hearing Susan's voice, and he was the first to speak, "Yeah, I get that. Me mum, always told me that magic was to 'elp living things, not kill 'em."

Triene added vehemently, "I agree. I don't want to kill anyone with magic."

Jael frowned and asked, "But without using the magic we won't be able to do enough, and why else would the prophesy include us?"

Wolf yawned, then shifted into his human shape. He spoke in a measured tone, "Life kills and fights to survive." He shrugged before adding, "The mother protects her young to ensure their survival, the eagle kills the fish to feed, the plant will kill the deer that tries to eat it, so future deer learn to avoid it." He leant back and waited for the others to contemplate what this meant.

Will looked confused, "So we can fight with the magic?" Wolf didn't answer.

Susan was frowning, her eyes pensive, "So we can fight for the survival of ourselves and each other, but not in anger, greed or revenge." She thought some more. "We shouldn't kill unless we have no alternative, as that wouldn't be justifiable for survival?"

"Perhaps we will need to focus on defence when using the magic," suggested Jael.

"I don't think that's quite right. I think we can attack first if that is necessary." She looked at Wolf whose expression remained mild. "I think it is what is in our minds that is important." she concluded tentatively.

Jael nodded slowly, and Triene grimaced but agreed. Hrel was the least concerned by the thought of killing and accepted this with a nonchalant nod. Wolf simply stated, "That is good," and settled back to sleep.

Susan muttered quietly to herself, "It sounds simple, but I bet it isn't in the heat of battle." Jael folded his arms around her, and she lay back against him and sighed.

## Chapter 30

Seven more days of training passed them by, and now it was time to leave the islands to head for the plateau. The friends packed their things and bid farewell to Bilqi, Bilqu and the other Spirit elders, promising to return soon, their doubts and fears buried behind their smiles and jovial air. Many of the Spirit elders felt the decision by their ancestors to disappear rather than prevent the first Mage War had been wrong, and a score of them boarded the Coral Skies, determined not to make the same mistake again.

Will's new friend, the young panther Baraq, bounded on board and scaled the new main mast to sit next to him on the highest yard while he awaited the call to unfurl the sails. She hummed with excitement as they bobbed along the eddies and through the passageway between the looming rock islands that protected her home. She had never been beyond her own islands. As the ship finally emerged from the narrow passageways of the archipelago, Baraq stood. Her emerald eyes sparkling as she spied the clear blue skies reflected in endless ripples all the way to the edge of the world.

Will and the other riggers unfurled the sails, adjusting them to catch the breeze and the bow sliced through the waves towards their destination. The crew's delight at being back at sea was expressed through a lively shanty that echoed from the top of the masts to the bottom of the holds. The song was both a cry of joy and a cry of defiance to the mages and soldiers they would soon have to face.

The first couple of days at sea were idyllic. The sun was hot, but the wind filled the sails and the sea remained calm. The third day, however, turned muggy, the air so thick that all movement felt slowed as if pushing against the sea itself. Even when night fell, there was no relief from the humidity. Triene wiped the sweat from her brow before it stung her eyes and recorded Uisca's sextant readings on the chart. She cast her gaze longingly over the cooler sea. Close to the horizon, the moonlight caught on the crests of some larger waves heading their way. They would be in for a bumpier ride soon. She drew Uisca's attention to them, asking what could be causing them. He stared at the approaching waves, "Could be a storm or a shift in the ground, we'll see soon enough."

"A storm?" questioned Triene. She peered at the clear night sky, trying to find a cloud, and failing. "Are you sure?"

"Aye," replied Uisca, turning back to his work.

Shortly before dawn, the order to secure all loose items and furniture had been given and it wasn't long after that the first of the waves reached them. They were rocked sideways as each wave hit, and by the afternoon and, to Uisca's disgust, they had to turn from their path in order to meet the stronger waves head on.

The humidity continued, and Susan was complaining of another bad headache and nausea. Even Triene felt an ache deep in her bones that made her irritable, snapping at Danin as he fussed when she helped him store his research. They had finally all sat down and were gloomily picking at their evening meal when the half-expected call of "Storm Ahoy" was passed down from the deck. Crew members rushed to ready the ship. Hrel sent Jael to help move the canons and

350

shot to the hold to act as additional ballast, and to secure it so it wouldn't burst through the hull. He instructed Triene to keep watch over the gunpowder since it was the most vulnerable location in a lightning strike. Hrel then demanded Danin's presence on deck as he bounded up the steps. Wolf, as the only human Spirit elder on board, went to help secure the others in their quarters. Susan's head was reeling and her stomach churning. She wasn't going to be much help. She tentatively followed Uisca to the Captain's quarters, in the hope that there was something gentle she could do. Unnoticed, Will snuck up to the main deck, determined to help with the sails.

The deckhands were already battening down the hatches as Hrel appeared on deck. He exchanged a brief nod with the boatswain, before greeting the quartermaster who was watching the darkening skies with a wary eye. Hrel followed his gaze, an ominous anvil shaped cloud filled with sparks and crackles was chasing them down. Loud rumbles of thunder followed in its wake.

Danin had come up behind Hrel and stared at the storm cloud blankly. Hrel explained what Danin had to do, "I need you to go to the lateen sail," he said pointing to it at the stern of the ship. Danin didn't respond. Hrel frowned, before realisation dawned. The thunder was getting louder. Danin would need his earplugs. He found a pair in his own pocket, they had all taken to carrying a set, and handed them over. Danin blinked at them, then promptly popped them in his ears before looking at Hrel expectantly. Hrel walked him to the lateen sail and pointed to it. He indicated that Danin should remove one earplug, which he did. "We need to keep an even flow of wind in this sail, so we steer directly into the waves, understand?" Danin nodded, but Hrel felt he needed more motivation. "If we run parallel to the waves we will capsize, and everyone will die." Hrel paused then added "and all your work will be lost." Danin nodded more firmly. He placed the plug back in his ear and focused on his magic while Hrel waved at a deckhand to help secure Danin in place.

Hrel headed to the foredeck and stood by the rail at the bow, watching the waves grow longer and wider. The swells heading their way were dangerously high. He prayed to the absent Rua that they wouldn't be tossed over, a real risk if things got much worse. He couldn't prevent that, but he could reduce any flooding of his ship. He called on the magic in the artifact to help him guide the breaking waves away from the deck. He wouldn't be able to keep all of them from crashing over the bow, but he would do his best.

In the Captain's quarters Uisca and Susan used the fixed furniture to climb their way to the leaded windows at the stern. The ship crested the next wave and plunged into the trough. Susan was thrown sideways , bumping her hip against the window ledge. Uisca was already pulling the wooden shutters closed and fixing the catch. Susan reached out and grabbed her own as she saw the ship heading towards the bottom of the trough. She braced herself against a chair as the ship then tipped upwards. It was like having to walk from one car to another on a rollercoaster, she thought. The shutters slammed in place and she fixed the catch just as the bow crested the wave in an explosion of spray.

Susan was feeling very nauseous and pressed the back of her hand against her mouth as she clung to the top of the chair with the other hand. It had been a long time since she had had sea sickness, but these were the worst conditions she had sailed in. Uisca yelled at her to tie herself to the wall, pointing to a rope set out for that purpose. She made her way over to it and wrapped it around her leg before slumping to the floor. Uisca had spotted her green tinge and handed her a large jug before leaving. It was just in time, as her stomach contracted and thrust its contents upwards and into the jug. Alone and shuddering, Susan worried about the others. She started. Where did Will go? God, he wouldn't be stupid enough to be on the rigging in this, surely?

Vicious gusts preceded the storm cloud which erupted in a crash of thunder and sheets of lightening as it approached. The boatswain had sent additional riggers to help furl the sails. The gusts were snatching at the cloth, shaking it like a dog with a rag in its teeth. It made the steering into the waves much harder, knocking the ship sideways then back again, as she perilously tipped one way then the other. The sails slapped against the riggers as they clung to the ropes. Will and Flim were the fastest on the ropes and had been sent up the main mast to the uppermost yard to help adjust the halyards and furl the top sail, although their speed was hampered by the need to keep themselves tied to the rigging as they climbed. The boatswain had been insistent saying, "Ye not be just risking yer own life but that of your mates, if ye join Davy Jones, the sails won't be furled and the Coral Skies will be dragged to his locker, fer sure."

Flim scampered up with Will following quickly behind. The sea spray, full of abrasive salt, pelted their exposed skin making it raw and sore. As they passed the first and largest sail, a gust caught it and it snapped, full of wind, pulling the ship into the trough. The ship tilted to a 45-degree angle and Will's feet flew off the wet ropes and dangled over the sea, while his hands gripped the ropes as tightly as he could. The rope around his middle pulled tightly holding him in place even as his hands slipped. They crested the wave and as the ship righted, the sail slapped wildly, catching Will's fingers. His heart pumping with exertion and exhilaration, he glanced at Flim who had been similarly slowed, Flim gave him a nod and they continued to climb.

Up top, three other riggers were already fighting the wildly flapping sail. Trey saw them arrive and headed towards the mast so they could master the starboard side halyards. The storm cloud was nearly upon them, the crackle of thunder and lightning almost overhead. They had to get the sail under control. Will managed to heave and secure part of the sail, but he needed to get to the edge of the yard to finish it. Flim had completed his section and was coming towards him to help. If Will were to just do a short scramble and leap he would get to the edge much quicker. Flim seemed to read his mind and shouted, "Don't ye bloody dare!" as he fixed his own rope to the next section. Will started guiltily then secured his rope, to make his way safely to the end of the yard.

On the quarterdeck, Hrel faced the oncoming swells, his magic and that of the artifact combining to combat the crest of the waves as they broke around and over his ship. He parted the spray as it crashed against the hull, sending it curling away from the deck. The force behind the waves had been building for a long time and he didn't have the power to control it completely. Water washed over the deck and back into the sea with too many of the waves they rode.

The ship creaked her protest at the pummelling she was receiving. A bolt of lightning struck the sea about a mile distant, electricity slamming into the fish that had remained too close to the surface. Lightning strikes were a danger he hoped they wouldn't have to contend with. He shook his head and focused on the waves, they were the immediate threat.

Flim and Will dropped down onto the deck and water washed over their feet. They had to unwind the rope tying them to the rigging so they could head below deck. Will was still struggling with his rope when Flim joined him, head ducking down, eyes blinking in the salty spray. He smiled, water from the rain streaming down his face and into his mouth. "Ye did good, lad!" he said as he stretched out his free hand to pat a beaming Will on the shoulder. A wave crashed over the side, slamming them hard against the rigging and wooden posts. As quickly as it came, it was sucked back to the sea, swiping Flim off his feet and dragging him with it. Will felt it tug at him too and he clutched at the drenched rope, but his hand slid off. He was borne towards the rail, desperately holding his breath as the water submerged him completely. His body jerked and stopped, the rope he had been struggling with had slipped down to his ankle and pulled tight under the force of the wave. Flim continued to slide past. Will reached out to grab hold of him, but their fingers only met for a glancing touch before Flim, wearing a mask of fear, was whipped over the rail and into the sea.

Will screamed as the water drained away. He scrambled to release his ankle. He fumbled and pulled desperately, trying to get free. Another rigger, Vocare, laid a calming hand on his and they rode out another, less ferocious wave, before he helped him stagger down the steps to the Captain's quarters. Vocare helped him sit next to Susan and fixed him in place. Will's face was white and drawn. Vocare braced himself on the desk and addressed Susan, "We lost Flim." he said starkly. Will's eyes flashed towards him and Vocare nodded sympathetically. "It happens, we may lose more afore this blows over." He then turned and left the room carefully shutting the door as he left.

Will bowed his head. Water dripped onto the floor.

"What happened, Will?" Susan asked gently.

Will took a gasping breath but didn't look up.

"Did you see it happen?" Susan continued, sensing that Will needed to find a release for some extreme emotion. He shuddered and gasped again. This time he looked at her, a hank of wet hair fell over his face and she couldn't distinguish between seawater and tears.

"I tried to grab 'im, but I couldn't reach 'im. 'E was struggling but the sea just took 'im. I couldn't save 'im, I tried, but I couldn't save 'im." The words burst out of him. When he finished, he wrapped his arms around his knees, pulling them close, and lowered his head again as sobs racked his body. In between the sobs came a repeated indistinct mumble, "I couldn't save im". It sometimes sounded like he was saying "I couldn't save 'er" but Susan wasn't sure. She held his hand and offered her silent support until the tears dried up and just a hollowness remained. Susan cradled him in her arms as the storm raged on around them. Will drifted into an exhausted sleep and Susan finally shed her own tears, for Flim and for Will.

Eventually, the storm blew over and the intensity of the waves diminished. Susan had cleaned up her sick which she had been unable to keep in the jug and was back next to Will when Uisca hurried into the cabin to collect his navigational tools. "I heard about Flim," he said gruffly. "The sea took him, as it takes all of us one day."

Will's bleary red eyes opened and peered at Uisca. He gave a half sob as he apologised, "I should have grabbed him".

Uisca gave him a stern look, "Think ye're stronger than the sea, do ye?" Will shook his head reluctantly. "Then stop ye're wailing. Flim got taken, he was a good man and will be missed. But we honour him by living and remembering him. Right?"

Will sat a little straighter and managed to say in a shaky voice, "Right".

Uisca glanced over Will's bedraggled form, and added, "Ye need to dry up." He aimed for his trunk and took out a warm sheet and some clothes. "Ye can use these fer now.". He threw them to Will who automatically moved forward to catch them, but his ankle collapsed beneath him and he plopped back down, swearing. Susan helped him pull up his trouser leg and winced in sympathy. Uisca came over to peer at it.

Will's shin, ankle and foot were purple and swollen and the skin was hot to the touch. Where the rope had ripped at his skin, it was raw and weeping and coated with crusts of dried blood. "OW!" exclaimed Will, adrenaline and grief having hidden the pain until that moment. Uisca tutted. "I'll send

357

the surgeon to ye. Strip and dry off, but don't go wearing my things until he's finished!" he waggled his finger sternly. "I'll not have yer blood staining them." He then left to call for Xilm before heading to the deck and Hrel.

Danin was slumped on the quarterdeck. He was soaked to the skin and shivering with exhaustion and shock. Hrel was still standing but his back was sloped and he was leaning heavily on the rail as he discussed the clean-up with the quartermaster. When he saw Uisca he said in a slurred voice, "We must get back on course. We have lost too much time. We need to get to the plateau!" Uisca nodded his agreement even as he beckoned over a couple of nearby deckhands. Uisca addressed the deckhands, "Get the Captain and the priest to their beds. Bring them some food and water then leave them to sleep." The deckhands nodded and immediately set about their task, Hrel tried to pull away at first, but Uisca spoke to him firmly, "Ye're a pile of wet rags, Hrel. Ye need to rest and eat or ye'll be no use to anyone."

Hrel's lips quirked up and he gave him a washed out smile, "You are right as always, Uisca." and he held out his arm so the deck hand could support him and take him away.

That dealt with, Uisca took his tools over to the quartermaster, whose stern face was tired and worn. He said to Uisca, "I fear the storm has blown us off course and taken most of the wind with it." He looked at the sails which were being unfurled by the solemn riggers.

Uisca acknowledged the difficulty, "Aye" then proceeded to unpack his equipment. "The wind will pick up and we'll be ready when it comes."

"Aye," agreed the quartermaster on a sigh.

## Chapter 31

The next day the riggers were still working tirelessly to catch the breezes that fluttered by, but the ship barely moved. Despite his weariness, Danin clambered up to the deck and called up a wind that had them moving steadily but slowly, until the exhaustion caught up with him. He swayed and crumpled into a limp heap. The boatswain hurried over and turned him onto his back. She placed her ear to his mouth and her hand on his chest. Reassured by the shallow breaths, she beckoned Nooj, one of her burlier deckhands, to join her. "Feed the laddie and put him abed." she said gruffly, then with a tight smile added, "Give him rum if he tries to rise afore he be ready." The man gave a tombstone grin, and hefted Danin over his shoulder like a sack of grain before bouncing him down the steps.

Without Danin, the ship dawdled, buffered more by the waves than carried by the wind. Susan paced in the communal quarters, anxiety knotting her insides, making her feel queasy again. "We need to get to the plateau. We only have four more days before the merging of worlds. Two of those will be used up walking through the rainforest! We are going to be too late and too exhausted to stop the mage!" She paused to frown in Will's direction, before pacing again. She was the latest visitor in a long line aimed at ensuring he remained in his cot until his broken ankle had a chance to heal.

"We still 'ave time," he said with an attempt at his old optimism, although his eyes remained sunken and distant. "We 'ad a couple of days extra in our planning so it'll be alright." He was propped up on his cot with his leg elevated

360

by a makeshift hammock. The break had been fixed and was strapped up with two wooden paddles on either side of the ankle. The wound had been cleaned, and Jael had helped the surgeon prepare a poultice that would prevent infection. Susan stopped and shuddered, looking at his leg, remembering the slippery leeches that latched onto Will's swollen ankle when placed there by the surgeon. The leeches had tripled in size before falling off. Admittedly they had reduced the inflammation, but Susan really hoped that she wouldn't be needing medical treatment any time soon.

Triene's head whipped around the open door, a wide smile on her lips. "We've finally got a strong following wind and we are absolutely flying over the waves!" she exclaimed excitedly. Then without waiting for their response she declared, "I must tell Jael!" and disappeared.

Will put his hands behind his head cockily and declared in a self-satisfied manner, "There ye go! No problem!" Susan rolled her eyes at him, they might be moving now, but would it be enough? She continued to pace.

Just before dusk the following evening, the lad in the Crow's Nest called out the anxiously awaited, "Land Ahoy!" prompting a cheer from the crew above deck. Uisca wasn't ready to rejoice just yet. He headed for the foredeck, armed with his telescope and map. He scanned the distant coast for any indication that they had managed to sail proximate to the plateau. Hrel joined him and raised his own glass to his eye. The coastline was a single line of pale sands which blended into the sea. Beyond the sands were the lush greens of the dense rainforest over which wispy clouds flowed like multiple waterfalls. The sun began to descend over the sea behind them, setting the sky on fire. Soon it would be too dark to see the coast. The bad weather had delayed them severely and they needed to get to the plateau. Where was it? Although the reds in the sky were now brightening the sand, the forest was swallowing all colour as it darkened. A glint of red flashed above the trees. Uisca focused his telescope on that spot. There it was! Emerging from within the forest and clouds to reflect the colours in the sunset was the tabletop plateau. Relieved, Uisca nudged Hrel and redirected his gaze. Lowering his eyepiece, Hrel whispered to Uisca, "You're a genius!" before he gave the command to sail starboard and prepare to disembark.

Baraq skulked into the communal quarters and lay on the cot next to Will; both looked sullen. Will was glowering at his leg while Baraq had her front paws crossed beneath her lower jaw and she grumbled her discontent. Will heard her and agreed with his own grumble, "Yeah! I get it, Baraq. What if they need us? I'm the one in the prophesy, I got the gemstones. I weren't too young then, was I? You got claws and teeth, I din't 'ave those even." They sat in silent agreement on the unfairness of life. Then Will's face crumpled, "I don't want to see more people dying though." he said quietly. Baraq pricked up her ears and looked at him. She then padded over to Will's cot and roughly rubbed her face against his. He reached out his hand and ran his fingers over her fur as unexpected tears rolled silently down his cheek. When he spoke it was a reluctant whisper, "I couldn't stop Flim from going over." Baraq fixed her sympathetic eyes on Will's face as he continued talking, "If I could 'ave just 'eld onto 'im…." Guilt flitted across Will's face before he forced out the thoughts that tormented him still, "I couldn't stop me dad from 'itting me mum till she died either." He gulped down a sob. "I grabbed 'is arm, but 'e threw me across the room. I went back and tried to get between 'em but 'e 'it me in the 'ead and I blacked out. When I woke, it were just me and me mum. I tried to get 'er to wake up, but she were dead." Baraq sprung up onto Will's cot and lay across him, snuggling him like her family would snuggle when one was hurting. Her pink rough tongue slowly licked away his tears and he tentatively stroked her, needing the comfort, but not sure how to accept it.

It took several journeys and half the night, for all but the essential crew members to be provided with supplies and be transported to the beach. Susan had suggested that the sea eagle Spirit elders reconnoitre the plateau and report on their findings before the others began the climb. The possible threat from an Air mage meant the eagles needed to be careful not to raise suspicion. Susan's evenings watching David Attenborough meant she warned them that all six flying together would not be normal. Now, she stared at the opaque border where the forest met the sand. Those nature documentaries had often been set in rain forests and Sir David had enthused about the rich diversity of the insects and arachnids that lived there. Susan really wasn't looking forward to experiencing the bugs first hand. The ship's surgeon had insisted they gather up certain unpleasant creatures that would be needed after a battle. His vivid descriptions of the land-dwelling leeches and the large headed driver ants, with sharp scissor like mandibles just added to her reluctance.

The plan was for them to walk in a long line, with the minimum of light so they didn't garner attention from any mages or soldiers on the plateau. Triene lit the few torches they would use, infusing them with magic that should keep them burning throughout the night. Jael was to guide them with his Earth magic. A few members of the crew took the lead, using the sturdy branches they had trimmed into hooks to pull aside the brush before slashing into it with their long machetes.

Jael and Susan stepped carefully over the hacked vegetation, keeping close in the subdued light. Susan pulled her arms in tight, not wanting to touch the large ferns and leaves lining either side of their trail. Skin rashes and ticks were not on her to do list. Susan tried to control her breathing, this was not that bad, she told herself. The animals would be moving away from their path, disturbed by the cracks of the machetes and the wet crunch of their boots. They were moving at a faster pace than she had expected, the efficient elbow flicks cut through the undergrowth with speed. The pirates chopped at the undergrowth twice. The first cut was a sharp angle at mid-height, the second lower to the ground, clearing the route for them to march upon.

It was a hot and humid walk, the limited light only emphasising the oppressive tunnel through which they walked. Susan's attempt at a positive attitude disappeared after an hour. She felt itchy and grubby, and very irritable. She had brought plenty of water with her but was getting through it fast. Her clothes were sticking to her, and her hair was heavy and lank. She stared at Jael's back as he walked in front of her. His circles of armpit sweat and the diamond between his shoulder blades just looked sexy, she thought grumpily. Even his hair was cute, curling wildly around his head.

Their column was forced to a halt by a tree that spanned several feet in diameter and disappeared high above the canopy that enclosed them. They would have to detour around it. Susan wondered why Jael hadn't directed them away from it earlier. He would have been aware of such a large tree in their path. In answer to her silent question, Jael indicated that they should wait and, carefully avoiding the needle-like spines that projected from its trunk, he placed his palm against the tree. His eyes drew closed as he combined the magic of the artifact with his own and allowed it to flow into the bark, enhancing the natural healing properties within it. When he stepped back, he instructed the men standing nearby to collect it. They obediently retrieved a knotted cloth and removed the bark, using the back of their machetes. When the cloth was full, it was tied together to form a bag which they hung from a stick.

Jael observed Susan's raised eyebrow, "It can be used to stop bleeding," he explained. Fear prickled her skin. This was what they were heading towards. A fight. A fight with swords and knives which would slice open flesh. She took a calming breath. She knew this already. She had chosen to do it. The world was relying on them, even if they didn't know it.

Watching them from the canopy above their heads a small brown creature hung upside down from a vine. It stared with large black eyes as it sniffed the air and its small round ears twitched at the scraping of the bark. It didn't have a tail to wrap around the vine or to use for balance, so it crawled along, monkey hands holding tight, until it reached the next tree and disappeared.

Once the bark had been collected, they continued walking.

365

Susan's body was heavy, and she could feel her heart stuttering as she fought to keep going. Small cramps were jumping in her legs and her mouth was sticky and dry. She opened her next waterskin and gulped down some of the warm liquid. It wasn't enough. Bloody hell! She thought angrily, she needed an electrolyte supplement, where the hell was she going to get that? Could it get any worse?! As if in response to her complaint, a flash of light, so bright it burst through the thick canopy and lit up the forest floor. Temporarily blinded, Susan stood still and swore roundly, her words drowned out by the powerful crash of thunder that accompanied the sheets of rain tearing through the trees. The rain congregated on wide leaves before bouncing off in even larger drops, to plop onto the rapidly saturated ground. The salty sweat from her brow dripped into Susan's eyes, stinging before it washed away. She stuck out her tongue trying to catch the salty water in her mouth. She continued marching; her boots splashed and squelched bringing up the scent of mulch with each step. The rain continued for the rest of the night and into the early morning, blocking all attempts by the sun to light their path. Eventually, the rain stopped, disappearing as quickly as it had begun. Dappled light filtered through, picking out the brightly coloured begonias and fungi. Flashes of blue and white birds flitted among the trees. She could see the creepers and liana lacing the canopy, a highway for the numerous red monkeys swinging and leaping between the trees as they foraged for insects, fruit and fresh new leaves to eat.

The sun had reached its highest point in the sky when they reached a clearing. A large tree had fallen, breaking smaller trees on its way down. The forest floor had only just begun the race for dominance. The tree provided a convenient

366

place to sit and rest. Susan sighed with relief as she lay down on the trunk and felt the sun attempt to dry her drenched clothes. Hrel called up to her, "Here, fill your waterskins!" and she promptly sat up eager to do so, until her spinning head made her lie down again with a groan. Jael pulled out her skins and Hrel released some of the fresh rainwater he had gathered, into them before moving on. Susan sat up more cautiously this time and Jael passed her some water and salted dried fish. She had reached the point of nausea again, but forced herself to eat it, knowing the salt would help with her dehydration.

Danin had found a wide branch to sit upon, and while he ate, he watched some red ants weaving a sticky nest on one of the larger leaves. They appeared to be using secretions from their larvae to create the weave. He remained fascinated by their endeavours while the others plotted the final stretch of their walk. The ants concluded their nest and Danin searched the ground for something else of interest. There was a moving shadow among the wide leaves. He got down from his branch and wandered over to investigate. A line of thousands of black ants, with disproportionately large heads, were heading away from the tree. Lining their route were soldier ants with huge horn like mandibles, standing upright as they scouted for trouble. Danin straightened and pushed back his glasses before announcing his discovery. "I do believe that I have discovered some driver ants." A few of the pirates, including the ship's surgeon, Xilm, were soon headed his way bearing large glass jars with pierced cork lids.

"Yep, that's them." said Xilm, "Let's scoop them up. Get some of those soldiers as well." Danin retreated. Those mandibles indicated a certain aggressive nature. He backed up a bit more as the pirates removed the lids and bent over the marching ants. "On the count of three," Xilm said. "we'll scoop 'em up, then jump out of the way before they cotton on. One, two and three." They dived in with the jars, leaping back and using sticks to brush off any ants that clung to the outside of the jars. They crammed the lids on as they ran away from the frantic soldier ants seeking out the source of the attack.

Most of the pirates got away with their booty before they were spotted, but one cried out, "Sonnoabitch, one bit me!"

Xilm, shouted, "Don't touch it!" but it was already too late, the pirate had tried to knock the ant off. Its body had fallen to the ground, but the head and jaws remained locked in place. The pirate was trying to pull it off, but the skin was tightly pinched and the jaws deep. Xilm sighed and taking out his knife headed for the swearing pirate.

Their rest was ended too soon, although the extra water and food helped renew their energy levels. The plateau above the distant trees, appeared much closer now, and it gave the much needed motivation to start walking again. They continued their march even as the sun set and continued walking in darkness again. Finally, Jael passed a message through the line that they were close to the cliffs and the dell at the base of the plateau. The torches were extinguished as they emerged into the moonlight. The cliff face's pale grey mottled rock jutted out of the ground and soared high above the trees. The rock was sheer and hard and smooth. Jael placed both hands on the granite, sensing its composition and structure. Earth elders used to crack the rock, he thought. He centred his attention on a small section and with

368

a pop it split, and he knocked it down to the ground. The crisply cut ledge was at knee height and would make a perfect step for climbing.

Susan placed her hand on his shoulder, "Let's hear what the Eagle Spirit elders have to say and take the time to rest and recover." Jael nodded but he crooked his neck back as he gave a final look at the rock towering above them.

Soon the eagles joined them and Wolf translated as they gave their report, "Soldiers, many more than our number, sit on the plateau, waiting. There is one tent which is lit from inside, and many campfires. They have swords and clothes of blood red," Wolf explained.

"How far from this edge are they?" asked Susan thinking about the noise they would make if Jael had to create steps.

"Half a mile or so." One of the eagles obviously had more to say about that since Wolf paused to listen then added. "A thicket lies between them and the edge." Susan sighed with relief. That was going to be her next question, they needed to be able to disguise their approach or they would be fighting before they finished the climb.

So, what did many more, mean? The last time they had seen the crimson clad soldiers there had only been around 50, obviously more had been recruited. There were about 140 of the crew so how many more could there be? Hrel asked the question and Wolf answered, "Five to our one." Susan gasped. That was not good, not good at all! Even the pirates seemed intimidated by those odds. They spent the next hour trying to work out a way they could improve their chances, but other than their previous plans with the magic, they had no solutions.

They had no choice but to rest and wait for what the dawn would bring.

## Chapter 32

Two hundred foot up and half a mile from the edge, a crimson army camped. They had arrived a week ago and since then nothing had happened but heat, rain and training. A group sat by one of the fires, drying their sodden clothes, while their meal cooked. They were bemoaning their inaction.

"I can't see why we couldn't 'ave longer in that last village," said the one with acne scars as he struck the stick in his hand with his knife. He was whittling it to a sharp point.

"Yeah, I mean we been stuck 'ere doing nothing for days. We could 'ave been 'aving a bit more fun with those women," said the man sitting next to him with a leer.

The younger man sitting closest to the fire rubbed the sweat from his face as he muttered angrily, "Or we could've been finding more of that gold they 'ad."

The first man gave a growl of frustration. "They 'ad it decorating their 'omes, like it were nothing. I only got 'alf of what I could've before 'e set fire to the lot!"

"It's not like we 'ad to get 'ere quickly!" complained another.

The man sitting furthest away mumbled something, and the first man looked at him and said, "What's that?"

He spoke a bit louder, raising his chin defiantly, "I said, we shouldn't be questioning the Commander. 'e wouldn't like it."

The first man scoffed loudly, "Wot 'e don't 'ear, won't 'urt 'im!"

The other man muttered again, "It weren't 'im getting 'urt that worried me."

Despite that initial show of defiance, they no longer spoke, instead they eyed the flames suspiciously as they waited for the monkey meat to finish cooking.

There was only one tent in the camp, and the Commander was currently sitting in it, studying the translation that came with the ancient's book. He had one hand resting on the Eye of Rua, making the magic inside the artifact recoil. He already knew what he had to do to trap the magic, the text had been helpful in that respect. Oh, the ancients had written it as a caution since it went against the magic's "purpose", according to their religion, but it had shown him how to force it into the artifact and store it there against its will. His own magic would bind it and channel it. Once in the artifact it couldn't escape until he had a use for it. The ancient's had been fools, limiting their power and the power of the artifacts in the name of their fictitious Goddess. The mages during the war had it right. Those with power over the magic should have power over the people. Back then, though, during the war, they had had to share the magic, fighting over their petty squabbles. Not so for him, soon he would be the most powerful mage Ruanh had ever seen and no one would be able to challenge him. He smiled to himself. He was looking forward to showing them what he could do.

It appeared that his plan to destroy the other mages and to keep the knowledge of the magic's return secret had been successful since no one had arrived to challenge him for its power. That was what his army was for, of course, to kill any challengers. He would have no need for them after this. He might even use them for practice.

He had first used his magic to kill when he was only five years old. He had torched his mother and found that he liked seeing the fear and pain, hearing the sizzle and pop and smelling the burning flesh. It was like an addiction, killing and forcing the reluctant magic to obey. He closed his eyes and recalled that sweet moment.

He had been sitting on the bare floorboards, coated with dust, examining the dead mouse caught in the mousetrap. The spring had broken its back, folding the creature in two, and piercing its skin. The blood was congealing already. He opened the jaws of the trap so that he could remove the mouse and tossed it aside. He then examined the mechanism. It was a powerful spring.

His mother was splayed out on the chair drunk again. She had been singing a melancholy melody to herself, but soon she would remember his presence. And there it was, that realisation she wasn't alone. She slid out of the chair and swayed as she approached him, "Look at you, you disgusting little shit!" she slurred, beginning her familiar tirade. He kept quiet and continued to examine the mousetrap. Perhaps he could leave it somewhere where she would stand on it. Perhaps it would break her toes like it broke the mouse's back. He would like that.

She threw her empty mug at him and he moved having expected it. It shattered against the wall. Soon she would hit him, then she would cry and babble about how sorry she was. He hated her sloppy kisses and hugs, more than the

373

fists. He looked up at her just as she was stretching out to slap him around the head. He raised his hand automatically, to soften the blow. He was still holding the mousetrap and it snapped across her fingers.

Screaming, she struggled to remove it from her misshapen digits, the purple bruising already bubbling up to the surface. She dropped it to the ground as she spat out, "You fucking little bastard!" She grabbed him with her good hand and hauled him to his feet by the front of his tunic and swung him against the corner of the table. The impact had him gasping for air. She was coming for him again, eyes wild. She wasn't going to stop this time.

His cherubic face scrunched up, "I want you dead!" he shouted, as he thrust his own fist in her direction. A flame burst from his hand, heading straight into his mother's face. The skin around her nose and cheeks burnt first, peeling back to reveal the cartilage and bone beneath them. The eyelids and eyes were next. She clutched at her face, desperate to put out the flames, but her hands caught alight. She staggered back onto a pile of dirty clothing knocking over the remaining cask of gin. The alcohol spilled over the rags and the fire wrapped her in its grasping tendrils. She writhed and kicked, no longer able to scream.

He felt his magic recoil from the violence, but he forced it to continue, his control over the magic strong even then. He watched her skin and flesh blacken and shrivel, watched the way her pale bones were revealed as the muscle contracted. He smelt the roasting flesh, noting it bore a resemblance to the beef they had stolen a few nights before, until an acrid stench made him screw up his nose and move back. When she stopped kicking, he allowed his magic to return and hide.

374

He left the remaining fire to spread and destroy the thatched hut that had been his home. He stood outside, watching it catch the thatched roofs of the closely packed homes of his neighbours. Watched them yell and run to escape the ferocious flames. He heard the screams from those trapped inside.

The old couple that took him in, gave him shelter, food and clothing, had felt sorry for him, thought he had been traumatised. He remembered the look of disbelief and fear on their faces when he left five years later. He had trapped them in a circle of flame so they could watch their precious home and belongings burn around them before they too went up in flame. He had taken their coin and travelled after that.

Yes, he thought, he was used to forcing the magic to do his bidding. It barely resisted now.

## Chapter 33

The company at the bottom of the plateau stirred with the rising of the sun. Sleep had been elusive for many, but at least they had fed and rested. Weapons were now sharpened, limbs stretched and minds readied as they silently prepared for the final part of their journey and the battle that awaited them. They retreated from the cliff face where Jael stood, hands and forehead resting against the rock. It had been agreed that Jael should attempt to work on the whole of their climb rather than in small segments, in the hope that the army on the plateau would believe it to be a natural shift in the ground and so not be warned of their arrival. Two of the eagle Spirit elders were sent to observe the soldiers' reaction and report back.

From beneath the rainforest's canopy, Susan watched Jael's hands slide along the rock, feeling the fine bumps in the surface of the granite. It was still cool, the sun hadn't reached that part of the cliff yet, but as he sent the magic searching for the fault lines and softer rock, he felt the heat of the morning sun as it was absorbed into the granite higher up the wall. The magic began to rearrange the rock. Ledges and hollows appeared, accompanied by loud pops, cracks and shudders. Stones and rubble bounced and tumbled to the ground, landing with loud thumps all around the dell. As the shifting rock settled, Jael stepped back to await the eagles' report. Susan slipped her arm around his waist and gave him a reassuring squeeze. He hugged her back then checked her cutlass and dagger were safely stowed. "You must keep back, away from the fighting." he reminded her for the third time that morning. "The weapons are for defence only." Susan nodded again. She had no intention of throwing herself into the battle, but she was going to help where she could. If Jael thought she was here to just hide, he was very much mistaken.

Eventually the eagles returned and the news they bore was good. Although the soldiers had been alarmed by the shaking and the noise, there had been no sign that they suspected anything but natural causes. Even better, they had moved further from the edge, no doubt concerned it would be unstable. The eagles also had a warning, many of the soldiers were already armed and training so would be quick to respond to their approach.

The mood was solemn as they began the climb. The wide ledges made it relatively easy, even for the panthers who had been worried by the inability to dig their claws into the rock. The riggers swarmed the cliff face confidently, but others clung tightly, all too aware of the drop. Susan had done what she could to reduce the risk, the eagles were ready to push anyone who slipped back against the wall and Danin and Hrel were ready to slow any fallers with a puff of air beneath a bubble of water. She had wanted to use vines in the climb too, but the crew had rejected her plan of tying them to one another as they said it would restrict them if they needed to fight as soon as they reached the top.

The undulating wave of bodies scaled the cliff, reaching the clifftop in fives or tens, only to crawl and nestle among the wide leaves and tall ferns that shrouded them from sight of the awaiting army. They had to move slowly and stealthily; any noisy rustle of the undergrowth would alert the soldiers on guard. Fortunately, the sounds of shouted commands, boots stomping, and swords clashing were loud enough to mask their arrival. They halted to take stock of the army before them, a crimson carpet of malice. The reality felt like a blow to the solar plexus depriving Susan of air. We're going to die! There's too many of them. Oh my God! So many will get hurt. The thoughts tumbled until she steeled her spine and took a deep breath, the world needs us to win, and we shall win. Her chin tipped upwards.

There was a blurring of light, a moment of darkness and red desolation, as a low hum resonated across the plateau. Suddenly the magic was with them. A condensed ball which exploded in joy, shooting out towards the life surrounding it. It seeped into the earth, soared into the sky and infused the insects, lizards and mammals with its essence. The trees and ferns vibrated with energy as the magic soaked into them. The soldiers stood still, stunned by the joy and strength surging through them. The pirates grinned as they too felt the power flow through their veins. Susan could feel the aches from the climb and her fears of failure dissipate in the onslaught.

The elders not only felt the rush but could taste the magic around them, Jael's connection to the Earth meant he could even sense the magic filling the stems on the smallest of plants and being carried around the wide leaves, feeding the plant's lifeforce. Hrel could feel every drop of moisture in the ground as it evaporated in the heat of the sun and rose up to the sky. Danin looked up as the air shifted above him, he could visualise the currents that supported the bird's wings, and the clouds forming another storm far away over the sea. Wolf and the other Spirit elders felt the magic's power nudge them into expanding their animal forms. They embraced the change, doubling in size and strength. The

378

eagles stood six foot tall, with a wingspan of twice that size. The panthers now stretched out a full 10 feet long and flexed their enormous claws, making the men next to them eye them nervously and shuffle away.

Wolf had shifted into his animal form once he had completed the climb and had hunkered down next to Triene. As he too grew, his expanding body pushed Triene over. She sat back up and stared at him, her mouth dropping open in surprise. Wolf licked his lips and grinned at her, pleased with the advantage this change would give him. He had already been a large wolf but now he would tower over a horse. Triene reached over to scratch behind his ear and gave a bewildered smile in return, even as her own magic revelled in the influx of additional power. For the first time in her life, she could sense her magic's connection to the sun, that giant source of light and heat. She finally understood the link to life and fire and felt at peace.

From within the silence, a peel of delighted laughter rang out as the Commander felt the fire magic lick its way through his body. He sensed the power, not the life, and drew it into himself. He grabbed the Eye of Rua and opened the channel through which he would funnel the magic. He began to spin the magic, drawing it back towards him as it tried to spread out across the land.

Jael felt the magic struggling against the mage and indicated that they should encourage the magic to seek refuge inside the gemstones that made up the Hand of Rua. They had run out of time. They had to act now. Hrel shouted the command and they surged forward.

## Chapter 34

The surge of pirates took the soldiers by surprise, coming as it did when the magic first flooded their bodies and minds. One of the guards who recovered from his shock faster than his fellows, raised the alarm. After a moment's hesitation the soldiers' training kicked in, spurred on by their commander's laughter, always a worrying sound. They grabbed their weapons and formed a unit of ten lines, with the most eager taking the front. Those were the soldiers that could see the smaller number facing them, and they puffed out their uniformed chests, confident that they would easily defeat this ragtag bunch.

The pirates came to a halt some fifty feet away and kept their weapons lowered while they allowed their Captain to speak. The soldiers jeered and hurled insults as Hrel's amplified voice, washed over them, "We are here to protect the magic, not fight you. If you leave now, you will be unharmed."

A scarred captain sneered his retort, "Nah, my friend here wants to play." He shook his sword as cruel laughter and more jeers erupted from his men. The pirates grinned, they were ready to fight, but knew to wait. Hrel sighed, he would lose crew members, the numbers were too uneven for it to be otherwise. He signalled to Danin that it was time, and they worked on building up a rainstorm. Danin gathered the clouds while Hrel drew up the water from the forest and sea to fill them. The clouds grew heavy and dark, as Danin guided them closer to the plateau.

At the same time, Wolf and the giant panthers stepped out of the cover of the trees, past the foremost pirates, to take the lead. Their heads were lowered, and powerful shoulders hunched as they stalked their prey. Their snarling, bared teeth had the previously arrogant soldiers desperately backing up. The troops behind them couldn't see what was coming and angrily shoved them forwards, swearing and growling their desire to draw blood. With no way to escape, the first row of soldiers yelled and ran at the Spirit elders, slashing their swords and axes, attempting to maim and kill. They were quickly dispatched by the slice of claws and chomp of jaws.

During that initial clash, with Hrel and Danin working on the storm, Jael channelled his magic into the rock beneath them. It started to shudder and shake. Triene thrust up a wall of flame between the elders and the fight, a fortress within which they could safely focus on the magic.

The next wave of soldiers quickly followed the first, engaging before they had a proper chance to take in the new opponents. Blood splattered, coating the combatants in thick, warm liquid that clung to their skin and soaked into their clothes. The rock heaved and shifted, sending the soldiers stumbling backward. The pirates, with their sea legs and prior knowledge of the plan, used their advantage to finish off the staggering soldiers. Their dead or dying bodies were stomped on by friend and foe and kicked aside as the fighting continued.

The ground now sloped downward from the edge of the plateau and the trees, down towards the soldier's camp. The pirates had the higher ground. Susan nodded, the plan was coming together. She glanced overhead, they needed the rain.

The soldiers not yet engaged in the fighting took stock of the changed battlefield and monstrous creatures attacking their fellows. Sergeants shouted instructions and they regrouped. This time they circled the Spirit elders with pikes, rushing in together before retreating out of range. One of the panthers went down, and the soldiers poured over her, stabbing her repeatedly, even after she was dead. Her mate roared and slashed wildly. He was badly wounded before being replaced by a swathe of pirates who quickly finished off the remaining soldiers.

The eagles soared high above the battle, relaying information about the army's tactics to the other Spirit elders. Susan winced as she saw an eagle swoop down to grab an exposed soldier whose arms and legs kicked uselessly as they flew to the edge of the plateau. The eagle released him and he plummeted towards the rainforest below. Adrenaline surged through her making her body tremble and stomach clench. She tried to disassociate herself from the death and bloodshed, she had to keep her focus. She was here to guide the use of the magic. She looked up at the sky again. Where was the rain? She saw the approaching clouds and urged them to move faster, come on!

Triene stood close to Susan searching for the merchant. His rotund and grandiose appearance shouldn't have been hard to find, but there was no sign of him. Just outside the tent, though, there was a single soldier, a younger man, not engaged in the fight. He wasn't wearing a jacket and held something aloft. Triene squinted at him, but a group of soldiers moved across her line of sight. She shuffled to the side, dropping part of her flaming defence, trying to see. Jael stepped forward and sliced the throat of a soldier that had somehow made it that far.

"Where is he?" he snapped.

Triene stepped away from the fallen body and shook her head in frustration. "I can't see the merchant, but there is a soldier still in the camp. I think he might be the mage."

Down in the camp, the Commander was ignoring the fighting. That was the purpose of his army after all. They should distract his enemy long enough for him to trap the magic. He kept his focus on drawing in the magic, wrapping it up tightly and spinning it into a thin rope and dragging its unwilling strands into the Eye of Rua. He could feel the powerful thrum of the magic as it filled him and spun into the artifact. He laughed again.

A rumble of thunder and dark clouds appeared overhead, casting the battle in deep shadow. The Spirit elders and pirates immediately retreated up the slope as the rain was released. Many of the soldiers were swept off their feet and washed backwards as the torrent of water rushed towards their camp. The soldiers at the front, weren't caught up in the flood, but unable to see for the rain, brandished their swords wildly, some losing their weapons as they slipped out of their hands.

The Commander frowned at the water lapping at his boots and looked up at the tumbling river of soldiers heading towards the camp. Irritated by the distraction, he dragged the magic towards himself before thrusting it out from him to form a bubble of broiling flames that burned so hot the water sizzled and boiled before soaring in a gust of steam.

The soldiers that were washed too close scrambled to get away, their scalded skin blistering before peeling back to bleed. Their high-pitched screams drowned in the downpour. Their Commander ignored their suffering as he continued to focus on the Eye of Rua.

It was a Fire mage! They needed a more focused attack. Susan called out to Hrel, "Water tornado, attack the mage." Hrel held his hand up and spun his finger for Danin who nodded. The rain clouds instantly dissipated to fall naturally over the rainforest, and Hrel started gathering up the water on the ground. It rose above the pile of drenched soldiers who caught their breath and weapons as they tried to regroup. Their tangle slowly unravelling to form a sodden army that began another advance. At the base of the slope, broken bodies remained, dead or unable to move.

The Commander noted the cessation of the rain. He knew his opposing mages would attack again, but he reached out to the panicked magic vibrating in the Eye, he was already more powerful than they. The artifact was still filling, there was so much magic left to harness. He smiled widely before he syphoned off some of the magic for himself, time to be rid of the mages.

The whirling waterspout quickly gathered speed before heading towards the mage's protective sphere. Damn them! Before he could form his new flame, he had to reinforce his defence. A spinning water tornado was heading in his direction knocking soldiers out of its path or picking them up to form part of its attack. The flame in the sphere burnt violet as the tornado hit. Steam spiralled into the air with a loud hiss.

Danin and Hrel were tiring. Their tornado wasn't getting through, and it was becoming harder to keep refuelling it. Susan needed to get another attack going now! She looked around for Jael and Triene. It was their turn.

Jael had moved away from her and was battling a brute of a man who wielded a double headed axe with ease. Jael suddenly stumbled over a fallen body and dropped to his knee. She watched with horror as the giant axe came slicing down. Somehow, Jael managed to raise his sword and halt its descent, deflecting it to the side. Desperate, Susan raised her own weapon and charged, useless though it was. As she ran, she saw Jael sweep his attacker's feet from under him, then rise and plunge his sword in the man's chest. Susan slowed, lowering her arm in relief, she didn't care Jael had just killed a man, he was safe!

Out of the corner of her eye she saw two more soldiers sneaking up behind Jael. He hadn't seen them. Susan screamed out a warning, but her cry was lost in the noise of battle. Suddenly Triene appeared and thrust out her hand towards the two men. A flame burst from her, wrapping the men in its heat. It licked its way around their weapons and their heads until they collapsed, empty eye sockets staring from their blackened skulls. Susan looked at Triene fearful for her friend. Triene's face was impassive as she turned to face her. "Get back!" Jael shouted at Susan, anger roiling off of him. Susan recoiled instinctively, before she remembered why she had been seeking them out. She shook her head and shouted to them, "You need to throw heated rocks at the mage as soon as the waterspout fails. The protection of your flame might help them get through and he won't be expecting it." The siblings looked at each other

385

and nodded. Jael shouted "Go!" again, before turning to face the mage. Wolf trotted back from the fight to defend them, his sharp ears having picked out Susan's instructions.

Susan backed away to her safer vantage point and viewed the battle. Despite their best endeavours, they were still outnumbered, and the pirates were beginning to tire. Although they were ferocious and strong, they had had a hard trek and climb to get here and for each soldier they defeated another appeared. Her heart raced, she was responsible for keeping them alive. She was responsible for the strategic use of the magic, the others were too involved. She needed to find a way to end this battle quickly.

The Commander could feel the power behind the waterspout lessening. The other mages were weak, the magic was his. The artifact was vibrating dangerously now, but he continued to fill it. Greed for more and more power consumed him. He felt the pressure from the water tornado stop but it was immediately replaced by a pounding of rocks against his barrier. Most of the rocks were melting in the extreme heat but some were getting through. A flaming rock made his leg buckle. His trouser leg was on fire, he patted it out. Some of his flesh had blistered. That wasn't his flame, there was another fire mage! He frowned as he threw more of the magic into thickening his barrier.

Susan rubbed her temple in frustration. She needed a strategy that combined all the elements in the Hand of Rua to defeat this mage! She had tried and tried to think of an attack that did that, but she couldn't. How did the Spirit element combine with the others? That's what she couldn't get! A slow prickle made its way up her spine, towards the base of her head. She watched Wolf, a giant predator that pounced and snarled as he snapped at the attackers. As she stared her mind imagined his eyes flashing red and fire emerging from his mouth, his fur seemingly made of stone. She rapidly blinked clearing the image. Perhaps the Spirit element was what connected all the other elements. Perhaps Wolf should be the one that combined them…

Her idea was slowly formulating into a plan. That was it! She scrambled over to Jael and Triene and waved over Wolf, Hrel and Danin. Did Wolf think it possible? He cocked his head then gave a slow dip of agreement.

Triene was the first to try. She prayed to Rua that this wouldn't hurt him. She reached up and placed one hand on either side of his bowed head and concentrated. Calling on her gemstone, she encouraged a small portion of her Fire magic to flow into Wolf. When it didn't burn him, she poured in more of her magic, feeling it meld with his own. When it was done, Triene added her gemstone to his and stepped back. Even in her weakened state she felt a blaze of excitement at the flash of red in Wolf's eyes before they resumed their amber hue. Wolf could feel the flame of the Fire magic rushing through his blood, fuelling his muscles. It was strange but not unpleasant. He licked his lips and turned to Jael.

One by one, the different magics were added to his own, and soon all five elements lived within him. He now bore the Hand of Rua around his neck. His body felt prickly and itchy so he gave it a quick shake, and detritus from the battle flew from his fur. He focused his attention on the mage. He could sense the fear and disgust of the magic under the mage's control, it called to him to free it. He stepped away from the others, his eyes turning brown as he created an

387

armour of rock, to protect him from weapons and flame. He then bounded forward soaring through the air as he whipped up a wind to carry him above the heads of the soldiers and closer to the mage.

The Commander looked up to see a huge creature of rock and sharp teeth, flying towards him, orange eyes aglow. What on Ruanh?! He lowered his protective sphere as he flung a shot of flame at it. The blue fire burnt hot enough to melt some of the rocks and sizzle the creature's skin beneath, but it kept coming. The creature landed a few feet away and began to stalk towards him. Head lowered, hackles high. The Commander threw another flame towards it.

A jet of water blocked his flame, steam rising where they met. The next flame was met by a swirl of wind that whipped it into a fire tornado that tore towards him. The Commander staggered back, dragging in more magic from the Eye of Rua, to raise a shield. It was just in time to protect him from it and the following flames that flew from the creature's open mouth. What was this creature? It had access to all the elements, that was impossible!

Wolf was testing the mage. He was very strong. His shield of flame was defeating the combined attacks he flung at it. He needed more magic, but the mage had it trapped. This was not working. Wolf stopped the attacks and paced the shield.

The Commander grinned, the creature couldn't defeat him. He kept the magic flowing from the artifact to bolster his shield. He would tire it and then he would get to enjoy seeing it burn. With the commander's full attention on

Wolf, and the channel open, the magic in the Eye of Rua began wiggling free of his control, breaking away strand by strand. Each strand too small for the mage to notice.

But Wolf noticed. He called to the magic, seeking its help. The magic wanted to flee, to get as far away from the mage as possible, but it could sense the diminishing power in the Hand of Rua. The Spirit elder needed help. The loose strands of magic arrowed for the artifact around Wolf's neck. Power surged through Wolf, shifting the balance between him and the Mage.

Creating a great sword from the granite beneath him, Wolf encased it in a ripple of water fuelled by the Air magic. He got the magic to raise it high above the shield. The Commander desperately threw everything he had at his defence, realising too late that most of the magic had escaped the artifact. Wolf blasted the shield with a bolt of fire to weaken it then sliced down with the sword. The shield split, recoiling from the sword's path.

Wolf advanced, lips curling, mouth wide. With his own snarl, the Commander unsheathed his sword and hacked uselessly at Wolf's armour. Wolf pounced. The breath exploded from the Commander's chest as he landed on his back. The Eye of Rua tumbled free from his hand. His eyes widened as he saw the massive jaws open over his face. Wolf's teeth clamped down, piercing the flesh on the man's cheek. The Commander's body spasmed as Wolf twisted his head and pulled. The Commander's neck ripped, the spine popping apart, and the head was torn from his body.

Wolf sat back, a wave of exhaustion hitting him with the death of the mage. He spat out the head. It rolled away until it bounced to a halt against the dropped artifact. The magic remaining in the two artifacts soared into the sky and quickly disappeared. Wolf sunk to the ground, his rocky protection tumbling, his body shrinking to its normal size as the elemental magics within him were drawn back to their hosts. Wolf slumped into unconsciousness.

Triene felt the magic return to her as she fought. The mage's shield had dropped, she stabbed the soldier and ran back, eyes searching for Wolf. He was lying on the ground, unprotected. "WOLF!". She wrapped herself in flame and tore a blazing path through the soldiers until she reached him. Flinging a wall of fire around them, she sunk to her knees and draped herself over him. He couldn't be dead!

The mage's headless body lay beside them, in a muddy puddle of blood. She paid it no mind as she examined Wolf, she felt a shallow breath and his faint heartbeat. A small smile of relief made it to her lips as she checked his body for injuries. He only had a few burns, nothing serious to see. She cradled his head in her arms. It was obviously internal. Where was Jael?

Around her the soldiers were floundering. The elders were focusing their power on them now their Commander was dead. The waterspouts and flying rocks were decimating their numbers. Many ran, eager to escape the magical onslaught, many others were already dead. Those that remained, struggled to move past the bodies and were being picked off by the enormous eagles who ripped into them with their hooked beaks or threw them into the forest below; and by the determined if tired pirates, sensing victory in their grasp; and by the panthers with their knife bearing paws and jaws.

When Hrel's voice swept over the battered soldiers, calling for them to lower their weapons and leave, most of those still fighting did so with relief. The few that continued, their faces contorted with spite and fury, were quickly dispatched.

Soon the battlefield quieted save for the groans of pain and calls for help. The victors faced a mass of bodies swathed in blood and mud, some still moving, some permanently still.

## Chapter 35

Jael was shouting for Triene to lower her flame. Thank the Goddess he was here. Triene extinguished her fire wall and moved over so he could examine Wolf. Susan was with him, and they rushed forward. "Is he … dead?" asked Susan, her voice trembling as a tsunami of guilt and grief washed over her. She hugged her body tightly, taking a step back unsure of her welcome.

Jael immediately set to work, checking Wolf's eyes, breathing and pulse. "He's alive, but weak." he said. "He must have drawn on a lot of his strength and now needs to rest." He lifted his eyes to meet Triene's. "You know he's tough. He's going to be all right". Unable to hold it in any longer, a loud sob burst out of her before she took a deep breath and nodded. She trusted her brother and had faith in Wolf. "I'll put a poultice on those burns." Jael added.

Triene sat up straighter, "What do you need?"

"My backpack has some clay, herbs, and clean cloth. I'll also need a bowl and some fresh water for boiling"

Susan was concerned she was going into shock. She felt faint and nauseous, her body was shaking and her teeth were rattling. She gritted her teeth to stop the chattering and tried to get as much oxygen into her lungs as possible. She was still needed. "I'll get the bag!" she mumbled and stumbled back to the thicket where they had all stowed their packs.

"I'll get the water boiling." Triene jumped up, looking around her at the devastated campsite. There must be a pot and poles round here. The flood had washed most of the camp further along the plateau. She headed towards a muddy bundle of bedrolls, blankets, cups and general detritus, glad to have something she could do to help.

Danin sat at the top of the slope, looking down at the destruction. He was tired.

He had read the manuscripts, even some written by the Mages during the Wars, but he didn't understand their driving desire for power. There was no learning involved, no knowledge to gain. Rather, they seemed to divide their time and effort between trying to get more power and fearing they would lose what they had to the other Mages. A puzzling and self-destroying cycle.

He observed the dead soldiers and the wounded. Why had they helped the Mage? Surely, they had been aware it was wrong to do so? What had they hoped to achieve? Danin's thoughts then turned to the Mage they had fought. He had gained a great deal of power for a short period of time. He wondered if he had concluded that it had been worth it, just before he had died. He dismissed the thought since there was no way he could find out. He would, however, be able to question some of the wounded soldiers about their decisions later. More importantly for now, he needed to find and protect the artifact that had been in the Mage's possession. He thought it had looked like the Eye of Rua. He hoped so, for that meant he should also find the missing book on the artifacts. They needed to be protected.

He collected his pack and made his way past the dead, down to the remains of the soldier's camp. Ah, there it was. The Eye of Rua. The mage's crushed skull, with its ripped cheek and staring eyes was resting against it. Danin toed the head away from the Eye of Rua before picking up the artifact and examining it for damage. A small amount of magic remained. It appeared to be frightened. He sent a soothing tendril of his own magic to calm it, even as he sought a clean cloth to wipe its exterior clear of blood and mud. The only cloth suitable was either his own tunic or the Mage's shirt. He decided the latter would be best since it wouldn't be needed anymore. He then placed the artifact in his pack and wondered where he might find the ancient's book. He sincerely hoped the water hadn't harmed it or washed it over the edge of the plateau. He contemplated the broken tent. It was fairly intact, and it was possible that the book had been protected by the canvas. He headed for it, passing Wolf and Jael. He hoped Wolf would be well soon. He had been most helpful with the other Spirit elders and was one of the more pleasant companions on this journey.

Further up the slope, Uisca was keeping an eye on Hrel as he supervised the rescue of their wounded and the collection of their dead. Uisca didn't offer comfort, that would be needed later. For now, Hrel needed to maintain his detachment. That numbness would pass though, and Uisca would be there for him when it did. In the meantime, he helped Xilm prioritise the order of treatment for their injured as they arrived at the makeshift medical hub. They would provide care for the soldiers once they had tended their own wounded. Xilm had already directed his assistants to boil the mashed bark, set out the jars of ants and leeches, and to make up poultices. Strips of cloth were laid out and branches were trimmed to make paddles to help set broken bones.

The pirates with the most grievous injuries, those injuries where only death offered solace, were given plenty of rum, while Xilm concentrated on those he could assist. The gaping wounds were sloshed with rum and slavered with honey, before being sealed with a row of driver ant heads. Poultices and bark decoctions were spread on the cloths that then covered them, before being bound in place.

Xilm moved on to the dislocations and closed breaks after the wounds, oftentimes having to forcibly set them. His assistants had to hold the injured still, as even the toughest of pirates cried out in pain or fainted.

Hrel counted 29 dead and many more seriously injured. He knew every one of them, their hopes, their loves, their pain. They were his family. He would ensure they were remembered. He sent his crew out to scour the battlefield for weapons, coin and items of value. They were pirates after all. They would hand it over to the quartermaster once they returned to the ship. He would ensure a fair distribution.

As the sun lowered over the distant sea, Hrel ensured his crew took the time to eat and rest. There would be more to do on the morrow. It wouldn't be time for celebrations and grieving for a while yet. The quiet moans and whimpers of the injured pierced the night air, the firelight picking out the agony in their features. Hrel sat with the dying as they struggled through their last moments of life, speaking of his pride in them when they could hear, and reaching out to close their eyes when they could not. As they died, he took a personal something: a hunk of hair, a ring, a gold tooth, a lucky coin. He couldn't take their bodies home, but he could take a part of them. He would give them their proper burial at sea.

Wolf had been brought up to lay with the rest of the crew,

Triene remained by his side. Jael checked on him throughout the night, and although he remained unconscious, his heartbeat and breathing were stronger. Triene had wanted to be on her own while she sat with him. She spoke quietly, telling him that he had to get better. Telling him how much she cared. She busied herself as she spoke, by crafting a stretcher that would take his body, using thin tree trunks and a cleaned blanket from the camp.

Susan had insisted she work with the other crew members, who were making more stretchers and crutches. Her determination came from a fear of allowing her thoughts to take over. Jael understood and helped her, even though he wanted to rest. Eventually, Susan couldn't fight her exhaustion any longer and her work fell from her fingers as she slumped back against Jael, eyes closing. Relieved, he lowered her to the ground, and lay down beside her before quickly joining her in sleep.

Dawn arrived with an instant burning sun that sucked up the remaining moisture on the plateau. The pools of blood that had started to dry overnight, now blackened and shrank. Some nocturnal creatures had ventured forth in the night and had started nibbling on the dead soldiers furthest from their fires. They would be welcome to the rest when the pirates had left. Their own dead needed to be buried in the soft soil of the forest floor, but first they had to get down there.

Jael had a plan. He drew on the magic, there was so much of it now, and stored some in his gemstone. He used it to initiate a vertical fracture in the granite and to gradually crumble the rock beneath them. There was a grating rumble and an explosive crack. A deep fissure appeared, separating their part of the plateau from the rest. The ground beneath

396

them began to pitch and shake and puffs of dust plumed as they descended. The freshly shorn rock face beside them revealed colourful striations as it seemed to power its way to the sky. Dust covered trees and liana rose up on the other side, and it wasn't long before they shuddered to a halt. They covered their noses and mouths as the fine powder from the pulverised rock settled on the ground, coating the undergrowth. Hrel quickly pulled over some water to dampen the dust and then it was just a small step onto the forest floor.

Jael dug a large grave and their dead were carefully carried over and laid out. Hrel and the others remained silent as they watched. The celebration of their lives would be over the sea, as it should be. This was merely the disposal of their empty shells, their souls would be sent to the deeps for keeping. The dead panther would be provided with the honour of a pirate's burial as well. At Hrel's quiet instruction, Jael refilled the grave with soil and they prepared for their hike back to the shore.

No longer concerned with being seen, and now with the additional magic to draw upon, Triene sent a flame along their previous trail and Danin helped it reach the shore. The journey was faster along the wider and burnt path, even though some bore stretchers and others limped. The ground was firm and dry underfoot and the sun shone through the open canopy, lighting their way.

They arrived at the shore after night had fallen. The sight of the Coral Skies, lit up with lamps to welcome them home, raised their flagging spirits. They still had the journey by boat and it was made harder by the number of wounded. Hrel was ready, however. He separated them into groups and returned first to send crew from the ship to ferry them back. It would take longer, but they acknowledged the necessity, and were glad of the reprieve.

Chapter 36

They immediately set sail for slightly deeper waters, where they furled the sails and dropped anchor. The crew, even the wounded, crowded on deck. It was finally time to grieve and bid farewell to those they had lost.

Will had managed to get up the steps by leaning heavily on a tall, teenage girl, whose riot of black curls framed her heart shaped face. Baraq had been able to shift once the magic had been freed, and now all the other Spirit elders had also shifted to human form in a show of solidarity with the rest of the crew.

The riggers manned the yards, lining them as a traditional mark of respect for their fallen. Jael stood with Uisca, who watched as Hrel stepped onto the rail of the foredeck, one foot resting on the upward tilt of the bowspit. Danin sat with Susan on some barrels, and Triene rested on the floor, Wolf's unconscious head in her lap. She was already crying silent tears, but her head was held high, the magic giving her much needed strength.

Hrel tossed the first of the tokens, a gold tooth, into the sea and named the first, "Ryobe Adeyo, gunner and son, loved and missed by all. I commit ye soul to the deep until the blessed Rua has need of it." Ryobe's name was chorused by the crew and floated away on the breeze before Hrel tossed a dagger with an intricately carved handle, "Meg Grillon, rigger, mother, wife and daughter, loved and missed by all. I commit ye soul to the deep until the blessed Rua has need of it."

When all had been named, Hrel concluded the ceremony with, "Ye live on in our heads and our hearts. Be at peace." The pure sound of a note being sung by a tenor hung in the air before he began a song of parting, of sorrow and the call of the sea. As he sang, other voices blended with his, until the final verse was reached, and all the crew were singing. Silence fell after the final note had drifted away. The gentle lapping of the waves combined with the soft sway of the ship and the gentle creak of wood, while the hot sun beat down upon them. It was a moment for memories.

A moment that could not last. They were pirates! It was time to celebrate life and victory! A building, roaring cheer blasted out of the silence, and Susan quickly reached in her pouch for Danin's ear plugs, but he had beaten her to it, although he gave her a nod of acknowledgement. He remained seated rather than hurrying back to his books. He would go there soon, but for now he would stay with his friends.

Jael walked over to Susan and she stood up to melt into his embrace. She was sobbing loudly. She felt so emotional, even though she hadn't known all of the dead, she felt their loss intensely. She knew it wasn't her fault and she knew they had tried to prevent a battle and had given the soldiers the chance to leave, and many of them had, in the end. It was the Mage's fault and the fault of the soldiers that had decided to fight for him. It didn't help much, knowing that. She still felt the guilt and the blame. She blubbed into Jael's shirt, covering it with tears and snot. Oh God, and Wolf was still unconscious! Her plan had worked, Wolf had killed the

399

Mage, but he hadn't woken up. What if he never woke up? She gave a burst of renewed sobs into Jael's chest, and he held her with a slightly bewildered air. He knew it was a time of great sadness, but it was also a time of joy. They had saved the magic, it was free and filled Ruanh with its love. They had prevented a Mage from destroying hundreds, if not thousands in his greed. However, he decided, if Susan needed to cry on him, she could.

Uisca met Hrel, offering a supporting hand as Hrel stepped back onto the deck. Hrel gave a tired smile as he took it. His face was drawn, his eyes were shadowed. Uisca wanted to whisk him away and protect him. He would have to wait. Hrel was needed still. He grabbed two mugs of rum and handed one to Hrel who raised it in toast calling out, "To victory!" and his crew returned the toast with cheers and laughter.

They were a resilient bunch, his crew. They felt the pain of loss, but somehow managed to accept death and move forward to the next adventure with the same vigour and excitement as before. Hrel hadn't learnt that trick. He still felt every death, and every decision that led to it, deep in his soul. He felt responsible for so much loss, and sometimes doubted his decision to become a pirate. He was too soft, he cared too much. But then he had only look at Uisca, and think on how the pirates had welcomed him, accepted all of him, to know he had chosen well. He was part of their family now, and they were his. He pretended to drink his rum and greeted and hugged those who wanted his reassurance and love. They were tough, but they still needed love, they still needed comfort in their loss. He was their Captain, the one they looked to for guidance and support. He could and

400

would give them that until his dying breath.

Triene had got Susan, Danin and Jael help her carry Wolf down to their quarters. He was lying on a blanket beside her cot. She whispered to him, "Come on, Wolf! You need to wake up. You saved the world, and now we're heading back to the islands to tell the other Spirit elders. Think of all the children, kits and cubs that will want to hear your story. You need to be strong enough to tell it them." With that attempt to push Wolf into recovery, she lay under her blanket and closed her eyes. "And I need you too. I love you, Wolf." came a whisper so quiet it was almost a thought, but Wolf's ear twitched. The darkness was back, trying to get inside her mind, but she fought it. She wasn't giving in to it again! She wiggled until she was comfortable and squeezed her eyes even tighter. I have improved the now and the future, father, she thought as she tumbled into a light sleep, ready to wake if Wolf needed her.

In the next cot, Jael was lying uncomfortably. Susan had insisted he lay on her bed and she was draped over him. Her face was on his wet top, and her arms and legs hung on either side of him. He had his arms around her so she didn't fall and she was snoring quietly. He sighed and closed his eyes. Tomorrow he would get Hrel to hydrate Wolf again. Wolf seemed to be getting stronger and he was hopeful that he would wake soon. He gave another sigh. He really needed to sleep.

The bittersweet celebrations continued long into the night although the revellers gradually began heading for bed, or simply fell asleep on the deck, until only a few remained. Those few had reached that contemplative mood of slurred storytelling and reminiscences, that no body listened to.

Eventually, they also slept and all aboard was quiet.

Uisca had managed to get Hrel to go to his quarters when night had fallen, on the pretext that he needed his rest so he could work on the morrow. Upon spying the priest deep in study, he had gently guided Danin out the door and to his own bed, before returning and helping Hrel get ready. Finally, lying on his cot, head resting on his pillow, Hrel gave way to his grief, to the heaviness of responsibility. His tears were quiet but kept coming until he fell into exhausted sleep. Uisca watched over him as he worked through his grief, coming to terms with the decisions and the loss. He knew Hrel would blame himself for their deaths. He always did. In truth, he hurt too much for a pirate Captain, but the crew sensed his love for them, and they loved him back as a result. Uisca had been born on the Coral Skies. He understood the life and the death that came with it. Hrel had joined them as an adult. It was harder for him. Uisca was strong though, he could be strong enough for both of them.

The Coral Skies headed for the Wuhynga Islands once more and this time the weather remained favourable, especially, now Jael and Danin were able to influence the skies and the seas. It was a peaceful journey of recovery. The wounded continued to heal, and to everyone's great joy, Wolf woke two days in, demanding food. After devouring a whole pig, he shifted and grinned at Triene who had watched his consumption of the animal with pleasure. He was fine, he was more than fine! Wolf's first words typically ignored the worry she had suffered, "The magic is free!" he said with proud satisfaction at his own role in their success. She just grabbed hold of him, hugging him tightly, and didn't let him go until he said apologetically that he needed to pee.

Will's ankle was healing well and he was soon hobbling around the ship looking for other injured and sedentary pirates that needed entertaining. They spent many hours playing games, especially those involving cards. Susan was pleased to see him occupied and building friendships, that is she was until Jael pointed out that they were placing bets on who would win with coins and other trinkets. Jael had had to hide his laughter at her horror. "They are teaching him, a boy, to gamble!" she had exclaimed with disgust.

Jael had replied, trying to keep his voice serious, "I think it is Will that is teaching the card games, actually."

Susan had hurried to find Will and had sat him down to talk to him about the dangers of gambling. "It can become very addictive and before you know it you are dangerously in debt."

Will's response had been a wide grin and a pat of her outstretched hand. He had looked around to check they were alone then said reassuringly, "You don't 'ave to worry 'bout that!" and he gave a meaningful wiggle of his fingers and an exaggerated wink before leaving.

Jael found her still sitting there five minutes later. "Ah! There you are. I wondered where you had got to?" She just burst into tears and ran off to be sick. Jael followed her, he was concerned. She had been crying and complaining of nausea since their return to the ship. He didn't know all the illnesses you could catch in this part of the world. "I think you should see Xilm." he said as he held up her hair while she sat over a bucket.

"No!" she shouted. "I'm not having leeches put on me, or

ants or maggots!" She shuddered and eyed Jael askance, "Did you know he uses maggots to treat people? He puts them on wounds!" She heaved and brought up the rest of her breakfast.

Jael tried to explain, "Maggots are actually very helpful. They eat decayed and rotten flesh so they clean out infected wounds really well."

Susan glared at him and put up a hand to stop him from speaking. "No!" she said again. Jael shook his head in frustration. She needed help. As soon as she had stopped being sick he bent down and scooped her up into his arms. As he carried her to Xilm's rooms Susan's legs kicked and she slapped his chest with her free hand. She was frowning at him. "No, no, no! Put me down you great oaf!" she yelled. They passed a few crew members who didn't even bother to look their way.

"You need to be checked over. You are unwell." Jael said as he continued walking. Fortunately, Xilm was there sorting out his equipment when they arrived or Susan would have run. He plonked her bottom on the table, "She keeps being sick and she's tired and crying a lot. It has been happening every day since we got back on board."

Susan rolled her eyes. "I'm fine." she said trying to escape Xilm's attention. "It's probably a bit of sea sickness. I got sick in that bad storm and have been feeling nauseous every now and then since."

Xilm looked at her and then at Jael with a slight smirk on his face. "Were you feeling sick in the rainforest too?"

Susan squinted as she tried to remember, "Yes, but it was so

404

humid, and then the fighting...."

"Are you still eating well?" asked Xilm.

Jael answered for her, "Yes, she's actually really hungry and often asks for more."

Susan glared, "Thanks for saying I'm greedy."

Jael shrugged apologetically but said, "He wanted to know."

Xilm was smiling widely now as he finally asked, "Have you missed your courses?"

"What? What do you mean? Oh! OH!"

Susan's mind went blank, she was barely aware of the others in the room. She was pregnant! She had another life growing inside her. It would be just a tiny thing at the moment, but it would grow, and it would become a baby! Her blood started to pump around her body again and she gulped in a breath. A baby! She knew nothing about babies! She couldn't be a mother, she wouldn't know what to do? What if it cried? Oh God! Of course it would cry. She knew that! It would cry and be sick and poop, and it would be completely dependent on her! She bent down and put her face in her hands. Then it would get older, how would she treat it. Her own mother had passed her over to a Nanny, so was no role model to follow. She thought about it. The Nanny had been caring though, had soothed her when frightened, had taught her right from wrong, how to behave to others and so on. Looking back, she thought Nanny had loved her, even though she had to protect her heart. Well, Susan could love with all her heart, and she would give that to this child. She sat up and straightened her spine. She would be a fantastic mother, she would make sure this child was happy and safe!

She looked at Jael and felt a twinge of fear. He had said he loved her, but this might change things. She wanted to raise their child with him, he would make a wonderful father, but she knew that might be too much to expect. Xilm was speaking, what was that? Oh, he was going to leave so they could talk. Great! She wasn't sure that was something she needed right now, but she supposed it was necessary.

Jael rose his head and his questioning eyes caught hers, "Are you pregnant?" She nodded tentatively.

He was going to be a father! He was going to have a child with Susan! A family! Excitement and nervousness flooded him. His own father had been a wonderful man, he could only hope to emulate him. Susan would be a clumsy, eager and fun mother to their child. His own mother had been rather quiet and serious, so it would be interesting to see how that would work. He looked at Susan, she was worried. He wasn't having that, this was wonderful news! He jumped up and grabbed her, swinging her around, "We're having a baby!" he said joyfully.

She gave a nervous laugh, "I guess we are!"

"We must tell Triene and Wolf!" said Jael dragging her by the hand, as he hunted for his sister. Susan followed, more tears forming. Elation filled her as she placed her free hand on her belly. Looks like we're a family she told it.

As soon as they drew near the islands, the eagle Spirit elders flew ahead to warn the islanders of their return and to speak of Glanic's passing. They told of her body's burial under the rainforest soil and the pirates' ritual to send her soul into the keeping of the sea. The Spirit elders appreciated the pirates' care and grieved her loss. Some needed more time, and they headed into the forest for they knew it was necessary for the others to welcome home the survivors and to celebrate their success. The Spirit elders had known they had succeeded as the magic had washed through the islands, filling them with joy and elation as they experienced their first changes of form. They had celebrated then too, but it had been subdued for they had not known the cost of that success. Now they could rejoice with those that had survived.

They hurried to prepare a feast and to decorate the clearing with flowers and when the rowing boats bearing the victorious elders neared, the Spirit elders, in human form, ran through the surf to place flower garlands over their visitor's heads. More pirates were brought to the shore and they all headed for the communal living space, grins on their faces, crates of rum in their arms. More floral garlands, of frilly orange and red, spilled from the trees surrounding the clearing, while pink and white flowers with their captivating and complex scent decorated the spaces between the seats.

Food had been prepared and placed on wide glossy leaves that lined the clearing closest to the huts. Succulent meats and spiced vegetables were piled high. The pirates eagerly devoured the fresh fare. Huge bowls were filled with pineapple juice and sliced pale green limes. Copious amounts of rum were being poured into this mixture, Their previous visit having introduced this tasty cocktail of flavours to the Spirit elders. Hrel was the first to taste it, dipping his wooden cup into the bowl and taking a long sip. "More rum!" he said, pointing to the crates, and the racoon

407

spirit elder quickly opened another bottle. One of the pirates brought out a simple drum, another a flute, and finally, an older man revealed his three stringed violin. They began to play a lively tune that had the pirates tapping their feet and singing, the ribald lyrics making Susan blush. The youngsters danced in the centre, pirates joining them in an energetic reel, a vibrant celebration of life. Laughter sparkled its way to join the twinkling stars in the clear night sky.

Danin gathered Hrel, Jael, Wolf, Triene and Susan to one side. He pushed his glasses up his nose and addressed the closed notebook in his hand. "I have been contemplating the implication of the remaining artifacts and have determined that a Mage War is still a risk. We know the Heart, the Ear and the Mouth of Rua remain unaccounted for and there may be more artifacts, of course. I have come to the conclusion that these islands will be the safest location to keep them."

Hrel gave a wry smile as he leant back against the tree. "My ship is at your disposal, my dear fellow. My crew have declared a thirst for more noble adventures. What do you propose?"

Danin gave a rapid nod and pushed up his glasses again. "I have been looking at Father Culdric's annotations on the Book of Artifacts. Unfortunately, some of the pages have sustained damaged, but was pleased to note that many useful sheets remain intact. It appears that the Heart of Rua was last seen in the northern mountains of Dvinsk."

Hrel suddenly leant forward his smile disappearing. "Dvinsk." he stated flatly.

"Yes, indeed. Father Culdric had made several notes, presumably from other research, that plot out its most likely location. I think we should head there first."

A smile had returned to Hrel's lips, but his eyes were cold and distant. "Very well, Dvinsk it is." He stood abruptly. "I need to speak to Uisca." he said before leaving with a short bow.

Triene suddenly announced, "Wolf needs rest! Not going off and nearly getting killed again!" and she wrapped her arms around him as if to pin him down should he try to escape. Wolf raised his eyebrows and looked at her quizzically.

Surprisingly, Jael agreed with her, before adding, "Susan should also remain, she shouldn't be placed under further stress. It can cause problems with the pregnancy." It was Susan's turn to raise her eyebrows, until his next words had her swallowing nervously, "I will be better able to help with her pregnancy and the birthing pains here." Oh God! No epidurals! What if she needed a caesarean? She quickly agreed with his suggestion. Please be able to make it painless! she thought.

Wolf's rumbly voice then announced, "We are welcome to remain." and just like that the decision had been reached. They would not be going on the next adventure. They would be staying on the islands with the Spirit elders until the Coral Skies returned with the Heart of Rua.

The next night, the rowing boats were readied and bobbing in the shallows while they took their leave. Danin hoisted his bag onto his back and started to head for the boat until he was stopped by Jael and forced to accept various back pats and good wishes. Finally able to escape when their attention had turned on Will, he hurried to go sit in the boat. Will had limped over and given a cocky, "I'll bring back the 'eart of Rua, for you as a gift to the littl'un." Susan smothered him in a hug and admonitions to stay safe. He managed to wiggle out of her embrace only to be caught up in another from Triene. Jael's grip of his arm as he pulled him in, was a more manly version of a hug. Then, Wolf caught Will's eyes with his own as he said, "Rua's blessings. Be guided by her on your quest." Will surprised himself by answering seriously, "Yeah, I will." then he too got into the boat.

Hrel reassured them, "I'll take care of the lad. He is working with the gunners until his ankle heals. It will do him good to get to know the workings on the ship." He turned to the panthers standing close by and gave them his usual corkscrew bow before leaving. The panthers were bidding farewell to Baraq who had declared her desire to be a pirate. She then went to say goodbye to the others. She had been learning their language, so was able to understand their babbled best wishes. Wolf took her hand and spoke directly to her. Her eyes widened and hand trembled briefly before she nodded and stepped back. Then she too, went to sit in the boats.

The people on the shore watched as the boats were hauled up onto the Coral Skies. Once the ship left the confines of the islands. Uisca shouted orders, the clear night sky providing him with its heavenly map to start them on their journey north.

Baraq sat on the topmost yard, alone now the other riggers had returned to deck. They were underway and the wind in

410

the sails was even. She unhooked and opened the neck pouch Wolf had given her. She stared at the golden gem. Her large emerald eyes blinked slowly. What on Ruanh was she supposed to do with it?

# About the author

Rachel Dray was born in Kent, England in the 1960s.

At school she was a typical geek and as such she received her fair share of bullying. She consequently left school with a desire to become a lawyer so that she could "achieve justice for the underdog".

She married her childhood sweetheart, and they raised two wonderful children together, with Rachel dividing her time between nappies, school runs, court cases and litigious suits.

After gaining many years of experience, Rachel decided she wanted to share her love of law with other like-minded people and became a law lecturer, who tortured her students with the intricacies of contract and tort.

Rachel considers herself blessed to have had the opportunity to work with adult special needs students shortly before taking retirement. She found the experience enlightening and enjoyable. With that retirement came the realisation that housework wasn't satisfying, and she decided to fulfil a lifelong dream of writing a fantasy novel. Rua's Gift is the product of that ambition, and it has sparked a love of writing that has already led to a short story, Haven, and plans for numerous books set in the World of Ruanh.

Rachel loves reading as a means of escaping the realities of life, of finding satisfaction in the conclusion of a story that is rarely found in the real world. Her aim in writing this series is to create tales that she enjoys in the hope that there are like-minded individuals out there that will enjoy them too.

She thanks you for taking the time to read her work and plans to release further books for you to read without too much delay, since she hates having to wait for the next book in a series herself.

Printed in Great Britain
by Amazon

86516918R00235